MOORESTOWN LIBRARY
W9-COZ-587

A Heritage of Shadows

Books by Madeleine Brent

A HERITAGE OF SHADOWS

THE LONG MASQUERADE

THE CAPRICORN STONE

MERLIN'S KEEP

STRANGER AT WILDINGS

MOONRAKER'S BRIDE

TREGARON'S DAUGHTER

A Heritage of Shadows

Madeleine Brent

DOUBLEDAY & COMPANY, INC.
GARDEN CITY, NEW YORK
1984

Library of Congress Cataloging in Publication Data
Brent, Madeleine.
A heritage of shadows.
I. Title.
PR6052.R419H4 1984 823′ 914
ISBN: 0-385-19041-7
Library of Congress Catalog Card Number 83–45164

PRINTED IN THE UNITED STATES OF AMERICA
FIRST EDITION

A Heritage of Shadows

One

It was almost midnight. Louise, fat and bad-tempered, was putting dishes on my tray in the kitchen of La Coquille when Armand came through from the little restaurant, his waxed moustaches beginning to droop, his long white apron spotted with splashes of wine.

"Is he still there?" I asked.

Armand shook his head. "Gone."

We were speaking of a stocky, moon-faced man who had spent an hour over his meal at one of Armand's tables, and whose eyes had rarely left me as I went about my work. I knew he was not studying me simply because I happened to be a young woman, for I could easily recognize that kind of look. He had seemed rather to consider me without any personal interest, but with a brooding and speculative air I found disturbing.

Armand had told me the man was English but spoke French less badly than most of his compatriots. I did not feel it was his being English which made me uneasy, for I had long ago overcome the quick chill that any reminder of my native country had once roused in me, and I was a little annoyed with myself for allowing his attention to trouble me.

"A party of gold watches just arrived," said Armand, setting down his tray of dirty glasses. "Four of them, without a word of French between them, the barbarians. Père Chabrier needs you to translate, Hannah."

Armand and Père Chabrier always referred to English gentry as gold watches because so many carried in their waistcoat pockets a gold watch attached to a chain which looped across the front of the waistcoat. This, in Armand's view, proved that they were mad, for it offered irresistible temptation to the pickpockets and apaches of the quarter, especially with almost everybody so poor after the terrible winter we had just endured.

I felt myself truly lucky to have been working at La Coquille throughout that time, the worst winter Paris had suffered in thirty years, so the newspapers said. It had begun in the last months of 1890, and by January the whole city was frozen. Fires were kept burning in many squares and streets, shelters were set up for the homeless, and the *Assistance publique* kept great caldrons of soup simmering on the snow-covered Champ de Mars, to feed the hungry. Business everywhere had been very poor, especially in the cabarets and restaurants of Montmartre, but somehow La Coquille had survived, and Père Chabrier had kept me on.

Now, with spring approaching, many English people were again visiting Paris, and we were thankful to see them for they were free spenders. The English had been coming across the Channel in increasing numbers for the past two years, ever since the spring of 1889, when it seemed that the whole world was flocking to Paris for the great Exposition. I thought it likely that Père Chabrier had continued to employ me through the bad winter because he felt my fluency in both languages might be of use when better times came, so I was thankful to have him call upon me to act as interpreter.

I said to Armand, "I mustn't keep him waiting. Will you serve the corner table for me, please?"

Armand looked at my loaded tray and sighed heavily. Louise snapped at him. I went through the swing doors into the restaurant, where Père Chabrier was making a great fuss of seating four English gentlemen who were laughing at some joke one of them had made, and who had obviously been enjoying themselves among the many entertainments offered by the cabarets, dancehalls, and theaters of the quarter. Two wore top hats and capes, two were in knickerbockers and golf caps. All were smoking the bulldog pipes by which Parisians had learned to recognize English tourists.

Père Chabrier, beaming and talking, made large gestures to indicate that I would take the order. I was tired, but made a big effort not to let this show as I smiled, dropped a small curtsy, and said, "Good evening, messieurs. May I bring you an aperitif while you decide what you wish to order?"

There came the usual exclamations of surprise, followed by the usual questions. How well I spoke English! I *was* English? Remarkable! They wondered how a young English girl came to be serving as a waitress in a Montmartre family restaurant. They had seen no other waitresses anywhere, only waiters. What was my name, and how old was I? Hannah McLeod? Eighteen? Surely I must be Scottish rather than English?

I briefly told the story I had told in like circumstances before, almost none of which was true. My mother French, and a schoolteacher. My father a ship's officer, London born though doubtless with Scottish forebears. I had lived in London till I was twelve, when my father's ship was lost at sea and my mother died soon after. Her family in France had given me a home, but they were in poor circumstances, so I was very glad that I had been able to find work and help to keep myself.

It was a story which sometimes brought me a large tip, though I did not tell it for that purpose. I had made it up as the simplest and least interesting way to account for my presence at La Coquille. In their manner toward me as I smilingly answered their questions, the Englishmen were slightly flirtatious. I felt sure this would not have happened if I had been a tea-shop waitress in London, but we were not in London, we were in Paris, indeed in Montmartre, the haunt of bohemians, where English visitors threw caution and formality to the winds. Also, I did not sound like a tea-shop waitress, for I spoke good grammatical English in a voice of much the same quality as these English gentry would hear from their wives or daughters. It was because of my voice and my manner that I had been known as *la professeuse* by my fellow students at the College for Young Ladies, so strictly presided over by Mam'selle Montavon in Rue des Moulins.

By behaving diffidently and not responding too readily to their questions and chaffing, I managed to bring the English gentlemen fairly quickly to a study of the short menu written with violet ink in Louise's large flowing hand.

"There are the two kinds of soup, messieurs, the oxtail and the *catalane.* The *catalane* is made with onions, chopped ham, a little white wine, some vegetables, egg yolks, and herbs. I regret that we have few vegetables at this time because of the bad winter, but you will find the omelets very good if you wish only a light supper. If you have a good appetite, then I suggest the *côtelettes mousquetaires*—mutton chops marinated in oil, brandy, and parsley. Or you may prefer the breast of lamb, or the ragout, which is a kidney stew. The *coquilles Saint-Jacques* is a specialty of our kitchen . . ."

It was an evening much like most of my evenings at La Coquille, except that with the better weather we were now much busier. As I went to the kitchen with the order I hoped that these would be the last customers of the day. In summer the cafés and theaters, the cabarets and concert halls, would be crowded at this hour, but as yet the nights were still very cold, and most places of entertainment would be closing.

I did not think anymore about the moon-faced man, who had studied me so closely, until the day's work was ended. Armand mentioned him while we were stacking chairs on the tables before leaving, and I felt again that odd chill of unease. At half past one I put on my hat and coat, said goodnight to Père Chabrier and Louise, and walked with Armand to the corner of Rue Muller, where we went our separate ways.

The streets were dark and empty now, but I was not afraid to be alone. Any well-to-do visitor would have been unwise to walk at such a late hour through the maze of streets that wove around the summit of Montmartre, for this was the quarter of the apache, where a woman might lure a foolish and unsuspecting gentleman into a dark place for her man to stun him with a leather tube full of lead shot, and rob him. But I was not in danger, for I was myself a dweller in the quarter, a young woman in cheap clothes, clearly not worth robbing, quite apart from the tradition that the footpads of Montmartre usually refrained from preying upon local people.

I did not speculate about the moon-faced man as I walked, for I was too tired and cold. I knew my room would be cold, too. During the long hard winter I had used most of my small savings to buy coal for the barrel-shaped studio stove, stoking it for the day so that I would not have to break ice on the water jug when I came home from the restaurant in the early hours. I had stopped this as soon as the temperature became bearable, because I simply could not afford it on the three francs a day Père Chabrier paid me. This was a generous wage, but unfortunately I had recently had a lot of expense owing to shoes and clothes finally wearing out.

Despite my tiredness I still felt content as I reached the steep flight of stone steps running up between houses at the end of the street. Eighteen months ago I had been living in comfort with the other students at Mam'selle Montavon's very select college in Rue des Moulins, a foreign girl who had come from England almost five years before; Hannah McLeod, well enough educated, an eager reader and student, somewhat prim and reticent but not unfriendly, occasionally most willful and troublesome. Today was very different. Today I had worked since noon at La Coquille, I was going home to a small cold room at the top of six flights of stairs, I had only a few sous in my purse, and there were two days to go before I would receive my weekly pay. Yet I never wished for those days of comparative luxury in Rue des Moulins to return. They represented a chapter in my life that had now closed, a chapter I had no wish to relive.

From the top of the long flight of stone steps I had all Paris spread below me, a pool of light under a bright half moon, with thousands of streetlamps marking the broad boulevards and picking out the famous buildings, while the revolving searchlight on the apex of the Eiffel Tower moved its misty beam over the city. Behind me, a mass of scaffolding rose above the as yet unfinished Church of the Sacré-Coeur, which stood on the very summit of Montmartre.

I paused for only a few seconds to look down upon the city that was now my home, wondering briefly if I should move away to some town in the south and try to find work as a teacher or nannie there, or whether I might do better to overcome my foolish qualms and return to England to seek employment. Of course, I would first have to save for the fare, and for lodgings while I sought work. It would not be easy . . .

I tucked my cold hands under my armpits and moved on through the warren of steep passages, courtyards, and archways leading to my home. To my left, the gaunt black skeletons of two ancient windmills rose against the sky, decayed remnants of the time when windmills had been thick on the summit of Montmartre.

I was a hundred paces from my home in Rue Labarre when I turned the corner of an alley and saw three figures less than a short stone's throw away in the light of a wall lamp. One lay on the ground, a man whose top hat had rolled into the gutter that ran at the foot of the wall bordering one side of the alley. The other two were crouched over him. I could not see them clearly, but I knew they must be footpads, apaches, going through the pockets of a victim who lay unconscious. He had probably come up from the Moulin de la Galette, the dancehall that lay lower down the hill, and lost himself in the maze of Montmartre. If so, he had been foolish to explore alone, for this was an area for the local people of the quarter, not visitors or tourists. Most of the inhabitants would be suspicious of strangers, and some would be dangerous.

As I stood still for a moment, staring, the two figures rose, and I saw that they were a man and a woman. The man was examining something, holding it close to his face, a wallet perhaps. Then he kicked the limp figure on the ground. The girl said something to her companion in an angry voice, and I caught the name Henri. For a moment I thought she was remonstrating with him, but then she too kicked the man on the ground. Henri spat, then kicked again, hard.

I pulled my skirt up to my knees and broke into a run. I hated apaches. There was a great fashion at present for making heroes of them in stories, but they were not heroes to me. I saw the apache as a selfish, vicious creature who lived on his woman and beat her if she failed to earn sufficient money from men to keep him in idleness, well fed, and well supplied with wine and tobacco.

I can say with truth that when I began to run toward the scene I was only a little afraid. This was not because I was courageous but because I was so angry and sickened by the sight. It touched chords of memory in me I had long kept buried, and set my heart pounding so furiously that I could hear it in my ears. On leaving La Coquille I had put my indoor shoes in a shopping bag hung on my arm, and I was wearing sabots. The clatter of wood on cobbles was loud, and at once the two figures stopped their kicking and stared toward me.

For a moment I thought they would run, but then they saw I was a young woman and alone. The man laughed and stood in a swaggering pose, hands on hips. He kicked his victim once more and said, "A rich foreigner with no watch, no rings, and only five francs in his wallet . . . bah!"

I stopped barely two paces from the apache, one hand raised to the side of my hat, glaring into his face with all the hatred I felt as I said, "Get back! Get away from him, you dirty *pigs!*"

He stared at me from a thin sallow face, then swung an arm to hit me across the cheek with an open hand; but I had seen the apaches set about their women, and I was ready with the six inch hatpin plucked from my hat, jerking back my head to avoid the blow and raking his hand with the sharp point. He gave a screech of pain, and as he clutched his wounded hand I stepped forward and kicked him hard on the knee with my heavy wooden sabot. He cried out again, alarm in his voice this time, and lurched sideways. Before his girl could think what to do, I swung the bag with my shoes in and hit her full in the face. She squealed with shock, and squealed again as my sabot cracked against her knee.

"Clear off, you animals!" I said furiously, and pointed with the hatpin. "I know *you,* Henri! Come near me again and I'll have your *eye* next time, sewer rat! I know where to find you, Henri, you and your *gigolette* here. Perhaps I will tell the police, or perhaps I will have my friend *Louis le surineur* come and talk with you!"

This was all make-believe, but as I spat out the words the apache and his girl began to back away. I did not know where to find Henri; I had simply heard the girl use his name. A *surineur* was a footpad who used a knife, a stabber as opposed to a garroter, and I had no friend called Louis in this trade or any other. But my words must have carried conviction, for abruptly the apache caught his girl by the wrist and began to limp painfully away, soon turning down a steep flight of steps and vanishing from my sight.

I stood trembling, suddenly terrified by what I had done, pushing my hatpin back in place with a shaking hand, then sinking to my knees beside the man who lay sprawled on the cobbles. His eyes were open, but as I bent over him they closed. In the lamplight he seemed quite a young man, perhaps in his late twenties, with dark hair and a neatly trimmed moustache. His topcoat and jacket were unbuttoned, the pocket linings pulled out by Henri and his companion in their search for money and valuables. One side of the man's face was covered with blood, and his breathing was labored. I wondered if he had some broken ribs from the kicking he had received.

I looked about me. The street was deserted. Here and there a dim light showed from a third or fourth floor apartment window, but I had little hope of summoning help. At this hour the fearsome concierges who guarded the ground-floor entrances to the houses would not leave their beds to answer the door.

I rested the man's head on my lap, patted him hard on the cheek, and said, "M'sieur . . ." Then I hesitated and continued in English. The French tended to think that all Englishmen were fair, but I knew this was not so. My own hair was as dark as this stranger's. The apache had evidently known the man was a foreigner, and in that event he was more likely to be English than any other nationality, so I said, "Sir Can you hear me? Please try to wake up. Sir?"

I pinched the lobe of his ear quite fiercely, for I was growing a little desperate. I could not leave the man, for he would surely die of cold before dawn. Somehow I had to get him to shelter, but I could not think how I might manage this alone if he remained senseless. I dug my thumbnail into the lobe of his ear and said, "Please, oh *please* wake up, sir."

To my infinite relief he stirred, mumbling something and trying to move his head away. I shook him, pulled his ear, and kept talking urgently to rouse him to consciousness. Slowly his eyes opened. He stared up at me blankly, and asked a question in English, but the words were so slurred I could not decipher them. For the next few minutes I tugged at him and cajoled him, trying to get him to his feet. I felt sure he was mentally absent, with most of his mind still asleep, for though he formed a few words as I heaved and coaxed, they were quite incoherent. But slowly he seemed to comprehend that I was trying to help him, and at last I managed to haul him to a standing position beside me, so that he had an arm across my shoulders while my own arm held him round the waist. We stood swaying for a few moments, then began to move slowly forward, reeling as if drunk.

I had remembered to pick up the bag with my shoes, but I forgot about the gentleman's top hat until we started to move, and then it was too late. I could not dare to let go of him while I picked it up. As we staggered along I kept panting words of encouragement and exhortation. "There now . . . steady, sir. Another step, and another, please. There's a good gentleman. Not much farther now. Come along, I've got you . . ."

Twice in the five minutes it took us to cover the short distance to my home at number eight, the gentleman sagged and nearly pulled me over, and by the time we reached the door of the tall dark house my right arm was burning with the effort of supporting him. The key was on a string round my neck. Somehow I managed to pull it out from under my dress, lift the string over my head, and unlock the door. An oil lamp, turned very low, stood on the table in the bare hall. This was always left out for me by Mme Briand, the concierge, and was a very special favor indeed. Like most concierges, Mme Briand was a morose and cantankerous character with a sharp tongue, but during the time that I had rented the room on the sixth floor she seemed to have taken a liking to me. Perhaps this was because she had seen me stamp hard on her husband's foot when he tried to be familiar with me on the stairs one day, not knowing she was watching from above. Her husband, Gustave, was a fat, idle man and she detested him, a feeling with which I fully sympathized.

I held my half-conscious companion against the wall while I got my breath back, and wondered how I could ever get him up the six flights of stairs to my room. There was nowhere else I could take him. Some of the other tenants were amiable enough in passing the time of day, but I would have been given a short answer if I had roused them in the small hours to take in a penniless and injured foreigner. The only one who would have helped me was the half Irish Englishman who rented the other room on my landing, Toby Kent, and he was away at sea.

The noise we made in mounting the first few stairs must have roused Mme Briand, for she appeared from her quarters on the ground floor with a candle, a thickset figure in a shapeless dressing gown and nightcap.

"Name of God!" she exclaimed, peering up. "Is it the mad Englishman returned? And drunk?"

"No, it isn't M'sieur Kent," I panted. "A tourist, I think, madame. I came upon him as an apache and his girl were robbing him. He is barely conscious, poor man. They kicked him brutally as he lay on the ground."

Mme Briand shrugged. "Because his wallet was too light for their liking, no doubt." She lifted the candle. "What will you do with him, girl?"

"I can't leave him in the street to freeze," I said apologetically. "I hoped you wouldn't mind if he rested in my room, and perhaps I can fetch a doctor to him tomorrow."

She snorted. "You have money for a doctor?"

"Well, no . . ." As I spoke, the man sagged to a kneeling position on the stairs, leaning against the wall, and I had to sink down with him to prevent his falling. "But I thought perhaps I could borrow a franc or two," I said hopefully.

"Not from me, stupid girl," Mme Briand said, though not unkindly "And how will you get him to your room?"

"I don't know. I was hoping he would come to his senses more." My eyes prickled with unshed tears, for I was beginning to feel helpless despair, and could not think what to do next.

Mme Briand's eyes lit up suddenly with a gleam of malice. "Wait, my little one," she said. "Gustave will help you." She shuffled back into her apartment, and a few moments later I heard her shrill voice and her husband's gruff one raised in voluble dispute. Sitting sideways on a stair with the half-conscious man leaning against me now, I felt very tired and allowed my eyes to close while I waited.

Two minutes later Gustave Briand came shuffling into the hall wearing slippers, a vest, and trousers supported by limp and ancient braces. His wife talked down his protests and gave instructions. Between us we managed to get the injured man upright, with his arms over Monsieur Briand's shoulders from behind so that his wrists could be held in front. Then we began the long ascent of the narrow stairs, Monsieur Briand bent double beneath his burden, gasping and cursing with what breath he could spare. The concierge and I helped from behind, supporting, pushing, whispering instructions, myself giving grateful encouragement, Mme Briand uttering waspish criticism of her husband's efforts.

To an onlooker we must have presented a comical appearance, and on the fourth flight, when Mme Briand in a hoarse whisper accused her struggling husband of trying to murder her by falling back on her with his load, I found myself close to giggling despite my tiredness. From time to time the hurt man groaned and muttered something in a slurred voice, which encouraged me to hope that he was gradually coming to his senses.

At last we reached my room. I unlocked the door and held it wide. Gustave Briand tottered through, the stranger's feet dragging on the floor behind him, then lurched sideways to drop his burden on my bed. The old bedstead creaked alarmingly but did not collapse. As I lit the lamp I whispered my thanks but he ignored me, standing with mouth open, shoulders hunched, panting as he glared malevolently at his wife.

"It is nothing," she said, giving my arm a little pat. "Gustave was glad to help." She ushered him out, and even when I had closed the door after them I could hear his wheezing as he plodded slowly down the stairs.

Two o'clock of a Saturday morning now; a cold Saturday morning. I hesitated, then set a match to the stove. It was laid ready for lighting tomorrow, Sunday, when I would not have to go to work. Now my room would be cold on Sunday, for I could buy no more coal until I was paid my next wages, but at least I would not shiver through tonight while my unsought companion lay warm under my blankets.

I set some water to heat on the stove, hung up my hat and coat, and took off the man's boots. Easing his arms from the sleeves of his topcoat, I managed to draw it out from under him, then I rubbed my hands to warm them a little before starting to take off his jacket, waistcoat, and shirt. To my shame I felt more resentment than sympathy. He was a fool to wander alone in such an area at such an hour, and he had paid dearly for his foolishness, but I was also paying for it in time and trouble.

It was not easy to get his shirt and undervest off, and as I struggled, bending over him, supporting his head in the crook of an arm, he half opened his eyes and said thickly, "Clara? That you, Clara . . . ?"

He spoke in English, with an accent I found unfamiliar. I replied in the same tongue, trying to be reassuring. "No, I'm not Clara, but please don't worry. You're quite safe now."

He grunted something, then his eyes closed and his head became heavy on my arm. When I at last had him undressed I found as I expected that there were some angry abrasions about his ribs. The skin was broken in places, the flesh beginning to show heavy bruising where the apache and his woman had kicked him.

Very gently I felt each rib in turn. Some might be cracked, I could not tell, but I could feel no sharp break. Relieved, I took from my small cupboard the jar of ointment I used to keep my hands from chapping, and spread a little on the abrasions. I knew nothing of medicine except what I had gleaned from a medical student who had been a regular visitor to the College for Young Ladies, a nephew of Mam'selle Montavon. At her request I had on several occasions spent an hour or two with a textbook in my hands, testing the young man with questions to which I held the answers. Perhaps I was chosen for this because I had won the nickname of *la professeuse,* but whatever the reason I quite enjoyed it, and if I had not learned very much at least I knew that the kick to the head sustained by my present companion was likely to be more dangerous than the damage to his ribs.

Again I was relieved when I found no sign of bleeding from the ears or nose. The blood which had now dried on the side of his face came from a wound where the welt of a shoe had torn the flesh over his cheekbone. I bathed the dried blood away, found a clean rag in my sewing drawer, spread a strip of it with ointment, and secured it over the wound with a piece of court plaster.

The gentleman, whose clothes marked him as such, opened his eyes, gazed blankly at me, and muttered, "Cold . . . cold."

"There now, don't worry, sir, you'll soon be warm," I said, and drew the sheet and blankets over him. I was spreading his topcoat over the blankets, and wishing I had a little brandy to give him to warm him from within, when there came a tap on the door and it opened to admit Mme Briand, puffing a little, with a small brown bottle in her hand.

"Cognac," she said brusquely "Sit the fellow up, girl. Don't want to choke him."

I brought a spoon from the dresser drawer, and between us we managed to prop the gentleman up. As we did so his eyes opened again and wandered vaguely over the room. "I heard . . . ," he mumbled, "in the street . . . heard what you said." His gaze rested briefly on my face, then his eyes closed again and he shivered violently. "Cold . . . ," he whispered, stammering. "C-cold . . ."

I held him with his head tilted back a little while Mme Briand poured out a spoonful of brandy and trickled it into the corner of his mouth. "Good," she said. "M'sieur swallows without choking." She tipped the bottle to pour again. When the gentleman had swallowed half a dozen spoonfuls, barely losing a drop, I said, "Perhaps that will be enough, madame. We had better not give him too much cognac."

She nodded grudgingly. "Perhaps. But it is not all cognac. There is laudanum also."

Hastily I lowered the gentleman's head to my pillow and tucked in the blankets. Laudanum was a strong drug, and I had no idea what its effect might be when mixed with brandy. "Is it safe to have given him so much, madame?" I asked, trying not to sound critical.

Again she shrugged. "I gave as much to my fool of a husband when he had the grippe, and it did not kill him." She corked the bottle. "Well, almost as much. He will sleep for a day, perhaps, and that is the best thing for him. And for you." She turned to shuffle out and I went to the door with her, thanking her with greater warmth than I felt.

When she had gone I made myself a cup of hot coffee and sat by the rickety table to drink it, watching the man in my bed. He lay on his back, his head turned toward me, and seemed to be in a deep sleep now. This was not surprising after Mme Briand's ministrations, but still he was shaken by bouts of shivering from time to time.

I had a few nice clothes left from my years at the college in Rue des Moulins, and when I had finished my coffee I undressed, put on two warm nightdresses and some woolen bedsocks, brushed out my hair and tied it back with a ribbon, then put on my dressing gown and sat in the chair close to the stove. By noon I would have to be at La Coquille once more, ready for the day's work. The room was still cold, and I began to realize that I would get little sleep sitting up in a chair for what remained of the night. If later today I was clumsy and broke some crockery, the cost would be taken from my wages. That was a thought to chill me further, for I had no reserves of money after the hard winter.

It occurred to me that I ought to find out the name of the gentleman and perhaps of the hotel where he was staying. I got up, and with much unease went through the pockets of his topcoat, jacket, and waistcoat. There were two keys on a ring, a cigar cutter, a handkerchief, a silver pencil, a crumpled bill from a restaurant I did not know, and one or two torn cabaret tickets.

I folded the clothes, turned out the lamp, and sat down again with a feeling of dismay. I had hoped that when daylight came I could go to his hotel and tell somebody what had happened, either a relative or the manager, but the gentleman had been robbed of his wallet and anything else which might have identified him. I would have to wait for him to wake up and tell me what to do before I could be free of responsibility for him, and if what Mme Briand had said was true, the brandy and laudanum would keep him asleep until long after I had left for my day's work at La Coquille.

I must have dozed for an hour, but woke feeling chilled, and found that the stove had gone out because I had forgotten to adjust the damper. When I lit the candle beside me, the clock on my dresser told me that it was half past three. I could not rake out the stove and relight it now. I looked enviously at the gentleman in my bed. He lay on his back as before, his mouth slightly open, his breathing slow but not labored, punctuated by an occasional faint snore. Obviously he was in a very deep sleep.

Half asleep myself, I decided that since nobody would either know or care what I did during the next two or three hours I might as well be as comfortable as possible. With the thought I took off my dressing gown, blew out the candle, lifted the edge of the bedclothes, and slid carefully in beside the Englishman.

Two

The bed was narrow, but not too narrow to hold us both when I had nudged him aside a little. I lay with my back to him, thankful for the warmth that soon began to encompass me, and very soon I slept.

Usually I was asleep by two and did not wake till past eight o'clock, but on this morning I woke at a few minutes before seven. Neither of us appeared to have stirred during the night. Sunlight was filtering through the thin curtains at my window, and the gentleman beside me was still breathing heavily with a gentle snore every now and again. I turned my head to look over my shoulder. A huge bruise had come out on the side of his face, and I winced at the sight.

Moving with care to avoid disturbing him, I got out of bed and went behind the curtain in the corner of the room where my enamel washbowl and jug of water stood. When I had first come to live here I had expected to find it disagreeable to take my bath standing in a bowl of cold water, even in summer, for at the college I had known every comfort, but I quickly grew used to the five minutes of gasping and shuddering every morning, for to some extent I had acquired the gift of being able to close my mind against mental or physical distress, so that it was as if some person other than myself were suffering whatever the affliction might be.

I toweled myself dry, put on clean clothes, brushed and combed my hair, and tied it in two plaits. The gentleman slept on. I put on my coat and hat, picked up my purse and shopping bag, and went downstairs. The sun was well up, but life in the court where I lived had begun at soon after five o'clock, with the clatter of milk bottles and the rumble of bread carts. Along the row of houses the concierges would drag out the ash bins in readiness for the garbage cart, whose coming would be announced by the sound of the bell hung round the neck of the leading horse.

In my first week here, before I began work at La Coquille, I had been quite bewildered by the dawn hustle and bustle, so different from all I had known in the previous few years. Now I was used to it, and could almost tell the time by the sounds from the court, for the pattern never varied. Once the ash bins were out, the gleaners would appear, both animal and human. The dogs came first, working in packs of half a dozen, digging through the garbage for scraps of food, working their way methodically along the court, and rarely fighting.

Next came the humans, singly or in families, and the strange thing was that each person or group would pick over the garbage for one particular item, some seeking old boots perhaps, others cast-off clothing, or paper and rag, or a category encompassing broken glass, crockery, and bones, while yet another group might sift the ashes for pieces of unconsumed coal. Following the gleaners came the street cleaner, a giant of a woman with a broom to match her size, sloshing water over the cobbles and roaring abuse at any gleaner who scattered refuse in the gutters.

At seven o'clock the court was busy, sabots clacking on the stones, buckets clanging. From the nearby wine cellar came the rumbling sound of casks being cleaned with chains and water, and this mingled with the ring of hammer on anvil from the ironworkers' shop beyond. Seven was the hour when the street vendors would begin to arrive from the great market of Les Halles, many of them women bearing huge baskets. They would have been at the market by four o'clock to bargain for their particular wares, one offering cauliflowers, another potatoes, others fruits of various kinds.

There was always order underlying the apparent confusion. The woman selling fish and mussels would arrive before the woman with the three-wheeled cart selling cream cheeses, and both would arrive before the artisans, the chair mender, the window repairer, and the porcelain mender. Later, when the bustle had died down a little, came the street musicians, the singers, and the beggars.

On this Saturday morning I was concerned only to buy fresh crusty bread and a little milk, and five minutes later I was in my room again, preparing my usual breakfast of bread with butter and honey, followed by coffee with milk. I was able to buy the honey very cheaply because Père Chabrier had a brother who kept bees, and I used it for sweetening my coffee in preference to sugar.

When I had finished and cleared away, I decided it was time I tried to wake the Englishman. Looking at him closely, I saw that his face was pale and moist with sweat, but when I felt his pulse I found it strong and regular, though slower than my own. I pushed back one of his eyelids. The pupil was very small, and I recalled from the time when the medical student had visited our college that this meant something, but could not remember what it was. I patted his unhurt cheek quite sharply, and shook him by the shoulder, but without effect. Evidently he was drugged by the laudanum Mme Briand had dosed him with so lavishly, and I could do nothing till he recovered. Meanwhile I had work awaiting me.

Lest he should wake within the next hour, I took a piece of paper and bottle of ink from the drawer of the rickety table and wrote in English:

> Sir,
>
> Please do not be alarmed. You were attacked and robbed by apaches near this house during the night. I found you and brought you to my room. There was nowhere else to take you for shelter. I shall return by nine o'clock.
>
> Yours truly,
> Hannah McLeod

I stood my chair by the bed, hung a towel over it, and pinned the note to the towel, so that if the gentleman woke he could not possibly miss seeing it. Then I picked up my basket of dirty washing and went down to the communal washplace with stone troughs, a minute's walk along the street.

The usual faces were there at this hour, and the women greeted me with the slight wariness that was natural in them toward one who was not only foreign but also came from a very different background. In the early days they had been suspicious and almost hostile, but as they found I caused no trouble and kept to myself they came slowly to accept me.

By ten minutes to nine I was back in my room, clambering out of the window onto the flat roof to hang my clothes on the line there while the sun was out and a breeze blowing. The Englishman was still asleep. I went downstairs again with a bucket and large jug to fetch water from the pump. On my way out I saw Gustave Briand, who glowered at me, and on my return I met his wife, who asked after my unexpected guest.

"He's still asleep, madame," I said. "He carries no wallet or papers to tell who he is, and I'm wondering what to do. Should I go to the police now, or wait for him to wake?"

"I want no policemen here, mam'selle," she said dourly, and the fact that she addressed me so formally told me that she meant it. "When he wakes, give him his coat and tell him to go. You have done enough."

"Well . . . I don't know. He looks very pale, madame. I don't like to turn a sick man into the street. Do you think Doctor Clouard would come if I promised to pay him the week after next? I mean, if the Englishman didn't pay, though I'm sure he would, as soon as he can get in touch with his friends or family."

Mme Briand sniffed. "Doctor Clouard? That old fool has killed more people than Doctor Guillotine. But he is not such a fool as you, young lady. He will want his money before he climbs the stairs." She flapped her long apron in a gesture of contempt, and turned back into her apartment.

I made my way up to my room, halting twice to rest, for the water was heavy. The sleeper had not stirred. A few minutes later, as I was raking out the stove, there came a tap on the door. I thought it could only be Mme Briand, but when I opened the door I found a man standing there, and I knew him at once, for it was the stocky man with the moon face who had been watching me so closely at La Coquille last night. He wore a short cloak in brown and white check over a plain brown suit with a fancy waistcoat, and in his hand he held a gray bowler hat with a low crown and a curly brim.

"Miss McLeod?" he said. "Miss Hannah McLeod?"

I was taken aback to find this man at my door, and felt a touch of foreboding as I answered in English. "Yes, I'm Hannah McLeod. I think you must know that, for you were studying me at La Coquille last night."

"That's a fact," he said, and now my ear recognized the short flat vowels of the more northern English counties. "Might I have a word with you, Miss McLeod? It will be to your advantage, I believe." He handed me a card on which was printed:

THOMAS BONIFACE
(General Agent)
22 Chancery Lane,
London

I said, "This doesn't tell me very much, Mr. Boniface."

He made a slight bow. "I'll be happy to explain further, miss, if you can spare five minutes."

I hesitated, then stood back. "Very well, Mr. Boniface. But I can't imagine—" I broke off abruptly, feeling color rush to my cheeks. I had forgotten about my sleeping guest until I saw Mr. Boniface's eyes go past me as he began to enter the room. He stopped short, looking embarrassed, and said, "Ahem!"

I said quickly, "Please don't have a false impression, Mr. Boniface. I found this gentleman just after he had been attacked by an apache and his woman last night." I went on to explain what had happened, but in a very few words, because after the first shock I had decided that what Mr. Boniface might think was quite unimportant to me. "Please sit down," I said, indicating the wooden chair by the table. "I apologize for not offering the easy chair, but the legs are very weak and you have to lean sideways against the wall in it, or it collapses."

Mr. Boniface did not sit, but moved to stare down at the gentleman on the bed. "Has he not come round in all this time?" he said.

"No, but he's just in a deep sleep," I replied. "The concierge brought some brandy to warm him and it was heavily laced with laudanum, which I didn't know till after he'd swallowed quite a lot."

My visitor stood with head a little on one side, as if making some calculation. After a few moments he said, "And you've found nothing about his person to tell you who he is?"

"No. I shall have to wait till he wakes up before I can find out."

"This attack you mention. Where exactly did it happen, Miss McLeod?"

"Only a little way from here, by the lamp just before the alley leading down to Rue Bertrand." Perhaps because I was tired I felt suddenly irritated by his questions, and said, "I must go to work at noon, m'sieur, and I have much to do before then. What do you wish to say to me?"

He stood lost in thought for a moment or two, then said, "Yes, let's come to that, Miss McLeod." He moved to sit down, hat resting on his knee, looking at me with curiosity in his gaze. "I'm in Paris on behalf of Mr. Sebastian Ryder, an English gentleman with business connections here. He is a widower, living in the Hertfordshire village of Bradwell, with a son of eighteen and a daughter of fifteen. Among other commissions I have to perform for him here, he instructed me to find a young lady of good education, preferably English, but completely fluent in both English and French, to be tutor to his children in teaching them to speak and write French."

I was so taken aback that I almost sat down carelessly on the easy chair, and only just remembered in time to push it against the wall first. Wondering if I were dreaming, I looked about the small mean room, then down at my patched apron and worn sabots. At last I said, "I don't think you can be serious, m'sieur."

"I'm entirely serious, Miss McLeod," he said rather sharply. "I've been here over a month now, and I can tell you it's devilish hard to find *anybody* who is completely fluent in both languages. A few among the gentry perhaps, but I can't offer such a position to gentlefolk. In all Paris, you seem to be the only young lady who fits the bill, and you fit very well, being English."

I said, "How did you happen to find me, Mr. Boniface?"

"I didn't happen to. I've been looking hard, asking questions." Mr. Boniface's manner was abrupt, but I now guessed from his accent that he came from Yorkshire, a county known for plain speaking. "Talked to an English chap a few days ago, and he said there was this lass at La Coquille, so I went along to ask the proprietor about you—what's-his-name, Père Chabrier."

"Oh. He didn't mention it."

"I paid him not to. Wanted to know more about you first. We had a chat, and next day I made a visit in Rue des Moulins."

I looked out of the small window at the gray sky, then at Mr. Boniface again, and said, "So you know I was a student at the College for Young Ladies there?"

"That's right. Had a talk with the principal, Mam'selle something-or-other. She spoke well of you. Said she thought you would do better as a teacher than as a student."

Yes, I thought, inwardly rueful. Mam'selle Montavon could well say that of me. Now that I knew Mr. Boniface had talked with her, I understood the look of curiosity in his eyes as they rested on me. I said, "Do you feel that my time as a student there provides a good recommendation for me to teach French to the children of the English gentleman?"

"My employer isn't concerned with references," Mr. Boniface said flatly. "Or rather he's only concerned with *my* recommendation. Your mother was an English schoolteacher, you were brought up in England until you were thirteen and she educated you herself. You've become completely fluent in French during your years at the college, and according to the principal and your fellow students you're widely read in both French and English literature. That's good enough for me, and I can promise you it'll be good enough for Mr. Sebastian Ryder."

I said, "Was it my friends who told you about my mother and my early life?"

He nodded. "That's right. Mam'selle what's-her-name let me have a chat with a couple of young ladies who had been special friends of yours."

"I see." That would be Annette and Marguerite, one a year older and one a year younger than I. Parting from them had given me my only sorrow when I left the college.

Mr. Boniface lifted a hand, palm up, in a questioning gesture, showing a touch of impatience. "Well, miss? You've only to put your few things in a case and we can catch the early train for Calais tomorrow. Cross-channel packet to Dover. Victoria by teatime, across to St. Pancras by cab, and we'll be in Bradwell by soon after six o'clock."

I stood up and said, "No thank you, Mr. Boniface."

He studied me with pursed lips, and gave a brief nod. "All right, you don't know me, and you don't want to go off abroad with a stranger. Natural enough. I might be telling you a cock-and-bull story. But as I said, Mr. Ryder has business interests here, and he's known to the British consul, who also knows I'm his agent. We'll go along to the consulate together, if you wish, and establish my bona fides."

I shook my head. "No thank you, Mr. Boniface. I don't wish to go to England."

He looked slowly about the room, then at me again. "I hardly think you're serious, lass," he said curtly. "You live in a garret and you're poor as a church mouse, so you'll not turn down the chance to live soft in a fine house. We've not spoken of money yet, so maybe you're bargaining, but that's foolish. Mr. Sebastian Ryder will be generous enough, but he might not take kindly to a young woman who's too greedy—"

I broke in sharply. "You're mistaken, sir. It's true I'm poor, but I manage well enough, and I have what is more important to me than anything else, my independence. I'm not trying to bargain. I simply do not wish to go to England, and there's an end of it."

He stared at me from stone-gray eyes that held no expression, yet I sensed anger and frustration simmering within him. "Don't be a fool, girl," he said at last. "Here's a chance for you to get out of this slum and start a completely new life. Chance in a million if you ask me."

"I expect it is, Mr. Boniface," I said, "but please offer it to somebody else."

"There isn't anybody else," he said, his annoyance showing in his voice. "Damn it, I've spent a month searching, and you're the only one to fit the bill."

"Then I'm sorry, but I have no intention of going to England. Will you excuse me now, Mr. Boniface? I really can't spare any more time."

He got slowly to his feet, jaw set. I thought he was going to argue further, but he stood for a moment, hat in hand, looking with narrowed eyes at the unknown gentleman still asleep in my bed, then he shrugged, walked to the door, and said, "I'd be obliged if you would let me know in the event that you change your mind, Miss McLeod. I'm staying at the Hotel Plaisance, and I'll be there for another week. You'll find I've written the address on the back of my card." He opened the door, clapped his hat on his head, and went out.

I found I was trembling a little, and realized that the notion of returning to England had touched me more deeply than I thought. The offer of a teaching position in Mr. Sebastian Ryder's house in Hertfordshire was quite startling in the way it had come to me, but I had little doubt it was genuine, for Mr. Boniface had been ready to have the British consul himself confirm it. My refusal had been quite instinctive and without reflection, but I knew that time to consider would have made no difference. My decision would have been the same.

I made up my mind to shut Mr. Boniface's visit out of my thoughts and get on with the morning's work. Long ago I had found that the best way to dispose of any particular memory was to decide that it had been experienced by someone other than Hannah McLeod, not by me but by a girl I knew very remotely who had told me about it. It was in this fashion that I was able to put away memories which would otherwise have haunted me.

By half past ten I had done my cleaning and mending. The gentleman still slept. His forehead was rather hot, his lips dry, but I felt that the long sleep was helping him to recover from the hurt he had suffered. He mumbled but did not wake when I peeled the pieces of rag from his body to look at the abrasions. They were raw, but showed no sign of festering. I washed them gently with warm water, then dusted them with boracic powder, deciding that this was more antiseptic than the ointment. As I was doing the same to the jagged cut on his face, he opened his eyes suddenly and said quite distinctly, "Who are you?"

I said, "I'm Hannah McLeod, sir. Can you tell me your name and where you are staying?"

I had the impression that he did not take in my question, but he seemed to listen carefully to my voice, and after a moment he said slowly, "Ah . . . I remember. You are the girl who . . . who . . ." His eyes closed, his voice trailed to silence, he gave a sigh and was asleep again. I found myself smiling a little as I dusted the gash on his cheek with boracic, but was not quite sure why. Truth to tell, I felt far from charitable toward the gentleman, for he was giving me a great deal of trouble that I would have been thankful to pass on to somebody else, had there been anyone willing to accept it, but I had the grace to acknowledge that this was not his fault, poor man.

Soon I would have to leave for the day's work at La Coquille. I would be home again by midnight, for this was a Saturday and we closed early on Saturdays, but I was in a quandary as to what I should do about my unexpected guest. He would surely wake before I returned, and would be alarmed to find himself stripped of most of his belongings and lying in a shabby Montmartre garret. I recalled from the scraps of knowledge I had picked up when helping the medical student in my college days that if the gentleman were suffering from concussion there might be a gap in his memory, beginning from some time before he had been attacked, and this would surely increase his alarm.

And suppose he was still unconscious when I returned? This would mean his condition was serious, and I would have to fetch a doctor at whatever cost, lest the gentleman died and I be blamed for his death. I tucked in the blanket and sat pondering my problems for a while. Henri, the apache, had missed the cuff links his victim was wearing, and I had taken them out before washing the shirt with my own clothes. I went to the drawer where I had hidden them. Yes, they were gold. I could pawn them for a good few francs to pay for a doctor and food for my sleeping guest, but I dared not do so for fear it might be said I had stolen them.

I went to the cupboard that served as my wardrobe, lifted the floorboard, and took out the small tin box where I kept my valuables—my birth certificate; my mother's birth certificate and wedding ring; the letter she had left for me when she died; her prayer book; her purse in which I had kept what small savings I had brought with me from the college, empty now; and the ring of Mexican silver, too large for any of my fingers, engraved with the initials R.D. This I could pawn, for it belonged to me, but on the day it had been given to me, almost two years ago now, I had made up my mind that I would never part with it. Remembering, I smiled and felt my eyes grow moist, then was annoyed at my stupidity in permitting myself such sentiment. I put the cuff links in the box and hid it under the floorboard again. My room was empty for at least twelve hours every day, and though it was unlikely to attract a thief, I could not afford to take any risk.

When I climbed out onto the roof again I found that a stiff breeze and a surprisingly warm sun had almost dried the clothes. I brought them in, heated my iron over a tiny spirit stove, pressed the clothes, put my own away, and hung the gentleman's shirt and undervest with his suit over the back of the kitchen chair.

There were eleven sous in my purse, and I decided that before leaving for La Coquille, I would go out and buy some cream cheese and a plate of oysters, the cheapest of all shellfish. These I would leave on the table with bread, milk, and honey, so that when the gentleman woke there would be something for him to eat and drink if he wished. I would also write a longer note explaining what had happened and saying that he was welcome to rest until I returned at midnight.

This still left several problems, for neither he nor I had money for a cab, and although I would be free tomorrow since it was Sunday, and could walk to his hotel or lodging for assistance if he were unable to do so, there remained the question of what to do about sleeping arrangements for the night. If he was awake, I could not possibly do what I had done last night, and if he was still unconscious when I returned there was nothing I could do but go straight away to tell the police, even at the risk of displeasing Mme Briand and losing my room.

Deciding I would do my shopping before I wrote the note, I put on my hat and coat, took a last look at my visitor, then picked up my shopping bag and went downstairs, leaving the door unlocked because it seemed wrong to lock the gentleman in my room. On the ground floor I knocked on Mme Briand's door and told her that the gentleman was still asleep and I intended to leave him some food with a note when I went to work. She listened, pulling hairpins from her tight bun of gray hair and thrusting them in a new place, a habit of hers when agitated, then wagged her head and told me I was stupid to have brought the foreign man home.

There was no point in arguing with her, so I agreed apologetically and went on my way, saying I would be back in ten minutes. As it happened I was delayed because I found one of the stall holders roasting pieces of chicken over a brazier, and I waited for some to be ready, thinking that a portion of cold chicken breast would be very welcome to a man who might wake feeling famished.

When I finished my shopping I had three sous left, but this was quite satisfactory since I had food for myself in the cupboard to see me through Sunday, and tonight I would eat well in the kitchen at La Coquille when I was allowed half an hour off duty from half past eight till nine o'clock. On Monday I would be paid my wages and all would be well. I was lucky to be working for Père Chabrier, for from the beginning he had paid me weekly in advance, a rare concession, but one he had been glad to offer at a time when his business was depending heavily on English visitors and he badly needed somebody who knew the language and could deal with them.

As I returned through the passage which led to Rue Labarre I saw to my surprise a carriage standing outside number eight, almost blocking the narrow street. It was a four-wheeler drawn by two well-groomed horses who, though strong, looked almost dainty compared with the giant Percherons who dragged the double-decked omnibuses known as *impériales* up the long slopes to Montmartre. The driver sat with long whip in hand, head turning as he kept a watchful eye on a few ragamuffins who had gathered to stare.

No doubt I was slow witted, but it did not occur to me that the carriage might have something to do with my nameless guest until, as I reached the third landing, I found Mme Briand there, staring up the well to the top floor where a great scuffling was going on against a background of two or three voices, one of them a woman's voice.

Mme Briand's head jerked round as I stopped beside her, and she stared at me with frightened, accusing eyes. "I told you so!" she exclaimed in a fierce whisper. "Did I not say? Now they have come for him, his wife or sister, I don't know, but she is a rich foreigner, and from the way she glares and storms she will have us all guillotined if she can!" With that my concierge went scuttling downstairs as fast as she could go, calling back to me that it was nothing to do with her.

I went on up, very uneasy now, aware that several people were coming down. Below, I heard the door of Mme Briand's apartment slam. Above, a man's rather rough voice was saying in French, "Steady, m'sieur . . . wait, Gaston, let me go first. Now . . . I have him. Gently now . . . ."

And mingled with this a woman's voice, very much a lady's voice, was saying in English but with an accent I associated with American visitors to Paris: "I'm here, Andrew, I'm here, my dear. It's all right, you're quite safe now; don't try to talk, we'll soon have you home—oh, be *careful* with him, you silly men! I mean—er—*prenez garde! Faites attention!*" The last words were in badly accented French.

They came to the fourth landing together, a young woman moving backward, beautifully dressed, head constantly turning to watch her steps, talking, encouraging, exhorting as she moved. Following her, two men in the livery of hotel servants were supporting the stranger between them. His eyes were half open but he seemed barely conscious, his feet trailing, an arm across the shoulders of the servant on each side. They had managed to put on his topcoat and button it, but the young lady carried the rest of his clothes and his boots.

I said, "Oh, thank goodness you've come, mam'selle, I've been very worried—"

I stopped short, for she had whirled round and I found myself under the glare of two cornflower blue eyes filled with such fury that I almost flinched. She was a beautiful lady, fair of hair, with a strong chin and lovely mouth, though at this moment her lips were set hard. Young, no more than twenty I was sure, she had an air of authority far beyond her years. "What?" she snapped. "Who are *you?*"

I said, "I'm Hannah McLeod, mam'selle, and—"

"Ah, you speak English. Good." Her gaze became even more fiery and she pointed up. "That is *your* room where we found Mr. Doyle?"

"Yes, I brought him home last night because he was attacked in the street, and unconscious—"

Again she cut me short, and though she did not raise her voice, her words were like knives. "You expect such a tale to be believed?" she said on a rising note of incredulity. "Oh no, young woman! I think you are a liar, a slut, and a thief. I've no time to say more to you now, but be sure that once I have made all necessary arrangements for Mr. Doyle, I shall take this matter further. Now stand aside!"

I felt my face go pale with shock as apprehension seized me. "No, mam'selle," I stammered, "I've been trying to help your friend, but I couldn't discover who he was. Please believe me—"

One of the servants reached out and pushed me aside. They all moved past, Mr. Doyle with head lolling, still barely awake. On they went down the next flight, with the young lady giving orders to the servants and encouragement to the gentleman. I followed them down, trying to explain to the lady, then to the servants in French, but I might have been invisible for all the notice they took. Reaching the ground floor, they carried Mr. Doyle out and put him in the carriage. The lady and a servant climbed in with him, the other servant joined the driver, who immediately whipped up the horses and took the carriage clattering away over the cobbles, watched by a curious crowd till it turned the corner, when they transferred their curiosity to me.

I felt inwardly very shaken, but I had long ago learned to hide my true feelings and present a calm face to the world if need be, so I was able to smile when I went back into the house and Mme Briand opened her door in answer to my tapping. "I'm sorry you were inconvenienced, madame," I said. "The young lady has a wrong impression of me, but I'm sure that will be put right when the gentleman comes to himself. You need not concern yourself about the police."

"Ha! So *you* say." Mme Briand was transferring hairpins in her bun at a great rate, very agitated. "But she is like a wild cat, that foreign woman, all teeth and claws."

"She was overexcited," I said, "but when she is calm again, and has spoken with the gentleman, there will be no trouble here for you to worry about. Did you explain to her what had happened, madame?"

"I tried," Mme Briand said, not very convincingly. "Naturally I tried." She scowled suddenly. "How do *I* know what happened? I was not there."

I managed to keep smiling. "But you were there when I was trying to care for the poor man, madame. Did you tell the young lady that?"

"Tell her? What chance was there to *tell* her anything? She does not listen. She speaks continuously on and on and on. Even if she listened it would serve no purpose, since she does not understand a civilized language."

"Yes, it was very difficult for you," I said in what I hoped was a soothing tone. "Do you know how they discovered that the gentleman was here?"

"I know nothing, girl," Mme Briand snapped sourly. "You think such a woman would stop to explain to me? I do not know what she said, I only know it was very unpleasant. I do not have to learn English to understand that." She transferred a final hairpin and wagged a finger at me. "Let us hope for your sake that we hear no more of this."

The door closed. I stood feeling drained and unhappy, then suddenly realized how late it was, and went hurrying upstairs to put my shopping away and get ready to leave for La Coquille. Apprehension was strong within me. If Mr. Doyle remembered nothing, and if the lady went to the police, it would be hard for me to prove that I had taken no part in the robbery. Mme Briand would be of little help.

I ran downstairs and out into the street. Twelve hours of work lay ahead for me, and I could not afford to be distracted and make mistakes. This was a moment when I felt thankful to have acquired the faculty for blotting out any thoughts, memories, or speculation that might distress me. It was an ability which had served me well in the past, but on this occasion it was to serve me ill, for it caused me to forget something I had done that morning, a small action but one that was bound to have disastrous consequences.

Three

I woke at eight next morning to the sound of banging on my door, and felt my heart quicken with alarm at what this might portend after the threats made by the young woman yesterday.

"Wait," I called, trying to keep my voice steady. "A moment, please." The banging ceased. I slid my feet into the slippers beside the bed, pulled on the winter dressing gown I had brought with me from Rue des Moulins, and went to the door. "Who is it?" I said.

There was no answer. Puzzled, I drew the bolt and warily opened the door, then gave a gasp of relief and threw it wide. Red hair, green eyes, freckles, and a wide grin showing through a darker red beard, a big man in a seaman's jersey and calico trousers stood there in the passage, his face brown and weather-beaten. "Wishing a very good morning to you, Hannah McLeod," he said. "How are you, me beauty?"

Toby Kent was half Irish, and it had become his habit to call me, as he had just done, "me beauty." He was my only neighbor on this floor, and I saw that across the landing his door stood open now. I pushed back my plaits, hugged the dressing gown about me, and said, "Oh, Toby, you gave me such a fright. I thought it was the police."

His eyebrows twitched upward. "The police? But why?"

I shook my head. "I had a difficult day yesterday, but I'll tell you about it later. It's good to see you home again."

"Only for two days, while the ship unloads and loads again at Le Havre, then I'm off for a few weeks on a run to Bombay. Now listen, you're invited to breakfast if you'll cook it for us. An English breakfast with eggs and bacon and kidneys and heaven knows what else I've brought with me."

I smiled. "I never had such a breakfast myself in England, but thank you, Toby. Give me twenty minutes to wash and dress, then come in with your fatted calf and I'll gladly do the cooking."

"No, come to the studio, Hannah." He gestured across the passage. "I lit the stove an hour ago, so it'll be nice and warm, and there's more elbow room for you there."

"All right. In twenty minutes."

"Fine. Do you like the beard, young McLeod?"

"Not much, Toby. I'm used to you without."

"Then I'll have it off before breakfast." He laughed and swung away across the landing. I closed the door and hurried to warm some water on the spirit stove for my standing-up bath, happy to have Toby Kent home again but regretting that it was for so short a time.

We had known each other for eighteen months now, and were friendly neighbors, perhaps because we were both English. Toby had a much larger room than I, a studio with a small bedroom adjoining, and he had been there long before I came. It was during my first week, when I was settling in and getting a few sticks of furniture together before starting work, that he knocked on my door, introduced himself, and announced cheerfully that if I needed help and failed to ask him he would be greatly put out.

I was wary of him at first, as was natural for a young woman of eighteen years living on her own in such a place, but as the weeks went by I found him a good friend, and quickly came to know that I need never be uneasy about his intentions. He knew I had been a student at the College for Young Ladies, and as we came to know each other better I told him of my earlier years in England, and how I had come to Paris soon after my mother died. In turn I learned Toby Kent's story.

It was plain from the beginning that he was an artist, for he usually smelled of paint, his clothes were often daubed with it, and his room was cluttered with pictures. The first time I saw him was through the landing window on a raw morning soon after dawn as he stood in shirt-sleeves on the flat part of the roof between the gables, an easel before him, one moment utterly still as he stared south toward the Seine and the panorama of the city below, the next attacking his canvas with enormous energy in a flurry of brush strokes.

He did not paint only landscapes, but would paint whatever took his fancy, a flower, a street scene, a portrait—he had done several of me—a ragamuffin, a sunset, or an overflowing garbage can. It saddened me that with such enthusiasm he should be so poor a painter, but to me his pictures never looked like the subject he was painting. They were very bold, even though the colors were often delicate, and great splotches of paint stood out from the canvas as if he had smeared them on with a finger, which he sometimes did. Strangely, I found that if I half closed my eyes, his pictures took on a quite different aspect and were intriguing in a way I could not fathom. When I told him this he chuckled and said there might yet be hope that he could cure me of being a Philistine. He knew I thought his paintings not very good, for I had no gift for pretense with him, but he was not in the least hurt by this, so I was able to respond that painting pictures for half-closed eyes was a funny thing for an artist to do.

Toby had been born in England and schooled there, but his mother was Irish, and a time had come when the family moved to Dublin and Toby went up to Trinity College to read law. His father was a very successful barrister, and his two brothers, both older than he, were following the same profession, but when Toby was twenty he rebelled.

"I wanted to paint," he said simply, one morning as he sat on the only safe chair in my room while I sat on the bed sewing over some frayed parts in the cuffs of his best pair of trousers. "More than anything in the world I wanted to paint, Hannah. And less than anything in the world did I want to be a lawyer. There was an almighty row, I'm telling you. My father's a man who knows what's best for everyone; in fact he rather doubts that God made the universe quite right, and is sure he could have done better himself given the chance. He has no liking for me, and I've none for him, but the brothers go in fear of him, and they tried to persuade me to do as I was bid. My mother would have tried too, poor dear, if she hadn't died six months before, but it was only for her sake I ever went up to university."

He drank from the coffee he had made and brought in for us to share, grimaced as he swallowed, and said, "Dear Lord, don't I make awful coffee, Hannah?"

I said, "Yes, Toby, it's the worst I've ever tasted."

"Do you think boiling it for ten minutes is not long enough?"

I stared. "You *boil* it? No wonder it's so bad. I'll write out the way to do it for you. Now go on with what you were saying."

He shrugged. "There's not much to it. The devil of a row, and Toby Kent, the black sheep of the family, is cut off without a shilling and told he has ceased to exist as far as the family is concerned." He chuckled and ran fingers through his red hair. "So I did cease to exist. I enlisted in the *Légion étrangère* and spent the next three years marching about Algeria."

I stopped sewing and only just managed to prevent my jaw from dropping. "You were in the Foreign Legion? Oh, Toby, you really must be as mad as Mme Briand thinks. How could you practice painting as a legionnaire?"

"I couldn't, me beauty," he said, rather soberly for him. "But I felt I'd best become a man before I tried to become a painter. I'd lived soft for twenty years and I knew little enough about the world or about myself."

"Yourself?"

"Surely. For it's when you're lying on a ridge of sand with a handful of other men, looking over the sights of your Lebel at a great crowd of yelling Tuaregs charging up at you that you find out what sort of fellow there is inside you."

"And what did you find out, Toby?"

He laughed. "That I'm as frightened as the next man, but that with practice you can shut it out and carry on. You must have found that out for yourself, Hannah. But it wasn't just the danger you learn from. There were men from all over the world there, men who'd been rich or poor, good or bad, gentleman or peasant, saint or sinner, civilized man or brute. So when I'd served my time I felt I'd gathered enough understanding to begin learning to paint, and for that there was nowhere else to settle but Paris. I studied under Gérôme at the École des Beaux-Arts for two years till my money ran out—"

He broke off with a sudden shout of laughter. "You'd never believe the pranks students play on one another, Hannah. They'll light a fire of paper under your stool while you're painting, or run a ribbon of paint round the collar of your painting blouse, or maybe add some awful things to your picture while you're away. There was a fellow who spent an hour trying to paint with currant jelly from a tube he thought contained lac."

"What's lac, Toby?"

"Oh, a dark red transparent resin. What was I saying?"

"Your money ran out." I bit the thread off and laid the trousers aside.

"Well, you know the rest. Whenever I run out of money I go to Le Havre or one of the other ports and sign on as a deckhand on any cargo ship I can find." He grinned. "If you're not fussy about conditions you can always find a berth. Sometimes it's for two or three weeks, sometimes for nine or ten. I never go further than French Somaliland one way and Mexican Gulf ports the other way, but whether it's a long or short voyage I come back with enough money saved to see me through for a few months here."

At the end of my first six weeks as Toby Kent's neighbor, he invited me to dine with him one Sunday evening at a good restaurant in Montparnasse, in Rue de la Gaieté. By now I knew that he sought nothing of me but a companionable friendship, and I was glad to accept. We both put on our best clothes for the occasion and spent a very pleasant evening together, taking a cab both ways from Montmartre. I suspected later that he had used the last of his money to give us a luxurious evening, for next day he left on a five week voyage to Casablanca.

I was always sorry when Toby left on a voyage, and always glad to see him return safely, for I had no other friend, and sometimes had time to feel lonely when he was away, his room empty. I found him a happy man, and was grateful for a companion I could be at ease with, a companion who made no demands. Because of my work, we did not see a great deal of each other, but sometimes he would take me out to lunch or to dine on a Sunday, as he had on that first occasion. In return, although he expected no return, I was glad to do his mending, to clean his studio, and from time to time prepare a meal for us to share, as I was about to do now.

Throughout the neighborhood there was a very natural belief that I had become Toby Kent's woman. It was the only thing I had ever known to give him concern, which was on my behalf, and he broached the matter to me plainly one day. I was quick to reassure him. "Toby, I'm glad for people to believe it, as long as you don't mind. A young woman living alone as I do in a place like this has no reputation to lose anyway, and I'm not troubled by what people think. To be honest, I'm sure it helps protect me a little from other men who might press their attentions on me."

This was perfectly true. Toby Kent was a big man whose years in the Legion and as a seaman had made him far too formidable for the average apache to risk trouble with him, and in well over a year there had been only three occasions when I had been approached by an importunate man. Young though I was, I had little difficulty in sending such men about their business, but I was thankful to have the problem arise so seldom.

When I explained this to Toby he sighed with relief, then gave one of his chuckling laughs which always made me want to laugh myself. "Right then, me beauty," he said. "I'll walk you on my arm to La Coquille this noon, if you'll permit, to reinforce the notion hereabouts."

On this Sunday morning of his unexpected return I began to feel almost glad that so much had happened to me in the past thirty-six hours, for I rarely had much of interest to tell Toby, while he of course would return with strange and marvelous stories to tell of foreign lands he had visited. He sometimes declared that he made up half the tales, and that the dock area of one big port was just as dull and dirty as the dock area of another, whether in Port Said or Panama.

Today I had some tales to tell myself. First there was Mr. Doyle, the gentleman I had brought home barely conscious after the apache and his woman had attacked him. I imagined how Toby would laugh when I told of the way Mme Briand had dosed the poor man so liberally with laudanum and brandy that I had been quite unable to wake him. Then there was Mr. Boniface, who had appeared that same morning with his extraordinary offer of a private teaching position in England. Finally there was the fierce young lady, probably American, who had come to take Mr. Doyle away and had abused me in such strong terms. That was not a very amusing story, in fact I had been frightened by her threats, but now, with a new day beginning, I felt sure she would realize she had been wrong to think ill of me.

When I had bathed and dressed, I brushed my hair, pinned it up neatly, put on my apron, and went across the passage to tap on the door. My mouth was watering, for Toby usually brought home a fine parcel of food wrapped in oilskin, and I knew we would soon be enjoying a splendid breakfast.

When I entered in answer to his call, the studio was already growing warm from the heat of the stove. Toby, clean-shaven now, was in the corner where he kept his brushes and paint, busily scraping hardened paint from a palette. Already I could smell turpentine, and I said despairingly, "Oh, Toby, you're impossible. Do you want to ruin our lovely breakfast?"

He looked at me, frowned suddenly, and said almost accusingly, "You've pinned your hair up."

"Of course I have." I went across to cork the bottle of turpentine. "I always put it up if I'm invited out."

"I like the plaits better."

"No you don't; you said they make me look fourteen and I'm not. You *asked* me to put it up last time you painted me."

"Ah, well, yes, sometimes I like it up, but today I like the plaits." He was not being flattering, and although he was staring at me as if I were an object rather than a person, he was not being impolite, either. I recognized the look in his eye. He had been seized with an immense urge to paint a particular subject, and at this moment I was that subject. I had seen it happen to him once or twice before, and I could not help smiling now as he gestured impatiently and said, "Plait it again, Hannah, plait it."

I said, "You invited me to breakfast."

"Oh, dear God, I'm sorry. Look, there's the stuff beside the sink. Go on, make it, make it, quick as you can."

I said firmly, "I'll make it when you've put that bottle of turpentine in the cupboard, thrown that turpsy rag out of the window, washed your turpsy hands, and gone down to get some milk."

"Milk?" His green eyes were glazed. "Why?"

"Because we're going to have coffee with our breakfast, and I have only a little milk left."

"But it's Sunday."

"I know it's Sunday. Now listen hard."

Toby cocked his head. Faintly to our ears came a sound from the street below as a reed pipe was played. This signaled the arrival of the goat's-milk vendor who came each Sunday morning with his flock of eight goats, very hairy but amiable creatures who would stand to be milked into a customer's bowl.

"It's the walking milk cans," said Toby, and picked up a jug.

"The turps first!" I cried. "And that rag and your hands, Toby. We don't want our coffee ruined."

He rolled up his eyes, grimaced, opened the roof window to fling the rag out, and rushed to the sink. "It's a terrible woman you are, young McLeod," he declared grimly. "God save us all, to think I sometimes wished I'd had a younger sister. I wager she'd have been just like you."

"And if I'd had an older brother like you—" I began, then broke off because my throat closed suddenly and tears came to my eyes. If I had been lucky enough to have an older brother like Toby Kent, then my life would surely have been very different. He came to me, drying his hands then throwing the towel aside, taking care not to touch me as always, and said contritely, "I'm sorry, Hannah. Did I hurt you?"

"No, no," I said impatiently. "I just had a silly thought that took me by surprise, but I'm quite all right now. Off you go, or you'll miss the goats."

Twenty minutes later we sat down to a magnificent English breakfast, or Irish breakfast as Toby called it, since the bacon and kidneys came from Ireland. We spoke little while we ate, I because I wanted to concentrate on savoring the delicious food, Toby for a different reason. From the way he ate, he can hardly have tasted anything, for his whole concentration was focused upon me and he was in a world of his own, staring, moving his head from side to side, drawing it back a little, narrowing his eyes, chewing his lip, muttering under his breath.

I was too busy enjoying my breakfast to be embarrassed by this, and in any event it was only Toby Kent. He finished eating, gulped his coffee, and began to fidget, but I would not be hurried. "Toby, if you want me to sit for you I will," I said, "but you'll have to wait. When I've finished eating, I'm going to have another cup of coffee, then probably another cup, and we'll talk as if we were gentlefolk with a bevy of servants to wait on us. Now tell me about New Orleans."

"New Orleans?"

"That's where you've just been, isn't it?"

"Oh, yes." His fingers drummed on the table. "Well, we went there and . . . er, then we came back."

"And nothing interesting happened?"

"Not really. I can't remember anything."

"Why are you home for only two days this time?"

"Because I signed on with another line for a trip to Bombay. Longer than usual, but I want to get as much money saved as possible so I won't have to go away during the summer." He gestured toward the big studio window. "Longer days. Better light. More time for painting."

I poured myself more coffee and said, "Whyever did you trouble to come all the way down from Le Havre? You could have stayed there more easily."

He looked at his hands, flexing the fingers. "I had to come back to my paints, even for only two days." He smiled suddenly. "I was starving for them, Hannah. Do you think I'm a lunatic?"

"No, of course not. I just wish—"

I stopped short. He lay back in his chair and laughed. "Wish I weren't such a dreadful painter?"

"Oh, Toby, no. It's just that I don't quite understand your way of painting. Now will you listen for a while, because I have tales to tell you."

He folded his arms, composed his expression, and said, "Proceed, me beauty."

At first he was inwardly paying little attention, but then he began to take notice. "A hatpin?" he interrupted. "Dear Lord, where were your wits, you daft girl? He could have knifed you!"

"No, he was too distracted. I almost broke his knee with my sabot. Anyway, everything was all right, so don't fuss."

Toby laughed when I told him of the brandy laced with laudanum, and again at my tale of how I had crept into bed with my sleeping guest rather than freeze. When I came to the arrival of Mr. Boniface and his offer, Toby looked surprised. "Why didn't you take it?"

"Oh, you know I don't want to go back to England. I never want to be reminded of the way I left there."

"All the same," he said slowly, "you'd be a great deal better off, providing the job is genuine."

"He offered the consul here as a reference."

"Good enough. Why not take the plunge? Once you were there you'd soon get over this feeling you have about England." He hesitated, then went on, "I know you associate England with all that happened after your mother died, but you could just as easily associate France with the fact that you were unhappy at the College for Young Ladies."

I said, "I know it doesn't make sense, but I can't help that. It's just the way I feel, Toby. Anyway, I'm not going, and I wish you'd stop interrupting because I haven't finished my stories yet. Later that morning I had another visitor."

I went on to tell of the young lady with the two servants who had come to take away the man I then learned was named Mr. Doyle, still barely conscious. "I think she was American," I said, "and she was certainly a very angry lady. Oh, Toby, it was awful. She was convinced *I* had robbed the gentleman, and she fairly stormed at me, calling me a slut and a thief. I was so taken aback I hardly managed to get a word in, but she wasn't listening anyway. And Mme Briand was no help. She hid herself away till it was all over."

"That old fool," said Toby, and struck the table with his palm so that the crockery jumped, an angry glitter in his eyes. "If this American idiot had a grain of sense she'd realize you don't rob a man then give him a bed for the night and wash his shirt. What the devil were you thinking of to bring him home anyway, young McLeod?"

"I had no choice," I said indignantly. "I couldn't leave him there unconscious; he might have frozen to death."

"Then maybe he'd learn not to wander alone in a place like this at such an hour."

"Oh, don't be so heartless."

"He was the heartless one. Oh, it's a fine adventure for a foreign tourist to prowl the streets of the apaches, but if you invite danger then you should damn well take the consequences, with a slashed face or a knife between your ribs. And to cap it all, this American vixen then comes here and blames the girl who saved his miserable life."

Toby rose abruptly from the table, almost overturning his chair, and paced across the studio, the freckles standing out on his face because it had paled beneath the tan. "She'll not come back with the police," he growled, "for if she hasn't already realized her story makes no sense, they'll be quick to point it out to her. But I wish she would come back, by God. She'd not talk *me* down, and I'd give her a tongue-lashing to take the starch out of her, so I would."

I got up and stood in front of him so he had to stop his restless pacing. "If she won't come back, then that's an end of it and I'm very glad," I said. "But please calm down, Toby. It's all over and done with. I didn't mean to make you angry; I thought you'd laugh about it."

He stared down at me with a baffled air, then slowly his expression changed until once again he was looking at me with that fierce, impersonal concentration I had seen in him before. He glanced at the window and at the skylight. Outside it was one of those bright mornings, sunny and cloudless, which sometimes come toward winter's end. Turning, he began to gather up our breakfast crockery with feverish haste and put it in the sink.

"The light's perfect," he muttered. "Help me clear these things, Hannah."

"I'd better wash up before you start painting."

"No, no," he said impatiently, "I want a sink full of crocks. Now wait a minute." He clutched his chin, staring at me. "I want plaits. Yes, change your hair to plaits and . . ." His eyes lit up and he slapped a fist into the palm of his other hand. "Go and put your dark blue dress on for me. Please, Hannah. The one with the wide neckline, scooped out, I don't know what you call it."

"But that's my oldest dress," I said. "Surely I could wear my best one?"

"No, no, no," he exclaimed. "The blue. Please, Hannah, there's a good girl." He lunged toward the door and opened it for me. "Quick as you can, now. I'll be mixing paint."

I could not help laughing at his urgency as I went out, but he did not respond, and as I looked back from my own door I saw him push the table aside with his foot and snatch up a chair to place close to the sink. When I returned almost ten minutes later, he was setting up a canvas on his easel.

"How do you want me?" I asked. I was clean and tidy, but hardly looking my best in plaits and my old dress. This did not trouble me, however, for Toby's paintings bore little likeness to the subject.

"On the chair, me beauty, sitting on the chair," he said. "No, wait." He tugged at a handful of his hair. "Look, I'd like the shoulders bare. Would you mind if we had the neck pulled down off the shoulders a wee way, Hannah?"

I smiled, perhaps a little wryly. It was considerate of Toby to ask if I minded, but the fashion among the gentry today was for ladies to be far more daringly décolleté than I would be with the neckline of my dress running across only two inches below my shoulders. I unfastened two buttons, eased the neckline down, and said, "No, I don't mind. Is that all right?"

"Too much. Up half an inch. Fine. That's fine." He stepped back three paces. "Now turn round slowly. Hold on; you have something odd on your right shoulder."

"You'll have to put up with it," I said. "It's a birthmark."

"A birthmark?" His voice lifted on the word. "Surely not. It's so regular."

"Well I can't help that, Toby, and I haven't painted it on. Look for yourself." It was on the back of my shoulder, near the point. I could see it in blurred fashion by craning my neck, but I had often seen it in the looking glass in my bedroom at the college, a pale golden brown mark an inch across, not raised from the flesh, shaped like a butterfly, each symmetrical wing with rounded corners.

Toby came close to peer. "Good Lord, that's remarkable," he said softly. "And so pretty."

I made a face. "I don't think it's pretty."

"You're a Philistine. It's like a beauty spot, but far better, and it's actually part of you. If you mixed with the high society ladies, they'd all soon be painting golden butterflies on their shoulders."

"I'll remember that. Now how do you want me to sit?"

"Looking toward the window over the sink, looking out over the roofs and chimney pots. Good. Turn a little more to your right. Whoa! Yes, that will do. Now, one foot forward a little. Good. Knees together, hands resting loosely in your lap. Wait. Now keep your head just as it is, but turn your body a tiny bit more toward me. That's fine!"

There came the sound of scuffling as he moved the easel slightly, then the clatter of palette, brushes, tubes of paint. After a while, silence. Complete silence. I was in profile to Toby, and could see him only from the corner of one eye, but I knew he was just standing and staring, as I had seen him do on other occasions. At last he sighed, and his hand moved to make the first brush stroke.

I looked out over the rooftops of Montmartre to the bright blue sky beyond, closing my mind to awareness of Toby Kent, for I had found that this was the easiest way for me to hold a pose. If I thought about what he was doing, I became tense, and he would alternately shout at me and apologize. I did not in the least mind his shouting, but felt it could hardly improve his painting.

It was pleasantly warm in the studio, and outside the sun was shining. A hard winter was almost past. I had work, and tomorrow I would be paid. I was independent and beholden to nobody. I had just enjoyed a wonderful breakfast, and I had one good friend, a man who respected me. It was hard to think what more I could want for, and I felt very content as I sat there with random thoughts drifting through my head.

Books . . . I had brought a number of books with me to Montmartre, but had pawned them all during the hard winter. I had been offered hardly anything for them, but I was glad of that now, because over the coming weeks I could save a few francs and redeem them. If I was lucky with tips, I might even be able to save up for one or two new books. I missed having them about me, and had well earned my nickname of *la professeuse* during my time at the college. Toby had two shelves full. He had given me leave to borrow at will, and I had taken him at his word, but I still longed to have books of my own in my own small room.

For half an hour I was vaguely aware of sounds coming from Toby's direction, heavy breathing through the nose as if from anger, a muttered curse, the sound of palette knife on canvas as paint was scraped off, some more effortful breathing, a snort of contempt. I had heard all this before, and taken no notice, but now came something new, a silence followed by a half-throttled cry that seemed to hold exultation, then the furious clatter of knife on palette as color was mixed. I rolled my eyes round to the corners and glimpsed Toby as he almost flung himself at the canvas. My head must have moved slightly, for he shouted, "Still, Hannah! Keep *still!*"

I looked out of the window again. More sounds came, but this time they were mutterings of effort rewarded and grunts of satisfaction. I gathered that Toby was pleased with his progress, and felt glad for him, but could not help wondering if anybody else would share his feeling of success.

Time passed. It was an easy pose, and I was very comfortable. This was Sunday, the best day of the week, when I would not have to be on my feet for close on twelve hours at La Coquille but could do as I wished, some cleaning and mending, some preparations for the coming week, and if the weather continued kind, I might take an omnibus down into the city that afternoon and walk by the Seine for a while, for the fare was only three sous.

There must have been a long time when my mind slept, but I was only aware of it when I slowly roused to wakefulness again and saw that the sun beyond the chimney pots had moved quite a way. Now I was stiff, for I had not moved a muscle in all that time. I listened, but could hear no sound of Toby, no movement or breathing, nothing at all. Puzzled, I peered from the corners of my eyes. There stood the easel, but of Toby there was no sign. I turned my head, quite bewildered now.

Two brushes and a palette lay on the floor by the easel. Behind me, Toby sat at the table, slumped over it with his head pillowed on his arms. I got up quickly and moved to shake him by the shoulder. "Toby? Are you all right?"

He lifted his head and looked at me soberly. His eyes were quiet, but wide open and aware, so I knew he had not been asleep. I said, "What is it, Toby? What's wrong?"

He shook his head and sat up straight, his eyes beginning to sparkle. "Nothing's wrong. Are you listening now, young McLeod?"

"Listening? Of course I am! Whatever do you mean?"

"I just want to be sure you take notice of what I'm going to say, so here it is now, Hannah McLeod. If you ever need a favor, if you ever need a friend to do anything at all for you, even if it means going down to hell and back, just come to Toby Kent. You understand?"

I stood back with a little laugh of wondering surprise. "Toby, you're mad as a hatter, just as Mme Briand always says. What on earth makes you say such a funny thing?"

"You do, me beauty." He threw back his head, gave a joyous laugh, and stood up. "By God, this is the finest day of my life, so it is. I've broken through, Hannah. I've found the way of it, found what I've been struggling for all these years." He slapped a palm to his brow. "It's here now, in my head and my hand. Oh, sure, it'll never be easy and I wouldn't want it so, for there has to be the passion and the pain, but I've found . . . dear God, what have I found? Not a secret, no, nor a touchstone. I've found the way between my head and my hand, and it was through you that it came, Hannah. Through you. I'll never forget that. Now come and see."

He moved across the studio with eager strides, and I followed, turning to look upon the picture, filled with hope by his enthusiasm. But as I gazed, my heart sank. The painting seemed to me to be just like all his other pictures, thick layers of paint dashed on the canvas with a hasty brush, and some of the background unfinished—part of the floor, the sink, and the wall beside the window. I could only just recognize the girl seated in the chair as myself, and there was something about her that made me feel uneasy, a sad, haunting quality. It was there, and strong, but I could not see how it had been achieved.

I said reluctantly, "I don't really think it's very much like me, Toby."

He laughed and stretched his arms lazily. "Dear Hannah. If you want a picture that looks exactly like you, then I'll have your photograph taken. Haven't I explained to you half a dozen times about the impressionists?"

"You've said a lot about the quality of light, and . . . wait a minute, yes, about the juxtaposition of pure colors arranged according to—er—oh yes, according to the optical laws of the complementaries, whatever that may mean. I can't remember the rest, but you said the impressionists were so obsessed with light they lost all sense of form. Is that right?"

"Not bad," said Toby, "except you've only remembered the words, but that's a start at least. Now step back, me beauty. More, more. Now look again. Don't tell me some of the background needs filling in, because I know, and I can do that at leisure in half an hour. Just look. Not with your eyes and your brain, because I want you to stop being realistic and practical for a few moments. Look with your eyes and open your heart; that's the way to see a picture."

I wanted to obey and stood gazing, trying to empty my mind of thought. At first nothing happened, but then slowly I began to glimpse something quite strange. What I had seen close-to as daubs of color seemed gradually to blend and come to life in a new way. It was like an optical illusion, except that the illusion seemed to lie in the way I had first seen the picture. Now I could see that the face was much like mine, perhaps more so than I imagined since we see our own faces only in a looking glass, and there was something about the seated figure which reached out to touch me in a most curious way.

I moved closer, and the picture became a conglomeration of blobs again. "How do you do it, Toby?" I said, intrigued. "How do you know it will look right when you stand back?"

He laughed. "I only found out for myself today, Hannah, and I couldn't begin to explain. But if you can see that much, then maybe I've started your conversion from a Philistine at last. Do you like it better now?"

"Yes," I said slowly. "Quite a lot better. But why have you made me look so sad? I don't mean my face exactly; I'm not quite sure what it is."

"Look again."

I moved back and contemplated the picture once more. Surprise touched me. "Oh, no. I'm not sad now; it's in the past, isn't it? I've put it behind me and . . . I'm content in a quiet sort of way." I turned to look at Toby. "Is that how you see me?"

He nodded, not taking his eyes from the picture. "You don't mind?"

I had to smile. "If you know me as well as that picture shows you do, then you must know I don't mind. I think it's very clever, and I'm glad you're pleased. Now I must wash up, and while I'm doing that you can put out anything that needs mending. Are you listening to me, Toby?"

"Yes, of course I'm listening," he said absently. "What did you say? I was just thinking, Hannah . . . there are still three days to go before the closing date for admission of paintings to the spring Salon at the Palais des Beaux-Arts. The picture has to be framed for that, but if I finish it today, I could get old Depuis to frame it in the morning, in time for me to get it to the Salon in the afternoon before I leave."

I put a hand to my mouth. "Oh, Toby. Will I be on show at the Salon?"

"That depends. There's a jury made up of the greatest French artists. All the paintings pass before them in procession. If they lift their hands it means approval, if they do nothing it means rejection. But I won't submit it if you don't want me to."

I did not want him to, but he was so happy with what he had done that it would have been cruel to deny him, so I said quickly, "Of course you must submit it. I just felt shy at the notion for a moment, but really I'm flattered."

Toby took his eyes from the painting to look at me, head on one side, smiling a little. "Come to think of it," he said, "if I'd had a sister, she might just possibly have been worse than you."

We were both busy for the next hour or so. I washed up, did Toby's few bits of mending, and brought my own into his room to do. He spent little more than half an hour finishing the picture, working very swiftly but in a relaxed way now, and chatting with me as we went on with our tasks. When he had finished he went out to arrange for old Monsieur Depuis the carpenter to come next morning and make a frame. While he was gone I cleaned his room and began on my own, smiling to myself occasionally as I remembered the scenes two years ago on the final day for the acceptance of paintings by the Salon. It was the same every year, but on this occasion my friend Marguerite and I had persuaded Mam'selle Montavon to allow us to go out in a carriage to watch the fun.

This was the day when from every corner of Paris canvases came pouring in at the last moment for judgment at the Salon. They came from splendid studios and from mean garrets, from established painters and hungry students. Many of the poor ones had spent their last francs to have a painting framed, and some were enormous. The strange thing was that so many pictures were worked on until the very last moment. Marguerite and I had seen an artist putting desperate finishing touches to his picture as it was carried along the street on the back of a man hired for a few sous. Others brought their pictures in cabs, on hand-carts, and on the upper decks of the omnibuses, and many sustained damage on the way.

The manner in which the students dressed and behaved made the whole event like a circus; some were in top hats, some in what appeared to be fancy dress, some in paint-daubed smocks. Toward six o'clock, the closing hour, all was confusion outside the wide entrance to the Salon, and when the great doors closed at last, bands of students would sweep down the Champs Élysées, singing and dancing, howling with laughter at a belated entrant frantically trying to swim against the tide with his precious canvas held over his head. It was all great fun to watch, but I was glad for Toby's sake that he would not be taking his painting in on the final day.

I had almost finished my room when I heard him return. He thumped on the door and called, "Come and take a cold luncheon with me when you're ready, Hannah. I have some German sausage and a carafe of wine."

I opened the door and said, "Thank you, Toby. Give me a few minutes. I'll contribute a piece of cold chicken and some cream cheese. It's quite a feast day for us, isn't it?"

"A day of days, me beauty, not even counting the food."

I completed my cleaning, washed my hands, changed my dress, and went across to Toby's room with the piece of chicken and cream cheese I had bought to give Mr. Doyle the day before. Toby lay sprawled on his bed. Only ten minutes had passed since we spoke, and no doubt he had intended just to lie down and rest while waiting for me, but he was sound asleep. It occurred to me that he had probably slept hardly at all last night, for he had arrived at dawn after docking at Le Havre and traveling down to Paris overnight. Then had come the hours of work on his painting, feverish work into which he had poured his whole spirit, so it was little wonder that he slept now.

I unlaced his boots and eased them off without waking him, then put a blanket over him, fed the stove with more coal, and settled down with a book from his shelves, a fairly recent book by Émile Zola called *La Terre.* More than two hours passed before Toby stirred, opened his eyes, blinked dazedly about him, then sat up with a start, a hand to his head.

"Holy saints, what time is it?" he demanded muzzily.

I put down my book. "Almost five, and you've had a nice sleep, Toby."

"Five? Why the devil didn't you wake me?"

"Why should I? You needed to sleep."

"Have you eaten?"

"No, but after that breakfast I wasn't especially hungry, so I thought I'd wait for you."

He got up, went to the sink, bent over it, and poured a jug of cold water over his head. Busy drying his face with a towel, he marched across the room and turned to look at the painting again, anxiously at first, then with a sigh of relief and pleasure. "Ah, I didn't dream it, then. Now listen, Hannah. Since you've not eaten, you daft girl, and since it's too late for luncheon now, why don't we have a bite of bread and cheese, then take the omnibus down to the Boul' Mich', stroll awhile by the river, walk down to Montparnasse for an hour at Le Soleil d'Or, and finish with a good dinner at Maison Darblay?" His face emerged from the towel as he finished speaking. "Well?"

It was an attractive prospect. I would enjoy the ride and the walk, for there was still warmth in the air from the day's sunshine, and Le Soleil d'Or was a café where bohemians of all kinds, writers, artists, poets, musicians, gathered to perform for each other, to play or sing, to read prose or verse. Some were quite good and some were quite awful, but on the two or three occasions I had been there before with Toby, I had always enjoyed myself.

I said, "I can't sponge on you for dinner as well, Toby; you know that."

"I know you're too damned independent," he said irritably. "No, you're not. I'm sorry I said that. All right, you'll not let me pay for dinner, but have you no money yourself?"

"Not till tomorrow."

"So." He threw the towel aside. "You sat for me for three hours today, and I pay a franc an hour. That's your dinner paid for. It's all settled."

I said indignantly, "I don't charge money to sit for you."

"Oh, don't you?" He pointed a menacing finger at me. "So it's charity, is it? Well you can keep your damn charity, young McLeod. Am I a man without pride, that you think you can play Lady Bountiful for me? Will you patronize me with your charity just because I'm a poor seaman? By heaven, you're a cruel and heartless wench to treat a man so, but I'll overlook it this once provided you don't prolong the offense. Now go and get your coat on; there's a good girl."

This was a memorable evening for me, not that anything special occurred, but it was good to have company, and I knew that pleasant memories of those few hours would remain with me and warm me for many weeks to come. Perhaps I savored the occasion all the more because I knew Toby would be going away again next day for a long voyage, and I would have nobody to talk to except during my working hours at La Coquille. This lack of other friends did not trouble me greatly, for in some ways I had been alone with myself for years, and was used to it. Indeed, I rarely thought about Toby while he was away, for we were no more than neighborly companions, but I realized that life was always more cheerful for me when he was at home.

We returned at ten o'clock that night, and knowing that Mme Briand would peer out from her door when we entered, I held Toby's arm to confirm her belief that I was his woman. The more widely it was thought that the big mad Englishman was my protector, the safer for me. On our landing I thanked Toby for a very enjoyable evening and went to bed. At soon after seven next morning old Monsieur Depuis arrived to measure Toby's new canvas for a frame of pine, to be painted black with a gold cornice.

Shortly before noon I said good-bye to Toby and wished him bon voyage, for he would be leaving for Le Havre that evening. At La Coquille, business was slack as usual once we had served luncheon, with only the occasional handful of customers for coffee, drinks, or snacks throughout the afternoon and early evening, but by nine o'clock, with the better weather still holding, every table was occupied, four of them by groups of English gentlemen dining before going on to Le Moulin Rouge or one of the other cabarets.

At ten o'clock I was in the kitchen loading my tray with soup bowls, cutlery, a basket of bread, and a tureen of vegetable soup, when Père Chabrier appeared from the restaurant looking flushed and angry. "The two men in the corner, one English one French," he snapped. "Have you spoken with them?"

"No, Père Chabrier," I said, not ceasing in my work for both Armand and I were very rushed at this time. "I will take their order as soon as I have served this course at the window table."

"I have already taken their order," he said irritably, and slapped the slip of paper onto the spike jutting from the wall for Louise to deal with. "The Englishman speaks French of a sort. Do you know him? Is he one of these fellows to make foolish jokes? He says I will soon need a new girl, since the police will come for you tomorrow."

I caught my breath, and felt the flesh of my cheeks creep with shock. "The police?" I said, dry mouthed. "Why does he say that?"

"How should I know?" Père Chabrier stared in alarm. "My God, is it true? What have you been doing?"

"Nothing. Nothing," I said, very flustered. "There is some mistake, I assure you." I was thankful now that on Saturday afternoon, while we were preparing to open the restaurant, I had told Louise of my attempt to help a gentleman attacked by apaches, and of the fierce young lady who had come to take him away next morning. Père Chabrier was with us at the time and heard my story, so now I said, "It must be something to do with that English gentleman I gave shelter to, but I stole nothing from him, I promise you."

He looked uneasy, and jerked his head toward the door. "Go and talk to them. I will take your tray."

The two gentlemen had a table by the wall and had ordered a carafe of wine to pass the time while waiting for their first course. One was fair, in his middle thirties I thought, with a beaky nose and a haughty expression. The other was perhaps ten years older, dark, with a narrow face, a goatee beard, and spectacles. As I came to the table, the fair one gave a laugh and said in English, "Ah, here she is, Jacques. You were right, damn you. I was sure she'd do a bolt out the back way."

The other shrugged and said in French, "Where could she go that we would not quickly find her?"

"That's the question." The Englishman looked at me and said, "I suppose you *are* Hannah McLeod? Living at an address in Rue Labarre?"

I dropped a curtsy and said, "Yes, sir. May I have leave to speak to you, please?"

He glanced across the table and raised an eyebrow. "You're the policeman, Jacques. I'm only a poor underling at the embassy. May I listen?"

The older man replied in French, "It's all the same to me."

Each was using his own language, but there was nothing strange about this, for a foreign tongue is always far easier to understand than to speak. The fair man looked at me again and said, "All right, my girl. What is it?"

"The patron says you have told him that the police will detain me tomorrow." I heard my voice shake with agitation. "Is it true, sir? I swear I have done nothing wrong."

"That will be for the proper authority to decide," he said rather pompously. "It has nothing to do with me. I am with the British embassy here, and this gentleman is Inspector Lecour, who happens to be a friend of mine. When charges were laid against you late this afternoon on behalf of a certain Mr. Doyle, the inspector felt it proper to inform the embassy, since you are a British subject. We have taken note of the matter, of course, but unless you request assistance, we shall not be involved."

"But I do request assistance, sir," I said, stammering a little as I tried to cope with my whirling thoughts and my fear. Drawing a deep breath I began to tell what had happened that night, but the gentleman from the embassy silenced me with a wave of his hand.

"Don't waste your time and mine," he said, though not unkindly. "I've already told you; the matter doesn't rest with me. I understand you've lived here for a good few years, so you must know how the French system of criminal justice works. An accusation has been made, so you will be detained by the police and taken before an examining magistrate. He will assess the evidence and decide whether or not to send you for trial."

I said desperately, "Yes, sir, I understand that, but won't you please help by persuading my concierge to speak for me? She knows what happened, but she's terrified of having anything to do with the police, so—"

This time it was the inspector who stopped me by interrupting, but it was to his friend that he spoke, and in a somewhat admonishing tone. "This is quite out of order, my dear Charles. It might be thought indiscreet of you even to have mentioned this affair to the patron if it were not so trivial, but you really must not involve yourself with the accused until the examining magistrate has made his decision."

"Have no fear, Jacques; I don't intend to," said the fair man with a laugh, picking up the carafe to replenish his glass. "And my apologies for mentioning the subject here." He leaned back in his chair and looked at me. "Now run along about your business young lady. If you're innocent then you have no need to worry."

I barely heard his words, for in the last few seconds my senses had been numbed by a new and terrifying shock that left me sick with despair. My gaze had followed the gentleman's hand as he reached out for the carafe, and my eye had been caught by the glint of silver cuff links.

Memory exploded like a photographer's flare in my mind, illumining with horrible brilliance both my stupidity and the complete hopelessness of my situation.

Cuff links.

The gold cuff links I had taken from Mr. Doyle's shirt were still hidden away in my room, in the little box under the floorboard, and I had forgotten all about them.

Four

Much later I came to see that my foolishness had perhaps not been so extreme as it appeared to me in that moment. I had taken the links from the shirt in order to wash the blood and grime from it. I had hidden them in my secret place to safeguard them when I decided that I should not lock my unknown guest in the room while I went shopping.

On my return I had found him being carried downstairs by the two hotel servants under command of the wrathful young American woman who had called me a thief and threatened to report me to the police. It was little wonder that all thought of the cuff links had been driven from my mind by shock and surprise. Only moments later I had been hurrying to La Coquille, fearful of being late for my day's work. After almost twelve hours on my feet at the restaurant I had returned home soon after midnight, too tired to think, and I had been awakened in the morning by Toby Kent, who had brushed aside my fears when I told him about the young woman's threats. We had been together for the rest of that day, busy in one way or another, and I had put aside all thought that the fierce young woman with cornflower blue eyes might report me to the police.

Taking all things into account, it was not surprising that I should have forgotten about Mr. Doyle's cuff links, but at this moment, with freezing fingers seeming to grip my heart as I stood by the table in La Coquille, dazedly hearing the English gentleman say something I did not take in, I felt I must have been mad not to remember so vital a matter.

But it was too late now. If I produced the links and said I had forgotten about removing them, I would never be believed, and I could not pretend they had been taken by the apache together with Mr. Doyle's wallet and other valuables, for I had no gift at all for deception. I might try to lie, but would at once display every symptom of guilt. In fact it was likely that I would look just as guilty even when telling the truth about what had happened.

The voice of the man from the British embassy said, "Are you all right, girl?" My vision cleared and I saw the two men frowning up at me. No doubt my face looked as white and drawn as it felt.

I said, "Yes. I was giddy for a moment. Please excuse me, sir. I will go and attend to your order."

My legs felt stiff as I walked, and once in the kitchen they almost gave way beneath me. Louise was laying marinated mutton chops in a baking tray with cubes of onion, mushrooms, and parsley. Père Chabrier followed me in from the restaurant with a tray of dirty dishes and said, "Well? What did they say?"

I pulled myself together with a great effort and said, "It was as I thought. They have made a mistake, but everything will be all right, Père Chabrier. The English gentleman is from the British embassy, and he understands what truly happened."

Fat Louise darted a suspicious glance at me, but Père Chabrier was too preoccupied to wonder if what I said was true. I had not meant to lie to him, but I needed time to think, and for the moment it was better for me that he should imagine all was well. "Good. Good," he said, nodding his head vigorously and beginning to load a new tray with dishes Louise had prepared. "Three gold watches in the back corner, Hannah. They speak no French. Hurry and take their order now."

I picked up my small pad and pencil, and went out into the restaurant again. For the next hour the work I did was almost entirely automatic. I took orders, smiled, answered questions, translated, carried trays, served dishes, brought more wine, all without conscious thought. Astonishingly I made no mistakes, and even received two good tips in that time.

The English gentleman and the French police inspector finished their dinner and left. Neither had spoken to me again except to call for more coffee and order some cheese. I took a fresh order from two American tourists, and lingered to respond to the familiar questions. I was eighteen, and my mother had been French and my father English, and I was born in London but had lived in Paris since I was twelve . . . and yes, it was unusual for a young woman to be a waiter, but the patron was pleased to employ me since I was fluent in both languages . . .

Behind this facade my mind was numb except for one small part which darted and fluttered like a trapped bird seeking escape. No magistrate would believe I had removed the gold cuff links and forgotten to return them. No matter what I said, I would be found guilty of theft and put in prison. I was sure of that now, and the very thought sent waves of sick fear sweeping through me. Once I had served a prison sentence as a thief, nobody would give me work.

I thought of running away, of catching an early morning train to a distant town, but I would have only the money Père Chabrier would pay me as wages before I left La Coquille tonight, and that would never be enough for me to pay my fare, rent a room, and contrive to live while I found some kind of work. Besides, even though the gentleman from the British embassy had been indiscreet in letting slip that I was to be detained, the French police inspector had seemed quite confident that if I attempted to run away it would be in vain.

I had known many moments of near despair in my life, and had fought hard to overcome them, but I had never been so close to complete hopelessness as I was now. As I waited in the kitchen for Louise to fill some vegetable dishes I recalled Toby Kent's very deliberate words of the day before, when he had told me that if I ever needed a friend to do anything at all for me, I was to come to him. I had no doubt he meant his words, and it was a bitter blow to know that by a few short hours he was beyond reach of any call for help I might have made.

When I entered the restaurant again I saw Armand taking an order from a man sitting alone at a table for two. It was the moon-faced man who had called at my room to make me that strange offer of work in England, and at sight of him I felt my heart jump within me as I realized there was one place I might run away to and be safe from Inspector Lecour. Suddenly my reluctance to return to England seemed a very puny emotion compared to the dread that gripped me when I contemplated the horrors of a French prison.

As Armand moved away, Mr. Boniface glanced at me without particular interest, then his gaze roamed on round the room as he took out his pipe and lit it. I hastily served the table I was dealing with, and almost ran back to the kitchen to intercept Armand. He had put the order on Louise's spike and was pouring a tankard of beer which Mr. Boniface had presumably ordered. I hurried to him and whispered, "Is that for the Englishman who was watching me the other night?"

Armand nodded without looking up and said, "He asks for English beer, and is annoyed that we do not have any. The man is a fool."

"Please let me take it to him, Armand. I have to speak to him."

Now Armand looked up, troubled. "Is something wrong, Hannah?"

"Yes, but don't ask me about it, I beg you."

"As you wish." He lifted a shoulder, handed me the tankard on a small tray, stroked his long droopy moustache as he gazed at me with a mournful air, and said, "Good luck, my little one."

I thanked him and went through to the restaurant with the tray. As I set the tankard down before Mr. Boniface, I said in a low voice, "Sir . . . I have changed my mind. I would like to take the teaching position you spoke of, if it is still open, but I can only do so if I leave Paris tonight." My voice quavered on the last words.

He looked up in surprise and said, "What? What was that?"

"The matter you came to see me about," I whispered, trying for Père Chabrier's benefit to smile and look as if I were exchanging my usual remarks with an English customer. "The family in Hertfordshire, sir. A Mr. Ryder, I think you said. Have you found anyone to fill the job yet?"

"Eh? No, not yet," he said with dawning interest, "but what's all this about leaving Paris tonight?"

I felt my heart sink as I said, "The police believe I stole from that man you saw in my room. I've been told they intend to detain me tomorrow morning."

I had no choice but to tell the truth, for even if I could have concocted a plausible lie, I could never have told it convincingly. Yet even as I spoke, I realized that the truth must surely destroy all chance of my being accepted by Mr. Boniface on behalf of his employer, and I felt hope drain from me as I stood watching his face.

"So they think that, do they?" he said, and drank thoughtfully from his tankard. I looked about me. Père Chabrier was busy with a party of French customers, and nobody else was paying attention to me. I noticed that Armand was serving a table I had now neglected, and I blessed him in my heart. Mr. Boniface set down his tankard, wiped his mouth on a napkin, and stared at the table. "There's a train out of Gare du Nord soon after five A.M. and it connects with the Channel steamer," he said slowly, then shot me a sudden upward glance. "You be at the station by a quarter to five. I'll meet you there with tickets for the two of us." His voice was suddenly hard, and an ugly look touched his small brown eyes. "And don't mess me about, girl. It's putting me to a lot of trouble to leave at such short notice, and I won't take kindly to your changing your mind again."

"Oh I won't, sir, I won't," I promised fervently. "Gare du Nord at a quarter to five. I'll be there. But . . . I'm sorry, I won't have much money with me. A little over twenty francs, no more."

"I'm not concerned about that," he said curtly. "Can you manage your luggage?"

"I shall have only one suitcase, sir. Yes, I can manage."

"Right." He nodded toward the kitchen. "Then you'd better tell your waiter friend to hurry with my supper. I've to be up early in the morning."

For the next two hours I went about my work feeling as if I were dreaming. That I got through the rest of the evening without mistakes and without upsetting any of the customers was thanks only to Armand, who kept an eye on me and lent an unobtrusive helping hand whenever he felt it was needed.

Mr. Boniface finished his supper and left. Others came and went, but slowly the restaurant emptied, and by soon after one o'clock we were able to set the chairs up on the tables and sweep the floor. I put on my hat and coat, and stood waiting while Père Chabrier opened his cashbox and counted out my wages for the week to come. Armand was paid on Saturdays for the week completed.

I felt guilty at knowing that tomorrow I would not be arriving for work at La Coquille, but I dared not tell Père Chabrier what I intended. He might well be in trouble with the police himself if they found that he had known but failed to tell them.

Armand was waiting for me by the door, and as usual we walked to the corner together. There, as we paused under a lamp, he sighed, tugged at his moustache, and said, "Will you be all right, Hannah?"

Somehow he had guessed that I was going away, and I did not try to deceive him. I said, "Yes, I'm sure I shall be all right, Armand. Thank you for helping me this evening."

He smiled his sad smile. "The lonely ones must help each other. Remember me sometimes, Hannah." With a little bow he turned and walked away into the darkness. For a moment surprise made me forget my anxieties. Armand and I had worked together for well over a year. I knew he had no wife, but it had never occurred to me that he might be lonely, and my surprise was tinged with shame that I should realize this only now.

By two o'clock I was in my room and busy packing my belongings in the suitcase I had brought with me from the college. I worked as quietly as possible, and when I had finished I sat down at the table to write three letters. One was to Mme Briand. My rent was paid in advance, and I simply said that I was leaving Paris tonight, that I hoped she would tell the police what had happened when they came to ask questions concerning the man I had helped the other night, and that she was welcome to my few pieces of furniture, but M'sieur Toby Kent was to have my blankets, my bed linen, and all small chattels, and would she please put them in his room.

The other letters were more difficult. I had taken from my box of valuables the cuff links belonging to Mr. Doyle and wrapped them in a piece of cloth, securing it with a few stitches. Now I took a piece of paper and wrote:

> Dear Mr. Doyle,
>
> I took your cuff links out to wash your shirt, but I forgot about them when the lady came to take you away, because I was upset by her belief that I had taken part in robbing you. I fear I shall not be believed, and I know the police are coming for me, so I am running away, but what I have said is the truth, and I am leaving your cuff links with this letter to be returned to you.
>
> Yours sincerely,
> Hannah McLeod

It seemed a feeble letter when I read it through, but I was too tired to compose a better one. I folded it and sealed it in an envelope with the cuff links. On the envelope I wrote: *To the Police—for Mr. Doyle.* I felt sure the word *Police* would discourage Mme Briand from any notion of prying. This letter I left on the table with the one for Mme Briand herself.

The third was to Toby Kent, and I wrote:

> Dear Toby,
>
> I was very stupid, and forgot I had taken some gold cuff links from Mr. Doyle's shirt to wash it, and I know that the police are coming for me in the morning. I cannot prove my innocence, and have decided to run away rather than be put in prison. I must not say where I am going, in case by chance the police find this letter. I have left a letter in my room for them with the cuff links. Do you think you could speak to Inspector Lecour to make sure Mr. Doyle received them safely? I mean, if it is not too much trouble.
>
> I have asked Mme Briand to put some of my things in your room. Please do me a great favor and sell them for me. There should be enough to raise the eighteen francs I owe Père Chabrier to repay a week's wages in advance.
>
> Thank you for the kindness you have shown me, and I hope your paintings will bring you great success.
>
> Your friend,
> Hannah McLeod

I wrote Toby's name on the envelope, sealed it, then tiptoed across the passage and slipped it under the door of his room. It would be many weeks before he returned to find the letter, but I thought it would be safe till then. Mme Briand had a key to his room, as she had to all rooms, but I did not think she would touch a letter belonging to Toby, of whom she stood in some awe.

I lay down on the bed for an hour, but did not dare to sleep. At four I rose, put on my hat and coat, picked up my case, and went out into the passage. I locked the door, leaving the key in the keyhole, and crept down six flights of stairs, wincing whenever a board creaked, thankful when Mme Briand did not appear as I reached the hall, and thankful again when I had eased the front door shut behind me and found the night dry and not bitterly cold. With my suitcase to carry I was glad to be going downhill for most of the way to the Gare du Nord, and although the station was less than a mile from my home I had to stop and rest for a minute or so twice during the journey. The city was far from silent at this hour, for already carts and wagons were trundling through the streets on their way to the great market of Les Halles.

By the time I reached the station approach, I was breathless, perspiring, and fearful that Mr. Boniface might not be there. Perhaps he had changed his mind. Perhaps he had told the police that I was running away, and they would be waiting for me . . .

I jumped with alarm as a figure stepped out from the shadows, then let out a gasp of relief as I saw that it was Mr. Boniface. "I've tickets for the two of us," he said in a low voice, and thrust some coins into my hand. "Go and buy a single ticket for Orleans, then if the man remembers you and the police come asking questions he'll put them on the wrong track. When you've done that, join me on platform two. Understand?"

"Yes," I said. "Platform two."

"Don't approach me or speak to me. Just get in the same compartment." He turned and moved away.

As I followed his instructions I felt like a criminal. There were few people about, but in my imagination everyone was watching me, and behind every pillar a policeman lurked waiting to pounce. I was so tired and frightened I wanted to cry, but I had wept for the last time five years before and had promised myself never to shed tears again. The train was waiting at the platform, the locomotive emitting an occasional slow hiss, as if of impatience. Mr. Boniface stood leaning on his walking stick, a leather suitcase beside him. I stopped a little way from him, and after a moment or two he looked at his watch, picked up his case, then moved to open a carriage door and climbed in. I followed. He moved along the corridor and entered a compartment, leaving the door open. When I reached the door, he was sitting in a corner with his back to the locomotive, opening a newspaper, his suitcase on the rack above him. There was nobody else in the compartment.

"Sit in the corner on the same side as me," he ordered without looking up, "and don't speak until the train leaves."

With something of a struggle I managed to lift my case onto the rack, then sank down thankfully in the corner adjoining the corridor. It was a relief to rest, but the twenty minutes before the train pulled out seemed to last for an age, and again I found myself imagining that at any moment a gendarme would appear and arrest me.

At last came the sound of the guard's whistle and a ponderous *chuff* as the pistons began to move. With a clank and a jerk we were away. Mr. Boniface looked up from his newspaper, frowning. "Are you all right?" he said. "You look like a ghost."

I shook my head. "I'm not ill, Mr. Boniface. But I've had no sleep, so I'm tired. And I was frightened, too."

"Well, you've nothing to worry about now," he said brusquely. He felt in his waistcoat pocket, then leaned toward me. "Here's your ticket for when the inspector comes round. We'll travel as strangers till we go aboard the boat at Calais." He looked me up and down. "Your clothes aren't too bad, so it won't be out of place if we travel together from then on. Have you any money?"

"About twenty francs of my own, and fifty centimes change from the money you gave me for the Orleans ticket."

He grunted. "Not exactly a fortune, but never mind. We'll have a damn good breakfast as soon as we're aboard. You look as if you can do with it."

He returned to his newspaper. I took off my hat, leaned my head back in the corner, and closed my eyes. Again a feeling of unreality crept over me. I was running away from the police, returning to my own country against my will, in the company of a stranger, because the master of a household in Hertfordshire wanted an English girl, fluent in French, to teach his two children the language. It was a queer situation. Mam'selle Montavon and my friends at the college would have thought me mad to go off alone with a man I knew nothing of, but I was not apprehensive on that score for I was quite certain Mr. Boniface had no sinister designs on me. Everything that had happened went to confirm that he was simply acting as an agent for Mr. Sebastian Ryder in the way he had described, and I had been at liberty to refer to the British consul for assurance in the matter if I so wished.

Weariness and the rhythmic sound and movement of the train must have lulled me to sleep. When I woke the sun was well up and I was huddled in my corner, head muzzy, neck stiff from the awkward position in which I had slept. With a belligerent roar the train raced through a small station. I glimpsed the name Rue, and as I sat up straight I tried to recall where I had heard it before. Then it came to me. My friend Annette had been born in Rue. It was a village only forty or fifty miles from Calais, which meant that I had slept for the best part of two hours.

Nobody else had entered the compartment, and I supposed that the ticket inspector had been kind enough not to wake me. Mr. Boniface had laid aside his newspaper and was gazing out of the window, arms folded. He glanced at me as I stirred, then looked away again. I went along the corridor to the toilet, washed my hands and face, tidied my hair, then returned to the compartment and sat looking out on the huge flat fields of Picardy stretching to the horizon on each side.

An hour later we descended from the train in Calais. When Mr. Boniface hailed a porter to carry his case, I threw caution to the winds and did the same, for I did not even know if I would be able to change my French money on the boat, and the two sous I would give the porter could make little difference to me now.

It was not until we reached the office on the quayside where tickets were stamped that Mr. Boniface gestured for me to join him. A thought occurred to me, and I whispered apprehensively, "Do I need papers? An identity card, or something of that sort?"

He shook his head impatiently. "No. Why should you?"

"It's only that I read in the newspaper last year about the National Assembly discussing the idea of passports for traveling from one country to another."

Mr. Boniface sniffed. "Damn stupid notion," he grunted. "Nothing came of it anyway, and you can take it from me, nothing ever will."

He spoke no more to me until much later. When we had set sail and were eating breakfast in the dining room he said, as if continuing our quayside conversation, "So you read the newspapers, hey?"

I did not particularly want to talk at this moment, for since we were on an English ship, *Invicta,* we had been served an English breakfast, and I was thoroughly enjoying two plump kippers, the first I had tasted for years. "I don't read as much as I used to," I replied, "but that's only because I've had less time since I left college."

"You'll have plenty of time in Bradwell, I fancy. I doubt that teaching the Ryder youngsters a bit of French will prove exacting."

I said, "Good," and concentrated on my kippers. Five minutes later Mr. Boniface said in a changed and rather unsteady voice, "Blasted boat . . . blasted Channel . . ." He got up with a napkin pressed to his mouth, and as he moved hurriedly away I saw that his face had become white and mottled. It was only then I realized that the sea was choppy, causing the ship to roll and pitch quite vigorously, so much so that I now understood why the waiter who poured tea for us had only half filled our cups. I felt no hint of sickness myself; in fact, breathing the sea air after my sound sleep on the train had combined with relief at my escape to make me feel very well and of hearty appetite. I noticed that Mr. Boniface had not touched one of his kippers, and decided he would not return to it, so I transferred the fish to my own plate and settled down to enjoy it.

Later I went out on deck and walked about, relishing the excitement of the rough sea and the sharp breeze. I did not allow myself any speculation as to what would happen when I finally reached my destination. That would be revealed when the time came, and there was no point in entertaining hopes or fears about it now. When the line of the Dover cliffs emerged from a light mist which kept visibility to no more than a mile or two, I gripped the rail hard and felt my heart lurch with that touch of dread which always came when some thought of England slipped past the barrier in my mind.

"Don't be such a little fool, Hannah McLeod," I muttered to myself. "What did Toby Kent say, and wasn't it true? If you get kicked by a horse in Paris, there's no sense in blaming France." He had said that to me long ago, when I first told him how I came to leave England and wished never to return. When I explained that it was a feeling I could not help, he had shrugged and answered, "That's only because it springs from memories, Hannah. Go back and lay those ghosts. Replace memories with present reality. It's people who hurt you, places don't, and it's bad for you to be troubled by the mere thought of the country you were born in. No matter whether or not you want to live there, it's important to get the fear out of your system, and there's only one way to do that. By facing up to it."

I had known then that he was right, and I knew it now. I could even feel glad that events had driven me to do what I might otherwise never have forced myself to do. If Toby could have known he would be pleased, I thought, and with the thought I began to feel my unease diminishing a little.

I did not see Mr. Boniface again until the ship had docked and the gangway was being lowered. Our two cases were still beside our table in the dining room, and I went to sit by them as disembarkation began. When Mr. Boniface appeared, I said how sorry I was he had felt unwell, and hoped he was better now. He did not respond, and seemed resentful that I had not suffered the same distress, so I made no further attempt at conversation. He called a porter to take our cases, and twenty minutes later we were on a train bound for Charing Cross.

I did not sleep on this part of the journey, but watched with slowly growing pleasure as the countryside flashed by. I had seen little enough of England beyond the mean streets where my mother and I had lived, but on three occasions the Sunday school I attended had taken a party of us to the seaside for a day. I had been entranced then by what I had seen as the train rattled toward the coast, the green and gold fields, the little winding lanes, the cottages and farms and windmills. Now it all came back to me, and with it a sense of belonging, so that the ghosts I had feared became yet more remote and insubstantial.

By noon Mr. Boniface was well recovered from his seasickness and we took luncheon in the dining car. "We'll not stop to eat in London," he said on one of the few occasions when he spoke to me. "I sent a wire to my partner, Mrs. Hesketh, and she'll meet us off the train. Then it's straight to my house in Chancery Lane."

I stiffened, and said warily, "Your house? Why, sir?"

He looked up from his soup and waved a hand irritably. "Oh, you needn't worry, girl. We have our office there too, but the house is a convenient place for Mrs. Hesketh to see what you have in the way of clothes. You'll need more than what's in that suitcase if you're to dress as you'll be expected to dress at Silverwood. As soon as Mrs. Hesketh has made a list of what you need, we'll be off to the Army and Navy stores for clothes and shoes and whatever else she decides, including a trunk to pack them in."

I said, "Who is to pay for all this, Mr. Boniface?"

"Your employer, girl, who else? Mr. Ryder has an account there and I have his authority to buy such items as you require."

I stared. "That seems extremely kind of him, sir."

Mr. Boniface shrugged. "I doubt it. He's rich enough to pay for what he wants, and he wants a suitably dressed young woman about the house, not a shabby Montmartre waitress."

"Well, that's splendid," I said. The coat and dress I had worn for the journey were not really shabby, but I had sold most of my good clothes during the winter, and the rest had seen better days, so I was pleased to think that I should start my life in England with a new wardrobe. I was fairly sure Mr. Boniface had meant to hurt me by referring to me as a shabby Montmartre waitress, perhaps because he was annoyed that I had not been seasick, but he did not know that I had long ago learned to be invulnerable to sneers.

Mrs. Hesketh proved to be a brisk but pleasant woman, about forty years old, who met us at Charing Cross and took charge as soon as we arrived, proceeding to talk about Mr. Boniface as if he were miles away instead of in the carriage with us on our way to Chancery Lane.

"I expect he has been bad-tempered," she said confidingly as she sat beside me. "He's a grumpy man at the best of times, Boniface is, but crossing the Channel always makes him worse. Fifteen years now I've been his partner and I've yet to see him smile, but never mind, let's have a look at you." She leaned forward and craned her neck to study me. "My word, you're very young to be a tutor. Still, that's up to the client, isn't it? Now let's see . . . no, I don't think that's quite the dress and coat for you to arrive in, but you can change at the Army and Navy when we've found something just right. What about shoes? Have you any others in your case? No, never mind; we'll see to everything when we get home. What time is it please, Mr. Boniface?"

He drew a watch from his waistcoat pocket, eyed it gloomily, and said, "Twenty-seven minutes past one o'clock, Mrs. Hesketh."

"And I trust you took luncheon on the train, Mr. Boniface?"

"We did, Mrs. Hesketh."

"Then we can leave for the stores by two o'clock, complete our shopping for Hannah by half past three, and you can catch the four-fifteen train with her from St. Pancras. That will bring you to Bradwell by five-twenty, and I have arranged for a carriage from Silverwood to be awaiting you at the station from five o'clock onward. Are you attending to what I say, Mr. Boniface, or are you gazing out of the window at something more interesting?"

"I am gazing out of the window at Her Majesty's Royal Courts of Justice," said Mr. Boniface heavily, continuing to gaze at a splendid building like a fairy-tale castle that we were passing, "and I am also attending to what you say, Mrs. Hesketh."

"And do you find the arrangements satisfactory, sir?"

"I do, madam."

"Then I am gratified." She turned to me. "It is probably dyspepsia which gives Boniface so morose a nature, but if he will insist on eating such large quantities of pickles, what else can he expect?"

A few minutes later we reached the house in Chancery Lane. Mrs. Hesketh took my case and led the way through two offices and up some stairs to a large bedroom. When we entered the house I was on my guard and a little suspicious, but everything fell out as Mr. Boniface had said it would.

"Hat and coat off, dear, and open your case," said Mrs. Hesketh. "Now, let's lay out your clothes and see what's to be kept and what more you need. H'mm . . . that's quite a nice dress. Some very pleasant underwear. No, this won't do. Nor will this . . ."

As she sorted my belongings I looked round the room. It was clearly a bedroom used by a man and a woman, for there were female toiletries on the dressing table and a man's valetstand in one corner. "Boniface will not intrude while we're here," said my companion, looking doubtfully at a blouse. "If he wants to doze for half an hour following his luncheon, then he can do so in the office chair instead of on the bed. I think you should have a fresh dress for the last part of your journey"—she held up my dark green day dress—"but shall it be this or one of the new dresses we shall be buying at the stores? I think this is quite pleasant, and you will feel more comfortable in a familiar dress. Yes, change into this one, dear girl, while I continue to list what we shall need."

I took off the dress I had worn since leaving Rue Labarre in the early hours, and before putting on the green one I asked if I might wash my hands and face to freshen myself after the journey. "Of course, of course," said Mrs. Hesketh, and moved to pick up a large copper jug beside the marble washstand. "Has that girl brought up hot water? Ah yes, she has. Here's soap and towel, and if you wish to use a little eau de cologne, you'll find some there on my dressing table." Evidently this bedroom was shared by Mrs. Hesketh and Mr. Boniface. Remembering the exchanges between them in the carriage, I could not help marveling at such a curious partnership.

Less than twenty minutes later Mrs. Hesketh and I were again in a carriage, this time on our way to Victoria Street. There, in a huge emporium called The Army and Navy Co-operative Society Ltd., we spent almost an hour and a half in different departments as she worked her way through the list she had made, buying me blouses, skirts, two dresses, corsets and underwear, stockings, shoes, two hats, and an ulster topcoat, as well as some toiletries and small items I lacked. All these things were assembled and packed in a compressed cane trunk, and a total of forty-six pounds seven shillings and eightpence three-farthings was charged to Mr. Sebastian Ryder's account.

I felt quite shaken by all this. Even before reaching the house I had cost Mr. Ryder more than a year's wages for two housemaids, and I did not feel I had much to offer in return. I could speak and write fluently in French and English, but I had no teaching experience. The thought that the money Mrs. Hesketh was now spending on me might be deducted from my wages over a long period made me realize with a touch of dismay that Mr. Boniface had not spoken of wages and I had never inquired. I pondered asking Mrs. Hesketh about it, then mentally shrugged the matter aside. Time would answer the question, and in any event I had no choice but to accept whatever situation I found. Meantime I should be thankful that I was here, and free, instead of in a police cell in Paris trying to convince an examining magistrate that I had not intended to steal the gold cuff links from Mr. Doyle's shirt.

Mr. Boniface was waiting for us at St. Pancras station when we arrived in a carriage with my suitcase and my new trunk. "Have you not secured a porter for us, Mr. Boniface?" demanded Mrs. Hesketh sternly as we alighted.

"Porters will not wait for luggage which has not yet arrived, Mrs. Hesketh," her partner informed her lugubriously.

"Porters are here to do as they are told," she replied, and lifted her voice. "Porter! Porter! Yes, you there, you! Over here with that trolley at once, if you please. No, never mind that gentleman waving his cane at you; it is of no interest to me that he hailed you first. Just take this trunk and suitcase, my good man, and off you go. What? Are you addressing *me?*" This was to an angry gentleman with a cane who had approached. "Have we been introduced, sir? Then how *dare* you accost me in this way! One more word and I shall call a policeman. It is quite disgusting, the offensive behavior a respectable lady has to endure in a public place, but I know your kind, sir, and I'm well able to deal with you!"

The gentleman hurried away. Mr. Boniface and I followed Mrs. Hesketh and the trolley. The train was waiting at the platform. Mrs. Hesketh saw my luggage safely into the guard's van, patted my arm, and said, "There you are, dear. I hope you will be very happy at Silverwood. Don't trouble yourself to make conversation with Boniface during the journey. He has nothing to say that is of interest to anybody. Good-bye, dear, good-bye."

She turned and walked briskly away. Mr. Boniface sighed, took off his hat, looked at it with a frown, and put it back on his head again. "She's upset because I won't marry her," he said absently. "Been like that for fifteen years now. All right, let's find the dining car and have a pot of tea."

I did not think it likely that I would ever see Mrs. Hesketh again, and in this I was wrong, but I felt sure I would always remember her with a blend of respect and admiration. As she had recommended, I did not exercise myself to make conversation with Mr. Boniface during the journey. We took tea together in silence as the train pulled out through dark and soot-grimed suburbs of north London to pastures and newly ploughed fields beyond, and for the next forty minutes or so I sat in something of a dream, letting my mind rest as I watched the countryside flash by.

A cloudy sky had brought early dusk when we left the train at Bradwell. The groom sent to meet us was waiting on the platform to see that a porter took my luggage and loaded it onto a fine carriage standing on the cobbles of the little station forecourt. Despite the dusk I could make out something of the surrounding country as we drove up a hill and along a lane that wound through woods. A little later, when the woods became less dense, I saw the trunks of scores of tall slender trees gleaming whitely, and I guessed that Silverwood had been named from the many silver birch trees which predominated here.

Our journey from the station took no more than ten minutes. We turned into a broad drive and I saw through the window of the carriage a house with a wide facade and a colonnaded porch. It stood three stories high, with a short tower rising from each end. Lamps hung in the portico, and faint light showed from behind curtained windows of several rooms on the ground floor and first floor. I could discern little detail in the half-light, but it seemed to me that the walls were of dark gray stone. Apart from the portico, the facade was flat and unrelieved. This, together with the rectangular windows, the flat line of the roof parapet, and the squat square towers, made a cold and forbidding impression on me.

Light rain had begun to fall, and as the carriage came to a halt the great door opened and a man hurried out carrying a large umbrella. He was not in livery, but I guessed he must be one of the footmen. When he opened the carriage door, Mr. Boniface got out and walked past him. The footman, not much older than I, gave me his gloved hand to help me alight, and that small courtesy brought a touch of pleasure to ease this moment of nervousness for me.

A second or two later we were in the paneled hall of Silverwood. Here a man in his forties, with thin dark hair, wearing a black suit and black bow tie, was speaking rather coolly to Mr. Boniface. "Good evening, sir. The master will see you in a few minutes." Then to me, and more pleasantly, "Miss McLeod? Welcome to Silverwood, miss. I am Farrow, the butler." He indicated an oak settle nearby. "If you would be seated for a few moments, Mrs. Matthews will show you to your room." As he spoke, the groom and the footman appeared with my trunk, followed by a boy with my case. "Upstairs to Miss McLeod's room," said the butler briskly. "Hetty's there to unpack for her. Wipe your boots first, Lang! That's better. Now off you go."

A door opened on the far side of the hall and a man stepped out. At first I judged him to be very old, for his hair was white, but as he moved from the shadow of the doorway there was lightness in his step, and I saw that the square face seemed to tell of no more than fifty years. His white hair was very thick, the eyes alert, the jaw firm. Broad shoulders made his body seem as square as his face, for he was no more than two or three inches taller than I. He wore a smoking jacket over a white shirt and black bow tie, and carried a cigar between the fingers of one hand.

"Ah, there you are Boniface," he said in a deep voice with a flat northern accent. "Brought the girl? Good. I'll see you now."

Mr. Boniface said, "As you wish, sir," and began to walk across the hall, hat in hand. The white-haired man looked toward me with a long and penetrating stare which lasted until Mr. Boniface had moved past him into the room beyond. Then he said, "All right, young lady, we'll have a talk later. Carry on, Farrow."

"Very good, sir."

As the door closed I whispered, "Excuse me, Mr. Farrow, but was that Mr. Sebastian Ryder?"

"Yes, miss," said the butler, "that was the master, and since you will be living above stairs with the family and Mrs. Matthews, I must ask you to address me simply as Farrow."

"Oh. Yes. Thank you for telling me."

A plump lady, of middle age and wearing a sober brown dress, came down the broad curving stairway. The butler said, "The young lady has just arrived, Mrs. Matthews. I have sent her trunk and case up to her room."

"Thank you, Farrow," said the lady, and her voice held the soft drawl I remembered hearing in the speech of country folk during my childhood. I stood up, and as she came from the stairs to take my hand in greeting I saw she had a round, almost unlined face and a tranquil gaze. "Welcome to Silverwood, m'dear," she said with a smile. "I'm Mrs. Matthews, the housekeeper, and you must call me Mattie, same as the master and the children do. All the way from Paris today, is it? My word you must be weary, but that's a nice cheerful smile you have just the same. Come along now and I'll show you to your room so you can rest for a while before dinner. Bless my soul, you look scarcely older than Miss Jane. I think it best if she and Master Gerald call you Hannah rather than Miss McLeod. Will that be all right now?"

"Oh yes, of course. Thank you." I was grateful for such a pleasant welcome, and began to feel less nervous as we made our way upstairs, though as yet I could only think of the housekeeper as Mrs. Matthews, and knew I would have to overcome some embarrassment to address her as Mattie.

My bedroom was almost at the end of a broad passage, and was as large as Toby Kent's studio and bedroom combined, besides being very amply furnished. I was overjoyed to see a hip bath in one corner with two large copper containers beside it. My trunk and case stood open, and a young housemaid in a black dress and long white apron had begun to unpack my belongings and put them away in the wardrobe and chest of drawers. She was a thin girl with a snub nose and very big eyes, her hair drawn tightly back in a bun under the frilled cap she wore. I remembered the name Farrow the butler had spoken, and said, "Hello, Hetty."

She paused in her work, giving me a startled look, and whispered, "Good evening, miss."

Mattie said, "This is Miss McLeod, and you will be looking after her room, Hetty. Now carry on with the unpacking; there's a good girl."

The curtains were drawn, but Mattie said the window looked out on lawns and part of a small orchard, offering a beautiful view especially in blossom time. "Perhaps you'd like to take a bath and lie down for an hour, m'dear," she said. "My room is just along the passage, so suppose I come and tap on your door at half past seven o'clock, then we'll have nice time for me to show you round Silverwood so you know where you are. We dine at half past eight o'clock regular, that's the master and the children and you and me, but we gather in the drawing room a few minutes before, so that's when you can meet the others. Lord knows what the master's thinking of, suddenly wanting Miss Jane and Master Gerald to speak good French, but that's his affair, and I'm pleased you're to join us at Silverwood, I am to be sure. You seem a nice young lady and I hope we'll be company for one another."

I said, "Oh, I hope so too. Are you sure it will be all right for me to take a bath now? Mr. Sebastian Ryder saw me down in the hall a few minutes ago and said he would talk to me later, but I'm not sure when."

"After dinner," said Mattie. "That's when he'll talk to you, Hannah, m'dear. After dinner." She turned to the maid. "Quick as you can with the unpacking, Hetty, then make ready Miss Hannah's bath and put out towels before you leave. She'll rest when she's bathed, so don't disturb her, just come and clear away here while we're at dinner."

Ten minutes later I was alone in the room, taking off my clothes and marveling at what appeared to be my amazing good fortune. Less than twenty-four hours ago I had been waiting at table in a Montmartre restaurant, working twelve hours a day and living from hand to mouth in a tiny garret. I had not by any means been unhappy or discontented with my lot, and would never have come to England if it had not been for the disastrous situation brought about by my attempt to help Mr. Doyle, but in a single day my life had changed completely. I had a fine bedroom in a fine house and a maidservant to look after me; I had a good wardrobe, the prospect of a good dinner this evening, and no doubt good meals three times a day to follow. It was true I possessed only a few francs in money, but I would surely be paid some small wage as a tutor in a mansion such as Silverwood, and in any event I could think of nothing I would need to spend money on for a long time to come.

With my hair tied up in a towel to prevent it getting wet, I sat in the hot bath, lazily soaping myself and counting my blessings. It was extraordinary how my deep-rooted fear of returning to England, or even thinking about England, had dissolved completely in the few hours since I had set foot ashore from the Channel steamer. Toby Kent had been right, I reflected. I had laid the ghosts that haunted me by replacing old memories with present reality, and present reality was far and away better than I could ever have dreamed it might be.

There came a faint click from the door. I looked round quickly, and saw that it stood slightly ajar. When it moved no further, I realized that it could not have been properly latched, and a draft must have moved it. I was annoyed with myself, for I should have made sure the door was firmly closed and then turned the key. It was unlikely that

Mattie or any of the servants would enter without knocking, but I had no wish to invite embarrassment on my first evening here. The door had swung only an inch or two, and since it was hinged on the side nearer to me there was no danger that I might be seen by anybody passing along the passage, but I thought it best to shut and lock it.

I climbed out of the bath, wrapped a towel about me, rubbed my feet on the bath mat to avoid making wet marks on the rugs and polished floor, then padded across to the door. As I approached I heard voices from the passage. At first I could make out no words, but I recognized Mattie's soft country burr and the rather plaintive drone of Hetty's voice. It seemed they were moving along the passage, perhaps with Mattie giving some sort of instruction to the maid.

My hand was almost on the doorknob when a dozen words came quite clearly to my ears. Hetty was speaking, and they must have just passed my door, probably without noticing it was ajar. She said, "Yes, Mrs. Matthews, I'll put them in the airing cupboard." Then, in a hushed voice, eager with furtive curiosity, "I suppose Miss Hannah must be the butterfly girl, eh?"

Five

If Mattie made any reply I did not hear it, and in a moment she and Hetty were beyond earshot. Gently I closed the door and turned the key, bewildered and a trifle uneasy.

The butterfly girl, Hetty had said.

When I turned my head, I could make out the shape of the golden butterfly birthmark on the point of my shoulder. It seemed impossible that any living soul in Silverwood could know of this, but Hetty must have heard somebody speak of "the butterfly girl," or she would never have asked the question I had just overheard.

I walked slowly back to the bath and stood on the mat, drying myself on the big fleecy towel. Mr. Boniface knew I had spent several years as a student at the College for Young Ladies, and he had talked with my special friends there. My curious birthmark had been no secret from them, for we often used to wash each other's hair wearing only a chemise, but I could not imagine that Annette or Marguerite would have told Mr. Boniface of so intimate a matter.

I began to wonder if I had misheard Hetty, but decided I had not. Yet the only connection between my old college and Silverwood was Mr. Boniface, so however unlikely it might seem, he must have spoken of the butterfly girl to somebody in Silverwood. How Hetty, a housemaid, had come to hear the words I had no idea.

It was all very strange and unsettling, but there was nothing I could do about it at the moment. I decided that as soon as I could find an opportunity, I would speak to Mattie about it, for she seemed genuinely friendly. After I had dried myself, I put on a dressing gown and lay on the bed, trying to rest without thinking of anything that might be disturbing.

When the wristwatch Mrs. Hesketh had bought for me in the Army and Navy stores told me that half an hour had passed, I got up, did my hair nicely, and put on fresh underclothes and one of my new dresses. Mattie tapped on my door two or three minutes after seven, and seemed pleased to find me ready and waiting for her to take me on a tour of the house.

It was a very large house which had been built by Mr. Ryder some twenty years ago. We did not go to the top floor, for this was occupied by the servants' quarters. There were fifteen servants living-in, Mattie told me, and she had been given the position of housekeeper nine years ago, on the death of Mr. Sebastian Ryder's wife, Mary. On the first floor were the family bedrooms and a number of guest bedrooms, two of which were occupied by Mattie and myself now. There was also a music room, a nursery, a study each for Miss Jane and Master Gerald, and a library.

As we moved along the passages and down the handsome staircase, we encountered several of the servants, both maids and footmen. Mattie introduced me to each briefly, and I made an effort to remember the names. The dining room and drawing room were large and expensively furnished, but in a way which produced a rather dour and heavy effect to match the impression I had gained on first sight of the house. The master's study, as Mattie called it, was on the ground floor, and there was also a smoking room, a sewing room, a breakfast room, a large room with a billiard table, and a ballroom which could have contained a small orchestra and fifty couples.

Finally we went below stairs to the kitchen, where Mrs. Fletcher, the cook, was presiding over preparations for dinner, but we stayed only long enough for me to be introduced as this was a busy time. We had not encountered any member of the family during our tour, but I learned that Miss Jane attended a very select day school for girls just outside St. Albans, and that Master Gerald had left his public school but was not going on to university.

"Mr. Ryder has no time for too much book learning," said Mattie as we mounted the stairs again. "A self-made man he is himself, and proud of it, too, so he's letting Master Gerald go on with his music till after summer, then he's to start work in one of the factories, learning how to do things, as you might say."

"Is Master Gerald musical then?" I asked.

"Oh, yes indeed, m'dear. Beautiful to hear him it is when he's playing the piano. Mind you, it's not much to Mr. Ryder's taste, because he thinks playing the piano is more the thing for a girl, really, except Miss Jane has no gift for it at all. She did have lessons when she was younger, but her heart was never in it. Now would you like to rest in your room till the gong calls us to dinner, or shall we sit in the library and chat a little?"

I said, "Oh, I'd like to chat and I'd like to be in the library. I'm so looking forward to seeing what books are there, and perhaps reading some of them if I'm allowed."

"Of course you'll be allowed, Hannah, and I'm sure you'll find some nice books there. I have to cut out the pieces they write in the newspapers about new books, and then order half a dozen of the best ones from Linden's, the booksellers, every few weeks. Mr. Ryder doesn't read books himself, only the newspapers and business papers, but he likes his library to be up to date."

We had entered the library now, and were seating ourselves in two armchairs by the coal fire that burned cheerfully in a mellow brick fireplace at one end of the room. I marveled that a fire was kept going in a room which it seemed was hardly ever used by the master of the house.

"Do you think Master Gerald will be sad if he has to give up his music and work in a factory?" I asked.

Mattie pursed her lips. "Now that's something it's not for me to say, m'dear. In many ways I'm looked on as one of the family, but I have to remember I'm the housekeeper and no more. When Mrs. Ryder was alive, bless her, I was cook-housekeeper, and when she died Mr. Ryder asked me to find a cook and take over the household myself. It needed a woman here, and he wanted nobody new, because the children were fond of me and I of them. Oh, I was nervous at first, but I managed well enough, and as time went on I settled down." A smile touched her homely face. "Nine years ago, that was. Now I sit at table with the family, and they treat me very nicely, like as if I was part nannie, part housekeeper, part auntie to the children. But I never forget my place, and it's the same for you, really, m'dear, for we're both paid servants lucky enough to have family privileges."

"I do appreciate that," I said. "I would hate to be overfamiliar, Mattie, even unintentionally. I'm sorry if my question about Master Gerald was out of place."

"It wasn't at all," she replied with a little wave of her hand, "and of course he won't be working *in* a factory, really. I mean, not doing things with his hands. He'll be learning all the business of how to run things, the way Mr. Ryder's managers run them."

I gathered from this that Mr. Ryder owned a number of factories and had managers to run them under his guidance. "What sort of factories are they?" I asked.

"They make guns and things," Mattie said, a touch of awe in her expression. "Armaments, they call them. Rifles and cannons and suchlike. Thousands and thousands of them, and not just for our own soldiers, either. People come from all over the world to buy guns from Mr. Ryder."

Making guns seemed to me a cruel business to be in, but then I reflected that if you were a soldier, somebody had to make the guns you needed to fight for your country, and we were all thankful to be protected by our soldiers and sailors in time of danger. I was suddenly surprised at myself to find I was thinking in terms of "our" soldiers and sailors, when I had left England as a child and returned with reluctance only a few hours ago.

Mattie had relapsed into silence and was gazing into the fire, hands in her lap. I had taken a great liking to her, and after a brief inward debate with myself, I said, "Please may I ask you something, Mattie? It's not about the family, and I don't think it's out of place."

She looked up with a touch of placid surprise. "Well, go on then, m'dear."

"A little while ago, when you and Hetty were passing my room, the door was ajar and I heard something Hetty said to you. She said, 'I suppose Miss Hannah must be the butterfly girl, eh?' That's all I heard, and I didn't mean to eavesdrop—it was quite by accident—but . . . well, can you tell me what she meant, please?"

Mattie frowned slightly, as if trying to remember, then her brow cleared and she gave a nod. "That's right, she did say something about you and a butterfly, Hannah, but I wasn't paying much attention, really; she's such a scatterbrain and always making up silly tales. I expect I just told her to hold her tongue and get on with putting the pillow slips away." She frowned again. "But I don't want her making up silly tales about you. Butterfly girl, indeed."

I suddenly saw in her face a look which showed another side to her. She might well have a placid and kindly nature, but there was iron in her, and she was able to run a large staff of servants with a firm hand when need be. Getting up from her chair she moved to where a speaking tube of polished wood rested in a cradle on the wall. Pulling the whistle free, she blew down the mouthpiece. It was evidently connected to the kitchen, for a moment later she said, "Is Hetty down there with you, Farrow? I'd like to see her in the library at once if you can spare her. Thank you."

She restored the speaking tube to its place and returned to her chair. "A very good butler, Farrow is," she said, her voice soft again. "Much better than old Mr. Benson who was here before. When the mistress died, poor soul, and the master asked me to take charge of the household, he dismissed all the servants so we could engage new ones. He said it would be easier for me to move upstairs if he took on all new servants who hadn't been below stairs with me, and right he was about that."

"It was thoughtful of him," I said.

"It was indeed, m'dear." She nodded slowly. "He put his trust in me, and he's been a good friend and master ever since." She looked at me sideways with a small, half-smiling grimace. "But as he says himself, he's a bad enemy, especially in business. My word, I've known him ruin folk who tried to do him down, and that's not telling you anything he'll not cheerfully tell you himself."

There came a tap on the door and Hetty entered, looking apprehensive as she bobbed a curtsy to Mattie. "You wanted to see me, Mrs. Matthews?" she said, a hint of whine in her voice.

Mattie said briskly, "Come here; stand still and don't fidget, Hetty. I just want to ask you what it was you said to me a little while ago about a butterfly girl. You remember?"

Hetty darted a furtive glance at me, her cheeks grew pink, and she twisted her fingers in her apron. "I didn't say it in front of Miss Hannah," she whispered.

"I know you didn't, girl," Mattie said patiently. "Nobody's cross with you, not yet, anyway. But I don't like you making up fairy stories about people, so you just answer my question now and tell me what you said."

"Well . . . I on'y said I supposed Miss Hannah must be the butterfly girl," Hetty replied tearfully.

Mattie looked at me, then at the maid again. "And what did you mean?"

"Mean? I don't know, Mrs. Matthews. I thought you knew."

"Knew what?"

"I don't know," Hetty said desperately, and pressed a hand to her mouth in fear. "Will I get into trouble, Mrs. Matthews?"

"Only if you're making up stories. Now what made you ask about the butterfly girl?"

"Oooh, I didn't make it up, honest I didn't," Hetty said earnestly. "It just came out when I was talking with Albert last week. He'd been serving a whiskey and soda to the master in his study the evening before, and that man was there who came with Miss Hannah this evening, Mr. Bonny-something, and Albert heard the master say, 'Bring me the butterfly girl, Bonny-something, and I don't care what it costs.' Well, I'm not sure exactly, but it was sort of like that, and when he came this evening, I mean that man, not Albert, I remembered what he'd said, so I asked you, Mrs. Matthews, because I thought you'd know and I was going to ask what it meant."

Hetty stopped, breathless from her outpouring. Mattie looked at me with a baffled air as if inviting me to continue the questioning. I smiled at the frightened girl and said, "It's quite all right, Hetty; I was just curious to know what you meant. Is Albert one of the footmen?"

"Yes, miss."

"And did he know what the master meant?"

"Oh no, miss. It was a sort of puzzle, really. That's why I asked."

I was puzzled myself, and a little troubled. It seemed very strange that Mr. Sebastian Ryder had referred to me as the butterfly girl, and equally strange that he should be so determined to secure my services at Silverwood. Perhaps some explanation of this enigma would emerge when he talked with me after dinner, but if not, then the mystery would have to remain, for I could see nothing alarming about it and I certainly did not intend to antagonize my new employer by questioning him on the matter. The thought occurred to me that if he wanted

Hannah McLeod for teaching French to his children regardless of cost, then he might well propose to pay me a wage as well as provide my keep. This happy thought must have shown on my face, for Mattie said, "Bless me, what are you smiling at, Hannah? Have you guessed what the master meant?"

I said, "No, I've decided not to guess, Mattie. I expect when men are alone together they may well speak of young ladies in funny ways that we don't know about, but it's quite unimportant anyway, so I think it's best if we all forget about it. The main thing is that Hetty wasn't making up a fairy tale, so there's nothing to be cross about."

Mattie eyed me with a surprisingly shrewd gaze for a moment or two, then gave a little nod. "Very well, m'dear. I expect you're right." She looked at the maid. "But don't you go about repeating things you don't understand, Hetty. It's almost as bad as making up stories, I do declare."

"Yes, Mrs. Matthews, I'm ever so sorry."

"Very well. Off you go now."

Hetty's relief was obvious. She shot me a grateful glance and scuttled quickly from the room. Mattie sighed. "Albert's very young and very slow-witted," she said. "I wouldn't be surprised if he muddled up something he heard the master say, but anyway I'm sure we'll hear no more about it now." She looked at the library clock. "We must be going down to the drawing room, m'dear. The family will be gathering there soon."

I did not think Albert had muddled anything up, but I was glad to drop the subject. It seemed clear that when Mr. Boniface had visited the College for Young Ladies, he had somehow come to hear me referred to as the butterfly girl. Perhaps he did not even know why I was so called. Having traced me to La Coquille, and then ascertained that I had the particular qualifications Mr. Ryder demanded, he had returned to report this to his employer. Apparently Mr. Ryder had been so impressed by the report that he had sent Mr. Boniface back to Paris at once to engage me, and I could now understand Mr. Boniface's persistence, and his chagrin when I refused the offer.

As I made my way downstairs with Mattie I reflected that if I was wrong in my speculation, and if there was something sinister in Mr. Ryder's forceful demand to have the butterfly girl brought from Paris, then the truth of the matter must soon emerge and I could deal with it when the moment came. Until then, I would not worry. I had long ago learned to accept, without being crushed, whatever could not be changed or prevented, and knew I would find no difficulty in putting out of my mind all concern about a problem which might well not exist.

As we entered the drawing room, I saw a young man standing near one of the bronze gaslamps beside the fireplace, studying a large thin book. He was slender of build with a gentle face and thick fair hair falling over one eyebrow. He looked up, and a puzzled expression touched his eyes as he saw me. Mattie said, "Good evening, Master Gerald."

He said politely, "Hello, Mattie dear. Er . . . ?" His brow cleared suddenly. "Oh yes, of course. This must be—er . . . oh dear, I've forgotten the name . . . the young lady from France?"

"You'll forget your own name one of these days, Master Gerald," said Mattie, and I could hear the affection in her voice. "Now let me introduce you. Hannah, this is Master Gerald Ryder. Master Gerald, this is Miss Hannah McLeod and you're to call her Hannah."

He smiled apologetically and offered me a slim, long-fingered hand, a very beautiful hand, yet one in which I sensed surprising strength as I took it and dropped a little curtsy. In the same moment I realized that the book he held was in fact a musical score, and remembered that Mattie had said he was a fine pianist. As we shook hands he studied me very intently with a friendly gaze, saying, "I'm so glad you've come to Silverwood, and I hope you'll be very happy with us, Hannah."

Warmed by his manner and his words, I responded to his smile and said, "Thank you for such a kind welcome, Master Gerald."

His eyes went blank for a moment and his head tilted slightly as if he were listening carefully. "Most pleasant . . ." he said vaguely, as if to himself, and the fingers of one hand danced for a moment as if on an imaginary keyboard. "Such a pretty voice." His eyes focused again. "I hope I shan't be too much of a trial to you, Hannah, but I must warn you that French was my worst subject at school. I seem to have no gift for it, but Papa has suddenly decided I must learn it well for future business purposes, so I hope you will bear with me."

Mattie had told me Gerald was just eighteen, so he was only a few months younger than I, but I felt many years older than this gentle and artistic boy. I had taken an immediate liking to him, as I had to Mattie, and now I said, "I expect they gave you too much book work at school, Master Gerald, but with your quick ear I'm sure you'll make very good progress with spoken French, and that's what I would like to concentrate on."

He was about to reply when the door opened and a girl entered, followed immediately by Mr. Sebastian Ryder. She wore a very pretty dress in pale cream, her hair was dark, and both in features and build she bore so close a resemblance to my employer that I knew she must be the daughter, fifteen-year-old Jane Ryder. I guessed then that as she had taken after her father, so must Gerald have taken after his mother in looks and perhaps in nature.

Mattie introduced me formally to Mr. Ryder and to Jane, and we exchanged a few polite words. They were both pleasant enough, but I felt nothing of the same warmth I had sensed in Gerald. They were brisk in manner, and when they asked if I had had a good journey, they seemed mainly interested in the punctuality of ship and train, and the quality of service provided en route and at the Army and Navy stores. During this rather businesslike conversation, Gerald resumed reading his musical score until his father spoke to him sharply.

"Can't you put that stuff aside for five minutes, boy?"

"I beg your pardon, Papa." Gerald closed the score and put it down on a side table. "I didn't intend to be impolite."

Mr. Ryder stood with his back to the fire, hands behind him, a short stocky figure but with a very strong presence. He looked at me and said, "The lad's a dreamer. I'll expect you to call him to order if he lets his mind wander when he's at lessons with you, young lady." He jerked his head toward his daughter, who had moved to seat herself beside Mattie on a big leather settee. "You'll have no trouble with that one's mind wandering, though. She's a chip off the old block."

"That doesn't mean I always agree with you, Papa," said Jane, slipping her arm through Mattie's.

"You wouldn't be a chip off the old block if you did," said Mr. Ryder shortly, "but you'd best keep any disagreements to yourself till you're a bit older."

Jane laughed. "You'll be saying that when I'm ninety, Papa," she said, and it was clear to me that she was not awed by her father as was her brother Gerald. Mr. Ryder began to talk with Jane about a pony the vet had attended a few days before. I noticed Mattie did not join in the family conversation, and decided this was how I too should behave, keeping silent until one or other of the family invited a response. Gerald sat on an upright chair, his hands between his knees, gazing at the floor, and I thought he was probably playing music in his head.

Two minutes later Farrow entered to announce that dinner was served. Mr. Ryder said, "Come, Mattie," and led the way to the dining room with her beside him. Jane followed, and I lingered to come last, but Gerald gave me a quick smile and offered his arm. I had no idea if this would be approved by his father, but I could not decline, and I was thankful when we entered the dining room to see no annoyance on Mr. Ryder's face as Gerald led me to a chair.

Mr. Ryder sat at the head of the table, with Jane on his right, Gerald on his left, and Mattie at the foot. I sat on Mattie's left, next to Jane. As soon as we were seated, Mr. Ryder said briskly, "Grace." We all bowed our heads and he thanked the Lord for what we were about to receive, but in a manner which seemed to hint that he would have managed very well even without the Lord's help.

Dinner was served by two footmen supervised by Farrow, and it was a splendid meal of roast beef, Yorkshire pudding, roast potatoes, parsnips, and spring greens. I had never eaten so well during my childhood in England, and for the last five years I had known only the French style of cooking, so this was a new experience for me and I greatly enjoyed it. Some of the conversation now touched on domestic matters, and here Mattie took part. It was clear that both children were not only very fond of her but also held her in great respect, and I thought what a credit it was to her that she had achieved this.

I did not volunteer any remarks, but simply answered, with a smile, any question put to me. For much of the time now, I had a light-headed feeling that I was not myself, not Hannah McLeod. This was hardly surprising, for it was still only sixteen hours since I had crept from a cold garret in Montmartre, and it was hard for my poor brain to accept such a swift and dramatic change. In a way this helped me not to feel too nervous now that I found myself sitting at table in a fine mansion with a very rich family.

Gerald had lost his absentminded air, and during a pause in the conversation he said, "Do you ride, Hannah?"

"I'm afraid not, Master Gerald," I said, leaning back for a footman to remove my plate, and with a fleeting memory of the mountains of washing up I had done at La Coquille. "No, I've never been on a horse in my life."

He looked surprised. "Oh. But surely people ride in France?"

"Yes, they do, but I had no opportunity to ride."

He glanced at his father. "Papa says you spent your childhood in England, so surely you rode then?"

Mr. Ryder made a sound of contempt, and I said quickly, "It's only well-to-do people who can afford to ride, whether in France or England, Master Gerald. My father died soon after I was born, and I was brought up in rather poor circumstances."

Mr. Ryder said, "And so was I, but this lad doesn't know what the world's like, Hannah. He'll be finding out soon though, when I put him to work."

Gerald was looking at me in a puzzled way, and hardly seemed to hear his father. He said, "But you must have been *well* brought up. I mean, you speak very nicely and have good manners."

"Thank you," I said, a little embarrassed. "My mother was an educated person, a teacher. After she died, I was sent to France and spent five years at quite a select school for young ladies. They were very strict about our behavior there."

"I see." Gerald thought for a moment. "Our school fees here are frightfully high, Papa says. However did you manage if you were in poor circumstances?"

"I won a scholarship in England," I said, and smiled brightly as I lied.

Mattie said, "Talking of manners, Master Gerald, I wonder if asking personal questions might not be inquisitive? That would never do now, would it?"

He flushed to the roots of his hair and said hastily, "Oh, I'm so sorry. I didn't mean . . . it was just I . . . oh, please excuse me, Hannah."

I was about to reassure him that I was not offended by his interest when Mr. Ryder gave an unsympathetic chuckle and said, "You'll never get on if you don't learn to think before you speak, lad. Oh, you wouldn't know how to be rude if you tried, but you sounded rude and that's a fact."

Mattie said placidly, taking a sip from a glass of water, "I did correct Master Gerald, sir. No need for us both to do it."

Mr. Ryder glared down the table at her, but she met his gaze serenely, and after a moment he shrugged and laughed. "And now you've put me in my place. All right, Mattie, I stand corrected."

I greatly admired Mattie in that moment, realizing that she had the courage to do what she believed to be her duty, even if it angered her employer. Gerald sat staring down at his untouched baked rice pudding in misery. A few moments ago I had decided I would do best to keep silent and wait for a new topic of conversation, but I felt so sorry for the boy that I changed my mind and said, "Master Gerald." I waited for him to look up, then smiled and said, "It's quite all right." That was as much as I could say without seeming to challenge Mattie's correction, which was the last thing I wished to do, but Gerald looked relieved at my words and murmured, "Thank you."

Beside me Jane said, "Gerald and I both like riding, so we'll teach you if you like. I'm better at riding than he is, but he's more patient than I am, so I expect he'd be the better teacher."

I glanced at my employer and said, "That would be very nice, if your Papa has no objection."

Mr. Ryder shook his head. "You won't be spending more than three hours a day giving French lessons, and for the rest you're welcome to Silverwood's amenities."

"Three hours!" Jane exclaimed indignantly. "But, Papa, I leave for school at eight and I'm not home till four. How can I spend three hours at French? It's different for Gerald. He's left school, and anyway he needs to learn French if he's to go abroad on business, but I don't, and—"

"Stop prattling on, young lady," her father broke in firmly. "You won't be doing three hours. Hannah will take Gerald for two hours and you, separately, for one hour daily during the Easter holiday. When you go back to school, you can do just half an hour with her each day on your return. That won't kill you." He gestured for a footman to come and refill his wineglass.

Jane said, "Can we take tea while I'm having the lesson after school?"

"That'll be up to Hannah."

She turned to look at me, and I said, "We shall mainly be practicing conversation, so it will be very suitable to take tea then, if both your Papa and Mattie consent." I thought I caught a gleam of approval in Mr. Ryder's eyes at my last words.

Mattie said, "Oh yes, m'dear, I've no objection."

Jane gave a brisk nod. "That's all right then," she said, and I thought how like her father she was in her manner as well as in her appearance.

When dinner ended, Mr. Ryder ordered coffee to be served for himself and for me in the study. "Mrs. Matthews and the children will take theirs in the drawing room as usual, Farrow," he added as he got up from his chair.

Jane said, "I wish you wouldn't call us children, Papa. We're really quite grown up now."

"You're my children however grown up you are," her father said bluntly, "and besides, I'm not given to using two words when one will do. This way, Hannah." He turned toward the door. Farrow moved quickly to open it, a footman drew my chair back as I rose, and with a murmured, "Excuse me," to the others, I followed Mr. Ryder from the room.

His study was large and very tidy, with glass-fronted cabinets holding shelves of box files and a number of thick books which I took to be reference books of some kind. He indicated an upright chair in polished mahogany for me to take, then seated himself behind a broad desk with a tooled-leather top. There was nothing on the desk except a brass inkstand, a blotter with leather corners to match the desk top, and an evening newspaper which had apparently been placed there ready for his attention. He said, "We'll talk when the coffee comes," and began to read the newspaper.

I sat taking in as much of the study as I could without turning my head, for I did not wish to appear curious. The clock on the wall stood at half past nine. In Montmartre this would be the beginning of our busiest time at La Coquille. I hoped Père Chabrier had managed to get help for the evening, so that my absence would not bear too heavily on Armand.

I offered up a silent prayer of thanks that I had escaped arrest in Paris and found such a comfortable haven here in England. My employer, Mr. Sebastian Ryder, was not concerned to be particularly welcoming or friendly, but there was no reason why he should be. As Mattie had pointed out, I was not a guest but a privileged servant. That being so, I felt enormously lucky to have received such friendliness from Mattie herself, for she might well have been a dragon of a housekeeper and jealous of her position. Gerald, too, had given me a warm welcome, and if Jane's attitude was more like her father's, well, I could scarcely complain about that.

After two or three minutes the door opened and Farrow brought in a tray with cups and a silver coffee service. He set it down on the desk, poured a cup of black coffee for his master, then looked at me. "How will you take your coffee, Miss Hannah?"

"With a little milk or cream, if you please, and one knob of sugar."

Farrow poured, handed me the cup of coffee, and said, "Will there be anything else, sir?"

"No."

The butler withdrew from the study. Mr. Ryder pushed his newspaper aside, looked at me, and said, "I thought a café waitress might be timid with servants, but you're not. That's good."

I knew he was not being offensive but simply making a plain comment. After all, twenty-four hours ago I had been a café waitress. I smiled and said politely, "We had a staff of servants at my college, sir, so I'm not unused to them."

He nodded, stirring his coffee. "Right. Now we'll talk business. Have you any money?"

"No English money, sir. About twenty French francs."

He reached down to a newspaper rack close to his hand, took out a paper, opened it, studied something for a moment, then said, "Today's exchange rate is twenty-four to the pound. Bring your francs here after breakfast tomorrow and I'll change them for you. I'll add another ten shillings for you to put in your purse. Beyond that, you'll be paid three pounds a month, in arrears, on the last day of each month, with bed and board all found. This engagement can be terminated by me at a week's notice, but you will agree in writing to continue in my employ for a period of not less than two years on these terms. Agreed?"

I blinked, trying to work out sums in my head, for I was used to francs, not pounds, but in another moment I realized that three pounds a month must surely be a generous wage, and I said, "Oh, yes sir. Thank you." I hesitated, then went on, "I know a lot of money was spent to set me up in clothes and small items. How much of that am I to repay each month?"

"Nothing." He made a brushing gesture with his hand, and his rather forbidding features relaxed slightly in what might almost have become a smile. "You have a regard for equity, I see. That's commendable."

I was not quite sure what he meant, and could think of no answer, so I said nothing. After a moment or two his face took on its usual severe expression again and he said, "Whatever was bought for you today is yours. As regards your duties, you'll spend two hours with Gerald each morning and one hour with Jane each afternoon, at times to be arranged with Mattie. They both have school textbooks you can use, and if you need other books I'll order them. Understood?"

"Yes, sir. Where do you wish me to hold the lessons?"

"The children have a study each. Use them."

"Very well, sir. With only three hours of work a day I shall have time to spare. Are there any other duties you would like me to undertake?"

"None," he said abruptly. "There's to be no question of your mixing with the staff below stairs. It's possible you may be able to help Mattie in some way, but you must ask her about that. For the rest you're free to do as you please, provided you behave with decorum at all times." He eyed me sharply. "I hardly need tell you, I'll have no bohemian ways brought into Silverwood."

I said, "I expect you will know, Mr. Ryder, that for the past year and a half I have lived alone in Montmartre, which is a haunt of bohemians, but I do assure you that during this time I have lived a very proper life, and I shall not be a bad influence on your children."

"Boniface has already assured me of that, after full inquiries," said Mr. Ryder dryly. "What's your religion?"

"I was brought up Church of England, but at the college I used to attend a Catholic church, not for confession or communion, but just to be present during a service."

"Here we attend on Sunday morning for matins, and I shall expect you to join us. The local gentry don't like me much since I'm in trade, but they like my money and they're pleased with the new church organ I bought. Same with the shopkeepers and local artisans, so though we're still foreigners after being here only fifteen years, we're now acceptable foreigners. Mattie's well liked except by one or two toffee-nosed ladies, but as a housekeeper she neither pays nor receives morning calls, so that's of no consequence. She attends social occasions such as fetes, garden parties, concerts in the church hall, and so forth, and she'll introduce you to one or two pleasant people. Do you drive?"

"A pony and trap? No, sir, I've never done that."

"Get a groom or one of the children to show you. The ponies are well trained, so you'll find no difficulty. Have you any questions you wish to ask?"

I thought for a few moments, then said, "Nothing occurs to me at the moment, sir."

"Right. That's all, then." He drew the newspaper toward him again.

I had drunk three quarters of my coffee as we talked. Now I finished the cup, stood up, put it on the tray, dropped a curtsy, said, "Thank you, sir," and made my way out of the study.

In the drawing room Mattie sat in an armchair doing some crochet work. Jane was at a small table with what looked like a photograph album, a magnifying glass at her elbow, writing in a long narrow book. Gerald sat on the settee, once again reading his musical score. "Ah, there you are, m'dear," said Mattie. "We'll all be going up to bed in half an hour, but if you're tired after your long journey and want to go up now, you please do so."

I said, "Oh no, I'd rather be with the family, thank you. May I see what you're doing, Miss Jane?"

"Yes, all right."

As I drew near, I saw that the album held stamps. She picked up the magnifying glass, peered for a moment, then put it down and wrote something in the long narrow book. "It's my own collection," she said. "They're all colonial stamps and I have almost five hundred now, so I'm making an index. Do you know anything about stamps?"

I shook my head. "No, I'm afraid not."

"Oh, well." She picked up the glass again.

Gerald stood up and said, "Mattie, will you excuse me if I go up to the music room to practice for half an hour before bedtime?"

She looked up from her crochet. "Is it the piece by that Chopin?" She pronounced Chopin in a funny way.

Gerald nodded. "Yes, the Étude in E flat minor."

Mattie smiled. "I don't know one name from t'other, Master Gerald, but anyway you run along and practice. Perhaps Hannah would like to sit and listen."

Gerald flushed. "Oh no, I play it very badly, really."

"Nonsense," said Mattie, and looked at me. "He plays beautifully, Hannah, you'll see."

"I would very much like to come and listen, Master Gerald," I said, and meant it, for despite my denial I was beginning to feel sleepy now, and I felt that to sit and listen to music would be less demanding than making conversation.

"Well, all right," said Gerald, half doubtful and half pleased, I thought. He opened the door for me and we went upstairs to the music room. There he moved a comfortable easy chair to a point about six paces from the grand piano and shyly invited me to be seated. "I'll just play one or two things I know well and can manage not too badly," he muttered, opening the top of the music stool and sorting through some pieces of music within. "I won't stop if I play a wrong note; it's awfully boring for people to listen to somebody just practicing."

I assured Gerald that I would not be bored, and watched him take his seat, open the piano, and set up the piece of music by Chopin. Then he began to play, and I was astonished at his skill. The music was gentle, slow, and strangely haunting, and if he played a wrong note, I was certainly unaware of it. I listened quite entranced until the final chords, and when he drew his hands from the keyboard and sat with head bowed a little, I clapped softly and said, "Oh, Master Gerald, that was so beautiful, I can't tell you how much I enjoyed it."

His face lit up as he turned to me. "Did you really? I didn't play it as well as I have done, but I'm glad you liked it." He began to set up another piece of music. "Mattie quite enjoys listening when I play, but Jane and Papa aren't very keen. This is a movement from Mozart 40. That's one of his piano concertos. It's very lively and exciting. Just listen . . ."

He began to play again, and I thrilled not only to the music but to the sight of those long sensitive fingers flashing over the keys. It seemed to me that Master Gerald Ryder was a very fine pianist indeed, and I felt sad that he would be unable to continue his studies because his father required him to enter the family business. He played a third piece, a cheerful dance by Brahms, then asked what I would like by way of conclusion.

I confessed that I was unschooled in music, and said I would like to hear the Chopin composition again. He seemed pleased by this, and as he began to play, I leaned my head back in the chair and closed my eyes, letting the slow, delicate melody wash over me like a lullaby.

This was unwise. I had not slept the night before, and since dawn I had traveled hundreds of miles by rail and sea on a journey which began in fear, was continued in varying degrees of apprehension, and ended in relief. It was little wonder that I now fell into a doze.

The next thing I knew was a feeling of shock as I struggled up from sleep and opened my eyes to find Gerald on one knee by my chair, his eyes filled with laughter as he gently patted my hand. "Hannah," he was saying softly. "Wake up, Hannah."

I came upright with a start, clutching the arms of the chair, exclaiming in horror, "Oh, I'm so deeply sorry! Please excuse me, Master

Gerald. I—I don't know what to say. Please don't think I was bored, I loved hearing you play, but I just closed my eyes to listen, and . . ."

He stood up, shaking his head, "For goodness' sake don't apologize, Hannah. I'm pleased, not offended. I think you've been marvelous to stay so bright and cheerful this evening when you must be tired to death almost. Mattie told us that at midnight last night you were still at work, waiting at table in a Paris restaurant, and since then you've had all that long journey. I think most girls would have made a great fuss and gone straight to bed, but you haven't made any fuss at all."

"That's very kind of you, Master Gerald." I gave an inward sigh of relief, and smiled at him to show my gratitude for his generous words. "But it was very rude of me to fall asleep, and I do apologize."

He stood back a little, looking down at me, hands folded in front of him, head tilted a little to one side, and said in a soft, faraway voice, "You have the most beautiful smile I've ever seen, Hannah. When I first saw you, when you came into the drawing room before dinner . . . it was as if sunshine had suddenly come into this house."

I stood up quickly, a tremor of alarm bringing me sharply to wakefulness. Gerald's eyes were resting on me with an absorbed gaze, warm and tender. He was eighteen, not long out of school, and no doubt impressionable. To him, perhaps, there was something romantic about me. I was a decently brought up English girl, who had no parents and after schooling in France had been compelled to work as a waitress in Montmartre to scratch a bare living. That might indeed seem very romantic to a sensitive boy, and now I was to live at Silverwood to teach him French. I would be in his company daily, and he liked my smile.

This was dangerous indeed.

Six

I got to my feet briskly. The last thing I wished was for my employer's son to imagine he had fallen in love with me. "Thank you for allowing me to hear you play, Master Gerald," I said politely. "I can see you try very hard with your music, so I hope you will do the same with your French. Now if you will excuse me, I shall wish you goodnight."

The formal effect I hoped for was ruined by a prodigious yawn that overcame me on the last few words, and I had to turn away with a hand to my mouth, making an unsuccessful effort to hide it. Gerald gave a little laugh and said, "Oh, poor Hannah, you're so tired. Yes, do go along to bed now, and I hope you sleep well."

I thanked him and went downstairs, leaving him to put away his music. Mattie was still crocheting, Jane was closing her index book, and Mr. Ryder was now leaning back in an armchair almost hidden by his newspaper. At his elbow was a small table bearing a glass of amber liquid which I guessed to be whiskey and soda, or perhaps brandy and soda since I now remembered that it was an English way to put soda with cognac, much to the amazement of the French.

Again I excused myself, wished everybody goodnight, and went up to my room. It was a great pleasure to light the gas by simply drawing down the little chain. The bed had been turned down, and one of my nightdresses was laid out on it in readiness for me. I undressed, let down my hair and tied it back with a ribbon, put on my nightdress, lit the bedside candle, and was about to turn out the gas when I remembered my little box of valuables and felt a foolish pang of alarm in wondering what the maid had done with it when she unpacked for me.

It was there in the topmost drawer of the chest of drawers, quite safe. I took it out, sat at the dressing table, and opened it, not quite knowing why. Perhaps it was because the sudden and dramatic change of circumstance had combined with my tiredness to make me feel I was living a dream, and I needed to look at those small things which most deeply belonged to me, to reassure myself that I was Hannah McLeod.

I read through my mother's birth certificate, then my own, with blank spaces where the name and profession of my father should have been. I put them away and unfolded the letter from my mother.

Dearest Hannah,

Please be a brave girl. The doctor has told me I have very little time to live, and when you read this I shall have passed on. My greatest pain and sorrow is that I leave you alone in the world when you are only twelve years old. I love you dearly, and you have returned my love, so we have been happy even though our circumstances have always been meager.

I feel much guilt that I am unable to leave you provided for, but you know that I have always done my best, and so I believe you will forgive me. We have very little saved, and there will be no more than thirty pounds left after my funeral expenses have been paid, which I shall attend to in advance. This money I shall leave to Mrs. Taylor, who has promised to take you in and look after you with her own children for three years, but she will want you to help look after the small ones and teach reading and writing to the older ones. After three years you will be fifteen, and I pray you may be able to secure a position as junior teacher in a school for small children. I leave you all my books, and beg you to continue your studies as best you can.

I weep as I think how little I am able to do for you, dearest Hannah. Please be brave, and try to live as I have always taught you: work hard and be well mannered at all times; be strong in adversity and never complain; be unashamed of poverty, providing it comes not from idleness; be unashamed of those burdens life may bring you; be ashamed only of your own faults, and strive to amend them; beware of self-pity, for it can destroy you; beware of bitterness, for it can destroy you; and trust no man.

Should you ever find yourself in truly dire straits, then as a last resort you should go to Messrs. Finch and Lowther, solicitors of Warner Street, Clerkenwell. Give your name, say you wish to see them concerning the Tennant Charity, and seek their advice.

As I end this letter you are lying asleep in your bed. I look at you, my dearest child, and I could cry out in anger at the cruelty of my being taken from you. But I will not cry out, I will not let bitterness enter my heart. I only pray that God will bless you and keep you safe, and to His hands I now commend you.

Your loving Mother,
Kathleen McLeod

Slowly I folded the letter, and in my mind's eye saw my mother clearly, a slight figure with dark hair, neither pretty nor plain; disciplined in herself, strict in my upbringing, yet always loving. She had taught in a school near the house where we rented two rooms of the upper floor, and there was rarely a time when her eyes did not show the struggle and strain of keeping us clothed, fed, sheltered, and living in a clean and decent way.

To my shame and regret I had not always been kind or understanding toward her, sometimes sulking when she insisted on giving me an hour's extra tuition every evening, but for the most part I was affectionate toward her, and she knew that I loved her. It was not until after her death, when I first saw my birth certificate with no father named in it, and also found no marriage certificate, that I wondered if the story she had told of my father being a sailor who had died abroad was true. Her letter offered no explanation, and I was too young to grasp what I later realized must be the truth of the situation.

Our downstairs neighbor, Mr. Taylor, had spoken plainly enough about it, with many a drunken oath. He and Mrs. Taylor rented the whole small house, subletting two rooms to my mother. He was a porter in Smithfield, the meat market, a coarse burly man who always stank of beer and was feared by his wife and children. There were seven children, with about a year or eighteen months between each. Mrs. Taylor was a thin, workworn woman, well meaning and a good mother as far as she was able to be, but weak of character and not very intelligent.

It was easy for me to feel that my mother had been mistaken in leaving her small savings to this woman to pay for her taking me into her own family, but when I reflected on this I could think of nothing better she might have done. In the event, when my first heartbroken grief and loneliness had begun to pass, I think I was more content with the Taylors than I would have been in an orphanage.

Mrs. Taylor and the children liked me. She had a praiseworthy if rather pathetic desire for her children to "learn 'ow to live nice, like you an' your Mum done," and so I began to teach them a little of the behavior and manners I had learned from my mother. This was much to the contempt of Mr. Taylor whenever he was present. A gross man, he would sit at table in stockinged feet, wearing trousers, braces, and undervest, jeering at any attempt I made to instruct the children.

"Well just 'ark at Miss Posh with 'er fancy ways. Lah-de-dah-de-dah!" He would shovel some food into his mouth and point with his knife. "And 'oo is she, eh? Born wrong side of the blanket, for all 'er Ma's airs and graces."

His wife would protest timidly. "Now you've no call to say that, Bert. Don't speak ill of 'er Mum."

"You shut your gob, Daisy. 'Ere, pour me some more tea."

I never protested myself, and was always polite to Mr. Taylor, though I had as little to do with him as possible. I did not understand what he meant about my being born the wrong side of the blanket, and when I asked Mrs. Taylor about it later she was upset. "Oh, take no notice, duckie. He's a pig, that's what 'e is."

"But what does it mean, Mrs. Taylor?"

"Well . . ." she looked flustered. "It's a way of saying you didn't 'ave no father, really."

"Oh. I thought there had to be a father."

"Well, there does 'ave to be, but what I mean, what wrong side of the blanket means, is that your father wasn't married to your mother."

I was baffled. "I don't understand how there can be a father and mother not married to each other."

Mrs. Taylor pushed back a straggling wisp of hair in a harassed manner. "Well, there can be, lovey. You'll understand when you're a bit older."

I did understand in time, not because it was explained to me but because I looked up the word 'bastard' in my dictionary after Mr. Taylor had referred to me as such on several occasions, and also because I learned the crude facts about men, women, and babies from the Taylor children, who seemed to have learned it on the streets almost as soon as they could talk.

Seated at my dressing table in Silverwood, I laid the letter back in the small box and took out a prayer book. This had been my mother's, and the pages were limp with usage for she had read from it every day of her life throughout the years that I remembered. For me it was a talisman. If I gripped it in my hands and closed my eyes, she seemed to live again in my mind, to give me comfort and support. This, together with her worn purse and a thin gold ring wrapped in tissue paper, were all that I possessed of her belongings. She had worn the ring as a wedding ring, but I now felt sure that this had been for the sake of appearances, to give credence to her pretense of being a widow. Whatever the truth about my father and my birth, I thought no whit the less of her for it.

There was only one more item in my box. This was the other ring, the ring of Mexican silver engraved with the initials R.D. As I held it, I conjured up the face of Ramon Delgado, the hawklike features and the dark tragic eyes as he spoke with despairing passion of his country's plight, of the poverty and oppression which gripped Mexico.

He knew no French, but his English was good, which no doubt explained why Mam'selle Montavon appointed me to receive him when he visited the college. Perhaps I was a good listener, for he seemed to find relief in pouring out to me his ideas for bringing prosperity and freedom to his countrymen. I had been told that he was something of a revolutionary, and therefore in temporary exile, but that he might one day attain a position of power. It seemed to me admirable that a man who was clearly rich and could have lived a life of ease should be so deeply concerned about the poor.

I saw Señor Delgado several times during the month he spent in Paris that summer, and I was aware of a progressive change in him, for during that short period he seemed to move from the depths of despair to lively optimism. He chose to attribute much of this change to me, and just before he left Paris I was summoned to Mam'selle Montavon's study. Señor Delgado had called to say good-bye, and it was then that he took the monogrammed ring from his finger and presented it to me.

Now, as I sat with the ring in my palm, if I smiled a little it was because I recalled that Ramon Delgado was one of two men who had made me almost the same strange promise—a promise I could never imagine myself taking seriously. It seemed much longer than two days ago that a half Irish seaman and artist had finished painting my picture and had said, "If you ever need a friend to do anything at all for you . . . just come to Toby Kent."

Almost two years before, a lean dark man of fierce beliefs had put a silver ring in my hand and said, "While we talked together, when I have spoken perhaps a hundred words, you have spoken only five, yet thanks to you I leave Paris with new life, new hope, señorita. Here is a token of my gratitude. If ever I can be of service to you, call upon me." He had written down the address of a French lawyer who would send letters on to him wherever he might be, but I had later thrown this away. I had kept the ring though, for I had few enough possessions which meant anything to me, and this was a souvenir from a man of idealistic passion and compassion, a man I liked and respected.

I returned the ring to the box, fitted the lid in place, and rose from my dressing table to put the box away in a drawer. It was a joy to sink down in the soft feather bed, so different from the bed I had last slept in. Here, the sheets were unpatched and of best quality Irish linen, the blankets were of finest wool, light but warm. I snuffed the bedside candle and lay there in the darkness for a few minutes, recalling the strangeness of all that had happened to me in the twenty-four hours just past. At this time yesterday, in a small family restaurant in Montmartre, a French inspector of police and a gentleman from the British embassy had warned me that I was about to be arrested for theft, and there had seemed no possible way for me either to prove my innocence or to escape. But now . . .

"You're a lucky girl, Hannah McLeod," I told myself. Closing my eyes, I said a prayer of gratitude, then another brief prayer for Toby Kent and for my friends at the college, Annette and Marguerite. While I was adding Armand and the others at La Coquille to my list for blessing, I realized that I ought to begin including all the family at Silverwood now, but before I could do so I must have fallen asleep.

By the end of my first week at Silverwood, I had found my way about the house, the grounds, and the village of Bradwell, and had fallen into a daily routine which seemed very undemanding compared with my days in Montmartre. I knew all the servants by name, and had the feeling that on the whole they liked me quite well, probably because I was careful to be courteous in my dealings with them.

My first impressions of the family remained unchanged. Mattie was a capable housekeeper and a kindhearted woman who helped me greatly in adapting to this new life in a country I had left as a child and half forgotten. Of Sebastian Ryder I saw very little, except when we came together for meals. He was not interested in conversation on domestic matters, but would talk about events reported in the newspapers to do with government, politics, and business. For the most part it was only Jane who knew what he was talking about. Mattie made no pretense of being interested in anything outside the home and village, and Gerald's thoughts were usually elsewhere, either on his music or, unfortunately, on me. But Jane invariably scanned the morning newspaper, and since her interests seemed to be much the same as those of her father, she was well able to maintain a conversation with him.

They both had a tendency to tease Gerald by asking his opinion on some matter they were discussing, and then subjecting him to banter because he knew nothing about it. After noting this, I began to study the newspaper myself every day, so that I knew at least something of what was happening in the world, and could occasionally deflect a little mockery from Gerald by putting in a few words myself, but I was careful to do so in the form of questions and not as an opinion.

Jane remained as neutral toward me as she had been on the first evening, neither friendly nor hostile, a little offhand, but never to the degree of being impolite. She applied herself well during my French tuition, and although she was sometimes irritated when I corrected her accent or grammar, it was always with herself that she was annoyed, never with me. I cannot pretend that I grew fond of Jane, but I respected her.

Gerald was clearly smitten by me, a boy in love for the first time, or believing himself so to be. This was obvious to anybody with eyes to see, but to my relief both Mr. Ryder and Jane seemed to regard the matter with tolerant amusement, and even more to my relief they did not tease him about it. On one occasion, Mr. Ryder spoke of it when he and I were alone together in the drawing room just before the rest of the family arrived to wait for dinner to be announced. Looking up from his newspaper, he said abruptly and without preamble, "You needn't worry about Gerald. It's no fault of yours, I can see that, and I don't doubt he'll get over it soon. If the boy makes a nuisance of himself, let me know, but you should be able to deal with the situation yourself."

I said thankfully, "Oh yes, sir. I was only worried about what you might think."

"Then don't be. If I've any complaint to make, you'll hear about it; be sure of that."

A moment later Gerald and Mattie arrived, and we said no more. Mattie herself was of course aware that Gerald had been smitten by calf love, and she was a little anxious until she understood that I did not take it seriously. "That's all right then, m'dear," she said. "It would never do, see now, him being the young master and you being just a teacher with no family or background."

"Oh, I know that, Mattie. Besides, Mr. Ryder has spoken to me about it and he knows I'm trying to discourage Master Gerald."

"Ah, that's all right then."

As the weeks went by there was little sign of Gerald being discouraged. He was far too timid to say anything or make the slightest advance, but no matter how cool and formal I was with him he continued to gaze at me adoringly.

After the first month I was well settled in at Silverwood. I had been introduced to the vicar and to several families of the local gentry, as well as to shopkeepers and workpeople in the village. I sensed that Mr. Ryder had been right when he said that the local gentry were not over fond of him, and I certainly had the impression that they tended to look down their noses, but at the same time they seemed somewhat in awe of him, probably because he was very rich and also a forceful person who did not mince words.

Gerald taught me to drive the gig, which was not very difficult since all the carriage horses and ponies at Silverwood were good-tempered creatures and well trained. He also began to teach me to ride, but after only a few days Jane decided to take charge of my tuition. I was glad of this, partly because she understood the art of riding sidesaddle, which her brother did not, and partly because Gerald was far too patient with me. I was rather nervous of horses, and he was indulgent about this, but Jane would stand no nonsense, either from the horse or from me, and under her firm guidance I soon began to acquire more confidence.

The family did not hunt, but there were two or three quite spirited horses in the Silverwood stables. I did not test myself on any of these, but left them to Jane and Gerald, who were both good riders, as was their father. After a month I was quite happy about driving the gig to the village, or going out for a ride on Willow or Patch, the two quiet mares I favored most. Jane gave me a riding habit she no longer wanted, and Mattie helped me alter it to fit. I fell into the way of riding for an hour each day, sometimes with Gerald or Jane, sometimes with both, and sometimes alone.

To my relief, Gerald proved to have a quick ear for French, and I was able to report as much when Mr. Ryder asked how he was getting on. He had learned French at school, but from an Englishman, and his accent was poor, but this improved rapidly now. Perhaps his ear for music helped him to imitate the nuances of my French accent, and certainly he paid attention and listened carefully during the lessons I gave. His written work was not nearly so good, but Mr. Ryder told me he was not particularly concerned about that. His main wish was for Gerald to be fluent in conversation.

Jane, on the other hand, made steady progress in her written work but had an appalling accent which nothing I could do seemed to improve. I reported this rather uneasily to her father when he inquired about her progress, and was again relieved when he simply shrugged and said, "We can't all be good at everything, and it's not important for Jane."

My only experience of teaching had been when I was taken in by Mrs. Taylor after my mother died, and had tried to teach the Taylor children letters and figures. Now I would spend at least an hour each evening preparing for the lessons I planned to give next day to Jane and Gerald. Even so, very little of my day was taken up by work, and I had a great deal of spare time. Some of this I spent out riding or walking when the weather allowed, and often I would drive into the village with Mattie when she did the household shopping.

There was much to be learnt from Mattie in my new life. I had no experience of keeping house except for the year and a half I had spent in a tiny room in Montmartre. Then I had lived from hand to mouth, with only myself to care for, and there had been no time or facility for any but the simplest cooking. Now, from Mattie and our cook, Mrs. Fletcher, I began to learn how to judge meat and poultry when buying, how to choose vegetables and fruit, and how to plan a menu for a family. Mrs. Fletcher was a bustling woman and a great chatterbox, but she was a splendid cook, and from her I learned a number of recipes which I wrote down in a book.

In a residence such as Silverwood, it was not difficult for me to fill the rest of my spare time. Sebastian Ryder's library was a treasure house for me, and when I discovered there was no index of books and authors, I asked if I might compile one, a request he granted with a brief, "Yes, if you want to," spoken without looking up from the newspaper he was reading.

Another interest for me lay in the spacious grounds. I scarcely knew one flower from another, and there was little to see at this time of year except for early blossoms on some of the trees, but I enjoyed putting on my coat and going out to spend an hour with Blake, the old gardener, or one of his assistants, to watch them at work in the big greenhouses where they were bringing on plants for the coming year. Sometimes they were surprised at the ignorance shown by my questions, but when they learned from other servants that I had grown up in France, they accepted my almost total lack of knowledge as being natural since I was a foreigner.

In one particular Silverwood was an odd household, for Mattie and I were neither upstairs nor downstairs people in all respects. Mr. Ryder sometimes entertained guests to dinner, not local people but business acquaintances, often from abroad. On such occasions Mattie and I dined in the small sitting room adjoining her bedroom. She would often invite me to join her there at other times, to sit and chat for an hour or so, or perhaps to play a card game she taught me called cribbage.

At the end of my second month, two Frenchmen arrived to stay as guests for the whole weekend. Mattie and I withdrew from the family for the occasion, but on the Saturday evening Mr. Ryder sent for me to attend him in his study. I felt suddenly alarmed that his guests might be policemen in plain clothes who had traced me from Paris, though it was hard to believe they would go to such lengths. In the event it transpired that they were businessmen who were negotiating to buy military equipment from one of Mr. Ryder's companies. Their English was labored, Gerald's command of French had proved inadequate for the discussion of details, and so I was sent for to translate.

It was an interesting experience, because by description and explanation I had to learn a number of technical French words regarding weapons and ammunition which I had not known before, and I later made a note of these terms for Gerald's future lessons. The sums of money and quantities of armaments I found myself translating were quite staggering to me, but I was careful to let no such thoughts show in my face, and simply translated as required in an impersonal fashion. My efforts must have satisfied Mr. Ryder, for he offered a word of commendation before giving me leave to go when my task was completed.

I rarely thought about my life in France now, but I remembered my few friends there when I said my prayers, especially Toby Kent, since I knew he must still be at sea with whatever extra perils this might bring. In Bradwell, Jane returned to her day school after the Easter holiday, Gerald continued to regard me with mute adoration, and spring flowers and shrubs began to bring great splashes of color to the green and brown gardens of Silverwood, first the daffodils, then the tulips, the aubrietia tumbling over dwarf walls, and the camellias with great blossoms of pink and red.

One evening in the drawing room I sat idly turning the pages of a magazine called *The Tatler,* when I suddenly froze with amazement, uncertain whether to feel pleased or uneasy. On the page before my eyes there were two photographs, each with a caption in black type beneath, and three or four columns of normal printing. One photograph was of a framed painting depicting a man in a shabby white jacket, and it meant nothing to me. The other was a photograph of the picture Toby Kent had painted of me that Sunday morning in Montmartre.

There I sat with hands in lap, the sink piled with crockery and pans, gazing through the window at the roofs and chimney pots outlined against the sky. Considering the size of the photograph and the absence of color, it was remarkably clear, yet I felt with a sense of relief that I could not possibly have been recognized from it. Indeed, I doubt if I could have been recognized from the original painting, for Toby had painted his impression of me, and not a careful likeness.

I looked up from the magazine for a moment. Mr. Ryder was not with us for he had gone up north on business for two days. Mattie was knitting, Jane was pasting some cuttings in her scrapbook, and Gerald was frowning over a textbook, trying to please me by improving his French. They all knew I had been a waitress in a poor quarter of Paris with barely a sou to my name, and there was no strong reason why I should not show them the picture and acknowledge that I was the girl in it, but I did not intend to do so. By harsh experience I had learned to look forward rather than back, and I had put my life in France behind me now, as I had done once before with my life in England. If I showed the picture, I would be asked all sorts of questions as to how I had come to sit for it, and I did not want to talk about such things.

I looked down at the magazine again, and read the caption: *Above is a photograph of the picture* Butterfly Girl, *by Mr. Toby Kent, which caused such a sensation when it was exhibited in Paris earlier this year.*

I stifled a gasp of pleasure at Toby's success. A sensation, the magazine said! And he had called it *Butterfly Girl* after the golden birthmark he had seen on my shoulder. This confirmed my decision to say nothing, even to Mattie—perhaps especially to Mattie, since she would be curious to know why both the artist and Mr. Sebastian Ryder had referred to me in the same way.

With an effort to appear unhurried, I turned back the page to find the start of the article. It was entitled "Some Modern Impressionists," and as I ran my eye quickly down the columns, I picked out several famous names Toby had mentioned when trying to explain to me what the impressionist painters believed and how they worked. Then I turned the page, found Toby's name, and began to read carefully.

> An Englishman, Mr. Toby Kent, aged thirty, has sprung to sudden prominence in Parisian art circles following a series of five paintings which began with the best known, entitled *Butterfly Girl*, a photograph of which is shown on the facing page.

I was bewildered. Five paintings? How could Toby have painted more pictures when he was away at sea, and without canvas, brushes, or paint? Perhaps the other four were earlier paintings, but the writer said that *Butterfly Girl* was the first, and I remembered the smiling fervor with which Toby claimed that in painting me that day he had at last found what he had been struggling toward for many years. In any event, if I remembered correctly, Toby had gone off on a long voyage and should not have been back in Paris even yet.

I put the puzzle aside for the moment and read on.

> Your correspondent was able to exchange a few words with Mr. Kent at the Montaigne Gallery last week, and put to him the questions which have stimulated much curiosity in artistic circles, namely, "Why is this picture entitled *Butterfly Girl*, and who is the model?" Mr. Kent is a young man whose manner is rather more amiable than his words would seem to indicate. In reply to my questions he gave the smiling response, "Why I call her *Butterfly Girl* is my business, sir, and the identity of the model is her business."

I smiled to myself, for I could almost hear Toby Kent saying those words, cheerful as ever but quite unconcerned to make an impression on this gentleman who was apparently an art critic of some importance. The next sentence almost took my breath away.

> It is rumored here that there was some competition for the purchase of this picture, and that it was sold to an American collector for a sum equivalent to £1,800 despite offers somewhat higher. When asked why he had accepted a lower price than he might otherwise have obtained, Mr. Kent is reported as saying, again most amiably, "What the h——l is that to do with anyone but me? And anyway it's leased, not sold." He could not be persuaded to enlarge on this cryptic statement.

I could hardly contain my delight at Toby's good fortune. One thousand eight hundred pounds! He was suddenly rich, but for me it was much more important that he had proved himself as an artist, for I knew it was this that would count for Toby.

I read on, but in a cursory manner because now the critic was writing about technical qualities in the paintings, referring to naturalism, analysis of tone and color, animating the surface of the canvas, and other such matters which I only half understood. It seemed to me that he did not greatly admire the impressionist school of painters, but felt that Mr. Toby Kent had diverged from that school in a quite admirable way to produce a number of most interesting and attractive pictures. These, he wrote, possessed "intellectual rigor—a quality hitherto lacking in impressionist painting."

My eye ran on, and stopped again at the final paragraph.

> Of the five paintings viewed by your correspondent at the Montaigne Gallery, two were portraits, two were street scenes, and one was a still life. We are able to show photographic reproductions of the two portraits, *Butterfly Girl* being perhaps of more interest, but the other, entitled *Waiter*, being of equal quality both in pictorial language and technical inspiration. Some may not like Mr. Kent's pictures, but your correspondent has no doubt that a successful career lies ahead for this artist.

I looked again at the other picture, but carefully this time, holding it a little away. For a moment it meant nothing, then suddenly the features which had seemed formless took shape, the body came to life, and this was Armand, my waiter friend at La Coquille, just as I had seen him a hundred times in his shabby white jacket, sleek black hair glinting with brilliantine, and long moustache down-curving, and the head tilted slightly as he stood with pad in hand to write down an order.

I stared entranced, quite shaken by the effect of it. Here in this photograph, so small compared with the painting, and with only shades of white, black, and gray for color, I could see the magic Toby's brush had wrought in putting on canvas the reality of Armand in a way no photographic likeness could have done.

Somebody was speaking my name, and I realized it was not for the first time. With a start I came to myself and looked up. Gerald stood gazing down at me with a puzzled smile. "My word, Hannah, you were miles away. What are you reading that's so gripping?"

"Oh, I'm sorry, Master Gerald." I closed the magazine slowly so that it would not seem I was trying to hide anything. "I was just reading a piece about artists in Paris. There were quite a lot on the Left Bank and up in Montmartre."

"Yes, I suppose there would be," he said without much interest. "I'm going up to practice the *Hammerklavier* for a little while, and I wondered if you would like to come and listen."

I searched my memory for what I had picked up during the past few weeks and said, "That's Beethoven, isn't it? One of his piano sonatas?"

Gerald beamed with pleasure. "Yes. In B-flat Major, opus 106."

"Thank you, Master Gerald, I would enjoy that, if Miss Jane and Mattie will excuse me."

Five minutes later I was listening to that beautiful music but not thinking about it in the way Gerald was always advising me to do if I wished to improve my understanding. Usually I did try, but on this occasion my thoughts were elsewhere, for I was wondering if I dared write a letter to Toby Kent to say how delighted I was to read of his success. After some reflection I decided against doing so. There could be little chance that the French police would come into possession of the letter and so be able to trace me, but I realized that Toby was now a person of some importance, and although he had always been most kind and friendly toward me it was hardly likely that he would be interested to hear from me now. For him the world had changed, as it had also changed for me, and we should both be looking forward, not back.

Perhaps it was the haunting music, but with that thought a curious sadness came upon me. I searched within myself for a reason, and found no answer, but that small *tristesse* remained with me while Gerald played. Later, in bed, I lay awake for a while wondering if the police had been given my letter and had returned Mr. Doyle's gold cuff links to him. In my letter to Toby I had asked him to speak to Inspector Lecour about this.

Perhaps after all I should write to Toby now and inquire . . . ?

No. With his success he would surely have moved to better lodgings, and even if the letter was sent on, which was most unlikely, it might only be an embarrassment to him. Whatever had happened, it no longer made any difference to me. The apache footpads, Mr. Doyle, the fierce young woman called Clara, my escape from arrest—that whole unfortunate affair was over and done with, and the people involved had passed out of my life now.

This was my conclusion as I lay in my comfortable bed in my well-appointed bedroom, drifting slowly down into sleep, but I was soon to be proved wrong.

At eleven o'clock one morning later that week I changed into my riding habit and bowler, and went down to the stables. Gerald's lesson had ended at half past ten, and when he learned that I planned to go riding he asked to go with me. I could hardly refuse, but I was glad when Mr. Ryder required him to attend a meeting in the study with some business people from the north that morning, for I found it rather a strain to be alone in Gerald's company for any length of time except when he was playing the piano. Gerald was attending his father's business meetings more often now. He confided to me that he was not expected to speak a word on these occasions but was simply there to listen and learn. I had the impression that he found it hard to concentrate on such matters, and was not learning very much.

After breakfast I had told Frank, the third groom, that I would like to go riding for an hour or so at eleven o'clock, and when I reached the stables he had Willow saddled and waiting for me. Five minutes later I was riding at an easy walk across the pasture to the north of Silverwood, enjoying a touch of warmth in the air which seemed to herald the coming of summer.

Beyond the pasture lay Quentin's Wood, an area of bracken, shrubs, and a variety of trees, with several footpaths and bridle paths winding through. As we reached one of the bridle paths, I decided I would practice my trot, and if that went well, I would put Willow to a gentle canter, something I had done only once before, and then under Jane's supervision.

I clicked my tongue, tapped Willow with my heel, and at once she broke into a brisk trot. Now it was a matter of remembering Jane's exhortations when she was teaching me. "Looser rein, Hannah! Just let her *feel* you're there. No, wait. Whoa! Now listen, you're not sitting properly, but I'm going to tell you the secret of riding sidesaddle, which you'll probably never hear from anybody else. You use your left leg just the same as a man. It's the position of the *right* leg that's important. You *must* sit with your right thigh parallel to the horse's spine, so that it bears the whole of your weight. That's better. Now off you go again."

Jane's instruction was very sound, even though her frequent reference to my thigh made poor Gerald blush and look away on the occasions when he happened to have joined us. I sometimes wished I could feel more affection for Jane, but she was a girl who seemed to have small need of it, except perhaps from Mattie, and although she would work diligently to do whatever she set her mind to, there seemed little warmth in her feelings toward others.

I felt rather pleased with my trot as Willow carried me along the grassy path through the woods. We were coming to a point where another path crossed ours, and I had to make up my mind whether to turn left or right, or continue straight on. I had just decided to turn right, so that we should climb Beech Hill and follow the ridge to Becksworth, when another rider emerged from the path I was about to turn into. Until this moment he had been screened by a mass of holly, so his appearance was a surprise both to me and to my mount.

Willow shied very slightly, but it was enough for a novice like me. Perhaps I might have held my seat if I had been astride the mare, but I was riding sidesaddle, and I began to topple backward. My left foot lost the stirrup, my hands lost the reins as my arms flew out in an effort to hold my balance. Only my right leg, drawn up and hooked between the horns of the sidesaddle, retained any useful grip. Willow stood like a rock now, but my balance was lost and my left leg rose as I tilted back helplessly. For a moment I teetered in that position, then my right leg slipped from the horns and I rolled over, sliding down the mare's side headfirst to land on my shoulders on the soft turf, my bowler hat being pushed right forward over my face.

I was quite unhurt, but since I was not wearing breeches under my habit I knew that my stockinged legs must have been much displayed, and I hastily pulled down my skirt and got to my knees before pushing back the hat that covered my eyes and looking up at the rider whose sudden appearance had brought about my downfall.

Toby Kent, on a big roan, sat with hands resting on the pommel, looking down at me with grave interest. "Would you mind running through that again, Miss McLeod?" he said. "I didn't quite follow the first time."

"Toby!" I stared up at him in amazement, still holding the brim of my hat. "But how . . . ? When did . . . ? Are you . . . ? Oh, Toby, how lovely to see you!"

He swung down from his horse, started to extend his hands to me to help me up, then hesitated. I laughed, put my hands up for him to take, and was pulled to my feet. We stood looking at each other for a moment or two, I in smiling wonder, he with head on one side, apprais-ing me.

"So you're all right then?" he said.

"Yes, of course I'm all right; I've been marvelously lucky." I was full of excitement at this unexpected encounter. "Oh, Toby, only the other night I read about you in *The Tatler,* and I was so pleased I could have danced. But did you get the letter I left for you? Have you been to the police? Why aren't you still at sea?" I spread my arms in a helpless gesture and laughed again. "Heavens, there's so much to ask and tell, but what on earth are you *doing* here?"

"Well, now . . . ." He took off his cap and walked round behind me to brush twigs and leaves from the back of my habit with it. "There, that's better." He came round in front of me again, putting on his cap, and now I saw he was dressed in good corduroy trousers and a tweed riding jacket. "What am I doing here?" he echoed. "Well, it's partly I had a fancy to see an old friend, and partly that I bring a message from a new friend. Name of Mr. Andrew Doyle."

"Mr. Doyle? But that's the man who—"

"Indeed it is," said Toby placidly. "The fellow you saved from those apaches."

"A friend?"

"Yes."

"Oh, thank heaven for that. You mean Inspector Lecour *believed* what I said in my letter, that I hadn't stolen the gold cuff links? And he was able to persuade Mr. Doyle of that?"

Toby eyed me somberly and rubbed his chin with the butt of the crop he carried. "No," he said. "It wasn't at all like that, which is another reason I decided I'd better make sure you were all right. Because the fact is, there's no such person as Inspector Lecour, and never was, and the whole business of bringing you here was a trick, young McLeod."

Seven

I looked about me, utterly bewildered, wondering if I might be dreaming, but this was the real world, with the woods all about us, a white and blue sky above, Toby holding the roan, and Willow standing with head lowered to crop a juicy tuft of grass.

"But I met Inspector Lecour," I said. "I spoke with him, and with an Englishman from the British embassy. It was in La Coquille, the night you left."

Toby shook his head. "The Englishman wasn't from the embassy. He's an assistant to a man called Boniface. And the Frenchman pretending to be a police inspector was an acquaintance hired for the job."

My mind was a complete jumble with all kinds of questions struggling to be asked, but all I could say at the moment was, "Oh, Toby . . . why?"

"I've no idea." Toby nodded toward the mare. "Shall we ride while I tell you as much as I know?"

I made an effort to throw off the almost numbing effect of what he had told me a few moments ago, and said rather confusedly, "Yes. Yes please, Toby. It's all so strange I can hardly believe . . . well, of course I believe you, but . . ."

"Where shall we ride?" he broke in gently.

"Oh . . . down through the woods and along the valley to Salter's Copse, I think. There's a hollow just below the copse where we can sit and talk if you want. I doubt if we'll meet anybody at all on that route. Does it matter if we're seen together?"

He smiled. "Not to me."

"Nor to me. You could have come to the house and asked for me. I'm sure Mattie would have let us talk in the drawing room, and Mr. Ryder wouldn't mind as long as it didn't interfere with his own affairs. Oh, Mattie is the housekeeper, Mrs. Matthews, and she's very nice."

"I'm glad to hear it," he said, "but since I've lurked for the best part of three days in the hope of seeing you alone, maybe we'd best take the ride you suggested."

I was recovering now from my surprise at meeting him and my shock at what he had told me. It was all highly mysterious, but in a way it seemed to match the phrase that Albert the footman had overheard Sebastian Ryder say to Mr. Boniface: *"Bring me the butterfly girl . . . and I don't care what it costs."*

Certainly the notion that I had been the victim of a trick to bring me to England seemed rather menacing, but I had been at Silverwood for many weeks now, and nothing had happened to cause me the slightest unease. Perhaps what Toby had to tell me would resolve the mystery in some quite simple way, I decided.

Dusting my gloved hands together I watched him take Willow's bridle and bring her up on my right. "How do you mount?" he asked.

I straightened my hat and said, "A groom makes a stirrup with his hands and gives me a leg up."

"H'mmm," he said doubtfully.

I laughed. "Toby, you're very thoughtful, but I won't burst into tears if you touch me."

His brow cleared. "In that case . . ." He did not offer a stirrup of his hands, but simply took me by the waist and lifted me easily to the saddle, then turned to mount his own horse while I settled myself in position.

It was extraordinarily pleasant to be moving through the woods at a slow walk with my friend from Montmartre beside me. I said, "I can't tell you how happy I am to know of your success, Toby. Did it really begin that day you painted me by the sink? If so I shall be very proud, because I shall tell myself I played a tiny part in it."

He pushed back his cap and looked at me with a blend of amusement and exasperation. "Well of course you played a part in it, me beauty, but how you can talk of that before all the rest I'll never know. Aren't you anxious to hear about the trick that was played on you?"

"Yes, naturally I am," I said, "but it's no more important than your success. I mean . . . oh dear, what do I mean? Well, if there was a trick, then either there'll be an outcome or there won't, and if there is an outcome, it might be good or bad for me, and if it's bad I might be able to prevent it or I might not, and if not, I shall just have to put up with it as best I can."

Toby looked at me, then up at the sky as if seeking understanding, then at me again. "Dear God," he said, "it's a fatalist you are, Hannah, a genuine fatalist. Oh, you can hear enough people claim to be, but they're not. Outside India, you're the first I've known. But I'm not surprised, now I come to think of it—"

"Toby," I broke in quickly, "I'm not much interested in all that. Now are you going to tell me what's happened since I left, or are you going to waste time describing me to myself?"

"It's my duty as a half Irishman to be loquacious," he said, "but since you're a Philistine, let's come to the point. You first, Hannah. What happened?"

My tale took only a few minutes to tell, even including a brief account of the Ryder family and my fortunate position in the household. Toby listened in silence and with a puzzled air. "So since Boniface brought you here you've had nothing to worry about? Nothing at all?" he said when I finished.

"No. Well, I was just taken aback at one thing on the first day. It came out quite by chance that one of the servants had heard Mr. Ryder tell Mr. Boniface to *bring him the butterfly girl*, no matter what the cost. It sounded strange, but perhaps it was just his way of being emphatic—I mean emphatic about wanting an English girl who was fluent in French."

Toby stared. "But that doesn't explain why he called you the butterfly girl. How would he know about that golden butterfly on your shoulder?"

"I've no idea, but perhaps he doesn't know. Perhaps it was just that one of my friends at the college spoke of me as the butterfly girl when Mr. Boniface was asking about me, and he simply took it as a nickname."

Toby shook his hea. "That doesn't seem likely to me."

"Well, it's never come up again, so for goodness' sake don't worry. Now it's your turn. I thought you were going to be at sea for months, and I'm dying to know what happened."

"That's easy," Toby said, and grinned. "We were in Le Havre preparing to sail, and some fool dropped a crate on my foot. It swelled up to the size of my head, and since it was clear I'd be useless as a seaman, the skipper laid me off. I spent two days in the hospital there, then they sent me home with the foot bandaged and a crutch under my arm."

I had winced in sympathy, and now I said, "Oh, I'm so sorry, Toby. And sorry I wasn't there when you got back to help you a little. How is it now?"

He glanced down at his right foot. "It still aches sometimes, but it'll do. Some bad bruising, but if a few small bones were broken they seem to have mended and I can walk well enough now, but it's only ten days ago that I was able to get a boot on. Anyway, that's how it was I came back to Paris to find you gone just a day or two before, and a letter waiting in my room. Oh yes, and Mme Briand in a fine panic over another letter you'd left in your room for her to give the police. You might have known she'd be too frightened to do that, me beauty."

"Yes, I suppose so, but I was so tired and afraid, I wasn't thinking very clearly. Did *you* take the letter to the police for me?"

"Holy Moses, no! Not till I'd made what we used to call a reconnaissance when I was a French legionnaire. I read the letter you'd left for me, then I opened the one to the police, with a touch of steam and a lot of care, and I didn't like anything at all about the whole business, so I went to the local gendarmerie, then to the municipal police, then to the First Bureau, and then to the *Sûreté,* inquiring for Inspector Lecour, but nobody had heard of him. Nobody."

"Oh, Toby, and with your bad foot. I didn't mean you to go to such trouble."

"Will you stop worrying about my foot, young McLeod? It's yourself you should be worrying about."

"Don't get cross. It makes your freckles stand out."

"I'm not cross. Just listen, will you? There was no Inspector Lecour anywhere, so I went along to La Coquille that evening, to talk to Père Chabrier in case you had said something to him that might throw a light on the mystery. Well, you hadn't, but he told me about the two men who were dining there the night before you disappeared, a Frenchman and an Englishman, and he said the Englishman had told him the police would be coming for you, and later you said the fellow was from the British embassy."

"Yes, that's right," I agreed. "The dark one with the little goatee beard was Inspector Lecour. His friend called him Jacques."

"The dark one with the little goatee beard was Jacques Lecour sure enough," said Toby grimly, "but he's an out-of-work actor, not a policeman."

I wobbled, and carefully eased my right thigh into the correct position again. "An *actor?* How do you know?"

"Because he was there the night I went along to inquire," said Toby, "and both Père Chabrier and Armand pointed him out to me. In fact Armand had overheard part of your conversation with those two, so *he* thought the fellow was an inspector, too. I suppose Lecour felt he'd played his part as ordered, and he'd been paid, and that was the end of it. There he was, bold as brass, sitting in the corner eating rabbit stew, but without his English friend, more's the pity."

"An actor?" I said again, quite bewildered. "But how did you discover that?"

Toby smiled and gave a contented sigh. "As he was paying his bill, I had Armand whisper to him that his friend from the British embassy was waiting in the yard at the back of La Coquille, and wished to speak with him secretly on a matter of great importance. As soon as the idiot came out, creeping furtive as a cat after a bird, I knocked him flat on his back, put the tip of my crutch on his Adam's apple, and invited him to converse with me. So that's how I learned he was an actor who'd been hired by a fellow called Boniface."

My thoughts were in a great tangle and I seemed to be trying to solve several puzzles at the same time. "But why?" I asked. "And who was the Englishman?"

"He was Charlie Grindle," said Toby, "an employee of Mr. Thomas Boniface, who is a partner in the Hesketh Agency, of Chancery Lane, London. Lecour didn't know that last part, though, and it wasn't till later I found it out for myself."

"Hesketh!" I exclaimed. "Yes, I met Mrs. Hesketh. She lives in the same house as Mr. Boniface."

"So she does," said Toby, and lifted his face to the sky as we emerged from the edge of the woods into spring sunshine. "Ah, it's a beautiful day. I'd forgotten how lovely England is. I ought to be saying that of Ireland, but the truth is it never stops raining there."

"Toby, how do you know about Mrs. Hesketh?"

"Well, the fact is, she was there in the office in Chancery Lane only a few days ago while I was holding Charlie Grindle by the neck and tapping his head against the wall in my quest for learning, Hannah. That's not my true nature, of course, banging a fellow's head against a wall, but I'm afraid I picked up one or two bad habits as a seaman."

"Toby, you didn't!"

"Oh, just one or two bad habits. For instance—"

"No, no! I meant you didn't bang his head against the wall, surely?"

"Oh yes, me beauty. I apologized to Mrs. Hesketh, of course, and she proved to be a very understanding woman. In fact I think she rather took to me."

"Even though you were banging poor Mr. Grindle's head? You really do amaze me, Toby Kent."

"And you amaze *me*, young McLeod, so we're even."

"Was your quest for learning successful?"

"It was. Mrs. Hesketh turned out to be a fountain of knowledge, in which I was invited to bathe."

"I see. But you've jumped an enormous gap, from La Coquille to weeks and weeks later in Chancery Lane."

"Then I'll fill it now." He paused as if setting his thoughts in order. "Here it is, then. Mr. Sebastian Ryder hired Boniface to bring you over from Paris to Silverwood, ostensibly to teach his children French. If that was the real reason I'll be surprised, but I don't know of any other yet. What's more, I'm sure it had to be you, Hannah, not just any English girl fluent in French. Again, I don't know why. Boniface came to your room in Rue Labarre and offered you the position, but you turned it down. However, while he was with you he saw, unconscious in your bed, a fellow you'd saved from footpads and brought home."

I nodded slowly. "Yes. It looked rather bad, so I explained what had happened."

"Mr. Boniface is a clever chap. He was desperate for a way of forcing you to take the job at Silverwood, and now he saw a possible chance. As soon as he left you, he went to the spot where you'd told him the attack took place. He knows the ways of thieves and rogues, does Boniface, and he started hunting through the dustbins in the alley there, because he knew that if they'd taken the man's wallet they would just strip it of money and throw the wallet away to avoid being found with it on them. And there it was, Hannah, behind the dustbins, with no money, but with some bits and pieces of private papers and a calling card with the name of Andrew Doyle on it. On the back, in pencil, was the address of a hotel in Place Vendôme, so Boniface went straight there to make inquiries, and maybe you can guess who he found there."

I remembered the name Mr. Doyle had mumbled, and I said, "Clara?"

"Miss Clara Willard, of Galveston, Texas. A very forceful American young lady, making a long tour of Europe with her parents, Benjamin and Melanie Willard, and her cousin Andrew, who at that moment was lying in your bed in Montmartre. When Boniface called at the hotel, Clara's parents were away at the gendarmerie reporting that Andrew had failed to return from a visit to Montmartre the night before. Boniface told Clara a vague story to the effect that he had by chance found the wallet in Rue Labarre, and had been informed that the owner was probably a foreign gentleman who had been rendered drunk and then taken into number eight by a street woman who had undoubtedly robbed him."

I said, "Oh dear, no wonder Clara stormed at me as she did."

"She might have asked one or two questions first," Toby said dryly. "But as you well know, she commandeered a couple of hotel servants, drove to Rue Labarre, and carted Andrew Doyle off, threatening you with the police. But listen now, Hannah, for I've a message to give you from Doyle and I'd better give it right away. He'd be telling you himself if he wasn't away in Mexico at this moment, but I'm to say he'll be coming to England soon and will call on you to give his thanks in person."

"His thanks?"

"Why, yes. That's the message, me beauty. I'm to thank you for saving his life, for he's quite sure you did no less."

"How can he possibly know that? He was unconscious all the time."

"Ah, no. Not all the time." We had reached the copse, and were skirting it to come to a grassy hollow beyond. "He says he was paralyzed by a blow to the head, but for much of the time he could see and hear everything, even though it seemed far away and like a dream. At times he thought you were his cousin Clara, but he certainly remembers everything from the time he was attacked until Mme Briand ladled brandy and laudanum down his gullet. I'll leave him to tell you all about it himself."

"Oh," I said uneasily. "Do you really think he'll come here to see me? After all, it happened many weeks ago, and I didn't do much. It was just that I happened to be there."

Toby laughed. "That's not what Andrew Doyle thinks. He's a fellow of mighty strong emotions, I'm telling you, and after what you did for him he can hardly distinguish between Hannah McLeod and Joan of Arc."

"Toby, don't tease me."

"I'm not. That's a good Irish name he has, and it would be more fitting if it were mine, but the fact is he's only one sixteenth Irish and seven sixteenths American, and the other half is Mexican, that half being from his mother, so it seems he's inherited the fiery Mexican blood."

I reined Willow to a halt, lifted my knee from between the horns of the sidesaddle, and slid to the ground, thankful that it would be easier for me to concentrate now I did not have to think about riding. The grass in the hollow was dry, and Toby sat down beside me on the gentle slope while the two horses grazed nearby. "Didn't Clara go to the police at all?" I said.

Toby shook his head. "Andrew was out of his wits for three days, but he kept saying, *'The girl saved me, the girl saved me . . .'* That put a different complexion on things. His uncle, Benjamin Willard, went to Rue Labarre to talk with you, but you were gone. He couldn't get any sense out of Mme Briand, and I was out hobbling round various police headquarters on my crutch. Then Andrew came out of it and was able to tell his story, and the next thing was that Clara and her parents appeared at number eight Rue Labarre again, seeking to trace you. Oh, by the way, I bring Clara's apologies. She's as forthright with her apologies as with everything else."

I said, "Were you there when they came that time?"

"I was, me beauty. It was the day after I'd shaken the truth out of Lecour, and an interesting chat we had when I handed over the cuff links, showed them your letters to me and to the police, and told them the whole business was a hoax, with Boniface behind it. Dear Lord, you should have heard what Clara had to say about him then." Toby chuckled and plucked a blade of grass to chew. "The Willards were quite distraught," he went on, "for they felt to blame that you'd been carried off by this scheming fellow for his own dark purposes, and there was no way of tracing you, or him, or his assistant who'd pretended to be from the British embassy. Clara was furious, and Mrs. Willard was almost in tears."

"They weren't to blame," I said, and took my hat off to enjoy the mild sunshine on my face. "Did you say Mr. Andrew Doyle was half Mexican? I'm not greatly surprised, for I remember he had quite a dark complexion."

"Mrs. Willard's brother married a Mexican lady of very high family," said Toby, "and Andrew is their son. The father died some years ago, but Andrew's mother is still alive. How is it you never ask the questions I expect you to ask, young McLeod?"

"I don't know. What did you expect me to ask?"

"Well, not about Andrew Doyle particularly, though he's a handsome fellow to be sure, and very rich, and quite a coming man in politics, I understand."

I laughed. "You know I'm not interested in men in that way, Toby."

"That's true. No, I suppose I expected you to ask how I managed to find you."

"All right, tell me."

"Well, first I tried to reassure the Doyles, telling them you were a fine sensible girl and well able to deal with the likes of Boniface if need be." Toby smiled. "Andrew himself agreed with that when we were all together a few days later, for he told us how you'd chased the apache and his girl off with a hatpin and a kick on the shins."

"Good heavens, did he remember that?"

"He did indeed, and he tells the story with admiration and true Latin passion."

As we sat there in the hollow, Toby went on to tell me that the Willards had been greatly concerned that they could take no steps to find me because they would shortly be moving on. Clara and her parents were to continue their travels since her father was visiting a number of European capitals on United States government business. Andrew Doyle was taking a ship for Veracruz and expected to be away for some ten weeks. On his return he would rejoin the Willards in London, where they were to remain for the summer.

"I told them not to worry and I'd trace you myself," said Toby, lying propped on an elbow, the sun glinting on his thick red hair now he had tossed his cap aside. "It was obvious I wasn't a fellow with money, so they offered me some with great courtesy. I didn't take kindly to that, mind, but we remained friends and they called once or twice to see me in the following days. I think it was the third time they came that I'd just finished a painting of your friend at La Coquille—"

"Armand!" I broke in with delight. "Yes, I saw it in *The Tatler* with the one of me. How is he, Toby? Did they find somebody to replace me at the restaurant? And if so, is it somebody Armand gets on with?"

Toby sighed. "Will you stop asking irrelevant questions, young McLeod? I've enough to tell without all that."

"I'm sorry, but how is he?"

"Armand is fine. He's something of a celebrity since I painted him, and that's made him happy. Now where was I? Ah, yes. Andrew and his Uncle Benjamin arrived, with Andrew looking well on the mend. The painting was there, and Benjamin took one look and became greatly excited. He's a collector, d'you see, and a great one for the impressionists, which I didn't know till then. To keep the story short, here was this quiet gentleman fairly dancing about he was so eager to buy the picture. What's more, he said he was an old customer of Jules Crespin, who runs the Montaigne Gallery, and he was sure they would want to exhibit any further work of mine if it was up to that standard."

I remembered something, and said, "Oh! Is Mr. Benjamin Willard the American collector mentioned in *The Tatler* article?"

Toby shook his head. "No, that was his nephew, Andrew, and he's not really a collector at all. What happened was this. Benjamin Willard brought M'sieur Crespin himself up later that day to see the Armand picture, and I spoke of how I'd found the way of it when painting another picture I'd entered for the Salon. Ten minutes later we were all in a cab on our way to the Palais des Beaux-Arts. The picture had been rejected, but—"

"Rejected? Oh, Toby!"

He grinned. "Crespin said it was a compliment, and that the best paintings always ended up in the Salon des Refusés. Anyway, we brought *Butterfly Girl* home, which I hadn't been able to manage yet, and then Clara's father and Andrew almost came to a duel over who was going to buy it, with Crespin demanding to put it on the open market. I could hardly stand up for laughing."

"But you said Mr. Andrew Doyle isn't a collector."

"That's right. But it's a picture of you, which is all he wanted. In the end I told them it wasn't for sale anyway, but that I'd lease it for a year to Andrew, since Benjamin had already bought *Waiter.*"

"I've never heard of anyone leasing a picture before, Toby. Whyever did you do that?"

"Holy saints, isn't it the first good picture I ever painted, and d'you think I'd sell it?" He grinned ruefully. "Truth to tell, I never intended to let it go at all. When Andrew was demanding and declaiming and declaring he must have it, and offering a fortune to boot, I only said I'd lease it for that amount because I was sure he'd be struck dumb at such an outrageous thing, but he seized on it, the crazy fellow, and it was myself that was struck dumb, for I couldn't go back on what I'd said."

We sat in silence for a while, and I tried to put into some sort of order all that Toby had told me. At last I said, "Did you tell them why you called the picture *Butterfly Girl?*"

He sat up straight, glaring. "No I did *not!* Damn it, I'd never speak of a private matter like that."

"No need to swear at me."

"I wasn't swearing at you. I was just . . . expressing feelings of indignation at a disgraceful slur on my character." He lay back and laughed, then sat up again quickly with a look of exasperation. "You're still doing it, you know, still asking any question but what a fellow might expect. Do you not want to know how I found you?"

"I'm sorry. You go on, Toby, and I won't say another word till you've finished."

"All right. Well, they both left their pictures with M'sieur Crespin to be shown in his gallery, and he told me to work hard at painting more, which I did over the next few weeks, seeing that I couldn't move about much because of my foot. Andrew went off across the Atlantic, and the Willard family continued their European tour. When I wasn't painting I kept trying to find out where you'd gone, as I'd promised. I saw Lecour again, but he knew nothing except that the man who hired him was named Boniface and came from England. He didn't even know the real name of the assistant who pretended to be an embassy man."

Toby paused, took a small pad and a pencil from his pocket, sketched quickly for perhaps thirty seconds, then showed me a very good likeness of the fair man with the beaky nose and haughty air I had spoken with in La Coquille. "That's the fellow, me beauty."

I was about to speak when I remembered my promise, so I nodded mutely.

"Charlie Grindle," said Toby, and crumpled the page. "His nose was a different shape when I left him. Well, the weeks were going by and I was no nearer finding where you'd gone. I wrote to an old friend in England asking him to trace a firm or detective agency or solicitors with the name of Boniface, but he had no result, or none that helped, for it's as the Hesketh Agency that the firm is listed in the post-office directory."

I would have liked to ask if Toby had seen Mrs. Hesketh and Mr Boniface together, and had the chance to note the extraordinary way she spoke of Boniface as if he were not there, but again I restrained myself.

"Then I had a bit of luck," Toby went on. "Your room was still empty; it hadn't been relet, and your bits of furniture were still there because Mme Briand was hoping the next tenant would buy them. One day I heard noises across the passage, went to have a look, and lo and behold, there was madame with a broom and a duster, actually giving the room a clean because somebody was coming to see it. So it was then I felt myself hit by sudden inspiration, and I told her not to bother about anyone else for I'd take the room myself."

Again I started to speak but managed to substitute a questioning hum of surprise. "Mm'mmmm?"

Toby laughed. "Well, why not? I was flush with money by then, and didn't wish to move, but I wanted no stranger up on that landing with me now you were gone. It made sense to take the room so I could spread myself a bit, and that's what I did. The very next day I found something which had slipped under the lining paper of your top drawer, Hannah."

He felt in his pocket and took out a small piece of white card to show me. It was the card Mr Thomas Boniface had handed me that morning when he had called at number eight Rue Labarre. On it was his name, the vague description *General Agent*, and his address in Chancery Lane.

"It was another couple of weeks before my foot was healed enough for me to make the journey," said Toby, "so meantime I wrote to the Willards in Vienna, telling them I was on the trail, and to Andrew in Veracruz, though heaven knows if and when he'll get the letter. I came across to England just under a week ago, and wended my way to Chancery Lane."

Toby's eyes sparkled with amusement and he gave a reminiscent sigh. "To my great regret I found when I reached the office in Chancery Lane that the much traveled Mr. Boniface was abroad again, in Spain this time, and on behalf of another client, but Charlie Grindle was there, looking very much like the description of him Armand had given me. As I told you just now, I was having a chat with him, explaining what I wanted and banging his head against the wall, when in walked Mrs. Hesketh. Being a gentleman I desisted and took off my hat, while Charlie Grindle fell to the floor groaning."

I smothered a giggle. Toby lay back, hands behind his head, eyes closed as if visualizing the scene anew. "She didn't bat an eyelid, Hannah. *'That's something I've often wished to do myself,'* she said, *'and it's a pity Boniface himself isn't here with his head for you to ring the changes. Now how can I be of service to you, young man?'* "

I lay back and laughed till the tears came, for Toby had contrived to imitate Mrs. Hesketh's precise voice so well that I could almost hear her saying the words, and my laughter set Toby off. Heaven knows what anyone would have thought to see us lying side by side in the grassy hollow, laughing up at the sky. After I had recovered a little, I propped myself on an elbow and said, "Oh, that was just like her, Toby. It's quite extraordinary; she shares a bedroom with Mr. Boniface—I know because I changed clothes there—but she seems to have no time for him at all."

"So I gathered." Toby sat up and wiped his eyes. "Well, I felt the moment had come to stop banging heads and start being gallant, so that's what I did, and most responsive Mrs. Hesketh was, the upshot being that I took her out to dinner that evening and listened to her life story, which I'll tell you about one day when we have a few hours to spare."

"Dinner?" I said. "Oh, Toby, you can take a lady to luncheon, but dinner is significant. Unless it's me," I added, remembering such occasions with him in Paris.

"Significant is the word," he agreed, "and there's no denying she took a fancy to me, which was most convenient, for it was from her I learned that Mr. Sebastian Ryder of Silverwood was the fellow who wanted you at all costs, ostensibly for teaching his son and daughter French. So I decided to find out about that for myself, and I came up three days ago. I'm staying at The Bull, by the crossroads just a mile or so away, and I saw you were safe and well when I watched you ride out the first morning I was here, but I've been waiting my chance since then to speak with you."

I sat up and looked at my watch. It was almost an hour since I had left the house. "I must start back soon," I said. "I can't tell you how touched I am that you came to see if I was all right, Toby, and I can only say I was wary myself at first. But in all these weeks there's been nothing amiss, and I'm sure now that what Mr Boniface and Mr. Ryder told me was true. I'm here simply to teach French."

I stood up. Toby rose with me and said, "Wait, you have bits of leaf and grass on your hair and jacket. It won't do to go back like that."

He moved behind me to pick fragments from my hair, then used his cap again to brush my back. I said, "I sometimes find it hard to believe my good fortune. It's true I'm a paid servant, but I'm very privileged, almost to the same extent as the family, so you really needn't worry about me, and you can reassure the Willard family."

"You can reassure them yourself," said Toby, and turned me round to see that the front of my habit was clean. "They'll all be in London soon now, and so will you."

"I will?" I looked at him in surprise as I put on my hat. "I don't understand."

"It's simple. The Ryder family will shortly be moving to a London house for the summer."

"How on earth do you know that?"

"Because Benjamin Willard, among other things, is head of a purchasing committee for the armed forces of the United States, and one reason for his visit to various European countries is to study the armaments those countries manufacture and make recommendations to his government. He's back in Paris now, and two days ago I went into St. Albans and sent him a wire saying you were employed as a French teacher in the residence of Mr. Sebastian Ryder of Bradwell, and that you appeared to be safe and well. He wired back at once to say he knew Ryder by reputation and had appointments with him in London shortly. I know the whole Ryder household will be moving down to London because mine host at The Bull told me they always do so for at least part of the London season."

I said, "Oh, dear. I don't want the Willard family or Mr. Doyle to make a lot of fuss about what happened in Paris."

Toby put on his cap. "From what I've seen, Americans have a strong sense of gratitude, so you'll have to put up with it. I'll tell the Willards we've met and talked, but if I were you I'd say nothing of this to Sebastian Ryder for the time being. It's none of his business anyway."

"I suppose not, and I'm sure he wouldn't be in the least interested. The children and Mattie might be, but I really don't want to talk about the past." A thought occurred to me. "Do you suppose Mr. Ryder *knows* Mr. Boniface played that cunning trick to make me leave Paris?"

"No. The Ryders of this world tend to tell their minions the results they want, then expect them to succeed by whatever means they can, but they wouldn't be concerned with details. Boniface certainly didn't tell Ryder how he'd hoaxed you."

"Can you be sure, Toby?"

He smiled. "Oh yes, me beauty, because after a very pleasant welcome to London from Mrs. Hesketh, and a most enjoyable evening, I put just that question to her next morning, and I'm sure the lady didn't deceive me with her answer."

I said, "You're a shocking fellow, Toby Kent, but it's been good to see you. When will you go back to Paris?"

"Not for some time yet." He scribbled on his pad, and handed me a folded sheet. "I've arranged to take a studio in Chelsea for a while, and here's the address. Write or wire me if ever you feel the need."

"Thank you," I said, and slipped the piece of paper in the pocket of my habit as he moved to bring Willow up beside me. "It's so kind of you to have been concerned about me, Toby, and you've gone to a lot of trouble. I don't know why."

"That's simple," he said soberly. "I'm in debt to my Butterfly Girl. Come along now, up with you." Again he took me by the waist and lifted me into the saddle, then helped me find the stirrup with my left foot while I settled my right knee between the horns.

His last words made me a little sad, and this was the price of vanity, for I realized now that I had sought a compliment, wishing him to say that we were old friends and he liked me, not that he was in my debt. "Serves you right, Hannah," I thought, and aloud I said cheerfully, "Don't ever feel in debt to me, Toby. All I did was sit in a chair and look out of a window."

He did not reply, but mounted his own horse, then looked at his watch. "Best if we say good-bye now. I'll leave first, as I'll be riding faster." He put the watch away and sat with hands resting on the pommel, frowning at me, green eyes no longer laughing, tufts of red hair jutting from under the cap he had slapped so carelessly on his head.

I said, "Good-bye, Toby. Perhaps I shall see you in London."

He nodded absently, then sighed. "I'll tell you something, young McLeod," he said. "I never had a parent or grandparent with second sight, and I'm not fey myself, for I've no gift in the way of clairvoyance, but I have a feeling in my bones this day that there's black trouble gathering, and I only wish I knew the source of it, but I don't. So have a care will you? Don't be so damned trusting. Be a little more wary of everybody. Yes, everybody. Of Sebastian Ryder and his family, of the grateful Willards when you meet them, and of Andrew Doyle." He stared broodingly for a moment. "And of me."

He nodded, touched heels to the flanks of his mount, and next moment he was moving away at a brisk canter, leaving me to gaze after him in bewilderment. Two minutes later I clicked my tongue and set Willow off at a sedate walk, trying to sit with my right thigh parallel to the mare's spine, and wondering why in heaven's name Toby Kent should warn me to be wary of himself.

Eight

Three days later Mattie mentioned that we would all be moving up to London shortly for the summer months. Belatedly I tried to show a touch of surprise, for I was not supposed to know this, but Mattie was too taken up with planning for the move to notice anything amiss.

It took me several more days to rid myself of preoccupation with all that Toby had told me. I did not dwell much on the way in which Mr. Boniface had tricked me, for that was past and done with now, but I found it hard not to wonder how my employer would respond if the Willard family and Mr. Doyle appeared on the scene in London, wishing to see me and thank me for what I had done. I did not think Mr. Ryder would be greatly pleased if they chose to regard me as anything other than a household employee, but there was nothing I could do about whatever might transpire, and so eventually I put the whole matter out of my mind.

Nobody noticed my preoccupation. Mattie was herself too preoccupied with arrangements for the move, and in this I was glad to help her a little. Gerald's thoughts were always either of music or of his idealized notion of Hannah McLeod, very different from the real person, while Jane and Mr. Ryder concentrated almost entirely on their own interests.

Sixteen days after my encounter with Toby the move was made, and on a cloudy afternoon we arrived in London by train. From St. Pancras the family traveled in one carriage, Mattie and I in another Our luggage had been sent ahead on an earlier train which had also taken Farrow and a number of the servants. It was Mr. Ryder's custom to rent a house in London for the season, supplying his own staff, and on this occasion he had taken a house in Portland Place, small compared with Silverwood, but splendidly appointed, and large for a London house so Mattie told me, with plenty of room for entertaining.

From Mattie I learned about the London season, when all the best people were supposed to give parties and balls and to attend particular events, such as the Ascot race meeting and the Henley regatta. Sebastian Ryder was not concerned to follow fashion. He gave one ball during the season, and a very splendid affair it was, but the people attending were mainly business acquaintances and their wives, since it was not Mr. Ryder's way to enter into social friendships. For the rest, he confined himself to giving occasional dinner parties for six or eight guests only, sometimes even fewer, and again these were invariably people in business or in government departments, some of them from abroad.

Until this year it had been part of Mattie's duty to keep the children entertained while in London by taking them out and about, perhaps to spend a day at the Zoological Gardens in nearby Regent's Park, or to take a boat trip up the river to Kew, or to visit some of the many famous places of interest in the city. This summer she asked my help in the task.

"I'm getting too old for it, m'dear," she said on our first evening in Portland Place, "and the master says he has no objection to you taking Miss Jane and Master Gerald out, so I'd be more than grateful if you would."

I said, "But I don't know much about London, and Master Gerald is almost as old as I am, so won't he feel insulted to be put in my charge?"

Mattie smiled. "I don't think you need worry too much about that. Besides, you can pretend he's in charge, and keep asking his advice, surely. But Master Gerald is such a dreamer; he really must have somebody practical with him, and Miss Jane is a wee bit young still. As for not knowing London, well, you're a clever girl, Hannah, and I have some nice books with maps you can study, so I'm sure you'll manage very well, much better than I did when I first had to do it."

Within a few days I discovered that it was really quite an easy task, for Mattie provided me with ample money, and the London cabbies were there to take us wherever we wished to go. We were not out on long trips every day, for on some evenings there were guests for dinner, and Mr. Ryder did not want the children to be tired for such occasions. On the morning of the first small dinner party, I was summoned to the study where Mr. Ryder was examining some blueprints. As usual, he wasted no words. "I shall be having four guests for dinner this evening, and I want you to be present, Hannah. Put that blue frock on."

I said, "Yes, sir. Shall I tell Mattie she will be wanted?"

"No." He leaned back in his chair. "Mattie won't wish to be present with guests there. These are Italian, and speak little English, but like most foreigners they speak pretty fair French. It's damned hard work entertaining people with only a smattering of English, so you'll be there to help translate and keep the conversation going generally. Understand?"

"Yes, sir. Will there be any business discussions? The Italian gentlemen may not know some French technical words."

"And you do?"

"I know some that I learned at Silverwood."

"Good, but you needn't worry. I'll talk business through my lawyers at the proper time. Dinner tonight is a social occasion, and you can steer them away from any business talk by telling them that my only wish is for them to enjoy themselves. Understood?"

"Yes, sir."

"That's all."

I was nervous as the time drew near for the Italian gentlemen's visit, but once they had arrived I found myself too busy to worry. They were shown into the drawing room where we were all waiting, and Mr. Ryder, who had met them before, introduced them to his family and to me. Their English was very meager, and it was clearly a relief to them to be able to change to French. I was helped far more than I had expected by Jane and Gerald, who had profited by my lessons and labored gallantly throughout dinner to converse with our guests in a mixture of French and English, which caused quite a little amusement. I congratulated them afterward and said in front of their father that I was very proud of them, which made even Jane go pink with pleasure. I knew Mr. Ryder considered the evening a success, for when I wished him goodnight in the drawing room as he sat with his whiskey and soda before going to bed, he looked up from his newspaper to respond.

On two further occasions I was required to join the family when there were guests for dinner, and all went well. Then, a few days after the second occasion, Mattie told me that an important American gentleman, a government representative and his family, were invited for the following day. "Speak English same as us they do," she said, "so the master won't be needing you, m'dear. I'll have Albert serve us dinner in my room, and we'll enjoy a nice game of cribbage later."

After what Toby had told me, I guessed that the visitors must be Mr. Benjamin Willard and his family, so I put on a nice dress in case I was sent for. I was in my room when the guests arrived, and sure enough it was only ten minutes later that Violet the maid tapped on my door. When I opened it, she said, "Mr. Farrow sent me, miss, to say the master wants you in the drawing room."

"Now, Violet?"

"Yes, miss. Right away."

"Very well." I went downstairs feeling more nervous than I had done at the prospect of foreign guests for dinner. The drawing room had double doors, and as I opened them and stepped through, every head in the room turned my way, except for Farrow's, and he was at the sideboard pouring sherry. I turned to close the doors behind me, then turned again toward the faces I had only glimpsed before. There was Clara, with her strong yet pretty face and firm jaw, looking at me with immense interest, her large cornflower blue eyes warm and friendly in contrast to the fiery anger they had held for me on the stairs of number eight Rue Labarre. She was sitting on a long settee, and at the other end was a woman I knew must be Mrs. Melanie Willard, her mother, for the likeness was clear. Both were most elegantly dressed, and Mrs. Willard was studying me with the same warmth and curiosity as her daughter.

Jane was seated on one of the Sheraton satinwood chairs, with Gerald standing beside her. Sebastian Ryder stood with his back to the fireplace. His face was impassive, but I had learned to read it since coming to Silverwood, and I knew he was taken aback, which was hardly surprising. I also felt he was trying to decide whether this unexpected development was to his liking or not.

He held a glass of sherry in his hand, and so did the two men flanking him. One was tall and lean, thick dark hair streaked with gray, and shrewd yet placid eyes. This, I knew, must be Clara's father, Mr Benjamin Willard. The other man's face I knew well, though his eyes had barely opened throughout the hours he had spent as my unexpected guest in Montmartre, but they were open now, dark brown eyes full of expression as they rested on me with a kind of wonder.

All this I absorbed in the moment or two before Sebastian Ryder spoke. "My guests have asked to see you, Hannah," he said. "It appears they have been anxious to find you since you rendered a service to Mr Andrew Doyle in Paris some months ago, and an acquaintance of theirs has recently managed to trace you through the Boniface Agency." He glanced round the room. "Ladies and gentlemen, this is Hannah McLeod, a tutor in the French language to my children."

Mr Willard set down his glass on a small table and spoke in a pleasant drawling voice to his host. "We shall be grateful to have you present us, sir."

Sebastian Ryder said, "Certainly. Hannah, I present Mr Benjamin Willard. His wife, Mrs. Willard. Their daughter, Miss Clara. And nephew, Mr Andrew Doyle."

I dropped a small curtsy and said, "Good evening, ladies and gentlemen."

It was then that Clara came out of her seat on the settee as if she could restrain herself no longer and almost ran toward me, reaching out to take my hands in her own. "Oh, I do hope and pray you'll forgive me, Hannah," she cried anxiously. "I said such awful things to you that day in Montmartre, and when I found out I was wrong and you had saved my dear cousin's life, you had *gone!*"

Feeling somewhat overwhelmed, I said, "Oh . . . please don't worry, Miss Clara. I quite understand. I'm just glad I was able to help."

Mrs. Willard had risen and was coming toward me. Her husband was also approaching. With a hurried glance I saw that Andrew Doyle was still gazing at me with the same wondering look, while Jane and Gerald were openmouthed with bewilderment and even Sebastian Ryder was unable to hide his surprise. He turned to Mr Doyle and said, "Saved your life?"

At the same moment Clara released one of my hands so that her mother could clasp it, and Mrs. Willard said, "We are truly grateful to you, my dear Andrew is my late brother's son, and as dear to us as if he were our own." She bent forward to kiss me on the cheek, then smiled and gave my hand to her husband, who took it in both his own and held it firmly, looking at me with steady eyes as he said, "My wife has spoken for us all. Thank you, Hannah McLeod."

By now I could feel my cheeks burning with embarrassment. Mr. Willard turned, smiling, and I saw Andrew Doyle moving toward me. He had set down his glass, and as he halted before me he reached out for my hand. I gave it to him and he bowed over it, raising it to his lips. He lifted his head, still holding my hand, and said in a soft deep voice, "As long as I live, Miss Hannah, I will remember your bravery, the bravery of a very young girl, quite alone, who should have run away, but who instead ran forward into danger, to save the life of a complete stranger."

I said desperately, "You make too much of the matter, I'm sure, sir. I had little to fear for myself."

Andrew Doyle shook his dark head, smiling. "Not so," he replied. "The apache tried to strike you down. I saw."

"Apache?" Jane echoed.

Sebastian Ryder said, "My children are gaping in astonishment, and I feel much in sympathy with them. We know nothing of this exploit of Hannah's, but I can promise you we shall be most interested to hear about it."

Andrew Doyle released my hand and turned to his host. "It will take several minutes to tell, and I fear I have already caused Miss Hannah some embarrassment."

"Oh, she's all right," said Mr. Ryder briskly, "and we're not dining till eight-thirty, so there's plenty of time. Let's all sit down and hear your story, young man."

I said hopefully, "Will you be needing me any further, sir?"

The Willard family all looked distressed, and Andrew Doyle said to Mr. Ryder, "Oh, please!"

"Sit down, Hannah, sit down," my employer said, quite genially. Then, to his guests, "Perhaps you would like Hannah to dine with us? She usually does, except when we have guests."

Benjamin Willard said, "In that case, sir, since we shall not be disturbing your domestic arrangements, we shall be honored to have Miss Hannah at table with us."

"Capital," said Mr. Ryder, and I knew he had decided that my popularity with the Willard family was to his advantage rather than otherwise. "See that an extra place is laid, Farrow," he went on, addressing the butler, "and that will be all for now."

"Very good sir," murmured Farrow, and withdrew.

Andrew Doyle said, "Miss Hannah," and held a chair for me. I thanked him and sat down, resigning myself to further embarrassment. The ladies resumed their seats, the two older men found chairs, but Andrew Doyle remained standing, head bent in thought. After a few moments he looked up and said, "Please try to picture a narrow street in the heart of Montmartre on a very cold winter's night. It is an hour past midnight, and a rather foolish young tourist has been exploring the cabarets and night haunts of this notorious quarter."

He gave a rueful shrug. "I was that foolish young man, but at least I had the sense to put very little money in my wallet for the occasion, and to carry nothing of value—oh, except for the gold cuff links I wore, which I did not think to remove. I went alone, which was unwise, and I lost my way in that maze of streets and alleys. It was in one of those streets that an apache stepped out from black shadows thrown by a streetlamp, and struck me down with a blow to the head from a club."

Gerald exclaimed in surprise, "An apache?"

"Not the redskin Apache of America," said Andrew Doyle. "The same name is now given to the criminals and footpads of Montmartre." He was silent for a moment, then made a small gesture of bafflement. "The effect of this vicious blow was strange. I lay quite paralyzed, unable to move, yet curiously aware, in some strange way able to observe the scene as if I had no part in it. The apache had a woman with him. That is quite usual, I understand, and they are as savage as the men. I watched them search my clothes, find my wallet, take out the small amount of money in it, and fling it away. They were furious to find so little, and they began to kick me, both of them, first my body and then my head."

He paused and looked at Sebastian Ryder. "This is not a pleasant tale for your young daughter, sir. I hope I am causing her no distress."

"I've not brought her up to be a niminy-piminy creature," said Sebastian Ryder bluntly, "and your story won't bring on a fit of the vapors, Mr. Doyle. I don't believe in hiding from young people the fact that this world can be hard and dangerous. Please go on."

"I felt no pain," Andrew Doyle said softly, as if remembering. "Perhaps they were drunk, for they could have stolen my topcoat, and that would have revealed my cuffs, with the gold links." He shrugged. "But they simply stood and kicked, and although I felt no pain, I knew that if they did not stop, I would soon be too badly injured to recover. Yet I could do nothing. And then . . . then I heard the clatter of clogs on the cobbles. Yes, I could hear as well as see. Next moment a young woman, a girl, small and slender, stood confronting my attackers, shouting at them in French. They laughed at her, and the man tried viciously to knock her down, but she tore the hatpin from her hat and raked his hand as he struck, so that he screeched with pain. Then came another screech, for before the apache could recover he received a kick on the shin from a foot wearing a heavy clog, and this took all the fight out of him."

I heard a gasp of indrawn breath from Gerald, and guessed that he was gazing at me with even more adoration than usual, but I did not look up; I continued to sit with hands in lap and lowered eyes, as I had done since the beginning of the story.

"It was quickly over," said Andrew Doyle. "That young girl, Miss Hannah McLeod, seemed to threaten the attackers in a stream of French I did not understand, and they simply ran away. She tried to revive me, and at last I found a shred of strength which helped her to lift me to my feet and support me, half carrying half dragging me along the street to . . ."—he hesitated, then said—"to the hovel where she lived. Yes, her home was a garret on the sixth floor of a slum building, and let nobody think the worse of her for that, for she opened her home to me, and that garret meant the difference between life and death, because if she had not taken me in, I would surely have died that night of the cold and my injuries."

It was very quiet in the room. I lifted my eyes to steal a glance about me, then hastily looked down again, for although Andrew Doyle was speaking, everybody was looking at me.

His voice continued. "With the help of a man and an old crone, whom we later found to be the concierge and her husband, Miss Hannah contrived to have me carried up to her room and laid on her bed. My mind was more confused now. Sometimes I was aware of my situation, sometimes I did not know what was happening, and believed it was Clara speaking to me, cleaning the blood from my face, tending the hurts to my ribs where the flesh was broken. Then, after awhile, the crone appeared once more, and I was given spoonfuls of warm spirit to swallow." He shrugged and spread his hands. "From that moment I remember no more, until I came to myself in a hotel bedroom some days later, with a nurse in attendance and my family around me."

I was thankful his memory ceased at that point, for I had been wondering if he remembered that I had climbed into bed with him to avoid being frozen. "To our great regret," he said, "my aunt and uncle and my cousin Clara were disgracefully deceived by a mischiefmaker who told Clara where I was to be found, but claimed that Hannah herself had been involved in the attack and the robbery. This resulted in my loyal cousin being less than kind to Hannah when she went with two hotel servants to bring me home, and I fear this brave and kind young girl must have felt great resentment to have risked so much and done so much, only to be thought guilty of that from which she had saved me."

I gave a small nervous laugh and said, "I might have felt that, Mr. Doyle, except that I was completely preoccupied by fear that the police were about to arrest me." I looked at Clara. "But it's all past now, and best forgotten."

"I will not forget," she said fiercely. "None of us will."

Benjamin Willard said, "When we discovered the truth, and went to thank Hannah, she had gone." He gave me a wry smile. "Perhaps her natural fear of arrest decided her to take the position I understand an agent of yours had offered her, Mr Ryder However, we met a neighbor of hers, a Mr Toby Kent, who has recently leaped to fame as an artist and who was also concerned to discover her whereabouts. My wife and daughter have been traveling with me in Europe, while Andrew has been across the Atlantic and back, so we were unable to track Hannah down ourselves, but by a fortunate combination of circumstances Mr Kent was able to do so, and he passed on the good news to us." He eyed Sebastian Ryder with a level gaze. "We were indeed glad to learn that she was in the safe care of a gentleman of impeccable reputation, and by happy chance one whose acquaintance I was expecting to make during our stay in London."

Sebastian Ryder sat regarding me with interest, nodding slowly. "That's a remarkable story," he said. "Why haven't you told us of it, Hannah?"

I hesitated, then said, "To use a hatpin and kick with a clog could sometimes be necessary in Montmartre, sir, but it isn't ladylike. Besides, all I could think of was the French police believing me a thief, and I didn't want to tell you that."

He gave a short laugh. "You show good sense. It must have been a shock when you walked into this room and saw Miss Clara and Mr Doyle."

This was not a question, so I looked down and remained silent. It was a surprise to hear Jane say enthusiastically, "I think it's such an exciting story! Did you really do all that, Hannah?"

I murmured, "Yes," and shot a look of appeal at Benjamin Willard, for I felt he was a perceptive gentleman who might well understand my feelings. This hope was realized, for at once he said firmly, "Andrew, you've told your story and thanked the young lady as you've been longing to do. Now I suggest we leave her in peace for a while. She clearly has no wish to dwell on the incident or to be thought a heroine, so as guests of our kind host I suggest we respect the wishes of a member of his household to whom we are indebted."

That was cleverly said, for though it was carefully worded to apply to the guests, it also had the effect of deterring the family from pursuing the subject. Mrs. Willard was quick to see what her husband wanted, and said, "You're right, Ben dear. I know Mr. Ryder said he wished to hear the story, but I guess he'll be wondering if Americans always monopolize the conversation as Andrew has." She gave a warm, pleasant laugh. "Now sit down, Andrew dear. I'm going to ask Jane to tell me about Silverwood, for I've heard it's a truly beautiful house. Is it very old and historic, Jane? Our history in the United States is quite short, so it's fascinating for us to come here and visit churches and castles and houses that are maybe a thousand years old."

Jane said, "Well, Silverwood isn't old at all, Mrs. Willard. My father built it not very long ago . . ."

I relaxed with an inward sigh. Mr. Willard engaged Sebastian Ryder in conversation, Gerald moved his chair to sit beside Clara and talk with her, and Andrew Doyle chose an easy chair close to where I sat. "Forgive me if I embarrassed you," he said quietly. "I will speak no more of that matter, Miss Hannah. Please tell me, are you enjoying your life here in England? It must surely seem pleasant after the very hard existence you led in Montmartre."

"Yes, I'm most fortunate, sir," I replied, "but please don't imagine I was unhappy in Montmartre. I had regular employment, and a place to live."

He gazed at me with a perplexed air. "It's strange that a young lady of your breeding should be content under such conditions."

I could not help smiling as I said, "I'm afraid you misjudge my breeding, sir."

He shook his head. "No," he said slowly. "No, Miss Hannah, I think not. There's much I don't understand, even though I have talked a great deal with your friend, Toby Kent." He lowered his voice. "You know I have his picture of you?"

I nodded, and spoke quietly. "Yes, he told me. I'm so glad he is having such success now."

"So am I. He is a most agreeable companion and my uncle thinks very highly of him as an artist." Andrew Doyle made a wry face. "I'm not a collector, or a student of art, but I'm very glad to have that picture, even on a year's lease, and I find it a marvelous piece of work. Can you unravel the mystery of the title? He refuses to say why he calls it *Butterfly Girl.*"

"I would rather leave it a mystery, sir, since that seems to be what Toby wants."

"Of course. I won't press you."

At that moment Farrow entered to announce that dinner was served. Sebastian Ryder offered his arm to Mrs. Willard and said to her husband, "Will you take my daughter Jane in, sir? Gerald will escort Miss Clara and perhaps Mr. Doyle will take Hannah in."

I did my best that evening, but I cannot pretend I enjoyed the occasion. All the guests were most kind to me, Clara in particular, but I was in a difficult position. This was not an evening when I was needed to help entertain foreign gentlemen, so I did not feel it was my place to initiate conversation, but on the other hand I could not respond with only a word or two when others spoke to me, and I found it trying to strike the right balance.

When the ladies withdrew, leaving the gentlemen to their port and cigars, Clara put an arm about me as we entered the drawing room. "It's not easy for you, is it, dear?" she said sympathetically.

"What isn't easy for her, Clara?" Jane said before I could reply.

It was Mrs. Willard who answered, taking Jane by the hand and leading her to the sofa. "It isn't easy being neither guest nor host nor servant," she said with a smile and a simplicity that endeared her to me. "Now you tell me all about English schools, Jane, while we leave those two to chat about whatever they want."

I was worried that Clara might ask me a lot of questions, some of which might be difficult to answer with Jane so easily able to hear us, for I had said nothing at Silverwood about my encounter with Toby Kent and the discovery of the hoax Mr. Boniface had played on me. I need not have worried, however, for Clara simply began to tell me about her home in America, in the state of Virginia, and the way of life there. I liked her voice, with its charming drawl, and was well content to listen and ask an occasional question. From my first encounter with her I knew she was a confident young lady who could be most formidable, but this evening she had treated me with openhearted friendliness and without for one moment being patronizing.

I learned that until three years ago she and her family had lived in Galveston, in the state of Texas, but had moved to Virginia when her father had accepted an appointment as head of a purchasing committee, so that he could be close to the seat of government in Washington. Her uncle, Andrew's father, had been a builder of railways in Mexico and had married a Mexican girl. Andrew had been born in Monterrey, which was only a hundred miles across the border from Texas, and his father had settled there. From childhood, Clara had made a long visit with her parents every other year to the family in Monterrey, and Andrew's family had visited Galveston in alternate years, so the cousins knew each other well.

I was thankful for the geography lessons my mother had given me, and for the reading I had done later at the College for Young Ladies, because although I could not have pointed to Galveston or Monterrey on a map, I at least knew where Texas lay in the United States, and could visualize the map with the Rio Grande forming the northern border of the great tapering piece of land that was Mexico.

"When Andrew's father died," said Clara, "his mother, my Aunt Maria, moved back to the family hacienda of her parents. Andrew spends part of his time there, but . . ."—she hesitated and looked rueful—"well, it's no secret, I guess. Andrew is something of a rebel. He's a man of strong ideals and I'm afraid he's quite a romantic. He hates the way things are run in Mexico, where the poor people work like dogs and the rich live like lords. He's fallen out with his mother and her family over this, which makes us very sad. We can understand the way he feels, but as my father keeps telling him, you can't change things overnight."

Clara glanced across the room to where her mother was talking with Jane, and lowered her voice. "There are rebel bands in the wilder parts of the country," she said, "and we believe Andrew has been in touch with some of the leaders to give them his support. It's truly dangerous, for his mother's family hold important posts in government, and of course they would be shocked and furious if they knew he was giving practical help to such people. The authorities regard them as brigands, but to Andrew they are patriots struggling for freedom." She sighed and shook her head. "I expect Andrew is right, but my father says he will achieve nothing by helping them. I was so glad when Andrew agreed to come away with us for a long tour of Europe. Perhaps it will have a settling effect on him."

I was not surprised to learn that Andrew Doyle was an idealist and a romantic, for I had seen this in the way he had told of my encounter with the apache, but all else that Clara had just spoken of seemed remote and fanciful. Sitting in a beautifully furnished drawing room of a fine London house, I found it hard to grasp the reality of a land where brigands roamed.

Speaking quietly so that Jane should not overhear, I said, "Toby Kent told me that Mr. Doyle returned to Mexico while you and your parents were traveling in Europe. That must have been a disappointment if you were hoping to keep him away for a long time."

Clara sighed again. "Yes, it was. Oh, sometimes he's impossible," she said. "We don't even know why he went back, except that he had a letter we think might have come from a man who's very much a leader of some rebel groups there. You must have read about Ramon Delgado in your newspapers."

I was very surprised but managed not to show it, and I shook my head. "I haven't read about him," I said, "but I don't suppose our newspapers print very much about Mexico unless something important is happening."

"I guess not," Clara agreed. "It's the same with our own newspapers, and maybe we wouldn't be interested ourselves if it wasn't for the family connection. Anyway, we figure Ramon Delgado was the man Andrew went to see, and when he came back he started asking Papa how he could buy a large quantity of rifles, so we think he had in mind to do some gunrunning into Mexico. Papa was furious with him, and Andrew never mentioned the subject again. I do wish he would settle down in America and forget about Mexico."

"Would his mother leave her own country?" I asked.

"I'm sure she wouldn't," Clara said slowly. "I love Aunt Maria, but since Uncle Hank died and she went back to her family, she's become very . . . well, very Mexican, I suppose. She and Andrew don't seem to understand each other the way they used to, and it's all very sad."

As she finished speaking the door opened and the gentlemen joined us. Gerald came at once to where Clara and I were sitting. He looked relieved to be able to break away from the older men, and at once fell into conversation with us. I contributed little myself, for I felt it was not for me to do so, but fortunately it transpired that Clara loved classical music and was quite knowledgeable about it, so they were soon talking happily together.

A little later I noticed that both Mr. Ryder and Mr. Willard were studying their pocket diaries, and the latter called to his wife, "Would you check that you have no social engagements for the twenty-first, Melanie? That's the week after next. Mr. Ryder has very kindly invited us to join a small river party he is giving that day, a trip up the Thames from Westminster to Kew, with luncheon on the boat."

"Why, that sounds delightful," said Mrs. Willard, taking a small diary from her handbag. "I'm sure I have no appointments that can't be changed, but let me see . . . no, both Clara and I are quite free."

"We shall hope for fine weather," said Mr. Ryder. "You'll find you can see a great deal of interest as we make our way up the river, and of course there are Kew Gardens to be visited before we return, if anyone wishes to do so."

"Papa, what a lovely surprise!" Jane exclaimed. "You didn't say a word to us about a river party. Who else will be coming?"

"I'm expecting only three other guests," said her father. "Mr. and Mrs. Hugh Ritchie, and Sir John Tennant."

I happened to be looking at Jane, and saw her blink in surprise. When I turned my head to look at Gerald he was staring in more obvious astonishment. Sebastian Ryder put away his diary and addressed his guests. "I think you'll find them interesting companions for the occasion," he continued. "Hugh Ritchie is a Member of Parliament and a junior minister who is expected to achieve very high office one day. His wife, Anne, is the daughter of Sir John Tennant, a landowner and squire of a Kentish village, among other things."

Clara clapped her hands. "A *sir!*" she exclaimed. "Now isn't that exciting? Is he what you call a baronet, Mr. Ryder?"

"Not quite, Miss Clara. Sir John is a knight bachelor."

"A bachelor? But surely you said Mrs. Ritchie was his daughter?"

Sebastian Ryder smiled. "A knight bachelor doesn't mean an unmarried knight. It originally meant a knight who was not a member of any particular order. I'm afraid our English system of titles is very confusing."

Mr. Willard said, "Am I correct in thinking that Sir John is president of Hayley & Tennant, the big shipbuilding company?"

"He is," agreed Mr. Ryder, "though in England we have company chairmen rather than presidents. It's possible you may be doing some business with Hayley & Tennant, I suppose?"

"I believe they hope that I shall," said Mr. Willard. "There's been some correspondence between their London office and our purchasing committee in Washington, but I haven't arranged any appointments yet."

"Oh, the river party is entirely a social occasion," Mr. Ryder said quickly. "There'll be no question of Sir John raising any matter of business."

Mr. Willard smiled and waved a hand. "I wasn't concerned on that score, sir," he said, "for I'm sure Sir John's propriety is beyond doubt, but in fact it's not at all a bad thing for us to have a look at each other socially."

He went on speaking, but I did not take in what he said, partly because I was tired with the strain of trying to be a guest without overstepping my position as an employed person in the household, and partly because my thoughts were divided. I was wondering what had surprised Gerald and Jane so greatly, and at the same time I was trying to remember why there was something vaguely familiar about the name of Sir John Tennant.

I was glad when, ten minutes later, Mr. Willard said that it was time he and his family "hit the trail" as he put it, using an American phrase which Clara explained to me. Although I had found the evening a little difficult, I had very much taken to the Willard family, for they seemed to be straightforward people who, despite their obviously high place in society, were warm, friendly, and without pretensions. I was the last to say goodnight to them, and intended only to curtsy, but they all offered me a hand to take. Andrew Doyle bowed over my hand, as he had done before, then said, "Shall we see you on the river trip, Miss Hannah?"

I did not know the answer to that question, but before I had time to be embarrassed Sebastian Ryder said, "She'll be there."

A few minutes later, when the guests had gone and I went up to my room, I saw a light under Mattie's door. She often sat up quite late, playing patience, and was always happy for me to visit for a little while after any dinner party at which I had been present. When I tapped and entered at her call, she looked up with a smile from the cards spread on the mahogany card table.

"Well, m'dear, did you have a nice evening?"

"It was a little awkward, Mattie, because one of the guests was a gentleman I'd helped when he was attacked one night in Paris—no, please don't ask me to tell the story now, I don't even want to think about it, and I'm sure Master Gerald will tell it all over again at breakfast tomorrow, so you'll hear it then." I sat down beside her. "Which patience are you playing?"

"Miss Milligan."

I looked at the cards set out, and saw she had but few left in her hand. "I don't think it will come out this time, Mattie."

"No more do I, but we'll see." She laid out another row of cards. "Was the master pleased?"

"Yes, I think so. Did you know he's arranged a river party for one day the week after next?"

"No, he hasn't said yet, but there's time enough if he wants cook to prepare a cold luncheon. Did he mention how many there's to be?"

"He said I was to go, I don't know why, and the guests will be the same four who came tonight, plus three others. A Mr. and Mrs. Ritchie and Sir John Tennant."

Mattie laid down the cards in her hand and turned her head to stare at me in utter amazement. "Tennant? Never, child! You must have heard wrong."

"No, I'm quite sure of the name. Sir John is head of a shipbuilding firm."

She sat looking at me blankly, slowly shaking her head, and at last she said, "I don't understand. I just don't understand."

"I thought Miss Jane and Master Gerald looked surprised, too. Why is it strange, Mattie?"

She said very quietly, "Because the master hates that Sir John Tennant more than anything in the world, and has done for many a long year. With good cause, too. Him it was that killed Mr. Harold."

"Killed?" I said incredulously. I had never heard of a Mr. Harold.

"Drove him to suicide," said Mattie, and picked up the cards with hands that trembled. "It's long ago now. More than twenty years. Mr. Harold was the master's stepbrother, quite a few years older, and Mr. Sebastian thought the world of him, so I'm told. It was long before I came to the family, but I heard all about it from the old servants."

"I didn't mean to be inquisitive, Mattie," I said. "It's nothing to do with me."

"Well, I've never spoken of it to the new servants who were taken on after Mrs. Ryder died, poor soul, but I'm sure you're no gossip, Hannah, and it's as well for you to know how things stand if that Sir John Tennant is really going to be a guest for the river trip. I've heard the master speak his name quite a few times over the years, and I'm sure he feels as strongly now as he ever did."

"The children must know," I said. "That's why they were surprised."

"Yes, they know, m'dear, though we never talk about it, of course. It was a business matter, you see. Mr. Sebastian had just opened his first factory, and Mr. Harold owned a small shipping line, and being very clever gentlemen in business they were both doing well, which was a great credit to them, for they started with little enough by all accounts. Now, I don't understand these things of course, but it seems Mr. Harold overreached himself, as you might say, buying more ships than he could pay for. Then Sir John Tennant played some kind of nasty trick, wanting the money sooner than he'd said, for it was his firm that built the ships."

Mattie looked at the cards laid out on the table and began to push them slowly together. "They fell out badly, Mr. Harold and Sir John. I don't know the ins and outs of it, but they say Sir John threatened to drive Mr. Harold into the gutter, and that's what it came to. Mr. Harold lost every penny, and his business. He was to have married a girl from a very good family later that year, but when all this happened her family made her break the engagement. Mr. Sebastian wanted to sell his factory and everything he had to help his stepbrother, but it wouldn't have been enough, and anyway Mr. Harold wouldn't let him."

Absently she stacked the cards together, patting them into place with little agitated movements. "I think to keep things going, Mr. Harold had done something he ought not to have done," she said in a hushed voice, "like signing a document or something of the sort, and Sir John was going to have the law on him. Well, one day Mr. Harold went out with his gun to shoot rabbits, and didn't come back. They found him later, shot dead, and from the way the gun lay with a thin branch caught up, it looked as if there might have been an accident, but Mr Sebastian knew it was no accident. He hated Sir John Tennant then, and he does now. He spoke about it to me once, when he'd taken an extra whiskey or two and read something in the paper that day about Sir John. *'Sooner or later I'll destroy him, Mattie,'* he said. *'The chance will come, and I can wait.'* "

A small shiver touched me. No matter what the cause, I shrank from the thought of hatred being nourished and kept alive for so many long years. "Do you think Mr. Ryder has in mind some way to hurt Sir John now?" I asked.

Mattie lifted her shoulders. "Who's to say? The master hasn't forgiven and forgotten, of that you may be sure."

"But surely it's strange for this man Sir John Tennant to accept a social invitation from a man who hates him so deeply?"

Mattie shook her head. "Oh, I'm sure he doesn't know, m'dear. After all, Mr. Harold and Mr. Sebastian weren't in the same business and they had different surnames, being stepbrothers. Same mother but a different father, you see. And what with it all being so long ago, it's not likely Sir John will ever have realized the connection."

"No, I suppose not."

We sat in silence for a minute or so. At last I said, "I would think the only way Mr. Ryder could hurt Sir John was in the way of business, yet this boat trip is a social occasion."

Mattie sighed and began to sort the cards into two packs. "Let's not worry about it, Hannah," she said. "Whatever the master has in mind, it's nothing to do with you or me."

"No, you're right." I patted her hand and stood up. "Goodnight, Mattie. Sleep well."

"And you, m'dear."

Later, when I was ready for bed, I stood in my nightdress by the window, holding the curtain a little aside and looking out over the London rooftops to a clear starry sky. The evening had held much that was strange for me, even more strange than Mattie knew. While she was telling me the story of Sebastian Ryder's stepbrother, I had suddenly remembered why the name of Tennant was vaguely familiar to me. It appeared in the letter my mother had written to me shortly before her death, when she said that if I ever found myself in truly dire straits, I should go to some solicitors in Clerkenwell and seek their advice regarding the Tennant Charity.

Perhaps this was nothing to do with Sir John Tennant. The name was not common but neither was it particularly rare, and by no possible stretch of the imagination could I conceive that my mother might have had any connection with a titled landowner who was also chairman of a big shipbuilding enterprise.

My thoughts turned to the other name I had heard during the evening. I looked toward the drawer in which I kept the small box containing my few special belongings. When telling me of the anxiety her cousin Andrew had caused the family, Clara had said they suspected him of meeting Ramon Delgado. I had no doubt that this was the man with proud aquiline features, tragic eyes, and a passionate ambition to right the wrongs afflicting his country, the same man who had once poured out his heart to a young student who knew nothing of such matters, and had given her a ring of Mexican silver, engraved with his initials, because she had listened with sympathy and because he believed her simple words of response had in some way transformed his despair into new hope.

After awhile I let the curtain fall into place and padded barefoot across the room to climb into bed. There was nothing menacing about the name of Tennant being familiar to me, nor in the fact that I had once sat listening to the outpourings of a man who was now half a world away, a man as idealistic and romantic as I knew Andrew Doyle to be. Yet as I lay in the darkness I had an uneasy feeling that the strands of an invisible net were very slowly closing about me.

Nine

By next afternoon I had thrown off my foolish forebodings and was enjoying myself with Jane and Gerald on a visit to the Natural History Museum in South Kensington. As I expected, at breakfast Gerald had been full of the story Andrew Doyle had told about me the night before, recounting it to Mattie with glowing admiration I found highly embarrassing.

Mattie was duly impressed. Jane, blunt and honest as ever, said she thought it was "jolly brave" of me, and let it go at that, for which I was grateful. Later that morning, when I was taking Jane for her French lesson, she said with a frown, "Did you know that I'm not to go on the river trip Papa spoke about last night?"

I was surprised, and said, "No, I didn't, Miss Jane. Why is that?"

"I don't know. Perhaps because there might be a quarrel. Papa regards Sir John Tennant as his deadly enemy, but I don't think Sir John knows that. Anyway, Papa says I'm to stay at home, so that's an end of it."

I did not want to be drawn into a discussion on the matter, and said quickly, *"Cela ne me regarde pas, Mam'selle Jane. Veuillez parler en français, s'il vous plaît . . ."*

Nothing more was said, then or later, and neither did Gerald raise the subject, perhaps because his sister told him I had made clear that it was none of my business.

After our visit to the museum we took a cab home by a roundabout route, down to the Chelsea Embankment and then along beside the river to Westminster before turning north for Portland Place. As we rattled through the streets of Chelsea in the growler, I thought of Toby Kent, and wondered if he was still living and working in Chelsea or had returned to Paris. The address he had given me was in my writing case, and I decided I would write to him on the weekend.

Next morning I received a letter, the first since my arrival in England, and at once recognized Toby's careless yet quite legible handwriting on the envelope. The letter was very short.

To Young McLeod—Greetings.
Will you sit for me again, please?
An afternoon if you can manage it. The light is at its best in my studio then.
Ton vieil ami,
Ex-seaman Toby Kent.

Hetty had brought the letter to my room with my morning tea, and I laughed as I read it. After breakfast I went to the room Mr. Ryder was using as a study and asked if he could spare me a few moments. He looked up from some closely written foolscap papers he was reading and said, "All right, what is it Hannah?"

"May I have a free afternoon one day this week or next week, sir?"

"What's stopping you?"

"I just wished to be sure of an afternoon free of any duties, sir."

"All right. Is it something special?"

"I've been invited to visit a friend of mine in Chelsea."

He sat back in his chair. "Who do you know in Chelsea?"

"A gentleman named Toby Kent, sir. He's a painter, and we knew each other in Montmartre."

"A painter, eh? How did he know you were here?"

"The Willard family and Mr. Andrew Doyle are acquainted with him, sir. Perhaps they told him."

Sebastian Ryder nodded thoughtfully. "I've heard of Kent myself. Made quite a name in Paris recently. They published photographs of two of his pictures in *The Tatler* a month or so ago. You were his model for *Butterfly Girl,* I take it?"

I stared in astonishment, then said, "Well . . . yes, I was. I didn't realize you knew, and I hope you're not annoyed, sir."

"I guessed, and why the devil should I be annoyed? I might be interested in some of that young man's pictures myself. Fellow at the club was saying he's got a big future."

"I didn't know you were interested in art, sir."

"I'm not. I'm interested in investment." Sebastian Ryder surveyed me with a glimmer of amusement in his hard eyes. "So you want to go off for the afternoon with a young man? Is that quite proper?"

I said, "Oh yes, sir. Quite. We lived across the passage from each other in Montmartre, and Mr. Kent always treated me with respect. Are you thinking it might reflect upon your family if I visit him without a chaperon? I could ask Mattie to accompany me perhaps—"

"Good God no," he said impatiently. "I don't give a damn for all that rubbish. When do you want to visit him?"

"I've made no plans as yet for any excursion tomorrow with Miss Jane and Master Gerald. If I write now, Mr. Kent should get the letter by this evening's post, so I could go tomorrow, if you approve."

"Yes. All right. Let me know which gallery will be showing his pictures."

"Yes, sir. Thank you." I went straight to my room and wrote a short letter to Toby, then put on my hat and gloves and went out to post it before starting Gerald's morning French lesson. Next day I asked to be excused luncheon so that I might leave in good time for Chelsea. I had begun to save a little money now, and did not want to incur the expense of a cab, so I went by omnibus, changing at Piccadilly Circus and walking the last half mile to Toby's studio in a street overlooking some gardens near Chelsea Embankment.

It was a warm day, and as I drew near I saw him sitting on a bench by the gardens, in shirt-sleeves, holding a big piece of bread and throwing crumbs to a flock of waddling pigeons. He stood up, threw the last of the bread, grinned at me, and said, "Hello, me beauty. I got your letter and there you are."

"Hello, Toby. It was nice to hear from you."

He stepped back, palms resting on his hips as he surveyed me, then scowled. "That dress hides your shoulders."

"Of course it does. I couldn't walk through the streets décolleté, could I? Besides, you didn't say what you wanted me to wear."

He sniffed. "It's a portrait I was thinking of, and you have a splendid neck and shoulders."

"You can't go on painting butterfly girls."

"I suppose not." He studied me dubiously. "The dress is pretty enough, and I suppose I'll just have to make do with the face. It's not all that bad."

I laughed. "You Irish, with your flattery."

"Come on up now. These pigeons have no sense of gratitude, I'm telling you." We began to cross the road. "How are you getting on with Ryder? No troubles? I saw Andrew Doyle yesterday, and he said you seemed well enough. Here's the door. Now straight on up the stairs. There's almost as many as at Rue Labarre."

It was a studio apartment, and a very splendid one, with a skylight and a big window facing out across the Thames. I had little chance to look round, however, for a blank canvas was already set on an easel, and Toby ushered me to an upright chair. "Hat off, Hannah, and sit down; there's a good girl. No, no. Facing the easel. That's better. Wait now, there's a piece of your hair has slipped a trifle, and it needs pinning."

"I'm not surprised, the way you're rushing me. Is there a looking glass handy, or can you see to it for me?"

"All right." His touch on my head was very quick and light. "So. That's fine. Are you comfortable?"

"Yes, it's an easy pose to hold. Where do you want me to look?"

"At me. And don't talk for a while. Later I'll be glad to work and talk, but I'll tell you when."

"Very good, sir."

He grinned. "You're the only sitter who never gets angry with me, young McLeod, and God bless you for it."

He began to mix paint, and soon he was at work, breathing hard, muttering under his breath, attacking the canvas, vanishing behind it for a while as he worked, then suddenly leaning out to glare at me ferociously for long moments. After twenty minutes he sighed, tossed his brush and palette down on the table, picked up the canvas, threw it into a corner and said very calmly and amiably, "D'you think you could make us a decent cup of coffee, me beauty?"

"I'll try, Toby. Is there coffee in the kitchen?"

"I'll show you. Most girls would have asked what was wrong and why I'd stopped and God knows what," he said, leading the way into a small but pleasant kitchen off the studio, "but you're a restful creature, praise be, and do you know I've not had a decent cup of coffee since coming back to England? What the devil do the grocers do with the stuff? By the same token, I never had a decent cup of tea in France."

I was opening the door of the larder, and said, "It's not the grocers, it's the water, Toby. I've tried several experiments with our cook, Mrs. Fletcher, and I'm sure it's the water. French water is good for coffee and English water is good for tea. Look, you have some tea here; shall I make a pot?"

"So young yet so wise," said Toby. "Yes, make tea but don't talk; I just want to watch you."

I felt no embarrassment as he sat astride a chair and watched me with great intensity while I went about the business of making tea, but it was hard not to giggle occasionally at his expression. When I had poured, we sat at the kitchen table to drink, but had barely started the first cup when he got quickly to his feet and said urgently, "Let's go back, Hannah. Quickly now."

We left our tea and hurried into the studio. As I took my seat, he set a new canvas on the easel and snatched up his brush and palette. Again came a period of muttering and heavy breathing as he worked with fierce vigor, then, perhaps twenty minutes later, he suddenly laughed, and though he continued to work swiftly and positively, I could see that the tension had gone out of him.

"How did you enjoy your evening with the Willards and Andrew Doyle?" he said.

"May I talk now?"

"Sure you may, except when I'm taking a hard look at you."

"Well, they were all very nice, but I found it a little embarrassing. They act as if I had been a great heroine and saved Mr. Doyle's life."

"It's possible."

"Oh, nonsense. He's a very romantic person, isn't he? But I think he's a good man. Clara was telling me he's very much taken up with trying to make things better for the poor people in Mexico."

"Dear Lord, I know all about that. One evening in Paris we went out to dinner together and he spent the whole time telling me how cruelly the peasants in his country are treated. Did you know he's besotted with you?"

I jumped in my chair. "What?"

"Keep still, will you? The fellow's besotted with you."

"Mr. Doyle?"

"Who else?"

"Oh, you're joking, Toby."

He appeared from behind the canvas and studied me absently for a few moments. "No, he's vastly taken, I promise you. It's partly because of what you did, and partly because you were a poor peasant yourself, and therefore all the more admirable."

"Oh dear."

"Why 'Oh dear'? He's rich and I've no doubt kind, and maybe he'll ask you to marry him, so then you can become a fine lady and divert him from dangerous and rebellious notions."

I smiled. "Now you really are joking."

"Maybe so, but I'm not entirely sure. As you pointed out, Andrew is a very romantic fellow."

I said uneasily, "You don't really think he might be so smitten as to want to court me?"

Toby stood back to eye his canvas. "And if he did, what's so bad about that?"

"Well, it will be embarrassing. You know very well I can't marry anybody, even if I wanted to."

"Then let's hope he doesn't ask. Tell me about life with the Ryder family."

"All right. Let me see now. Mr. Ryder is very brusque, but I don't mind that; it's just his way. I get on well with Mattie and the children. Gerald is rather lovesick, but I think I'm not quite such an obsession with him as I was at first, and all in all I lead a very comfortable life, with light duties and a lot of freedom."

"That's fine." Toby stopped painting to look at me. "Still no sign that Ryder's demand for the butterfly girl at any cost held some sinister meaning?"

"No, none at all. Oh, it came out yesterday that he'd seen the photograph of your paintings in *The Tatler,* and knew I was your model for *Butterfly Girl,* or rather he guessed. I expect Mr. Boniface must have told him we were neighbors, because he knew about your success and said he might be interested in seeing some of your pictures."

"He's not a collector, is he?"

"No. He seemed to feel they might be a good investment."

"Then be damned to him," said Toby, quite affably. "He's a worse Philistine than you are yourself, Hannah. But listen now. He spoke of the butterfly girl to Boniface before ever I painted that picture, so he must know of the golden butterfly on your shoulder, me beauty. Did you ask him how?"

"For heaven's sake, Toby, I can't ask my employer a question like that. Besides, I don't much care how he knows, as long as he treats me as decently as he has all along."

"So there's been nothing odd? Nothing at all?"

"No." I remembered my unease of the night before. "Well, just two odd coincidences, I suppose, and one of them had nothing to do with Mr. Ryder."

Toby said, "Go on."

I told him of the river party planned for the week after next, to which the Willards and Andrew Doyle were invited together with three other guests. "One of them is a gentleman called Sir John Tennant. I don't suppose you remember that letter from my mother I once showed you, but in it she mentioned the Tennant Charity." I did not go on to say that Sebastian Ryder bore an unrelenting hatred for Sir John, or to explain why, for I felt Mattie had told me this in confidence.

After a moment or two Toby said, "What's the other coincidence?"

I told him of Clara's suspicion that when Andrew Doyle was in Mexico he had met a rebel leader, Ramon Delgado, and I explained that this was a man whose acquaintance I had made when he visited our College for Young Ladies in Paris a year or two ago.

"Is that all?" said Toby. He was painting quickly, and only looking at me occasionally now.

"Yes," I said. "I'm not pretending either matter is important, but you keep asking if anything odd has happened, so I thought I'd mention those two coincidences."

"I'd hardly call them that," Toby said dryly. "There can't be many Mexican gentlemen who visit Paris, and if you've met a pair of them who happen to know each other, to wit, Andrew Doyle and Ramon Delgado, that's not entirely surprising. As for the other business, if Sir John Tennant has nothing to do with the Tennant Charity, then it's a very small coincidence that he has the same name. And if he does have to do with the charity, then it's not a coincidence, it's a mystery. Do you want to solve it?"

I thought for a moment, then said, "No. I wouldn't know where to begin, and I can't see the point. It would only mean raking up the past. I don't want that."

Toby stepped sideways to look at me soberly but with a touch of humor in his eyes. "You don't change much, young McLeod," he said.

"I'm better dressed than I used to be, Mr. Kent."

"So you are. Shall we go out to dinner somewhere immensely posh one evening?"

"Oh, I can't, Toby. This is England, and I'm employed in a respectable household. I wasn't even sure that Mr. Ryder would let me come and visit you this afternoon."

Toby grinned and ran a hand through his hair, leaving streaks of paint on his forehead. "I'm from a respectable family myself," he said, "and as a young man I've attended weekend parties in country homes both in England and Ireland, and I'm telling you, you'd not believe the scuttling between bedrooms that goes on at night among folks who occupy all the best church pews."

"Is that really so?"

"I do assure you. We're a land of hypocrites."

"Well, it's not like that at Silverwood, and I can't come to dinner with you, but it's very kind of you to invite me."

"Keep still a minute." He studied me, frowning, then resumed painting. "You'll be able to come and see me again, though?"

"I expect so. You mean to be painted?"

"Ah, Hannah, you're cruel." He paused and looked at me reproachfully, arms spread a little. "D'you think I only want you here as a model to sit for me? Perish the thought. No, I had in mind you might cook a nice luncheon for us one day, for I'm sick of going out to eating places, and what I make for myself is disgusting."

I laughed. "You don't change much yourself, Toby. You're still a terrible man. Is your foot completely better now?"

"Almost. Just a twinge or two if I run downstairs."

"I'm so glad. And have you seen any more of Mrs. Hesketh?"

He gave a shout of laughter, and shook his head. "No, I've not. I felt it best to resist that temptation. You know, Hannah, I thought she and Boniface were a rum couple, but after living in Chelsea for a while I'm inclined to think they're quite humdrum. Let me tell you about the folk who live on the next floor down from me . . ."

For the next hour we chatted as we had been used to in Paris whenever we spent a little time together, then Toby said I could stop sitting as he had all he wanted from me, and he was entirely parched, so would

I try my hand again at making a pot of tea, which I did, bringing him a cup as he worked, but taking care not to look at the painting.

After another half hour, which I spent sitting by the window and watching the Thames, he said, "All right. It's not finished, but come and see what you think."

The portrait showed head and shoulders, with my eyes holding a suggestion of a smile. In places the paint seemed to have been put on in thick slabs, and certainly there was no attempt at a careful likeness, yet this time I saw at once that the picture was of me, perhaps because I was now looking at it differently and not expecting a perfect replica in two dimensions. I realized also that although Toby painted at great speed and in a seemingly slapdash manner, every stroke of the brush had a precise purpose and every nuance of light had been faithfully portrayed.

"Go on," said Toby from behind me. "Tell me it's not like you."

"Oh, but it is," I said wonderingly. "It's very much like me."

"Ah. You're learning, Hannah McLeod."

"I didn't realize I was smiling."

"You weren't. That's just something you always have in your eyes, and I got it, by God." There was a note of exultation in his voice.

"I'm glad it came out right," I said, and turned, then burst out laughing as I saw that Toby's brow and cheek were now both striped with paint from his fingers. "You'd better go and wash," I said, and looked at my watch. "I told Mattie I would be back before six, so I must leave soon. No, don't wipe your face with a turpsy rag, stupid; you'll make it sore."

He threw the rag aside. "Ah, you're a bullying sort of girl, young McLeod," he said, and marched into the kitchen. While I stood in the doorway watching, he splashed and lathered at the sink, then buried his head in a towel. "I'll be taking you home in a cab," he said in a muffled voice, "so there's time enough for us to have tea first."

"Cabs are awfully expensive, Toby; I know because I take Gerald and Jane about. Sixpence a mile within a four mile radius of Charing Cross, so it would cost at least half a crown to take me home and come back yourself."

"I've lots of money," he said, his face emerging from the towel. "I keep painting pictures and people keep buying them. All the pictures I left in Paris have sold."

"Well, thank you very much, then. I'll put the kettle on again."

"I didn't mean a cup of tea. I meant four o'clock tea, with toasted muffins and Dundee cake, in an English teashop."

"Oh, I'd love that."

"Right, then. Give me two minutes."

He went through to his bedroom. I returned to the picture, studying it with interest. In less than two minutes he appeared with hair more or less combed, wearing a tie and pulling on a jacket. "What are you going to call this one?" I asked.

"Well now, it's just a portrait so there's not much scope for a title. I'll call it *Hannah.*"

I stood pinning on my hat and said, "I suppose it wasn't very sensible of you to do a portrait. After all, nobody's going to buy a portrait of a stranger, surely?"

"Not by a modern artist." Toby grinned suddenly. "But you're no stranger to Andrew Doyle, so I could always sell it to him; he'd take it like a shot. Besides, who said anything about selling? I'll maybe just scrape you off the canvas so I can use it again."

I pulled on my gloves, still looking at the picture, and said, "I'd be sad if you did that. Not for me, but for you, because it's your work and I know you're pleased with it."

"Then maybe I won't. Come on now; I'm dying for a muffin."

We took a cab to a teashop near Charing Cross and spent a pleasant half hour there talking of nothing in particular. Having missed luncheon, I was hungry now, and we both ate heartily as we sat at a window table watching the world go by outside. At ten minutes to six we arrived at Portland Place in another cab. Toby escorted me to the front door, waited till it was opened by Albert the footman, then lifted his hat to me and made his way down the steps to the waiting hansom.

That evening Gerald was somewhat sulky at dinner, no doubt because I had been to visit a male friend. Mr. Ryder asked one or two brief questions which brought out the fact that Toby had painted a portrait of me, and this seemed to interest him. "Is it for sale?" he asked.

Remembering Toby's comment when I had spoken of Sebastian Ryder buying pictures as an investment, I felt it was best not to encourage the prospect, and said hastily, "Oh, I think he just painted me for practice, sir. He mentioned scraping it off to use the canvas again." I did not say the suggestion had been made jokingly.

"There'll be other pictures, no doubt," said Mr. Ryder, and then to my relief the subject was dropped.

A few days later, when we were in a growler returning from an afternoon's outing to the Tower of London, Jane said, "Did you know Papa has invited your friend Mr. Kent to join the river party next week, Hannah?"

I was startled, and said, "Good gracious, no. Has Toby written to accept?"

"Oh, there weren't any letters. Papa went to see him. It's funny, isn't it? I suppose he wanted to look at any new pictures he'd painted. By the way, he still has your portrait, so he didn't scrape it off. Papa thought it was very blotchy. I don't think he liked Mr. Kent much, not just because he wouldn't sell him any pictures, but he said his manner wasn't respectful. It was very terse."

I stifled a laugh at the idea of Toby Kent being respectful to anybody. Gerald said, "Papa thinks the only one with a right to be terse is himself—but then he calls it not wasting words."

"That's true," Jane agreed, and turned to look at me. "It must have been very strange, living in Montmartre. Was Mr. Kent your lover there?"

Gerald went crimson and said, *"Jane!"*

I was dumbfounded with shock myself, and it was a moment or two before I was able to speak, then I said indignantly, "No, of course he wasn't! And you shouldn't speak of such things, Miss Jane!"

"All the girls at school talk about things like that," she replied, unabashed, "except for one or two priggish creatures. I'm sure it was the same with the boys at Gerald's school."

"Jane, stop it!" he exclaimed, scandalized.

"Well, it's silly," she said. "I'm convinced some of the things I've been told are absolute nonsense, and I wish there was somebody to ask all about it. I didn't mean to insult you when I asked if Mr. Kent had been your lover, Hannah, because after all, it's quite different in Paris, isn't it? I thought if he had, then I could ask *you* about these things; I didn't mean now, in front of Gerald, but just some time."

Gerald was holding his head in his hands in an agony of embarrassment. Oddly enough, and despite my admonition, I was in sympathy with what Jane had said, but I was not the person to answer her questions. I looked out of the window and said, "Mr. Kent and I were neighbors, and no more. I accept that you intended no insult, and now please let us drop the subject."

After a moment or two she said with a rare touch of contrition, "I beg your pardon, Hannah."

"Thank you, Miss Jane. Now I've just had an idea. I think one day we ought to go to the National Gallery and the Tate Gallery to look at paintings and try to understand about the different schools. Perhaps I could even ask Mr. Kent to come with us and explain all about it. . . ."

Gerald gave a sigh of relief, Jane responded with enthusiasm, and the iron-shod wheels of the cab rumbled on over the cobbles.

The day of the river party, the day when Sebastian Ryder began to reveal the true purpose for which he had brought me to England, was warm and dry when we gathered aboard the boat Mr. Ryder had hired for the day, one of the passenger boats that plied regularly between Greenwich and Hampton Court.

On the deck forward of the saloon, chairs had been set out and a striped awning erected to give a little shelter from the sun for those who wished. It was here that we received the guests as they arrived by carriage and made their way down the steps by Westminster Bridge. The Willard family and Andrew Doyle were first to arrive. I kept in the background while they were welcomed by Sebastian Ryder and Gerald, but they all made a point of greeting me as if I had been one of the family.

Five minutes later a very elegant carriage drew up and three people alighted. They came down the steps and along the gangway to be welcomed by Sebastian Ryder, who then began a series of introductions. Mr. Hugh Ritchie was a good-looking man in his middle forties with a brisk manner and an air of authority. His wife, Anne Ritchie, was several years younger, a handsome lady with very beautiful eyes. Her manner at first seemed haughty, but I sensed that this concealed a rather nervous nature, and it quickly faded under the easy friendliness with which the Americans greeted her. Sir John Tennant, her father, was in his late sixties and in no way resembled his daughter. He was a big, stoop-shouldered man, heavily built, pallid of face, with thin gray hair and eyes so heavily lidded that they seemed to be half closed. He was short in the neck, so that he carried his head sunk between his shoulders, which gave him a tortoiselike appearance.

When everybody else had been introduced, Sebastian Ryder turned to where I stood and said, "Finally, this is Hannah McLeod, my children's French tutor, who is accompanying us on this occasion."

I curtsied to Mrs. Ritchie and said, "Good morning, madam."

She inclined her head. "Good morning." Her gaze started to pass on, then came sharply back to me. She stared hard, almost as if trying to remember where she might have seen me before. "McLeod? You're surely not a French girl?" she said.

"No, madam, I was born in London, but my mother was French, and later I lived in France for several years."

"I see." She looked at me a moment longer, and I thought I saw shadows of remembered sorrow in her eyes as she turned away. Her husband gave me a nod and said, "Morning, young lady," then moved to speak to Mr. Willard.

Sir John Tennant stood regarding me from under those heavy lids, hands resting on the silver-knobbed cane he carried. The watery gray eyes were empty except for what I could only decipher as a strange wariness. I was conscious of Sebastian Ryder standing a pace or two away. The lizard eyes flicked toward him, then came back to me.

"McLeod?" he said in a deep toneless voice. "Was that what you said, Ryder?"

I glanced at my employer, and caught a flash of triumphant satisfaction in his gaze as it rested on the older man. "Hannah McLeod," he said smoothly; "that's right, Sir John."

I felt that in those moments something passed between the two men, something dark and menacing, but I could not fathom what it might be or what it could have to do with me. Sir John's heavy head nodded slowly. "I see," he growled. "Good morning, Miss McLeod."

Again I replied and curtsied. Andrew Doyle seemed to be the only one who had noticed anything odd, for the rest of the party had mingled and were talking together. He came to join me as Sir John turned away, and I could see he was somewhat puzzled, but he simply said, "What a pleasure to have you with us on this trip, Hannah." He glanced up the steps to the break in the parapet, where a hansom cab had just drawn up. "Here's our mutual friend, Toby Kent, if I'm not mistaken. Do you think you might persuade him to sell me that portrait of you he painted last week?"

This request, together with the intensity of Andrew Doyle's regard, recalled to me Toby's remark that he was "besotted" with me, and I was uneasily aware that his interest in me seemed more than casual. I said apologetically, "I'm afraid I have no influence with Toby Kent, and I doubt if anybody has, Mr. Doyle."

Toby came running down the steps. He was wearing a light gray summer suit, and looked more elegant than I had ever seen him. When he called, "Top of the morning to one and all," as he strode along the gangway, brandishing his cane and raising his hat, I realized with an inward smile that he had decided to be rather more than half Irish today.

He was introduced to the new acquaintances, greeted the Willards and Andrew Doyle warmly, then walked to where I stood a little apart, reaching for my hand and bowing to kiss it ceremoniously. "Your servant, Miss Hannah."

This, I knew, was to make clear that he regarded me as being in no wise inferior to anybody else on the boat, but since I found it embarrassing, I simply said, "Good morning, Toby," then muttered in French under my breath, telling him to behave.

He laughed, looked about him, then moved away and began talking animatedly to Mrs. Willard about a young American from North Carolina who had been one of his comrades during several years that they served together in the French Foreign Legion. Mr. Ryder called to the boat's captain, and two minutes later we were moving out from Westminster pier.

It was a glorious voyage we made during the next hour and a half, moving very slowly since the tide was ebbing. There was much to see, and apart from the captain and his crew of three, Sebastian Ryder had hired a guide who was able to recite the history of every point of interest as we passed.

Refreshments were served by two of the household servants who had accompanied us, and during periods when the guide was not speaking the guests mingled well. I found myself in conversation with Clara and her mother and father in turn, then with Andrew Doyle. I felt very comfortable talking with them, but was constantly aware of Sir John Tennant's eyes following me as he sat in a canvas chair smoking a cigar.

While we were drinking glasses of cool lemonade, Toby came across to me as I stood with Clara and said with a jerk of his head toward Sir John, "Why's the old fellow goggling at you, me beauty? That's for a painter to be doing, not a shipbuilder."

Clara said in a low voice, "I was wondering myself. I thought he would be making himself agreeable to Papa for business reasons, but he's more interested in you, Hannah. Have you met him before?"

"No, never. Perhaps we're just imagining it."

"Or perhaps he thinks that's a funny hat you're wearing, young McLeod," said Toby.

"It's beautiful!" Clara exclaimed indignantly.

"He's joking, Miss Clara," I said, "and even if he isn't, I'm used to him saying such things. He's a terrible fellow."

"I've not come here to be slandered," said Toby. "I shall take myself off and give Mrs. Ritchie the benefit of my extraordinary charm."

I passed only a polite word or two with Mr. Hugh Ritchie that morning, and none at all with Sir John, but as we drew near to Kew, where we were to disembark, I found Mrs. Ritchie beside me at the rail. "How was it you came to live in France for so long, Hannah?" she asked.

I assumed she had noticed how amiable the Willards were toward me, and had decided to show polite interest herself. Andrew was standing on my other side, and we had been talking for a while before Mrs. Ritchie approached. Now he said, "I've been meaning to ask that myself; in fact I did ask Toby Kent, but for a loquacious Irishman he can be very taciturn. He said he'd never asked because it was none of his business." Mr. Doyle's teeth showed white in his brown face as he grinned. "Which put me in my place."

This was a polite way of putting Mrs. Ritchie in *her* place, I realized, but I wanted to create no mystery, and so I told the lie I had so often told in La Coquille when English customers asked the same question—that my father had died at sea when I was twelve and my mother soon after, and so I had been taken in by her family in France, who were very poor but who had looked after me until I was old enough to care for myself. I did not elaborate, and when I stopped speaking Mrs. Ritchie said, "Your father was a seaman, then?"

"Yes, madam."

"You're well spoken, and seemingly well educated."

"My mother was a teacher, madam."

"I see." She studied me for a moment or two as she had done when I was first introduced to her, then gave a small impatient shake of her head as if finally discarding some vague and rather silly notion. After a little silence she murmured, "We seem to be approaching the pier," and moved away.

The next two hours were spent in Kew Gardens, and I enjoyed every moment. Mr. Doyle appointed himself my escort, Toby took charge of Clara, and Sebastian Ryder hired a guide to take us round these huge and remarkable botanical gardens. I was interested in the plants and flowers, for I had seen little of growing things before coming to Silverwood. The older men were interested in practical matters, such as the research here which had led to establishing the rubber plant in Malaya, and the cinchona tree, for quinine, in India. Toby was concerned with light and color, whether of a great tree against the sky or a tiny vivid plant against green foliage, and he found an attentive listener in Clara. Mrs. Willard shared my interest in the flowers, Mrs. Ritchie seemed just a little bored, and Gerald tried hard not to appear glum, though I knew he was put out at seeing Andrew Doyle play escort to me.

Halfway through our tour we rested and took cool drinks at the restaurant in the gardens, then at two o'clock returned to the boat for a cold luncheon while sailing back down the river to Westminster. The servants had set up a long table laid with fine white linen, sparkling glasses, and silver cutlery. A side table bore a variety of cold meats and poultry, with several huge salad bowls, a dozen bottles of champagne, and jugs of lemonade.

A festive mood prevailed throughout luncheon, but toward the end I heard Andrew Doyle, beside me, speaking across the table to Mr. Hugh Ritchie in a serious, almost bitter tone of voice. "No, sir," he was saying. "It's true that the war of the 1840s is still remembered by older Mexicans, but the bonds between the two countries are very strong today. American investment south of the Rio Grande is enormous, and it has helped develop railroads, ports, mines, and all kinds of industry. My father was one of the pioneers in this, and for me it is not difficult to be half Mexican and half American. What *is* difficult is to be Mexican."

Mr. Ritchie said, "I don't think I understand, Mr. Doyle."

"I simply mean that I find it hard to bear the repression of the Mexican people by the Mexican government, and of the poor by the rich."

"Oh, come now," said Mr. Ritchie. "During my spell at the Foreign Office I had occasion to study reports on Mexico, and there have been tremendous reforms since Porfirio Díaz became your president. Even before his time, if I remember aright, the Lerdo government proclaimed freedom of religion. It also enacted laws forbidding forced labor, and declared that man's liberty in labor, education, and religion was inviolable."

Andrew nodded ruefully. "It sounds admirable in theory, sir," he said politely, "so did the slogan of 'liberty, order, and progress.' But liberty has now been officially dropped in order to ensure progress, and the latest Díaz slogan is *'Pan o palo.'* Do you know what that means? It means bread or the club. In other words, do as you're told and you'll eat. Otherwise you'll suffer anything from imprisonment to death. Do you know that when the Yaqui Indians became troublesome, they were made to become army conscripts, and were then sent to be cheap labor on the sisal plantations of Yucatán?"

Mr. Ritchie sipped champagne, then said slowly, "A country must be stable if it is to make economic and social progress."

"It's too stable," Andrew Doyle said somberly. "Only two people in a hundred own land, and most of those properties are small ranchos, hardly big enough to provide for a man and his family. But then you have the rich with their great haciendas. I know of one estate in Durango that occupies more than a million acres, another in Zacatecas almost twice as big, another in Coahuila half as big as England. There is a railroad line in the state of Hidalgo and it travels through eighty miles of land belonging to one family. And there are some families who own several such haciendas."

From a little way along the table Mrs. Willard called, "Andrew dear, no hobby horses today, please."

Mr. Doyle leaned back in his chair with an apologetic gesture and said, "I'm sorry, Aunt Melanie. I began by answering a question, and got carried away."

She smiled at him, then turned to continue talking to Toby Kent, seated beside her. Mr. Ritchie said good humoredly, "We'd better close the subject. But try to remember that radical changes in a country always take time. A long time."

"For some people, a lifetime," Andrew Doyle replied a little grimly. Then he smiled, and glanced at me. "But I must say no more. Would you like to hear how the young lady beside me saved my life in Montmartre?"

I said quickly, "Oh please, Mr. Doyle, I so much wish you wouldn't."

Hugh Ritchie raised an eyebrow and said, "This sounds very dramatic."

"It was certainly that," said Andrew Doyle, and made a gesture of regret as he inclined his head toward me, "but it also appears to be another forbidden subject, sir." At that moment Clara, seated beside Mr. Ritchie, turned from her other neighbor to engage him in conversation, whereupon Andrew Doyle gave his attention to me and began to ask which London sights and places I would recommend for a visit beyond those which were well known.

Conversation continued generally along the table, though I noticed that Sir John Tennant made little effort to be sociable with those seated near to him. He drank several glasses of champagne, but only toyed with his food, and for the most part sat with a brooding air as if his thoughts were elsewhere, though occasionally I found his eyes on me with the same wariness I had noticed before.

Luncheon ended, the servants withdrew below, and since the ladies could not withdraw, they gave the gentlemen permission to smoke at the table. I had drunk only lemonade, and began to wish Gerald had done the same, for now he accepted a cigar, and as he began puffing away at it, I felt concern that it might upset him.

The boat moved gently on under the warm sun, with a touch of breeze to bring us fresh air under the awning. I was watching Gerald, hoping he would leave his cigar in the ashtray, when Sebastian Ryder spoke from the far end of the table in a voice which was sufficiently loud to capture everyone's attention. "Do you by chance know Paris well, Mr. Ritchie?" he asked.

Everybody's eyes turned to Mr. Ritchie, who sat with his chair pushed slightly away from the table, one arm over the back of it, a cigar in his other hand. "Not well, sir," he replied lazily. "My wife and I have spent a few days there, but that was three or four years ago, and I haven't at any time been attached to the Paris embassy."

"I understand it's a most fascinating city," said Mr. Ryder. "Our other guests greatly enjoyed their sojourn there, so they tell me, and Mr. Kent in fact chose to live there for some time, but I imagine nobody knows it better than Hannah, since she was a student at the Montavon College for Young Ladies for several years. Perhaps you have heard of this establishment?"

I had been feeling almost sleepy from the combined effect of the tour of the gardens, the excellent luncheon, and the warm sun, but on

Sebastian Ryder's final words I was instantly wide awake, greatly shaken, and with a sick foreboding of what was to come. Along the table on the far side, Toby Kent's head snapped round to look at me, and in his narrowed eyes I saw reflected my own startled unbelief.

Mr. Ritchie was saying, "I've had no reason to be concerned with French educational matters, and I can't say I've heard of the Montavon establishment. Is there something rather special about the college?"

I gave up a last shred of hope, and braced myself doggedly for what I would have to face in the next few minutes. My head felt muzzy, and I could not imagine why Sebastian Ryder was doing what I now knew he was going to do. The only thing clear to me was his reason for excluding Jane from today's river party.

"Oh yes," he said soberly, "there's something very special about the Montavon College for Young Ladies. To the people of Paris that title is well understood to be a euphemism, a pleasant way of referring to what we would call a house of ill repute. The so-called students are of course the girls who practice their profession there."

Apart from Toby Kent and Sebastian Ryder himself, every figure at the table seemed to freeze into total stillness. Toby looked slowly round at them with cold green eyes. Mr. Ryder continued speaking: "The Montavon place is properly licensed and supervised, of course; that's the French way, and I'm told it's regarded as a very elite establishment, superior to any other of its kind. They call it a *maison close* in French. Not sure of the pronunciation, I'm afraid. How do you say it, Hannah?"

I looked along the table at him and said with a French accent, "*Maison close.*"

He nodded, and picked up his glass of champagne. Toby Kent leaned back and gazed at the awning. Very slowly all other heads turned to look at me. In every face except Sir John Tennant's there was incredulity and shock. In his I seemed to see sudden comprehension and calculation. In the faces of Andrew Doyle and Gerald there was horror as well as shock.

I stood up and said to Mr. Ryder, "Do you wish me to withdraw, sir?"

He frowned. "If I wanted that, I'd tell you quick enough."

Clara had her head bowed and her hands pressed to her cheeks. Mrs. Willard looked imploringly at her husband, and Mrs. Ritchie at hers. Gerald was stabbing his cigar into an ashtray with savage, trembling movements, his face white and pinched. At last Mr. Willard spoke, slowly but with a hard edge to his voice. "I am amazed, sir," he said to Mr. Ryder, "utterly amazed that you should broach such a subject when my wife, my daughter, and Mrs. Ritchie are at your table."

Sebastian Ryder looked puzzled. "There's no offense intended, sir," he said. "Hannah McLeod sits daily at my table."

Hugh Ritchie stood up suddenly, two red spots of anger on his cheeks in contrast to the pallor of the ladies' faces. "It is that which is an insult, Ryder," he said in a voice that shook. "How dare you invite my wife to sit at table in the company of . . ."—he hesitated on a word, glanced briefly at Clara, and ended—"of a creature from a bordello!"

With a mildly pained air Sebastian Ryder said, "Oh, come now, Ritchie. Hannah left the Montavon *maison* almost two years before I brought her to England. She was already a reformed character. Would you criticize me for a philanthropic act of charity?"

"What you may do in the name of charity is your affair, sir; but you are quite out of order in thrusting such an aspect of it upon your guests." Mr. Ritchie glanced about him. "Since we are unable to leave, my wife and I will withdraw to the saloon. Come, Anne, my dear."

Mrs. Ritchie's lips were pressed tightly together, and her eyes glinted. She was evidently as angry as her husband. For a moment she glanced at her father as if expecting him to be equally outraged, but Sir John sat staring impassively in front of him. She frowned, stood up, moved to take her husband's arm, and together they passed into the saloon. Gerald pushed back his chair so violently that it overturned. His face was no longer white but crimson, and there were tears of rage in his eyes as he gazed at me and cried furiously, "How *could* you? Oh, I hate you!"

From the beginning I had kept my head up, and now I watched without speaking, hiding my inner weariness, as Gerald moved at a blundering run into the saloon. When I turned back to the table, Andrew Doyle and Mr. Willard were both standing. The former was nearest to me, gazing with horrified eyes as he said in a throaty whisper, "Is it true, Hannah? Is it *true?*"

"Yes, Mr. Doyle," I said in a flat voice. "I lived and worked in a *maison close* for four years."

"Oh, dear God," he breathed, and closed his eyes.

Sebastian Ryder sat with an unruffled air, slowly twirling his champagne glass between finger and thumb. I looked at him and said, "I ascertained from Mr. Boniface that you knew the truth about my background, sir, but I did not imagine you would make it public in this way."

He regarded me without interest and said, "The option has always been mine."

Mr. Willard said, "You have acutely embarrassed my family, sir, and if it were not for the fact that we sought out Miss McLeod for reasons of our own, I would condemn your behavior as unforgivable. We are not people who take a narrow view, but there are limits to our tolerance." He looked at his wife and daughter. "Melanie, Clara. We have no choice but to withdraw."

Mrs. Willard gave me a distressed look, shaking her head in bewilderment as she rose. Clara took her hands from her face and stood up, tears on her cheeks as she looked at me. "You must have been . . . little more than thirteen!" she whispered, then echoed Gerald's cry. "Oh, how could you, Hannah? I don't understand!"

Mr. Willard moved to take the arms of his wife and Clara, then paused to look at his nephew and said, "Andrew?"

Andrew Doyle opened his eyes but did not look at me as he replied in a low voice, "I shall not withdraw, Uncle Ben. Nothing can change the fact that she saved my life."

Mr. Willard inclined his head. "As you will," he said quietly, and led his wife and daughter away.

Sir John Tennant stood up, crushing out his cigar, casting a baleful glare first at me and then at Sebastian Ryder. "We have matters to discuss, Ryder," he said. "When?"

The other eyed him coldly. "This evening? At my house?"

"Very well. At what hour?"

"Half past nine o'clock."

Sir John nodded. "I'll be there," he growled, and turned to follow the other guests into the saloon.

"And then there were three," said Toby Kent in a strange tight voice. It was true. Apart from myself only three of the party remained on the foredeck. Andrew Doyle stood with his back to us now, gripping the rail, his body rigid. Sebastian Ryder sat placidly drawing on his cigar. There came a rattle of crockery and glasses as Toby suddenly crashed a fist down on the table, glaring at his host.

"You disgust me, Ryder," he said slowly and with deep loathing. "I wish to God you were a younger man, and even though you're not, I'm still toying with the notion of dropping you over the side."

I knew he meant it, and from the sudden alarm on Sebastian Ryder's usually impassive face he also realized the threat was not an idle one. I said sharply, "No, Toby. Do you hear me? No!"

Toby sighed and stood up. The freckles stood out sharply on his paler than usual face. "Andrew," he said, "oblige me by joining the others in the saloon. We'll be close behind you, for I've something to say."

Andrew Doyle hesitated for a moment, then gave a quick nod of his head and made for the saloon door. Toby bent to pick up his cane, which lay beside him. He moved round the table, stood facing me for a moment or two, then showed his teeth in a smile that was not a smile, and took my wrist in a gentle but strong grip. "Come, Hannah," he said.

I held back. "Toby, you know I'm not concerned to give explanations and excuses. They make no difference in the end."

"We'll see," he said softly. "I've obliged you with that," his head jerked contemptuously toward Sebastian Ryder, "so let's have no more argument, my little friend. I'm not in the mood."

The saloon door had been pushed to. Toby kicked it open and strode in, taking me with him willy-nilly and drawing startled looks from the already shaken guests. A long table stood in the center of the saloon. Andrew Doyle was still standing; the others had taken seats by the windows which ran down each side.

Before anybody could protest at my presence, Toby brought his cane crashing down on the table, making everybody jump, then he gazed slowly round. "And now, good people," he said in a voice that rasped with anger, "we shall have a short history lesson. All those who are cowards and hypocrites to their miserable backbones are invited to withdraw. Those who have some small respect for the truth will remain."

He paused, pressed me into a chair beside him, and glared round again, his red hair seeming to bristle. "There's no dueling here these days," he said with grim geniality, his gaze fastening intently on Hugh Ritchie, "but it can still be arranged across the Channel, so if any gentleman present is inclined to walk out, but feels insulted at being dubbed a coward and hypocrite, I'll be most happy to accommodate him."

Ten

There was a silence but for the steady throb of the ship's engine. I expected an angry response to Toby's cutting words, but it seemed that the suddenness and shock of Sebastian Ryder's revelations had left everybody stunned.

Toby paused for only a few seconds, then his voice softened a little as he went on, "I'll be glad to excuse Miss Clara from hearing the truth, for it's not pretty, especially for a young lady." He looked directly at her. "But before you withdraw, Miss Clara, I'll thank you for being the only one here with the wit to perceive that Hannah McLeod must have been a child of thirteen when it began, and to wonder how that could be so."

Sitting very upright, hands clasped in her lap, Clara said tautly, "I don't wish to be excused, Mr. Kent. I wish to be enlightened."

Her father leaned forward and said quietly, "Best that you leave, my dear."

"No I will not, Papa," she said flatly, her eyes on Andrew Doyle. "I have as much respect for the truth as anyone, and I have already done Hannah one grave injustice. If the truth is unpleasant, so be it. I am not a child. I know what a house of ill fame is, and what happens there. I have even had one pointed out to me in Monterrey by Andrew's sister, when I was on vacation there, for they are more open about such matters in Mexico." She transferred her direct gaze to Toby Kent. "Please begin your history lesson, sir."

I thought it probable that Mrs. Ritchie and Mrs. Willard would have left if it had not been for Clara, but now she had spoken so strongly they had little choice but to follow her example. It was of no importance to me whether they stayed or went. I knew that when Toby had spoken they might pity me, but it would change nothing in their eyes. I felt sad and tired, and if I could have prevented Toby speaking I would have done so, but I knew he would not be stayed.

Still standing, he laid his cane on the table and folded his arms. "Hannah and I were neighbors in Montmartre for eighteen months," he said quietly. "I knew she was from the Montavon *maison close,* for we were friends, and she chose not to hide her past from a friend by lies. I had no idea how she came to be employed there in the first place, until she told me one Sunday morning last summer, as we sat by the Seine. It's a story of which I've forgotten no detail, and I'll not be surprised if I'm the only one who knows it in full."

He glanced down at me with a lifted eyebrow. Strangely, I had begun to feel sleepy, perhaps in the aftermath of the shock that Sebastian Ryder's revelation had given me, and I had to rouse myself to say, "Yes, Toby. I've told nobody else."

Mr. Ritchie said coldly, "Do you know the story to be true, Kent?"

Toby turned away from the table, shoulders hunched, and I knew he was struggling to hold down his anger. After a moment he turned again, looked down the table at Mr. Ritchie with contempt in his eyes, and said mildly, "Listen to the story, Ritchie, then judge for yourself. And since I understand you were a practicing lawyer before you went into Parliament, maybe you can provide part of the story yourself. Would you care to enlighten the company regarding a classic court case of recent years? I'm speaking of the case of *Regina* v. *Stead.*"

Mr. Ritchie's eyes widened a little, and he glanced at me with dawning comprehension. For my part, I was puzzled, for I had no idea what Toby was talking about. After a moment or two Mr. Ritchie said, "It's scarcely a savory subject."

Toby nodded. "Especially for the victims," he said bleakly. "Now will you tell it or shall I?"

Mr. Ritchie shrugged. "Very well." He looked at Mrs. Willard and Clara. "I fear that between them our host and Mr. Kent have forced upon us a situation in which plain terms must be used, and for this I apologize. The court case referred to was a very curious one. Mr. W. T. Stead was the respected editor of a London evening newspaper, *The Pall Mall Gazette.* He was scandalized to learn that certain bawdy houses in London were in the habit of procuring young girls of thirteen for the use of dissolute clients whose—er—base desires tended toward —er—the use of young females."

"To use biblical language," said Toby brusquely, "we're speaking of men who lusted after virgins, the younger the better. And the age of consent was then thirteen. The newspapers referred to the case as the Sale of Virgins trial."

"The gutter press did so," said Mr. Ritchie with a look of disgust.

"The gutter press was exactly right," said Toby. "And let us all remember that the dissolute clients in question were not rough and uneducated men from the sweatshops of the East End; neither were they known libertines. The clients were invariably gentry, apparently respectable men leading apparently blameless lives." He waved a hand. "But please continue, Mr. Ritchie."

I remembered now that Toby had once studied law, which no doubt explained why he was familiar with this particular court case. I was not surprised that he had never mentioned it to me, for once I had told him my story he never referred to any part of it again.

"I don't propose to go into details," Mr. Ritchie was saying, "but in order to expose this shocking practice, W. T. Stead went to the East End and in fact bought a young girl of thirteen, the daughter of a chimney sweep, for the sum of three pounds. The girl was taken to a nursing home and then placed in the care of Mr. and Mrs. Bramwell Booth, who ran a mission in the East End of London and who later founded the Salvation Army. The girl was taken to the Paris headquarters of Mr. and Mrs. Booth, and W. T. Stead began to write articles in his paper to show how easy it was for any man to obtain possession of a young and innocent girl."

It was very quiet in the saloon. Most eyes were on Mr. Ritchie as he spoke, but every now and again I was conscious of a face turning toward me. From the women came looks of shocked pity, though Mrs. Ritchie's expression also contained much of revulsion. Mr. Willard sat grim faced, eyes narrowed as if in pain. Andrew Doyle was still standing, pale with rage, his hands clenching and unclenching. Sir John

Tennant sat with eyes closed, hands resting on his cane, face impassive. Gerald had his back to me, head bowed.

Mr. Ritchie said, "Unfortunately W. T. Stead showed some lack of judgment in the way he carried out his very laudable intention. He was prosecuted on a charge of abduction, was tried at the Old Bailey, and sentenced to only two months imprisonment in recognition that his motives had been impeccable. Probably as a result of this trial, a Criminal Law Amendment Act was passed in 1886, raising the age of consent to sixteen and laying down heavier sentences for what was commonly referred to as the white slavery of young girls." Mr. Ritchie looked at Toby. "Will that suffice, Kent? I take it this young woman was a victim of the practice I have just described?"

"It will suffice admirably," said Toby, "and Hannah was indeed a victim, as you surmise. Probably one of the last, since the Criminal Law Amendment Act came just too late to save her."

Benjamin Willard had been staring at the deck. Now he lifted his head and said, "I understood that Hannah was educated by her widowed mother, a schoolteacher. I cannot believe such a person would sell her child into obscene slavery."

"She did not, sir," Toby replied sharply. Then to me, with an air of frustration, "For God's sake, will you not speak up for yourself, Hannah? It's out of all order for us to be talking about you as if you weren't here."

"No, Toby," I said bluntly. "I made up my mind a long time ago that I would never try to excuse myself or defend myself. You've seen my mother's letter, and you know this is what she would have wanted of me."

Toby sighed and thrust a hand through his hair. Andrew Doyle said in a strained voice, "Please continue, Toby."

"Very well." Toby looked slowly round the room. "Hannah was twelve when her mother died. Kathleen McLeod knew she was dying and didn't wish her daughter to go into an orphanage. No doubt she knew the kind of life an orphanage child would lead. So she left her whole estate, of some thirty pounds, to a Mrs. Taylor, wife of a Smithfield meat porter, with seven small children . . ."

I sat looking through one of the saloon windows at the bank of the Thames as we moved steadily down river, ruefully listening to Toby Kent waste his breath. Nothing he said would make any difference in the end. I found that if I looked at any of the faces in the saloon, except that of Sir John, I would soon find eyes fixed on me with horrified wonderment, but as soon as I met that gaze it was averted, as if the person felt ashamed to be so curious about me.

I could well understand such curiosity. Here in the saloon, with these respectable people, sat a girl of eighteen who looked even younger than her years, well spoken, decently brought up, reasonably educated . . . yet for some four years she had known the embraces not of one man or two but of scores. No doubt the very thought was disgusting to them, man and woman alike, but in the way of human nature it also held for them a thread of macabre fascination.

Toby Kent was saying, ". . . and then one day when Mrs. Taylor was out delivering washing, her husband told Hannah that he had found her a job in service. She was to pack her few belongings, put her hat and coat on, and go with him at once. He took her on a knifeboard bus to what I think must have been Regent's Park. There they met a respectably dressed woman who gave Taylor money, took charge of Hannah, and called a cab to take them to a tall house in a London square. Hannah was never to know the name of that square . . ."

I could relive those first days now without the sweat of terror breaking out on my brow, for I had perforce learned the way of separating my inmost self from such emotions as might destroy me. At first I had felt only bewilderment. The house was much bigger than it first appeared, but it was not a family house. Apart from two or three male servants the household seemed to be made up of fifteen or twenty women. Mrs. Logan, the lady who had given money to Mr. Taylor in the park, was very much in charge.

To my surprise I was given no work to do, but spent an hour or two that evening in the smaller of two drawing rooms with several of the ladies. They were quite kindly toward me, but spoke of things which meant nothing to me in my ignorance. Sometimes one would be called from the room by Mrs. Logan and would disappear either for a little while or for the rest of the evening. I heard music from what I later found was the larger drawing room, and sounds of laughter from both men and women.

That night I slept in a fine bedroom, and next day I was taken out by Mrs. Logan to buy a lot of new clothes. Every now and then I would ask what my duties were, but her answers were too oblique for me to comprehend. For the next two days nothing much happened, but I felt a growing sense of nameless unease. The ladies who lived in Mrs.

Logan's house would sleep for most of the morning. After lunch they would put on rather garish dresses and gather in the drawing rooms until gentleman visitors began to arrive.

On the second day I asked Alice, a girl of about sixteen and the youngest of the ladies, to tell me what was expected of me in this strange household, for I was doing nothing to earn my bed and board. She gave me a rather pitying look and said, "If you don't know, you'll soon find out, lovey."

On the afternoon of the third day Mrs. Logan told me to put on a pretty white dress with lace frills she had bought for me. Before I did so she inspected my hands and face to make sure I was quite clean, and afterward spent some time putting my hair in two plaits to her satisfaction. She left me in my room for ten minutes, then returned and took me down to a small room I had not seen before, rather like a study. Here sat a very well dressed gentleman with a bushy moustache, heavily built and with a florid face. He smiled upon me, asked my name, praised me for my pretty face and dress, then said to Mrs. Logan, "Yes. Very good. Capital."

He picked up his hat, gloves, and cane, smiled at me once more, and told me to my surprise that he looked forward to seeing me again that evening. Then he nodded to Mrs. Logan and departed.

As soon as he had left, Mrs. Logan made me go to my room and take off the white dress, but I had to put it on again later, at about eight o'clock that evening, and only about ten minutes before Mrs. Logan conducted the same gentleman into my bedroom, referring to him as Mr. Smith. I was bewildered, and when she went out leaving the gentleman with me, my misgiving increased.

He was very friendly, taking off his topcoat and talking to me in a jolly fashion, but I was too nervous to respond sensibly. Then he took off his jacket and waistcoat and invited me to sit on his knee, but I answered with growing trepidation that I did not wish to. He laughed and seized me, reaching up under my dress, and it was only then that the things I had learned about men and women from the Taylor children penetrated my innocence, and I understood, albeit in formless fashion, what Mr. Smith intended.

Terror swept me. I broke free from him and ran to the door but found it locked. Banging on it frantically with my palms I screamed for help, not realizing how futile this was, for the whole truth of my plight had still not yet dawned upon me. Mr. Smith became angry. He seized me again, slapped my face, carried me struggling across the room, and threw me onto the bed, clamping a hand over my mouth. It was then that I got his thumb between my teeth and bit him as hard as I could. He gave a bellow of pain and dealt me such a buffet across the head that I was sent flying from the bed to lie stunned on the floor. As if in a nightmare, my head ringing, my sight blurred, I saw him stride across the room and tug on a bellpull beside the curtained window; then he snatched a towel from the washstand and clutched a corner of it about his thumb.

I had not thought to use the bellpull to summon protection, but now Mr Smith had used it himself and I felt almost sick with relief, for in my stupidity I could only think that he had attacked me in this way because he had suddenly gone mad. I lay still, not daring to move for fear of attracting his attention as he poured water into the washbowl and started to clean the blood from his bitten thumb.

It seemed an age later that a key turned in the door and Mrs. Logan entered quickly, followed by one of the male servants, a big man in a dark suit who closed the door behind him. Mr. Smith started shouting at her, displaying his hurt hand, abusing me bitterly and complaining that he had been cheated. I got to my knees, beginning to weep now, and tried to stammer out what had happened. Mrs. Logan gave me a vicious look and snapped, "Shut up, you stupid creature!"

To Mr. Smith she said apologetically, "I'm deeply sorry, sir, but you will understand that young girls who have the attraction of innocence may sometimes prove difficult. You may be sure I shall put the matter right." She glanced at the servant and said, "Very well, Tom." They both advanced on me, and I knew a terror beyond all telling.

I struggled wildly but in vain as Tom threw me on the bed, gathered both my wrists in one big hand, and with the other formed a pincer with his thumb and forefinger to dig brutally into the hinge of my jaw on each side, forcing my mouth open. From a handbag on her arm, Mrs. Logan took a bottle and a dessert spoon. While Tom held me helpless, she poured a dark liquid from the bottle and pushed the whole spoonful into my mouth. I choked and coughed, but could not prevent myself swallowing. Another spoonful followed, then Tom let go of my face but continued to hold me down. He was very strong, with a broad flat face, and did not seem to be at all interested in what he was doing.

Mrs. Logan put away bottle and spoon, and turned from the bed. "She'll soon be asleep, sir," she said to Mr. Smith. "Well, not quite asleep—you wouldn't want that—but near enough, if you understand me. Now I'll fetch my medicine box and see to that thumb of yours, and by then Hannah will be ready for you."

I came back to the present from a memory which no longer had power to touch me. How much of my story Toby had told I did not know, but he could have left little out, for as I began to listen again he was saying, ". . . and so they drugged thirteen-year-old Hannah McLeod in order that 'Mr. Smith' might have his will of her. Since she spared me further details, I'm glad to spare you them also, ladies and gentlemen. Suffice it to say that when she at last came to herself fully again, she was alone in her room, the sun had risen, and she had been violated."

A little moan of pity came from Mrs. Willard. Her husband reached out to put his hand over hers, and for a moment they both glanced at Clara. I could guess what was in their minds, for Clara and I were much of an age. Mrs. Ritchie sat with head bowed. Her husband had his legs stretched out in front of him, hands in pockets, and was frowning at his boots. Andrew Doyle stood gazing blankly out of a window, hands gripping the back of a chair, his knuckles white. Clara had tears on her cheeks. Gerald had turned and now sat with eyes tightly shut, shoulders hunched, his face drawn with revulsion.

"Now here's an interesting thought, gentlemen," said Toby, pacing across the saloon and back. "There's no table in England where Hannah McLeod would be accepted as a guest if the story I've just told were known. But I'll wager Mr. Smith belongs to one or more of the best clubs. White's? The Athenaeum? Boodles'? And he'll no doubt be received in the best of houses, too. He may even have been a guest of yours, Sir John, or of yours, Mr. Ritchie. You could well have welcomed a gentleman of substance who bears just a few little scars around his thumb from the teethmarks of a child."

Mr. Ritchie looked up and said, "There's no occasion to be offensive, Kent."

Toby gave him that smile which was not a smile. "Is the truth offensive, Ritchie? Will you deny you could have entertained the man without knowing his tastes? Will you set hand on heart and tell me that if his tastes *were* known he'd be ostracized by our noble male sex? Oh, by some to be sure, but there are plenty who'd just find his exploits amusing."

Clara said in a controlled voice, speaking directly to me, "How was it that you went from that place to Paris?"

I hesitated, but felt it would be churlish to refuse an answer, and said briefly, "I was insufficiently biddable, Miss Clara. They had to drug me for every occasion, and Mrs. Logan found that quite unsatisfactory. After three weeks I was taken in a semistupor to Dover and delivered to a French lady there. I later assumed that I had been sold by arrangement to Mam'selle Montavon's College for Young Ladies, in Paris, and that was indeed the case."

"But . . . but couldn't you have run away?" Clara asked with a baffled air. "Or told the police?"

I said politely, "Please don't ask me questions which compel me to defend myself, Miss Clara. I will not do it."

Toby Kent said quietly, "You must realize, Miss Clara, that in France such establishments are legal and under police control. What is more, Hannah had no access to the police, and no word of the language. Even with both, I can assure you she would have found no haven if she had run away. Bear in mind that she was only thirteen, but knew herself to have been despoiled. She was a stranger in a strange land, and a child at that. I will tell you what would have happened if she had become a stray in the streets of Paris. Do you know what a *mech* is?"

Clara shook her head, her eyes round and wide.

Toby said, "It is the name given to a young man in Montmartre, an apache, who takes a girl and makes himself her protector. He compels her to walk the streets and give herself to men for money, which he then takes from her. She is his property. He will beat her if she displeases him, and may take a knife to her face if she betrays him. I assure you that a *mech* would quickly have taken possession of Hannah if she had tried to flee the college, and there would have been nothing she could do to save herself. The girls at the Montavon establishment who took her under their wing explained that to her, thank God. It was then she knew that escape was impossible . . . until such time as she had made herself fluent in the language, and was old enough to leave the College for Young Ladies and find work to earn herself a living. A meager living it was, too," he added bleakly.

Without lifting her head, Mrs. Ritchie said with a shudder, "I would rather have died than submit."

"Oh, she had that option, Mrs. Ritchie," Toby said coolly. "The

Seine was always there at hand. But as you see, Hannah McLeod decided to live, and for myself I think that was the braver choice."

"But the shame," said Mrs. Ritchie in a low voice. "Oh, the unbearable shame . . ."

I said, "I'm not in the least ashamed of what was done to me, madam. I think that is something for other people to be ashamed of."

I heard Andrew Doyle say in a husky whisper, "Yes. Yes, by God." When I looked at him, I saw that he had turned round now but stood with the same strange rigidity as before. Gerald had not moved, but sat with face strangely puckered and feverish red patches showing on his cheeks.

Benjamin Willard said quietly, "I would like to be clear on what occurred in Paris. You spent the next four years at this . . . this college?"

"Yes, sir," I replied. "In a way I was fortunate, for Mam'selle Montavon was not another Mrs. Logan. She ran an establishment of some distinction, where we were expected to behave in most ladylike fashion with visitors. We used to have musical evenings and drawing room entertainments for our guests, in fact the whole notion of our being young lady students was maintained, except in our private rooms."

"You appear to remember this bawdy house proprietor with some affection," Mr. Ritchie said dryly.

"She was very considerate of my age and inexperience when I first became a student, sir," I replied. "I knew I had no choice but to endure several years at the college before I could achieve independence, but at least she saw to it that the other girls tutored me gently in what I would have to do. Soon after I was put to work, I managed to make clear to mam'selle that I would become very troublesome if I were expected to accommodate men with unusual inclinations, and she accepted this."

"Unusual inclinations?" Clara said wonderingly. "What do you mean?"

I shook my head. "You need never know, Miss Clara. Please don't pursue the question."

"But—"

Her father broke in sharply. "Leave it, Clara. Hannah is right." Then to me, with a look of mingled pity and sorrow, "So you led this life as a . . . student at the Montavon establishment, for four years?"

"Yes, sir." I could see a dozen questions in his eyes as he studied me, and I could have recited them myself, for they were the questions men so often asked in the privacy of the bedroom. Mr. Willard did not ask them. Instead he said gently, "Weren't you desperately unhappy throughout all that time?"

"Not exactly, sir." I hesitated for a moment, trying to put my thoughts into words. "At first I was terrified, then only frightened, but in time this passed, and I simply abhorred the ugliness of having to pretend, of having to act a part. But I knew the pattern of my life was inevitable, and I learned to . . . to separate myself from it in some way. I was taught by my mother that self-pity is a destroyer, so I was helped by not feeling sorry for myself. I could always think how much better my life was than it would have been if Mrs. Logan hadn't sold me."

I heard something like a sob break from Gerald, but when I turned my head I found no pity in his blotched face, only a wild anger that distorted his mouth and brought beads of sweat to his brow. I felt sorry for him, but mentally shrugged my shoulders. This shocking revelation was his father's work, and there was no way that I could shelter the boy from its impact.

Mr. Ritchie said incredulously, "Your life was better than it might have been? Are you serious?"

I looked at him and said, "Yes, sir. Mrs. Logan's house was an evil place. At the college I was decently treated. I would have only three or four duties a week, and for those I learned to become another person, not myself. I made friends with other students, and for the rest of the time I could be myself and live quite a pleasant life. But I always lived for the day when I could turn my back on that life forever, and be myself all the time."

Benjamin Willard said, "And this you achieved four years later, when you were seventeen? You were permitted to leave?"

"Yes, sir. Mam'selle and my friends thought I was foolish to go, but I was quite free to do so. By this time I was fluent in the language and no longer a child, so I could find work and keep myself."

"Hannah doesn't tell you that finding work at that time was harder than finding a four-leaf clover," said Toby, frowning at me. "Or that the best she could get was twelve hours a day serving in a Montmartre restaurant for three francs. Try living on that for a while if you've a fancy for an interesting experience, ladies. Oh, and of course the *mechs* tried to get her and she had to deal with them. When she saved your bacon that night, Andrew, did you think it the first time she'd given an apache a taste of her hatpin? Not by a long chalk."

Andrew Doyle muttered, "Oh, dear God," and closed his eyes as if in pain.

Mr. Ritchie said slowly, "You're most eloquent in defending this young woman, Kent—"

"I've not been defending her," Toby broke in sharply. "I've done no more than tell you what happened to her from the time she was thirteen. It's not Hannah McLeod who needs defending."

"But your account may be colored by bias," said Mr Ritchie. "You haven't declared an interest in the matter, but perhaps you should have done."

"I'm not sure I take your meaning," said Toby. He spoke very slowly, and I caught a malevolent gleam in his eye.

"You lived as neighbors in Paris," Mr. Ritchie said tersely. "I'm suggesting that this young woman was probably more than a neighbor to you."

Toby drew in a sharp breath as anger seized him, and his big shoulders seemed to grow broader before my eyes. I recalled his threat to Sebastian Ryder, and his way of showing displeasure by banging heads against walls, and I said quickly, "Stand still, Toby! Don't you *dare!*"

To my relief he obeyed, glaring. I looked at Mr. Ritchie and said, "I will answer your question, sir. I left the college to become my own woman and to be free of men. I have never given myself to a man of my own desire, and now, because I have long been despoiled and am what might be termed damaged goods, I can never marry, for no man would have me. Toby Kent is my friend, no more. Many would regard him as bohemian, but I tell you I have had greater consideration from him than from any other man."

As I stopped speaking, Gerald suddenly got to his feet and ran out of the saloon, slamming the door behind him. Mr. Ritchie took out a diary and began to flick through the pages, as if to show that he had now withdrawn from the whole matter. His wife sat staring into space with an expression I could not interpret. Sir John Tennant had not stirred but his eyes were open now, watching me, cold and reptilian. He was a man I could easily fear, and I marveled that he could have fathered a daughter so unlike him as Mrs. Ritchie. Across the saloon from where I sat, Clara and her mother seemed stricken with grief.

Andrew Doyle, still standing, had a dazed and uncomprehending look. Benjamin Willard sat shaking his head slowly, sorrowfully.

I began to think about my future. Sebastian Ryder had exposed my shocking past, but he did not appear to have done so for the purpose of getting rid of me. What his true purpose was I had no idea, but now I asked myself if that purpose had been served, and if he might now dismiss me. I very much hoped not. I felt sure I would be able to find work and keep myself, but my circumstances would be considerably poorer than those I enjoyed now.

Benjamin Willard cleared his throat and said reluctantly to the company in general, "With all the sympathy in the world, with all the good will in the world, there's no way to make things right for Hannah. Nothing can be undone. What happened to her . . . *has* happened."

I looked at him and said, "Yes, Mr. Willard, I don't deceive myself in that respect, and I know I shall always be regarded as beyond the pale by people who know the truth about me. You and your family have been very kind to me, but after today I'm sure we shan't meet again and I understand why. If I think of the evil brute who sold me, or of Mrs. Logan who bought me, or of the beast who then despoiled me, I still feel an undying hatred in my heart. But I try hard to feel no bitterness toward those who are scandalized by me now. This isn't because I have a forgiving nature, but quite simply a way of protecting myself. My mother taught me that bitterness is as much a destroyer as self-pity."

"Your mother must have been a very remarkable lady," Benjamin Willard said in a low voice. For a moment there was sudden alertness in Sir John Tennant's eyes, then it was gone, and his face was as expressionless as before. I wondered how Benjamin Willard's words could have touched any chord in the man, but my attention was caught by Andrew Doyle, who had moved across and was now standing in front of me, extending his hand to me. I thought he intended to shake my hand in polite farewell, but to my surprise he took it, bowed over it, and raised it to his lips. There was still pallor in his face, and he was in such a turmoil of emotion that his whole body seemed to be trembling, but his voice was steady when he spoke.

"For me, you will never be beyond the pale, Hannah," he said. Still holding my hand, he straightened up and turned toward his family. "Aunt Melanie, Uncle Benjamin, Clara . . . I ask nothing of you, but I unashamedly declare myself to be a friend of Hannah McLeod. You say that what happened to her cannot be changed, but I say it *has* been changed, transformed by her courage and fortitude."

Poor Mr. Doyle. His declaration had been so dramatic and well meant, I did not have the heart to say he was wrong. He turned to me and continued with equal fervor: "Your employer, Sebastian Ryder, disgusts me by what he has done today. To you I say this, Hannah. I will give you my address here, and in America, and in Mexico. Whatever help you may need, now or in the future, please ask it of me. You understand?"

I drew my hand gently from his grasp, remembering a time when another Mexican gentleman had said much the same words to me one early dawn, as he lay with his head on my shoulder, and later had given me a silver ring in token of his promise. "Thank you, Mr. Doyle," I said. "You're very kind. Now if you will excuse me, I must go and speak to Mr. Ryder."

As I walked to the saloon door, I saw that the boat was passing under Chelsea Bridge, and knew that we would soon reach Westminster pier. Toby opened the door for me and said, "No need to speak to him, me beauty. You can come home with me and I'll find lodgings for you somewhere nearby till you've decided what you want to do next."

I shook my head. "I don't yet know if I shall need to find a new position, Toby. I haven't been dismissed yet. That's what I want to ask Mr. Ryder now."

He stared down at me in amazement. "You surely won't stay on in the fellow's service after what he did to you this afternoon?"

"He told his guests that I had once been *une fille de joie,* Toby, and that's nothing but the truth. I think it was in poor taste to treat his guests so, but I can't complain myself. I doubt that he will want me to stay, because people will be scandalized when they hear about this—"

I was interrupted by Sir John Tennant's deep, harsh voice. "This episode will not be spoken of by me, or my daughter or her husband," he growled. "I hope the same can be said for Mr. Willard and his family."

"You may be sure of that, sir," said Benjamin Willard grimly. "We shall not forget the debt we owe to Hannah McLeod. I suspect Sebastian Ryder is aware that he counts on our silence."

Toby Kent said impatiently, "But for God's sake, Hannah, you surely don't want to continue under his roof? It's humiliating!"

I patted his arm. "Oh, Toby. How can anyone like me be humiliated? I've been through the very depths of it, and I'm beyond it now. Don't worry so."

The tension went suddenly out of him, and he grinned. "You'll come and sit for me again soon, young McLeod?"

"Yes, all right. If I can."

"Ryder won't forbid you; I'll see to that."

"You'll behave yourself, Toby, or I shall be very cross."

I went out onto the deck. Gerald must have taken himself off aft, for there was no sign of him. Sebastian Ryder sat alone at the table, smoking a cigar. As I moved toward him he said, "If you've come to complain or give notice, save your breath. You're bound by agreement to remain in my employ for two years."

I had forgotten that. Halting a little way from him I said, "I only wished to ask if you intend to dismiss me, sir."

He waved the hand holding the cigar. "No. Why the devil should I?"

"Because of my past, Mr. Ryder."

"I knew about that when I took you on."

"But others didn't. Now your guests know, and Master Gerald knows. He's bound to tell Miss Jane."

"It won't go any further than that," Sebastian Ryder said casually.

"Your children may find it distasteful to have me continue as their tutor, sir."

"Jane has too much sense. Gerald can put up with it." Sebastian Ryder looked at me hard. "You're legally bound to remain in my employ."

"I wasn't intending to ask to be released, sir. May I ask a question?"

"Go ahead."

"Do you intend to recount my past life to other guests on future occasions?"

He almost smiled, and knocked ash from his cigar. "No. This was a special occasion. Is that all?"

"I'm afraid there may be some difficulty with Master Gerald, sir."

"Then deal with it," he said brusquely. "Damn it, you're experienced, aren't you? Must know how to handle a boy like that, even without the help of a bed."

I said, "If you speak coarsely to me again, Mr. Ryder, I shall leave your employ regardless of any agreement."

He glared for a moment, then gave a sudden hard grin and nodded. "Fair enough, Hannah. It won't happen again. Satisfied?"

"Yes, thank you, sir"

"That's all then."

I moved to the rail and stood there for five minutes, watching as the boat slid under Westminster Bridge to reach the pier. The gangway went down. Sebastian Ryder stood by it. His guests emerged from the saloon. Benjamin Willard and Andrew Doyle shepherded Mrs. Willard and Clara to the gangway. All four moved past Sebastian Ryder without acknowledging his presence. Mr and Mrs. Ritchie followed. Sir John paused for a moment and spoke briefly, but I did not hear what he said.

Toby Kent appeared. He also paused at the gangway, and his words were very clear. "While she and I are both in London, I'll be wishing Hannah to visit me occasionally, Ryder. You'll be wise not to forbid her."

Sebastian Ryder said ominously, "Are you threatening me, Kent?"

Toby grinned. "Of course I am, you stupid fellow. I served a few years in the French Foreign Legion, and I'd not in the least mind a month or two in a comparatively comfortable prison for the pleasure of breaking your jaw, so why not be sensible?" He raised his hat to me, walked past Sebastian Ryder, and ran up the steps to the Victoria Embankment, where two or three hansom cabs stood waiting hopefully for customers.

My employer seemed not in the least put out. "Your friend has a persuasive way with him," he said thoughtfully, then lifted his voice. "Gerald! Gerald! Where the devil are you, boy? Come along, we're going home."

Eleven

Gerald did not speak as we drove home in the carriage, and did not once look at me. His father sat gazing out of the window with an air of being well content. It was half past four when we reached the house, and I went straight to my room to take a bath. Despite my efforts to show a calm face, the afternoon had been quite an ordeal for me and I was glad to lie down and rest for half an hour before putting on fresh clothes.

I was lying on the bed in my dressing gown, wondering what it was that Sir John Tennant was coming to discuss with Sebastian Ryder at half past nine this evening, and how it could in some way be connected with the events of the afternoon, when there came a tap on the door. I called, "Come in," thinking it would be one of the servants, or perhaps Mattie come to ask how we had enjoyed the day, but it was Jane who entered.

Her expression was very strange, a blend of shock and curiosity, and her manner was more diffident than I had ever seen in her as she said, "May I speak with you for a minute, Hannah?"

I guessed Gerald had already told her everything, but this was no more than I expected. He was too young and too emotional to have kept such a thing to himself. I rose from the bed and said, "Of course, Miss Jane. Won't you sit down?"

"No. No, it's all right. I won't be long." She paused awkwardly, frowning. "I just want to say . . . well, Gerald has told me about what happened on the boat this afternoon. I think it was very cruel of Papa, and I shall tell him so. I also think my brother Gerald is a fool to be so upset. I expect it's because he believes he's in love with you—anyone can see that. But he's very stupid. He can't seem to grasp that you had no choice in anything that happened. He's supposed to be so musical and sensitive, and I'm not, yet I can imagine just a little what it must have been like for you, and he can't. He just blames you."

I said, "Yes, I know, Miss Jane. I'm sorry about that, but he's a young boy and it's very natural. I'm sure he'll get over it. Your father insists that I remain here to carry on as before."

"I'm glad he does," Jane said bluntly. "All I came to say is . . . I'm sorry about the dreadful things that happened to you, Hannah, and I'm sorry Papa told about them. But I'm glad Gerald told me."

"Thank you very much, Miss Jane. I'm a little worried about what Mattie will think if she's told. I'm afraid she'll be greatly upset."

"Mattie won't be told," said Jane with a shake of her head. "Papa is up to something, I know that, but he won't want Mattie to be upset—neither do I—and Gerald would be much too embarrassed to say anything to her."

"That's a big relief, Miss Jane. I'm glad you're not too greatly shocked."

"Oh, I'm terribly shocked, but not at you, Hannah. Men can be pretty beastly, can't they?"

"Some can, I'm afraid."

"I'd be grateful if one day you would . . . explain some things I don't know. I hate to be ignorant."

I was taken aback for a moment, and said, "Oh, dear. I understand how you feel, but I'm not the right person, Miss Jane."

"I think you're just the right person," she said in her matter-of-fact way. "I have no mother and Mattie isn't any help. Oh, I know you're very correct in all you do, so you would want Papa's permission, wouldn't you? All right, I'll ask him."

For the first time since I had known her, Jane gave me a friendly smile. "I'll see you at dinner," she said, and went out leaving me scarcely knowing whether to feel pleased, perplexed, uneasy, or a little of each. I realized now that my greatest concern had been that Mattie might feel badly toward me, and I was thankful to know that nothing of what had been revealed about me would come to her ears. Jane had assured me of that, and I knew her to be reliable.

I put on fresh clothes, tidied my hair, and found Mattie in her room, eager to hear about the day's outing. It was easy enough for me to dwell on the sights of the river and Kew Gardens, with no mention of the hour of drama following luncheon.

In the drawing room before dinner, and later at table, Gerald spoke scarcely a word, and never once looked at me. Mattie became quite concerned. "My goodness, it's not like you to just pick at your food, Master Gerald," she said. "You've not got a temperature, have you? We don't want you sickening for something."

"Don't fuss, Mattie," said Sebastian Ryder, his voice more amiable than usual. "If the boy's sickening for something it'll come out, and if he's not it won't. What have you been doing with yourself today, Jane?"

"Thinking," said Jane. "Well, reading and thinking. I read the morning newspapers, then I called at the public library and went for a walk in the park to think."

"What about?"

"The best place for you to build a new factory, Papa."

Her father smiled. "And what did you decide?"

"Nothing yet. There's a lot to consider because all sorts of changes are happening. I believe you would do best to wait and see whether the Liberals get in at the general election next month."

"I had the same notion."

After dinner I sat with Mattie and Jane in the drawing room while Gerald took himself off to the music room. Later, as I went upstairs to fetch a book from my room, I heard him playing a wild, thunderous piece of music. I wondered whether to go and join him, as I often did, but decided it was better to let him find his own way of getting the shock and anger out of his system.

At a few minutes before half past nine we heard the sound of the doorbell. Jane looked up from a ledger she was writing in and said, "Who on earth can that be?"

"I think it must be Sir John Tennant," I said. "Your Papa made an appointment for him to call at this hour."

"Sir John Tennant?" Jane echoed, and looked at Mattie. "It's really very odd."

"None of our business, Miss Jane," said Mattie.

"Oh, fiddle-de-dee. Why shouldn't I be curious? You know how Papa hates that man, so to invite him on a river trip this afternoon and then to the house this evening means Papa must definitely be up to something. He usually tells me what he has in mind, but not this time." Jane looked at me. "Have you any notion, Hannah?"

"None at all, Miss Jane."

"Oh, well." Jane returned to her private bookkeeping.

After a quarter of an hour I excused myself to go to bed. I was passing through the hall when the door of Sebastian Ryder's study opened. Sir John Tennant stumped out, clutching his cane as if longing to strike with it, his mouth drawn down in a grimly furious expression. Sebastian Ryder followed, saying, "Allow me to see you out myself, Sir John." He was almost grinning as he spoke, perhaps not with amusement but with hard satisfaction. Sir John made no answer but walked on, then paused for a moment as he saw me across the hall. His eyes dwelt on me for a long second, and in them I seemed to see a hatred so venomous that it chilled me with its intensity. Next moment he looked away and was moving on.

I went to my room and prepared for bed, brushing out my hair and tying it back with a piece of ribbon, cleaning my teeth, putting on a nightdress and dressing gown. My head was busy with the events of the day, and I knew I would not easily sleep yet, so I sat at the small side table and spent half an hour with paper and textbook preparing the next day's French lessons for my pupils.

Soon I heard Mattie's door open and close as she went to her room. I became engrossed in a French play I was rereading to see if it might be suitable for study, *Le Misanthrope* by Molière, and it was almost eleven o'clock when at last I closed the book and moved to my bed, taking off my dressing gown. I had my back to the door, but heard it creak slightly as it opened. Turning quickly, I was startled to see Gerald enter. He had taken off his jacket and tie, but was otherwise dressed. His face was pale and stiff, his eyes wide as he closed the door behind him, staring at me.

I pulled on my dressing gown again and went toward him, thinking for a moment that he had been taken ill. "What is it, Master Gerald? Are you unwell? I'll go and call Mattie—"

As I spoke I reached up to feel if his brow was hot with fever, but he brushed my hand aside and stalked past me. "Master Gerald!" I said in a startled whisper. "What on earth are you doing? You shouldn't be here!"

"Why not?" His voice cracked as he spoke, and I realized that he was close to tears. He raised one clenched hand and opened it. On the palm lay a golden sovereign. "You . . . you do things with men for money, don't you?" he said in a trembling voice. "Well, go on, show me." He threw the sovereign on the bed. "Or isn't that enough?"

Slowly I tied the belt of my dressing gown, thinking how stupid I had been not to realize what he was about from the moment he entered my room. Because he thought he was in love with me, in love with a girl he could idolize as young men will, the revelations of that afternoon had driven shards of bitterness and outrage into his very soul. Combined with this dreadful unmasking of me, and in spite of it, he was beset by the inevitable curiosity and natural desires of an eighteen-year-old boy.

I should have known, I told myself angrily. In Paris, especially during the university vacations, it was common for a well-to-do man to bring a son of suitable age to the College for Young Ladies so that he might be initiated into the mysteries of women. These boys usually pretended to be cool and worldly in order to hide their apprehension, but in fact they were always very nervous, and Mam'selle Montavon found in the course of time that the English girl who had come to be known as *la professeuse* was more popular than any other with these inexperienced visitors. This was after I had been many months at the college, and had long learned to accept the inevitability of my situation. I suppose I felt a kind of sympathy for the apprehensive young fledglings presented to me by Mam'selle Montavon and I came to think of them as boys even though I was younger than they were. I would always try to put a nervous boy at ease and help him, so perhaps it was not surprising that *la professeuse* became highly recommended by word of mouth for this class of duty.

In a way it would have cost me nothing to transform Gerald's troubled hatred into wild infatuation, for he was so impressionable, and I would only have been exercising a proficiency I had perforce acquired over several years. But in another way it would have cost me everything, for it would have meant defeat in the battle I had fought and won to put those years behind me forever.

I braced myself for what I had to do, staring first at the sovereign on the bed, then at Gerald, screwing up my eyes in a glare of anger. Suddenly I swung my arm hard to hit him across the cheek with my open palm. His eyes grew huge with shock, and his jaw dropped.

"How dare you!" I said fiercely. "What have I ever done to deserve such an insult from you, Master Gerald? Yes, I was at the Montavon college in Paris, but you know how that came about. You know I have a heritage of shadows, long dark shadows thrown by my past. They are not of my making, yet I must walk in those shadows all my life. Would you be glad if I had taken the only alternative and thrown myself in the river? Do you wish I was dead? Is that it?"

"No . . . I—no . . ." He was completely confused, and I gave him no chance to gather his wits.

"You heard the whole horrible story," I went on in the same low but angry voice, "yet you condemn me. Your sister Jane has heard only what you chose to tell her, yet she came to give me her sympathy while you—you come to hurt me as cruelly as you can. Or perhaps you meant what you said? Perhaps you're no better than the men who despoiled me, is that it? Are you really offering me money to lie with you, Master Gerald? Oh, you should be *ashamed!*"

He stood very still, a dazed look in his eyes, hands pressed to the sides of his head, lips moving as if trying to speak. The mark of my hand stood out sharply on his white face. At last he managed to utter words, though in such a whisper they were barely audible. "I'm sorry . . . forgive me, Hannah . . . must have been out of my mind . . . oh God . . . such a fool."

I let my expression soften and said gently, "It's been a difficult day for us all, Master Gerald, but can we try to make the least possible fuss about it?" I picked up the sovereign from the bed, put it in his limp hand, and folded his fingers over it. "Would you be happy for me to forget that you came to my room tonight?"

"Oh yes, please, Hannah, please." He was shaking now. "I don't know what . . ."

"It's forgotten," I said, and turned toward the door. "In return, will you try to think of me the way you thought of Hannah McLeod before what happened today?"

"Yes. Oh, Hannah, I didn't mean it when I said I hated you—"

I stopped him by putting a finger to my lips as I opened the door, then said in a whisper, "We won't remember any of it, and we won't speak of it anymore. Goodnight, Master Gerald. Please try to be at peace with yourself." He showed sudden alarm, as if realizing what would be thought if any of the family or servants saw him leaving my room, then he tiptoed out, mouthing and gesturing apologies. I closed the door and leaned against it, letting out a long sigh of relief.

I thought I might lie awake that night, but in fact I slept soundly. Next day Gerald was rather shy and subdued, but otherwise behaved as usual toward me. After another three or four days I sensed with regret that his old calf love for me had if anything become stronger, probably because on reflection he began to see me as something of a heroine for having endured the ordeal of my life at the college.

A week later Andrew Doyle called and sent in his card. Mattie received him to take tea with us, though Sebastian Ryder did not attend, and with Jane and Gerald we chatted in the drawing room for an hour. Before leaving, Andrew Doyle invited us to accompany him to an exhibition of Mexican paintings at one of the London galleries the following week, and we were happy to accept.

Later, when our visitor had left and I was alone with Jane in the sewing room, she said thoughtfully, "Did you notice how Mr. Doyle looks at you, Hannah?"

I was surprised, and shook my head. "I didn't notice anything unusual."

"Perhaps he only looks at you in that way when you're not looking at him, but it's very marked. At first I thought he paid the call to show that he doesn't think any the less of you because of what happened in Paris, but I think it's more than that." She looked up from her embroidery. "I wonder if he's in love with you?"

She did not giggle as she spoke. The words came out in her usual businesslike way, and although they startled me I did not at once reject the notion, for I had a healthy respect for Jane Ryder's perception. "I suppose it's possible that he thinks he is," I said at last and with much reluctance. "It isn't something I've been aware of, but I have very little idea how men behave when they have courtship in mind. Oh dear, I do hope you're wrong, Miss Jane."

She gave one of her brief smiles. "Yes. It's bad enough for you having Gerald making sheep's eyes. Whatever will you do if Mr. Doyle wants to start calling on you seriously?"

I put a finishing stitch in the hem of my riding habit where it had started to come loose. "Gentlemen don't pay calls on servants, not even on tutors."

"He paid a call on you this afternoon."

"Officially he was paying a call on the family."

"Officially." She sniffed. "He came to see you, Hannah. I could almost be envious, I think. You're not plain, but at the same time you're not beautiful or even pretty, any more than I am."

I looked up and laughed. "No, I'm not. That's true."

"All the same, I think Andrew Doyle might be serious about you. He's very romantic, I can see that, and Papa told me he's something of a rebel."

I said, "Even so, he'll never think of me in the way you suggest. He's a man, so naturally he may be a little intrigued by me because of my past, but that same past means no respectable gentleman can ever consider me seriously. Not even a romantic and rebellious gentleman."

"I suppose not," said Jane, "but it seems a shame. Do you mind very much?"

"Oh no. Not at all, really. It's something I accepted too long ago for me to mind about it now."

Sorting through her embroidery silks she said, "I spoke to Papa about whether I could ask you questions and he said yes, he had great confidence in your sense of propriety."

"Well . . . that's very flattering."

"It certainly is, coming from Papa. Perhaps we could begin now. It won't embarrass you, will it?"

I smiled and picked up a blouse with a loose button. "No, Miss Jane. It won't embarrass me."

On the same day that Andrew Doyle called, I received a letter from Toby Kent asking me to visit him again as before. I was rather uneasy about asking Sebastian Ryder's permission after the way Toby had threatened him, but when I went to his study with my request he said impatiently, "You can do what you like outside your duties, and anyway I've no quarrel with Kent. Tell him I said so."

Toby laughed when I reported this, but made no comment about the happenings on the day of the river trip. He seemed to take the same view as I did myself, that it was past and done with, and there was no point in going over it all again. He had completed my portrait, and I could not hide my surprise when I studied it. "Oh, Toby, you've made me look . . . . what is it exactly? Something about the eyes, and not just the smile. Yes, you've made me look quite dignified."

He scratched his jaw. "I'm glad you see it."

"But I'm not a bit dignified."

"Maybe that's the wrong word. You have your own dignity, young McLeod, and there it is. Just another facet of you I wanted for that painting. Don't argue. You've never seen yourself as you are. Few of us ever do."

There were several more paintings, two or three of the Thames at different places, another of two urchins using a drinking fountain at one end of a water trough while a horse drank from the trough, three still-life paintings, a portrait of a chimney sweep, and a large canvas of Piccadilly Circus, painted as if looking down upon it from a tall building, full of cabs, carts, and the small figures of pedestrians.

On Toby's easel was another large canvas, unfinished, but showing a circus tent and a funfair, with a great horde of tiny figures, circus folk and customers alike. I said, "This and the Piccadilly scene are quite different from your others, Toby, but I like them very much."

"To be honest I'm not too disappointed myself," he acknowledged. "I've no wish to get into a rut."

"A circus must be very exciting," I said, gazing at a white-faced clown on a donkey, and wondering how Toby had managed to convey so much in a space no larger than a shilling.

"Have you never been to a circus?" he asked, surprised.

"No. I'd love to go one day."

"You'll go this very day," he said cheerfully, and took out his watch. "It's only at Clapham Common, and there's a performance starting in a couple of hours, so we'll have time to enjoy the sideshows first." As he spoke he was moving into the bedroom, putting on a jacket as he returned, then catching up the straw hat I had just taken off and laid on a chair. "Here, get your hat on, me beauty, and we'll be off."

I said rather breathlessly, "But I thought you wanted me to sit for you."

"I do, but that will have to wait. Since today is your birthday, you shall have a birthday treat."

I looked at him in astonishment. "How did you know that? I haven't told a soul."

He grinned. "You once showed me the contents of your little tin box, and I remember the date on your birth certificate, so many happy returns of the day. Now hurry yourself, Hannah McLeod, or I'll take some other girl."

Five minutes later we were in a cab rattling south over the Albert Bridge, and I could feel myself bubbling with excitement. "Toby, you must let me share the expense," I said. "I shall be very happy to, and I can afford it because I'm really quite well paid."

"Fine," he said. "I'll take it out of the sitter's money I owe you."

"I don't want sitter's money; you know that."

"It's your birthday, isn't it?"

"Yes."

"Then just shut up, you daft girl."

"All right. And thank you. Are your paintings still selling, Toby?"

"Like hotcakes, so I'm told. Here and in Paris, too."

"Then why are you scowling?"

"I'm not scowling; I'm frowning in a judicial kind of way."

"Why?"

"Because I think maybe the pictures are bought mostly by people who don't know good from bad, but who know that Toby Kent is a fashionable fellow of the moment in the art world."

"I see." I thought for a moment. "But you paint every picture to the very best of your ability, don't you?"

"To be sure, I do."

"Well, that's all you ever wanted to do, isn't it? In Paris, before you sold any, you never thought about who might buy them or why, so what does it matter now? I expect the fashionable attraction will pass, and then only people who really want your pictures will buy them."

Toby leaned his head back and closed his eyes. After a few moments he said, "I'm greatly obliged to you, Hannah McLeod. Can you remember how you looked when you said that?"

"You mean just now? No, of course I can't. What are you talking about?"

He opened one eye. "A look. Another facet of you, me beauty. A kind of wisdom. Never mind. I'm storing it in my memory." He closed the eye. "I have to go to Paris soon. Crespin wants to arrange another exhibition there, and he also wants to show me off in one or two other European capitals, so I'll be away for a few weeks. Would you like to come for a bit of a holiday?"

"To Paris? Toby, how can I? It's quite impossible."

"I mean just for a week, perhaps. You could come back on your own.

Surely old Ryder owes you a holiday? Oh, I don't have to tell you this isn't an improper suggestion."

"I know that, stupid, but it's out of the question anyway. Mr. Ryder would never agree."

"Ah, well. Let's enjoy today."

That afternoon was one of the happiest times of my life. We tried all the sideshows, played hoopla, rode on the switchback and roundabout, bought pies and sticky buns to eat, drank sherbet from a stall at one halfpenny a glass, and at last went into the great tent for the performance. I was enchanted by the liberty horses, astonished by the lion tamer, terrified for the trapezists, and laughed myself into tears at the antics of the clowns. In those few hours I stored memories which were soon to stand me in good stead, for I truly believe that if I had not been able to relive them again and again as a way of blotting out the ordeal that awaited me, I might easily have lost my mind.

It was half past six by the time we returned to Toby's studio. There he made me free of his bedroom to wash and tidy myself. This took me only five minutes, but when I entered the studio again Toby had set a drawing board on the easel with a big piece of cartridge paper pinned to it and was studying a charcoal sketch he had made with a few bold lines. There was my face, but without the same expression as in the portrait he had painted. The eyes were different, rather grave and quiet, I thought.

Toby threw the charcoal aside and said with satisfaction, "Got you. That's how you looked in the cab. All right, young McLeod, I'll take you home now."

Three days later I had a hastily scribbled note from him to say he was leaving for Paris that evening and would write to me again on his return. The following week Mr. Andrew Doyle paid us another call, and made a point of saying that Mr. and Mrs. Willard and Clara had asked him to convey their good wishes to me.

That evening Jane told me she felt sure he was in love with me. I had not noticed him looking at me in any special way myself, but I remembered uneasily that Toby Kent, on my first visit to his studio, had said blithely that Andrew Doyle was besotted with me.

I had another cause for unease at this time. On three occasions Sir John Tennant had called by appointment to see Sebastian Ryder. Twice I happened to catch sight of him, and he did not look like a man paying a visit by choice. I had the impression that he had been summoned by Mr. Ryder, and had come against his will. I also felt that whatever the reason for this, I was indirectly linked with it in some strange way.

A few days after Andrew Doyle's visit I found myself with no duties for the afternoon. Gerald had gone to his London music teacher, Jane was out riding, and Mattie had kept to her bed with a cold. It was a warm and pleasant day, and after making sure Mattie had everything she needed, I decided to walk to Regent's Park, where the band of the Coldstream Guards was to play that afternoon.

It was not a long walk, and soon I was sitting in one of the deck chairs set out in rows before the bandstand while the bandsmen began to tune their instruments. I had been there only a minute when I was aware that a lady had taken the chair beside me, and a moment later a voice said quietly, "Miss McLeod."

I turned, and was surprised to see Mrs. Hesketh, quietly but elegantly dressed in a gray two-piece dress trimmed with lace, and a matching velvet bonnet with ostrich feathers. My first thought was that she seemed subdued compared with the very forceful and confident lady who had met me when I arrived in London with Mr. Boniface, and who had taken me first to her office and home in Chancery Lane, then to the Army and Navy stores for shopping. My second thought was to recall Toby Kent telling me of his encounter with her, and his taking her out to dinner.

I remembered Mrs. Hesketh with affection, and my pleasure was genuine as I said, "Oh, how nice to see you again, Mrs. Hesketh. What an odd thing for us to meet here in the park. Are you well? And Mr. Boniface, too?"

"Boniface is in disgrace with me," she said, her eyes suddenly flashing with indignation, "and he is at present in Hull, lurking in great discomfort I hope, as he keeps watch on a gentleman whose wife has engaged our services. But that is neither here nor there. I wish to speak with you at some length and on a very serious matter, my dear. Will you spare me an hour for what I have to tell you and show you?"

I said in bewilderment, "You mean now? This afternoon?"

"If you please," she said anxiously. "I have recently uncovered matters I feel should be made known to you." When I hesitated, scarcely knowing what to say, she went on. "It is not by accident we have just met, Hannah. For the past three mornings I have sat in a cab near the Ryder house, hoping for a chance to speak with you alone."

I realized then that she must have followed me in the cab to Regent's Park before speaking to me, and I said reluctantly, "Mrs. Hesketh, I don't want to find myself caught up in anything troublesome or complicated."

"I fear that is already the case, child. Believe me, I am not acting for my own benefit, but simply because I feel you should know the truth."

"The truth?" I said wonderingly.

"About yourself. If you will ride home with me, we can talk in privacy. I beg you to trust me and to believe I have your interests at heart."

She met my gaze steadily, and after a moment or two I said, "Yes, I trust you, Mrs. Hesketh, and I have this afternoon free."

We moved away together just before the band began to play. A hansom stood waiting on Broad Walk, and as soon as we were seated in it, Mrs. Hesketh made sure the trap in the roof was closed so that the driver could not hear us; then she began to speak in a quiet voice.

"I have always tried to maintain certain standards in the work undertaken by the Hesketh Agency," she said, and her voice shook a little as if from distress. "It was just over a week ago that I was clearing out some old files when I came across a recent one which should not have been in the cabinet where I found it. This was a file which concerned you, Hannah, but I knew nothing of it because that deceitful man Boniface had kept it hidden from me."

I said, "But surely you knew all about me? You met us when Mr. Boniface brought me here from Paris."

"I knew that Mr. Sebastian Ryder wanted you in his service," she replied slowly. "I knew where you had come from, and I knew how Boniface had tricked you when you at first refused. No doubt your friend Toby Kent has enlightened you on that matter?"

"Yes. He told me."

Mrs. Hesketh smiled mistily and gave a little sigh. "A splendid gentleman, Mr. Kent," she murmured. "I greatly enjoyed meeting him." She was silent for a moment, then seemed to come back to the present with a little start, and went on briskly, "I should like you to know that I did not approve of the trick Boniface played upon you, and I told him so."

"It doesn't matter anyway," I said. "Everything worked out amazingly well for me, Mrs. Hesketh. But I don't understand why Mr.

Boniface hid this file among some old ones when there was nothing in it that you didn't already know."

Mrs. Hesketh put her hand on mine for a moment. "There was much that I didn't know, my dear," she said, "and much that you do not know yourself. You see, this was a file Boniface had compiled from a number of reports Mr. Ryder had commissioned from several inquiry agencies over many years. He must have given them to Boniface when engaging him to seek you in Paris, but Boniface kept all that part of the matter hidden from me, no doubt because the wretched man knew I would not have allowed the Hesketh Agency to accept the commission."

I felt I was being obtuse, and said, "How could these old reports refer to me? Apart from the man who sold me and the woman who bought me, nobody in England knew I ever existed. Mr. Ryder certainly did not."

"No," said Mrs. Hesketh slowly. "But he had cause to believe that *the butterfly girl* existed, a girl with a birthmark on her shoulder in the shape of a small golden butterfly."

I turned my head to stare at her blankly, and at last I said, "I don't understand. I do know from something a servant overheard that Mr. Ryder told Mr. Boniface to bring him the butterfly girl regardless of cost, but I thought he only referred to me in that way because Mr. Boniface told him I had sometimes been called that when I was at the College for Young Ladies."

"When we reach home," said Mrs. Hesketh, "I will give you the file to read, then you will understand. If Boniface has a virtue, it is that he writes a good clear hand; I can think of no other at the moment. Meanwhile let me tell you a story, naming no names, which may help to prepare you for what you will read."

She paused for a moment to collect her thoughts, and as the cab turned into Tottenham Court Road, she began to speak as if telling a parable. "There was a certain rich landowner, a widower, with a beautiful but headstrong daughter of twenty. Because she was headstrong he guarded her jealously, for he was determined that she should make a good marriage. She had little freedom, and was almost a prisoner in the great manor house where they lived. But one day, when out riding with her father, she took a fall and hurt her leg. A young doctor who had recently moved to the nearby village came to attend her and made several further visits, with the result that she fell desperately in love with him, and he with her."

I knew nothing of love, for it had long ago been set beyond my grasp by the life I had led, yet I could well believe that a girl who had been greatly restricted might lose her heart completely to a man who suddenly broke through the barrier surrounding her.

"I do not know what the girl felt toward her father," said Mrs. Hesketh. "Perhaps she wished to escape from him; who can tell? Certainly she knew he would never allow her to marry a poor country doctor. I will not guess at the agonies of decision they must have passed through; I only know that in the end they ran away together, and it is probable that they later married at a register office. Their flight was no impulse, but carefully planned, and a note was left for the girl's father. To protect her name, or perhaps his own, he at once gave out that the girl had been found to be suffering from a lung complaint and had been dispatched posthaste to a sanatorium in Switzerland. He then set about hunting down the runaways.

"The girl and her lover, or perhaps husband, let us call him that, wisely chose to hide themselves in London, south of the river, in Kennington, where the husband became junior partner to a doctor in practice there. The husband's real name was Anthony James Tudor, but the couple now called themselves Dr. and Mrs. Anthony James."

I noticed that Mrs. Hesketh had used names for the first time in her story, but those names meant nothing to me. She continued: "It took the various inquiry agents employed by the father seven months to trace the runaways. When they had done so, they were paid for their services and dismissed. I cannot tell you what the father's thoughts were, but to judge by his actions he decided that an attempt to persuade or coerce his daughter to return might well fail, and that stronger measures were called for. Do you know what 'shanghai' means, Hannah? Not the city, the verb 'to shanghai'?"

My friend Marguerite at the College for Young Ladies came from Marseilles, and from her I had learned that French seamen used the same word. "Yes, Mrs. Hesketh," I said, "it's a slang word for drugging a man or knocking him on the head and shipping him to sea while unconscious."

She nodded. "That is what the girl's father decided to arrange for Dr. Anthony James Tudor, and he was in a very favorable position to make such an arrangement, for he controlled a shipping line. Presumably he believed that if his daughter's husband vanished without trace for a year or two, serving under compulsion as a deckhand on a foreign cargo boat sailing in waters of the Far East, the girl's infatuation would be long dead by the time the man returned. Or perhaps it was intended that he should never return."

I said, "Why did the father think it was only infatuation?"

Mrs. Hesketh shrugged. "Who knows? But I doubt if such a man has any understanding of love. For the task of carrying out this wicked plan he chose a bailiff on his estate, named Albert Morgan, a brutal fellow by all accounts, who was feared by the villagers and had once beaten a poacher almost to death. Morgan went to London and paid two seamen to assist him. One night after dark, Dr. Tudor was lured to a house near Vauxhall Bridge on the pretext that a woman had been injured. It was there that Morgan and his cronies tried to shanghai the poor man. They had a boat waiting at Draw Dock to carry him down the river to the Royal Albert Dock. There a ship was to sail for the Far East with the next tide, under a master who was expecting an unwilling addition to his crew, a master who would ask no questions and give no answers."

Our hansom was halted in a queue of traffic waiting to turn into the north end of Chancery Lane. Mrs. Hesketh said with a troubled look, "The attempt failed. It seems the doctor must have fought back vigorously when the moment came, and in the end Albert Morgan drew a short club weighted with lead, and struck him on the head to knock him unconscious. He struck too hard, or in the wrong place . . . or perhaps both. Whatever the cause, it was a fatal blow. Within two minutes Dr. Tudor was dead."

I shivered, and said, "How truly dreadful. Oh, that poor man."

"Yes, indeed," said Mrs. Hesketh soberly. "No doubt his murderers were thrown into panic. They carried his body into the dark street, then fled. Police found him toward dawn, when his wife reported in alarm that her husband had failed to return from a call in that area after many hours."

The cab began to move again. I sat imagining what the doctor's young wife must have suffered, and felt a pain under my heart for her. When Mrs. Hesketh had begun her story, I wondered how I could possibly be a part of it, but by now I had almost forgotten that it was supposed to concern me in some way. She said with a sigh, "Morgan and his cronies never came under suspicion. It was believed that the doctor had been attacked by common footpads. His wife was of course distraught. Fortunately she was under the medical care of the senior partner of the practice, Dr. Langley, and two days later she gave premature birth to a seven-month baby. The shock of her husband's death caused her natural milk to fail, and Dr. Langley arranged for a wet nurse to feed the baby. He then decided he must inform the girl's family."

I said, "Did he know she had run away from her father to be with Dr. Tudor?"

"No," said Mrs. Hesketh, "he knew nothing of her background, and since the young woman was in a fever and quite delirious for a time, he could not question her. Dr. Langley felt it was essential to seek out her family so that she might be well cared for in the difficult time ahead, so he went through all the papers and documents he could find in the rooms Dr. Tudor and his wife had rented, and he found what he was seeking, the name of the wealthy gentleman who was her father."

Our hansom came to a halt, and the cabbie called out. Once again I stood on the pavement outside the house in Chancery Lane where Mr. Boniface had brought me after our journey from Paris. Mrs. Hesketh paid the cabbie, opened the door, and ushered me into the office. "We'll go through to the sitting room, my dear," she said. "Wait while I collect the file. Here it is. Oh, I'm so ashamed to think I have allowed a stupid man like Boniface to keep a secret from me. Come along through, Hannah. There, now let me take your hat and coat, child, and you can sit here and start reading while I go and make a nice pot of tea. I have dismissed the maid for this afternoon. Big ears, you know. Oh, what a pretty dress you are wearing. I must say, in view of the way Boniface contrived to deceive me in this matter, and no doubt was well paid for his pains, I am truly thankful that I have never troubled myself to be entirely faithful to the wretched man, and why should I? After all, he has never even hinted that he might marry me. I am not in the least indiscriminate, you understand, but I greatly enjoy an occasional wayward encounter."

While she spoke she had bustled about, hanging my hat and coat in the hall with her own, settling me in an easy chair, adjusting the venetian blind to give full light for reading, and placing a blue manila folder on my lap.

"Now, are you comfortable, child? Good. I shall go and make tea while you begin to read, and . . ."—she hesitated, then smiled down at me with an air of apology—"and I hope you will not be too greatly upset."

I said, "I can't think that anything I might read is likely to upset me, Mrs. Hesketh. Before I start, will you tell me if the poor young woman went back to her father?"

"Yes," she said quietly, and gestured at the file I held. "You will find it all there. She returned to her father because her spirit was broken and she had nowhere else to go."

"And the baby?"

"Her father persuaded Dr. Langley that it would be best if she were to believe that the baby had been stillborn. She had never seen or held it, for she was unconscious when it was delivered."

"Did the doctor agree?"

"So you will find when you read. We must remember that the father was a very forceful man, very powerful, very rich."

"And very ruthless," I said.

"Yes. That, too. He took the girl away to Switzerland for three months, then brought her back home. Everybody believed she had been in a Swiss sanatorium ever since her departure from the manor, but was now cured of the supposed lung complaint. Eighteen months later she married a man of good family and good prospects, carefully selected by her father."

"Did the baby live, Mrs. Hesketh?"

She nodded slowly, and I saw her eyes turn moist. "Yes. The wet nurse was another patient of Dr. Langley's, a woman who had suffered a misfortune and lost her own baby. It seems she developed an affection for the baby she was feeding, and a private arrangement was entered into."

"You mean the wet nurse kept the baby?"

"Yes." Mrs. Hesketh smiled, and indicated the folder on my lap. "Read, my dear. That will tell you all you wish to know."

She went quietly from the room, and I heard a faint clatter of crockery from the kitchen as she began to prepare tea. I opened the folder. It contained lined sheets of foolscap paper filled with square but very legible writing. The first page was headed: *A Compilation of Sundry Investigations into the Affairs of Sir John Bancroft Tennant.*

I read the title again. Sir John Tennant? That man with cold lizard eyes? I settled down to read on. The phrasing was stilted and a little ornate, and the document began:

> *I, Thomas Boniface, here set down a summary of that particular matter in which Mr. Sebastian Ryder has required my services. He has engaged me personally, and not as a partner in the Hesketh Agency, as he has the opinion that a woman is not good at holding her tongue.*
>
> *This summary I will follow with an account of the several investigations, heretofore made by other people, and thereafter I will show how these fit together.*

My eye caught a word some way down the page, and at once I skipped two paragraphs to read a particular line. I found my hands were shaking, and made myself go back to the beginning. Then, slowly and deliberately, I read the first page, holding shock and bewilderment in check, though I could feel my heart pounding a little. Halfway down the third page, the summary ended and there began an account of what Mr. Boniface called "investigations heretofore made by other people."

I lifted my head and looked dazedly about the room, vaguely surprised to find everything was as it had been before, for I felt that the whole world had changed in those few minutes since I began to read. Mrs. Hesketh was still making small noises in the kitchen as if setting cups and saucers on a tray, and from beyond the walls I could hear the rumble of a heavy cart in Chancery Lane, a brewer's dray perhaps.

I pressed my fingers to my eyes, trying to make myself take in a truth that seemed impossible. I had yet to read the proof of it in the remaining pages, but I knew there could be no doubt in the end, for Mrs. Hesketh with all her experience had accepted it.

The truth could be briefly told. I was not the daughter of Kathleen McLeod, who had loved me and cared for me and brought me up from the day I was born until the day she died. Only a week or two ago I had sat at table with the woman who was my true mother, now Mrs. Anne Ritchie, the daughter of Sir John Tennant, and I had felt not the smallest tug of blood or kinship.

The people in the story Mrs. Hesketh had told me were no longer faceless creatures. The wealthy landowner was Sir John Tennant, and his daughter Anne was the headstrong girl who had fallen in love with a young doctor, had run away with him, had borne his baby prematurely when he died, and had later married Mr. Hugh Ritchie.

I was that baby, and Kathleen McLeod was the wet nurse who had kept me alive at her breast, and taken me as her own for the rest of her hard short life.

Twelve

Mrs. Hesketh came in with a laden tray, set it down on a side table, and shot me a keen glance. "So you have the essentials of it now, my dear?" she said.

I nodded slowly. "Yes . . . but there's so much I don't understand."

She moved to a bureau, took something out, then came to me and put a photograph in my hands. It was of postcard size and showed a man of about thirty with a strong face and humorous eyes. "This was with the file," she said, "but I wanted you to read the summary first." She put a fingertip over the man's chin and mouth. "Can you see the likeness there in the eyes and brow? It's such a marked resemblance. He was your father, Dr. Anthony Tudor."

I sat looking at the photograph, and felt drawn toward this stranger. "I like him," I said, speaking my thoughts aloud. "I don't feel the same about Mrs. Ritchie—I mean my mother. I've met her, you know . . . and her husband and Sir John Tennant. Mr. Ryder invited them all on a river trip. But even now that I know she was my mother, I don't feel anything about her."

Mrs. Hesketh sighed. "People change," she said. "Give her credit for what she once was, child. To have a father like Sir John Tennant would be enough to crush most girls, and to defy him was a brave act."

"I know. It's just that I don't feel anything." I studied the photograph again. "She looked at me in a very odd way when we first met on the boat. I suppose it was a matter of her seeing somebody with a likeness to this gentleman, but I'm sure she just thought it was a coincidence."

"Of course. She believes her baby was stillborn almost twenty years ago, and she would never dream that you could be alive today." Mrs. Hesketh poured tea as she spoke. "Milk and sugar, dear? There. Now you sit quietly while I tell you some of what's to be found in the rest of Boniface's file. You can read it all for yourself, of course, but if you prefer to ask me questions while we're having tea I shall be glad to tell you all I know."

I took a sip of tea and tried to put my scattered thoughts in order. One thing I knew already. In my thoughts, Kathleen McLeod would forever be my mother. For me, the old saying that blood is thicker than water did not apply. I felt pity for Anne Tennant, the girl who had suffered so cruelly, but to me she seemed somebody quite separate from the cool and rather haughty Mrs. Anne Ritchie. The person I first wanted to know about was the woman I had always known as my mother, and I said, "Do you know how it was that Kathleen McLeod came to be my wet nurse?"

"She had herself given birth to a baby only two days before," Mrs. Hesketh said gently. "Your foster mother had been a governess in a big house in the Midlands. Perhaps foolishly, she believed that a local solicitor, a few years older than herself, was in love with her and intended to marry her, but he betrayed her. She had to leave her post, and she came to London intending to have her baby here and then to seek work as a teacher. In the event, the baby was stillborn. Kathleen McLeod was then under your father's medical care, and perhaps that is why she was willing to wet nurse his baby when his partner, Dr. Langley, asked her to do so."

I drank some tea, imagining how bereft and alone Kathleen McLeod must have felt. She might have seen the loss of her own baby as an alleviation of her misfortune, for it lifted from her the burden of bringing up a fatherless child, yet she had nursed me and kept me, perhaps because she needed someone to love and to be loved by.

I said, "I hate to think that Sir John Tennant is my grandfather. Did he make some financial arrangement to help my foster mother? She left me a letter in which she said that if ever I was in dire need I should go to some lawyers in Clerkenwell and ask advice concerning the Tennant Charity."

"It would have done you little good," said Mrs. Hesketh. "That disgusting man, having caused your father's death, then settled a sum of thirty pounds a year on your foster mother for a period of twelve years to cover your upkeep. He took the view that by then you would be old enough to work, either in service or a factory. By the time Kathleen McLeod died, the final payment had been made."

We sat in silence for a little while. The first shock was beginning to pass and I felt more myself. It did not matter who my father and mother had been, I decided. For better or worse I was myself, Hannah McLeod, with whatever virtues and vices I had acquired in my nineteen years. I revered the memory of Kathleen McLeod, and only wished I had shown my love for her more freely during my childhood. I did not like Sir John Tennant, but was unable to feel hatred toward him for causing the death of a man I now knew to have been my father; it was too remote. I could feel horror, but not hatred. For Mrs. Anne Ritchie I had no particular feeling, and regarding the rest of the story I felt only a measure of curiosity.

I looked down at the papers I had laid aside, and said, "How did all this come to be discovered, Mrs. Hesketh? I suppose Mr. Ryder was behind it?"

"Indeed he was, Hannah." She reached for my cup to refill it. "The fact is Mr. Sebastian Ryder has long been a most fearsome enemy of Sir John, though not openly, mind you. It seems he had a brother who committed suicide many years ago, and he holds Sir John responsible."

"Yes, I know. I was told by Mattie. That's Mrs. Matthews, who keeps house for Mr. Ryder."

"Ah, then you won't need to read about that," said Mrs. Hesketh. "It's enough that Sebastian Ryder has spent years seeking a way to be revenged, and he began in a very cool and sensible manner by employing agents to unearth every possible scrap of information about the Tennant family, hoping to find a scandal he could make use of. I imagine all the reports together would make a book, but most of the material was worthless." She looked at the folder of papers lying beside me. "The only items of value are in that file, Hannah, and even then there are some whose value only became apparent in the light of much later reports. For example, the first one you will read there is almost fifteen years old, and it reveals that Mrs. Hugh Ritchie, who was once Miss Anne Tennant, inherited a distinguishing mark which comes down to her through her mother's side of the family. It appears intermittently, in the female line only, sometimes missing a generation. She bears on her shoulder a birthmark in the shape of a small golden butterfly."

I put down my teacup. "Yes, it mentions that in the summary. Has Mr. Ryder known all these years that Mrs. Ritchie had a secret daughter, unknown even to herself?"

"Oh no, my dear. He knew nothing of your existence until fairly recently."

I touched my shoulder. "Did he find out through the butterfly mark?"

"Yes." She looked down into her cup. "Last year he was playing cards one evening in a Whitehall club he belongs to. One of the players was a young fellow who had visited Paris the previous year. He had seen the usual sights, and had also attended cabarets, dancing shows, bohemian entertainments . . . and the College for Young Ladies, in Rue des Moulins." Mrs. Hesketh lifted her head and looked at me apologetically. "There, he said, he had greatly enjoyed the company one night of a young girl who spoke fluent English and who was also an excellent conversationalist and pleasant companion. During their time together he discovered that she bore on her shoulder a most attractive birthmark, golden in color, shaped like a small butterfly. He returned a year later, hoping to . . . visit her again, and was disappointed to learn that she had left the establishment." Mrs. Hesketh's voice faltered.

I said, "Oh, please don't feel embarrassed."

To my surprise her eyes filled suddenly with tears. "But . . . oh, child, it must have been so *awful* for you."

"At first," I said, remembering. "But if you intend to live, you simply cannot allow things to go on being awful, and I found a way of making what I had to do more bearable."

She studied me curiously. "But . . . how, Hannah?"

"Well, I learned to play a trick with my mind, Mrs. Hesketh. Whenever I was with a man, I made myself believe that he was my loving husband and that I wanted to please him. Sometimes it wasn't possible because of the man, but mostly I was able to do it quite successfully."

After a moment or two Mrs. Hesketh said in a subdued voice,

"You're an unusual girl, Hannah. Will you save me the trouble of talking for a few minutes by reading the Pinkerton report you have there? You will find it marked number five in red ink."

I did not know what Pinkerton meant, but I found the report and began to read. The date showed that it was five years old, and before the report began there was a preamble which stated that shortly after Miss Anne Tennant's return from a Swiss sanatorium many years before, one of Sir John Tennant's bailiffs, Albert Morgan by name, had suddenly come into money and emigrated with his wife to America. Morgan was considered an unpleasant and even dangerous man in the village, and his departure caused all kinds of gossip.

This incident, the preamble continued, was only one of many scores reported by various inquiry agencies Mr. Sebastian Ryder had employed to delve into Sir John's affairs, both business and domestic. It lay fallow for years, but then, some five years ago when Mr. Ryder was reviewing his whole collection of reports, he decided there was something odd about Albert Morgan's sudden departure and that it would bear further examination. To this end he engaged Pinkerton's, the biggest and best-known agency in America, to trace Albert Morgan and try to discover the source of the money he had acquired and the cause of his departure.

Here the preamble ended and was followed by a report from the Pinkerton agency, copied out in Mr. Boniface's square hand. The style was very different from his, being dry and devoid of flourishes. It had taken three months to trace Albert Morgan in America, and it was then found that he had died six weeks before. On emigrating to the United States with his wife, he had settled in Philadelphia, in modest but comfortable circumstances, living on a small private income. He was disliked by his neighbors as an uncouth and aggressive man, and was also disliked by his wife, whom he beat from time to time. There were no children.

Possibly because there was no need for him to work, Morgan had taken to drink over the last two years of his life. His drinking became so heavy that he had suffered from delirium tremens. When undergoing an attack of this kind his character changed and he would become terrified, screaming to his wife to protect him from monstrous creatures he saw in his delirium. After one of these attacks not long before his death, he had made a confession to his wife.

The Pinkerton report then went on to recount this confession as told to their agent by Mrs. Morgan. Much of the story I had already been told by Mrs. Hesketh, how Dr. Anthony Tudor had run away with the daughter of Sir John Tennant, entered a medical practice in Kennington, and later died during an attempt to shanghai him led by Albert Morgan. Following this, according to Albert Morgan, the daughter had given birth to a stillborn child. Sir John had decided that it would be safer to have Albert Morgan on the other side of the world with his knowledge of these secrets, and had made provision for this accordingly.

I read to the end of the Pinkerton report, then looked up. Mrs. Hesketh sat with her hands loosely clasped in her lap, watching me. I said, "Albert Morgan's wife actually told the Pinkerton people what her husband had done?"

"With very little persuasion apparently," said Mrs. Hesketh. "As you see, they paid her only ten dollars for her trouble. Evidently she knew about the baby, but believed you had been stillborn."

I laid down the report and said, "I suppose she had nothing to lose by telling her story. Her husband was dead, and they say she disliked him anyway. But shouldn't something have been done about this, Mrs. Hesketh? Surely it was evidence that Sir John Tennant had committed a crime?"

She gave a wry smile. "There's no signed confession, Hannah. What you have just read is no more than hearsay, the ramblings of a drunken man, now dead, as retold by his wife in return for a fee. We can be sure it's true because it fits in with all the rest of the story, but it isn't evidence. If anyone challenged Sir John on the basis of that report alone, they would immediately be sued for libel."

I sat thinking for a few moments, then said, "When did Mr. Ryder find out that I had not died but had been fostered by Kathleen McLeod?"

"That was not long after the Pinkerton report," Mrs. Hesketh replied. "Still accumulating all possible information, he employed yet another inquiry agency to seek out Dr. Langley, who had been your father's senior partner in Kennington and had attended your birth, but they found he had died a year or two before, and his early records had been discarded by the doctor who had taken over the practice. However, they discovered that his old housekeeper was still alive, and they managed to trace her. She was quite old and almost blind, but she remembered Dr. and Mrs. James, as your father and mother were known. She also remembered very clearly a young woman named Kathleen McLeod, who had lost a fatherless baby at that time. It was the old housekeeper's opinion, whispered behind her hand, that the newborn baby which Kathleen McLeod had then taken as her own was in fact Mrs. James's baby."

I said, "Why should the housekeeper remember my . . . remember Kathleen McLeod so clearly?"

"Because she was involved with her, dear. It seems Dr. Langley asked her to help find a place for Kathleen McLeod and the baby to live, and the housekeeper arranged something with a Mrs. Taylor she knew, who had been a scullery maid under her in the doctor's house before leaving to get married not long before. The agency found Mrs. Taylor still living at the address given them by the housekeeper. Mr. Taylor, a brute of a man by all accounts, was in prison for assault and battery, but from his wife they learned that your mother had died and the Taylor family had taken you into their care. The report says there is no independent confirmation of this, though."

"It's true," I said. "My mother left them her savings to pay for my keep, but after a few months Mr. Taylor sold me to a woman who ran a house of prostitution in London, and very soon after that I was sold again, to Mam'selle Montavon in Paris."

Mrs. Hesketh bit her lip, and again her eyes brimmed with tears. "I thought something of the sort must have happened," she said. "Oh, Hannah, my poor dear. Mrs. Taylor told the inquiry agents that you had run away and never returned."

"I'm sure she had no part in what happened," I said, "but even if she guessed what her husband had done, she would never dare to speak out against him."

"They did learn something from her," said Mrs. Hesketh, "something of great interest to Mr. Ryder, since it linked up with a seemingly unimportant fact discovered years before. They learned from Mrs. Taylor that Kathleen McLeod's daughter, as you were believed to be, bore a butterfly birthmark on her shoulder."

After a brief silence I said, "So that was when Mr. Ryder knew. That was when he knew for certain that Dr. Langley's old housekeeper had been right in suspecting I was really Mrs. James's baby . . . and Sir John Tennant's granddaughter."

"Yes," said Mrs. Hesketh. "Then he knew the truth, but it wasn't enough. The word of a convict's wife and the suspicions of an almost blind old woman amounted to very little in terms of evidence, so he was still frustrated. Just imagine, Hannah. Sebastian Ryder knew that his arch enemy, Sir John Tennant, had caused the death of the man Sir John's own daughter had loved and eloped with, the man who later fathered her child. And that was not all. He now knew that Sir John had told his daughter the child was dead, though in fact he had disposed of her newborn baby to a foster mother in very poor circumstances. Imagine the power such knowledge could give Sebastian Ryder over his enemy . . . if only he could prove the truth of it."

Mrs. Hesketh lifted her hands, palms up, in a little gesture. "But to do that, he had to find *you,* Hannah. He had to find the girl with the butterfly mark that would prove she was indeed the missing daughter of the woman who had been Anne Tennant. Then and only then could he turn hearsay into fact. He must have felt there could be little hope of success, despite all his efforts, and in the end it was chance that brought him within reach of his goal, when he sat playing cards in his club one night last year, and heard of a young English girl who had worked in a *maison close* in Paris . . . and who bore on her shoulder the Tennant birthmark, the mark of a golden butterfly."

I said, "Was it then that he engaged your agency to seek me out and bring me to London?"

She nodded. "I was occupied by another matter at the time, and sent Boniface to see Mr. Ryder. I did not know about all this." She indicated the folder of reports. "Boniface kept that part of the affair to himself, deceitful creature that he is, and I have only just discovered it. I hope you will believe that."

"Yes, of course I do," I said quickly, "and I'm grateful to you for telling me the truth about myself. Do you know if Anne Tennant and Dr. Anthony Tudor were married?"

"No record has been found by Mr. Ryder's agents, my dear, and when Anne Tennant later married Mr. Hugh Ritchie, she was registered as a spinster, not a widow. But the inquiry agents made the comment that it would not be beyond the power of a man such as Sir John Tennant to ensure that any register-office record of an earlier marriage was destroyed. It is my feeling that your father was an honorable man, and that he and your mother were legally married, but I am afraid the question is one which may never be answered, for only Anne Tennant and her father know the truth, and they will never tell."

I was beginning to feel very tired now, but I managed to smile as I said, "Since I was old enough to understand, I've always believed myself to be illegitimate, so it doesn't matter anyway."

We sat quietly for a while, and I tried to put my thoughts in order so that I might understand what had happened. Sebastian Ryder wanted to be revenged on Sir John Tennant, and had worked for many years to that end. Now he had discovered the truth about Sir John's daughter, and about the way her previous husband or lover had died at the hands of men paid by Sir John to shanghai him. The confession of Albert Morgan could not be used against Sir John on its own, so the search for another weapon had continued. I, Hannah McLeod, was the daughter of Mrs. Hugh Ritchie, who believed I had died at birth. I had become an employee in Sebastian Ryder's household, and I knew that in some way I was the weapon he was at last using.

I said, "Did you know that on the river trip I spoke of, with Sir John Tennant and Mr. and Mrs. Hugh Ritchie present among others, Mr. Sebastian Ryder revealed to them the truth of my life in Paris at the College for Young Ladies?"

"I learned that from your friend, Mr. Toby Kent," said Mrs. Hesketh, a rather soft and faraway look in her eyes. "He called to see me one day recently. I was extremely angry to hear how Sebastian Ryder humiliated you on that occasion."

"I didn't feel humiliated," I said, and touched the file. "Does Toby know about this?"

"No, I hadn't found the file when I last saw him, and I wouldn't speak of it to anybody without your permission."

"I appreciate that very much, Mrs. Hesketh, but I have no secrets from Toby." I shook my head, perplexed. "It's very puzzling. I'm sure Sir John knows I'm his granddaughter. When I was introduced to him by the name of McLeod, he gave me a very sharp look. Perhaps at the same time he saw the likeness to my father. Later he must have become quite sure, when Mr. Ryder told everybody that I had spent several years working in a Paris bordello. I think Sir John realized then that Mr. Ryder had somehow unearthed the whole story and was deliberately making him aware of it. He was more or less ordered to call at our house that evening, and I expect it was then that Mr. Ryder told him plainly who I was and that I bore the mark of the butterfly." I paused, thinking about what I had just said, then ended, "But I don't quite see what Mr. Ryder is about. If that confession in the Pinkerton report is legally worthless, he still can't prove Sir John was responsible for my father's death, so how does he hope to gain his revenge?"

Mrs. Hesketh got up, moved to the window, and stood gazing thoughtfully out upon a tiny yard where three tubs bore a mixture of petunias, lobelia, and salvias.

"I can only guess the answer to your question," she said at last.

"Then please guess. I think perhaps you are very good at it, Mrs. Hesketh."

She half smiled. "I have had considerable experience of it in my work, child. It's quite true that the story might never be proved in court, but imagine the effect if it were told to Anne Ritchie and to her husband, who is a rising politician and a junior minister in the present government. Imagine the effect if Mr. Ryder were to say to Anne Ritchie, *'Hannah McLeod is your own child, kept from you by your father at birth, and sold to a French brothel when she was thirteen.'* The mark of the golden butterfly would be proof enough to the woman who bore you, and who bears the same mark herself. That is the key, Hannah. *You* are the key to Sebastian Ryder's revenge. I think Anne Ritchie, who knows her father, would need no legal proof to help her believe the confession Albert Morgan made to his wife. And if she believes, then the world will believe."

I felt a chill of revulsion and said, "But it would ruin her life, and her husband's, too. I . . . . I don't feel anything for her, perhaps I should, but I don't. At the same time, I would hate to have her go through all the agony of learning the truth."

Mrs. Hesketh turned from the window to study me. "You mean you would never wish her to know? You really mean that?"

"Well of course, Mrs. Hesketh. It would do no good to me or to anybody, and it would cause endless pain. In my heart, Kathleen McLeod will always be my mother, but Anne Ritchie never did me wrong, she suffered greatly herself, and I don't want her to suffer again. For heaven's sake, let the story lie buried in the past—" I broke off sharply with the realization that the decision was not mine to make. Putting a hand to my head I tried to set my thoughts in order, then I said, "If Sebastian Ryder wants revenge, why didn't he tell the whole story that day of the river trip? Why has he only allowed Sir John Tennant to know?"

"That is what I have asked myself," Mrs. Hesketh said quietly. "Again, I can only guess, but Sebastian Ryder has waited many years to avenge his brother's death, and I believe he wishes that vengeance to be crushing. He can of course bring pain and chaos to the family by uncovering the truth to Anne Ritchie and her husband, but they are not the real targets of his hatred, and in a sense it would allow him to strike only one blow. I believe this is not enough to satisfy him. I believe he will use his knowledge as a threat to make Sir John Tennant dance to whatever tune he chooses to call."

I only half comprehended, and said, "You mean in business matters?"

"Certainly in business matters. Both men are rich industrialists. Sebastian Ryder can now compel his enemy to enter into dangerous financial enterprises, to invest to his own detriment and to Mr. Ryder's advantage, to harm himself in countless different ways. I believe he will set out to ruin Sir John, gradually, painfully, and mercilessly. He will also be able to call on Sir John to use his influence with Hugh Ritchie. A minister at the War Office must have much influence he can exert to the benefit of a manufacturer of armaments such as Sebastian Ryder."

I said, "But surely Mr. Ritchie would not allow himself to be corrupted?"

Mrs. Hesketh gave a small lift of her shoulders. "Perhaps not. I don't know the man's quality. But in any event Mr. Ryder is far too clever to attempt simple corruption. He will use his power over Sir John to make him influence his son-in-law. In such matters a little influence can have large effects, and I do not think Mr. Ritchie will be able to resist his father-in-law's advice and suggestions. Sir John Tennant is a formidable person."

I had begun to feel a little sick to know that I was embroiled in such a vicious tale of hatred and revenge. I wanted no part of it, yet as Mrs Hesketh had said, I was in some ways the key to it. I said, "I can see there are many things Mr. Ryder can do to injure Sir John, but surely it can't go on forever. How do you think it will end?"

Mrs. Hesketh stood holding the back of her chair and looking at me directly. "I think Mr. Ryder seeks what he would see as a perfect revenge for the brother who committed suicide. He seeks to drive Sir John Tennant into destroying himself."

"Oh, dear God," I said tiredly. "What a dreadful goal. I ought to understand men, but it seems I've much to learn."

"They are both wicked men," Mrs. Hesketh said simply, "and as such they will always be beyond our understanding, Hannah."

The clock on the mantelpiece chimed softly and I saw that it was four o'clock. Slowly I picked up the file and handed it to Mrs. Hesketh. I no longer wanted to read through all those reports. I had heard more than enough now, and there was nothing more I wished to know. "I'm wondering why you have gone to the trouble of telling me all this, Mrs. Hesketh," I said. "I'm deeply grateful, but it was in no way your responsibility."

She took a long time to answer, but at last she said, "I'm forty years old, Hannah. I've never married, but I wear a wedding ring and call myself Mrs. because it carries more authority than Miss. I looked after an invalid mother until I was twenty-four, and by that time I was left on the shelf. It isn't easy for a young woman to set up in business on her own with only a small inheritance, but I managed it. Boniface was a one-man agency with a small practice and no business sense. I bought his practice, retaining him as a partner, and called it the Hesketh Agency. We have worked together for over fifteen years now, and I have been his mistress since the second year. In some ways he is very capable, in others extremely stupid. I cannot help loving him a little, heaven knows why, perhaps because even Boniface is better than nobody. After all these years I still hope that one day he will ask me to marry him. I would be a very good and faithful wife."

She paused and gave an impatient shake of her head. "But I haven't answered your question. You ask why I have gone to some trouble to tell you what I have discovered about your birth. I confess I hesitated, Hannah, wondering if it would be kinder to remain silent, but if I had, I would have felt guilty, because you are innocently involved in a battle between two ruthless men, and it is right that you should be aware of it."

I said doubtfully, "Yes, I understand that. But I'm almost a stranger to you, Mrs. Hesketh, so I don't see why you should feel guilty if you hadn't told me. And I don't see any connection with what you said just now about yourself and Mr. Boniface."

"Oh, that." She looked almost shamefaced for a moment, then began briskly to gather up our tea things and put them on the tray. "It's just that . . . well, I used to long for a daughter to love, and if I had married at twenty I might easily have had a daughter of your age now, Hannah. I know we only met for a few hours that day when you came to England, but I've often thought of you since, with both sympathy and respect." She picked up the tray and looked at me almost fiercely.

"If I had a daughter who endured what you have suffered, I would pra that people might be kind to her, and that is why I had to do what felt was right."

She turned and marched out to the kitchen. A minute passed befo she returned, and then she was herself again, a confident and ve independent lady. "You have decided that Mr. and Mrs. Hugh Ritch are not to be told, at least by you," she said thoughtfully. "Beyond tha have you formed any intention?"

My mind seemed sluggish, and it was several moments before realized what she meant. "You think I might tax Mr. Ryder with wha you've told me? And tell him I know that he's . . . well, blackmailin Sir John Tennant?"

"You might, my dear. I won't attempt to advise you, for I simp don't know what's best."

"I have no liking for Sir John," I said, trying not to let the wearine sound in my voice, "but I don't want him injured. I just want th whole thing to stop, so that I'm not part of this horrible feud." I stoo up, suddenly wanting to be alone with my problems. "I shall have t think carefully about it. I won't do anything in haste, Mrs. Hesketh May I ask you a question now? When Mr. Boniface returns from th matter he is working on in Hull, will you tell him that you found h hidden file and have shown it to me?"

"Oh yes, my dear," she said firmly. "You may be sure I shall com plain forcibly of his infidelity in hiding the matter from me. You ma also be sure that he will have no further communication whatsoev with Mr. Sebastian Ryder. I will not allow the Hesketh Agency to wor for such a man again."

I picked up my handbag, and most of my thoughts were elsewhere a I said, "When you admonish Mr. Boniface, don't make him lose face It's very important with men." I stopped short and looked up quickly "Oh, please forgive me, that was most impertinent."

She closed her eyes, and when she opened them again I saw the were moist. "No," she said in a voice not quite steady. "I know it wa well meant, and I'm sure it is very wise advice. I'm only sad to thin how such a child learned such wisdom."

I shook my head and smiled. "Don't distress yourself. The past dead, and it doesn't haunt me. May I come and talk with you agai Mrs. Hesketh?"

"Oh, yes please. I shall be delighted. Must you go now? Very well, le me get your hat and coat. I shall come and see you into a cab. The drivers sometimes pretend not to be aware of a woman hailing them, because they are persuaded that women give small tips—which is all they deserve, say I. However, he would be a brave cabbie who ignored *me.* Years ago now I gave a street urchin a penny to teach me to whistle."

She had been helping me on with my coat, and now she stepped back, lifted a finger and thumb to her lips, and startled me with a sudden shrill whistle of truly piercing intensity. "I can summon a cab from eighty yards with that," she said proudly. "Poor Boniface cannot do it, and is racked with jealousy."

There proved to be no need for Mrs. Hesketh to use her surprising accomplishment, for when we went through the office and into the street there was a vacant hansom halted at the curb. The driver saw us emerge, flourished his whip and said hopefully, "Cab, ladies?"

Mrs. Hesketh eyed him forbiddingly. "You will take this young lady to Portland Place," she said, "and since she is familiar with London streets you will take the most direct route and not some roundabout way of your own choosing. Furthermore, if she is so generous as to tip you, you will not *sniff* when you regard the tip. Is that understood?"

The cabbie blinked, then grinned. "Clear as a bell, marm," he said, and scrambled down to open the door. I said good-bye to Mrs. Hesketh and sank back into the seat as the cab pulled away. For a while I sat with eyes closed, trying to keep my mind blank, for I knew that when I began to think of all I had discovered in the past hour I would go through a time of confusion and distress as I tried to unravel my feelings, and I wished to be alone in my own room for this. Later, when I had thought carefully about all the people concerned, and all the implications of the long and complex tale Mrs. Hesketh had revealed to me, then I would have to decide what I should do, or indeed if I should do anything at all.

After a little while I opened my eyes, gazing obliquely out of the window but in an unfocused fashion. To keep my thoughts engaged elsewhere, I decided to concentrate on somebody interesting who had nothing to do with the subject I wanted to avoid, and the first person I thought of was Andrew Doyle. I made a mental picture of him sitting in the drawing room in Portland Place when he had last paid us a call. At one stage of the conversation he had begun to speak rather passionately of the way the peasants in his country suffered, in much the same fashion that he had spoken to Mr. Ritchie during our boat journey from Kew, but he quickly caught himself, and apologized for what he called his bad manners in speaking of a serious matter when paying a social call.

Later, Jane had spoken with some amusement of his idealism, but I could not agree with her. I liked him for it, and would have looked forward to his next visit if Jane had not made me uneasy by saying she felt sure he was in love with me. Surely, I thought, not even a man as romantic and rebellious as Andrew Doyle would seriously consider courting a girl with my history. And yet . . . ? But no, it was out of the question. Perhaps he had some vague notion of taking me as a mistress . . . but again no, that was an unkind and unjust thought.

The cab lurched as it turned a corner. I leaned forward to look out of the window and see where we were, then frowned as I found the cab was passing along a cobbled mews with stabling along one side. Pushing open the trap I called up to the cabbie, "Why have you turned off the main road?"

"Lot of 'eavy traffic piled up in Oxford Street, miss," he replied. "Quicker if I cut through 'ere."

"All right." I settled back in my seat, but I had hardly done so when the cab came to a halt. I waited, but it remained still. I looked out of the left-hand window. There was nobody about, and nothing blocking our way. As I sat back, about to call to the cabbie again, the right-hand door opened suddenly, and before I could move or speak, a burly man was in the cab, looming over me.

Alarm swept me and I started to cry out, but my cry was cut short. A big powerful hand clamped a pad of some kind over my nose and mouth, forcing my head against the back of the seat. Alarm became terror, and instinctively my right hand went up to snatch the long pin from my hat, but the man's other hand caught my wrist and held it fast, his arm across my breast, pinning my left arm with one shoulder. His face was only three inches from mine, a swarthy face with a stubble of beard, topped by a low-crowned brown bowler hat. I tried to bite, to kick, but the pad smothered my mouth and he was kneeling with one leg on my thighs, his whole weight pinning me down in the seat.

I fought wildly, writhing and twisting to break free, but he was far too strong. I could hardly breathe, and when I sucked in air through my nose, it held a sweet, sickly smell. I felt my senses begin to swim, felt the strength draining from my limbs. The man loosened his grip a little, allowing me to breathe more readily, but I no longer had the power to fight. I tried to turn my head away, to hold my breath, but my body would not obey me. The world began to spin round, faster, faster, and then I was drawn down through a dark vortex into oblivion.

Much time was to pass before I emerged fully from that oblivion, but there were periods when I was dimly aware of being moved, handled, and spoken to coaxingly. Somehow I knew I was not dreaming, and despite my stupor I could feel great fear, but I had no power to move or speak.

There was a time of being in a room, on a bed. Two people, one a woman, undressed me and put me in a long nightdress. Then my head was lifted, something was held to my lips, and I was told to drink. Another period of darkness followed, how long I could never tell, but then I roused to a dream or to the reality of being in a wheelchair on a big railway station, wrapped in blankets, a shawl over my head, being pushed along a platform. Hands lifted me, and I was in a compartment with the blinds drawn and two persons with me, one a woman wearing the white headdress of a nurse now. Again something was held to my lips, a hand tilted my head back, and a voice told me to drink. I had no power to resist, and soon the darkness swept down upon me once more.

There came another partial awakening, with a distant feeling that much time had passed. I could hear the rumble of wheels and jingle of harness. I was in a carriage, with a strong arm about my shoulders to prevent me falling from the seat. I smelt stale tobacco from the man's clothes. A woman's voice spoke. The man called out, the motion of the carriage ceased, and I was made to drink for the last time before reaching my journey's end.

Thirteen

The room was small, the stout door locked. If I stood on tiptoe I coul see, between the bars of the window, an area of coarse grass an heather stretching away to the horizon. A single dirt road curved int view from the right and passed across the side of the house, presumab to reach the front.

I could not see what kind of house it was. Looking from the windo I could guess that my room was on the fourth floor, which made m feel that the house must be large. Certainly it was remote, for the vie framed by that small window showed only empty moorland.

It was perhaps an hour since I had roused from the drugged stupor which I had lain helpless for I knew not how long. I felt sick, and m mouth was coated even though I had rinsed it and drunk from the ti mug beside a pitcher of water standing on a small table near the wasl stand. I wore a coarse linen nightdress, and had put on a worn woole dressing gown I found lying over the chair beside the narrow iron bec On my feet were bedsocks of thick wool, too big for me even thoug much washing had made them hard and shrunken. My hair had bee roughly made into a single plait and tied with a piece of string. Apa from what I wore I had nothing else at all, and I was very frightene

For a while after coming to my senses I had been too muddled t think clearly, but as the mists in my head slowly dissolved I began to feel with growing conviction and growing dread that I knew whose hand had brought about my abduction. Mrs. Hesketh had told me I was the key to Sebastian Ryder's vengeful hold over Sir John Tennant, so it would surely be Sir John Tennant who had removed that key from Sebastian Ryder's possession.

It could only be by chance that his hirelings had struck within an hour of my learning the truth about myself and about Sir John, but no doubt they had been seeking an opportunity to find me alone and lure me into the hansom of the cabbie they had bribed. Mrs. Hesketh was not the only one to have followed me to Regent's Park that day, and we must both have been followed to Chancery Lane.

I held my aching head in my hands and tried to think what kind of house this could be. It stood on the edge of moorland and was probably in the north of England. It might belong to Sir John himself, but I doubted it. Sebastian Ryder had clearly never dreamed that his enemy would dare to go to such criminal lengths, but now that I had disappeared he must surely be hunting for me. Sir John would be well aware of that, and so it was most unlikely that my prison was a house connected with him in any way. He would be sure to cover his tracks carefully.

A key turned in the lock and I jumped to my feet, trying to hide my fear as the door opened and a man entered, closely followed by a burly woman I would almost have taken for another man if she had not worn a skirt. She had a big chest, but like a barrel, without shape to her bust, and the sleeves of the gray dress she wore were strained tight on her muscular arms. Her hair was dark and cropped short.

The man was perhaps forty, well built but running to fat both in his face and body, with an egg-shaped countenance and thick sandy hair. He was very well dressed in a gray worsted suit with a waistcoat of lighter gray, a starched collar and a dark red silk tie. He wore a small rose in his lapel, and was smiling in a benign way that reminded me of our vicar at Bradwell.

"Ah, Miss Smith," he said genially. "I am Dr. Thornton. May I ask how we are feeling now? H'mm?"

Struggling to keep my voice steady, I said, "I am feeling greatly distressed, Dr. Thornton, because I have been abducted. My name is not Smith, it is Hannah McLeod. I was seized in London, drugged, and brought to this place. I sincerely hope you are an innocent party in the matter."

He lifted his hands in protest with a pained look. "Oh, come my dear Miss Smith. You are in good hands, and we must not invent silly tales, must we?"

"I am not inventing any tale, doctor. I strongly suspect Sir John Tennant is responsible for what has happened to me. Are you his dupe or his accomplice?"

Dr. Thornton sighed. "You must remember that you have been very ill, Miss Smith," he said gently. "Your mental condition has given great concern to those near to you, and now they have felt it to be in your best interests that you should be committed to this institution."

Horror made my flesh creep. *"Institution?"* I echoed, and my voice was no more than a whisper.

"Two doctors have certified that your mental condition required committal," said Dr. Thornton with a bland smile. He looked about him. "This is your room, and, as you have no doubt discovered, there is a water closet beyond that door in the corner. We serve excellent meals three times a day, with some rather nice tablets to help you sleep at night."

"No!" I exclaimed. "Stop! You can't—!"

Dr. Thornton continued as if I had not spoken. "I'm sure you will be very happy here, Miss Smith. You will find a Holy Bible in the table drawer to read for your comfort, and if you are quiet and of good behavior for a few months, we may be able to let you join some of the other patients in the common room for an hour or so each day."

"Months?" I said, beginning to tremble from a blend of anger and despair. "But you can't shut me up here alone for months!"

"Just till you settle down," said Dr. Thornton reassuringly. "I'm sure you will find it wise to be of good behavior. Our patients have a splendid time in the common room. We can't allow knitting or anything that calls for needles or scissors, but they chat together and walk about, and sometimes play cat's cradle or make little toys of papier-mâché to keep themselves occupied. Such fun." He stopped abruptly, took a watch from his waistcoat pocket, opened it, and frowned. "Almost four o'clock, and I still have my rounds to do." He turned to indicate the burly woman. "This is Nurse Webb. She will be looking after you. Good afternoon, Miss Smith." He put his watch away and went quickly out.

I called, "Wait!" and started to move after him. Nurse Webb caught me by the arm, and I gasped with pain at the crushing power of her fingers. "This way, dear," she said, leading me back to the bed. Even if I had not been weak from drugs and lack of food, I could never have resisted her. With a twist of her wrist she threw me on the bed as if I had weighed no more than the nightdress I wore, then she stepped back and folded her arms, looking down at me, her eyes dark and very small in her broad face.

"We want no trouble, do we, dear?" she said in a voice of iron. "You behave yourself, and you'll get along very nice, but if you cause me trouble, I shall have to calm you down, and that's not nice at all."

She contemplated me thoughtfully, and I lay looking up at her, my head swimming, speechless and frightened. "We'll be bringing you tea at six," she said, "and a pill to give you a good night's sleep at eight." Her mouth tightened and the small eyes looked suddenly vicious. "Don't make a fuss about taking it, dear. You can get hurt if we have to make you."

She turned and went from the room with a heavy stride. The door closed, the key turned. For a moment I was swept by the old terror I had known years before, in a locked room in the house of ill repute run by Mrs. Logan. I turned on my face, rested my head in the crook of my arm, and set my teeth, waiting for the panic to pass. After a little while a sound touched my ears, faint and from a distance, but unmistakably the sound of a church clock striking. I lifted my head and counted. Four o'clock. A tiny hint of relief helped to steady me. I did not know what day it was, and doubted that Nurse Webb or anyone else would tell me, but I would be able to tell when Sunday came by the ringing of the church bell. Better still, I now knew there must be a village not more than a mile from the house. I sat up, rubbed my eyes hard with the heels of my hands, and tried to think.

Sir John Tennant had contrived to have me seized and imprisoned in a remote mental institution on the edge of a great moor. Dr. Thornton might or might not be qualified, but he was certainly a corrupt man who knew very well I was no lunatic. If it was true that two doctors had certified me insane, then they had done so without examining me and must have been bribed by Sir John Tennant.

Sebastian Ryder would seek me, but would he go to the police? I doubted that. I was a pawn in his campaign of revenge against Sir John, and he would not wish the police to intervene. Even if they did, I had little hope that they would find me. With a shiver I realized that Sebastian Ryder might well believe I had been done away with, and that there was no point in seeking me.

Toby Kent? He was abroad now, somewhere on the Continent. Weeks could pass before he heard that I had disappeared, and then he might think I had decided to run away and begin a new life somewhere, following Sebastian Ryder's revelations during the river trip. Andrew Doyle might think the same. Much would depend on whether Sebastian Ryder told anyone how sudden and unnatural my disappearance had been. Grimly I made myself face the fact that there was little if any hope of escape from this prison except by my own efforts, and I could do nothing immediately.

I went to the window and stood on tiptoe again to look out. The bars were stout, and in any event I could have no hope of climbing down to the ground four floors below. There was no window in the water closet. Trying to hold my nerves steady, I sat down at the table, opened the drawer, and took out the Bible. There was nothing else in the drawer.

I decided that for a few days at least, perhaps longer, I must behave quietly, without protest, and do all I was told. During that time I would try to find out as much as possible about the house I was in, the surroundings, the staff, and the servants who must surely be employed to keep the rooms clean. There would be stables, I thought. One or two ponies, a gig, a larger carriage, perhaps. If I could escape from the house . . .

But where would I go? Would the village folk argue with Dr. Thornton if he said I was an escaped lunatic? No doubt there were genuine mental cases here to give credence to such a story. Despair tried to enfold me and I fought it off. A letter . . . I must contrive to write a letter which I would post as soon as I reached the village, in case I were caught and brought back. Somehow I must lay hands on paper, pen and ink, an envelope, a stamp. No, a stamp would not be needed. The person receiving the letter would be charged double postage, but if I wrote my name on the back . . .

Who should I write to? The Ryder family would eventually be returning to Silverwood, and my letter might not be forwarded. If I wrote to Silverwood it might lie unopened for weeks. Toby Kent? He was abroad. Andrew Doyle? He might soon be leaving London, and I did not know how long it would take me to prepare a letter and make my escape.

Mrs. Hesketh. Yes. She would be the best person to write to, for the letter would find her in Chancery Lane and she had shown that she liked me. I felt sure she would do whatever was best to help, and I knew her to be both experienced and formidable.

I did not allow myself to think how difficult it might be to achieve what I planned, to prepare a letter and then to escape from Dr. Thornton's institution, at least as far as the village. I only knew that Sir John Tennant's intention must be to keep me imprisoned here for as long as he lived, or perhaps for as long as Sebastian Ryder lived. Or perhaps for as long as I lived. And if I was to be kept solitary in this room, or to dwell among the mentally afflicted as one of them for untold years, then sooner or later I might genuinely lose my reason.

The distant church bells told me three days later that Sunday had come, and I marked it with a little scratch low down on the inside of the water-closet door, made with the tip of my spoon. It was the first of six Sundays I was to mark on my crude calendar before I was ready to attempt my escape, but within three days I came to know the routine of the nameless institution that was my prison.

I was served three meals each day. Breakfast was porridge and tea, the porridge lumpy but plentiful, the tea weak and lukewarm. At noon or thereabouts came the main meal of the day, and this was always stew in a bowl, again a good helping but with far more vegetable than meat. The stew was followed by rice pudding or semolina and another mug of tea. At six o'clock came a mug of cocoa with three slices of bread and jam, the bread thick, the jam thin.

Each meal was brought in on a tray by a plump, rather stolid girl called Stella, but it was Nurse Webb who unlocked the door and stood watching while Stella set the tray down on my small table. Later they would both return for Stella to collect the tray. At eight o'clock Nurse Webb would appear alone, with a half glass of watery milk and a white tablet. I had to put the tablet in my mouth, show my hand empty, and drink the milk down.

I knew Stella was not a living-in servant, for when she brought in my breakfast tray on the third day, she was in the middle of telling Nurse Webb that her heel was sore from walking to work from the village that morning, and she needed to get her shoe seen to. Stella took no notice of me, and though I hoped I might later try to enlist her help, I made no attempt to speak to her in Nurse Webb's presence. Following the general plan I had made, I tried to look miserably resigned, as if sti stupefied by the shock of finding myself here.

I was not sure that I convinced Nurse Webb, for as the days went b she continued to eye me very sharply with a suspicious eye. In the wal beside the bed was a small wooden knob attached to a wire which ra through a tube in the wall. This was a bellpull, and Nurse Webb drew my attention to it on my first night, when she brought me the pill t make sure I slept.

"The bellpull is for emergency use only, Miss Smith," she said wit emphasis. "If you become excited and use it without very good reason we may find it necessary to employ suitable treatment for calming yo down. Now put this in your mouth."

I took the pill obediently and swallowed it with the watery milk. Th result was that my sleep was unpleasantly heavy and I woke with headache and a bad taste in my mouth, but it was hopeless for me t resist. I had been through a similar ordeal as a child, when I was sold t Mrs. Logan, and knew I would have to acquiesce until I could find way to circumvent the nightly routine of a drugged sleep.

A week passed before I achieved this, and by then I had practiced fo several hours every day with a piece of bread crust the size of the pill Holding it on my palm, I would go through the motion of tossing i into my mouth and then showing my empty hand, but in reality I wa hiding it as a conjurer might, tucked in the fork between my thum and first finger.

I was nervous when I first put my labors to the test by hiding the pi from Nurse Webb in this way, but evidently I was deft enough, for sh suspected nothing. From then on I was able to think more clearly, m mind free from the lethargy the drug had imposed even during m waking hours.

My room was gaslit by a mantle set close to the ceiling, and the flow was evidently controlled by a tap outside the room, for after I ha taken the usual tablet and been locked in for the night, the gas woul go out. This left only a dim light from the passage showing through double panel of glass set above the door with iron bars between. Onc each week I was given clean sheets, nightdress, and bedsocks. Twic each week my room was swept and dusted. I was not the only inmat on this floor. There were five rooms off the corridor, all occupied. knew this because while Stella and another girl cleaned the rooms, w all had to sit on chairs outside our respective doors under the eye o

Nurse Webb, who walked slowly up and down between the end of the passage where my room lay and a stairwell at the far end.

My fellow patients were all women and all much older than I. One never spoke, but sat as if having withdrawn completely into another world. The other three seemed to know each other, but I soon realized they were genuinely afflicted. One would go from sobs to laughter within a few seconds, chattering nonsense. The remaining two conversed after a fashion, but what each said bore little relevance to what the other had just said. I made one or two diffident attempts to talk to them while our rooms were cleaned, mainly to give Nurse Webb the impression that I had accepted my lot, but their response was meaningless.

I was thankful for the hour of room cleaning, for it took me out briefly from the four walls that held me, and at least allowed me sight of other human beings. While sitting outside my door on these occasions, I tried to learn as much as I could about the house. It was clearly very big, and I thought there must be men inmates as well as women, for I could sometimes hear males voices from beyond the stairwell. The words were indistinguishable, and some might have been exchanges between male attendants, but I also heard an outburst of shrieks, a snatch of song in a quavering voice, and some high-pitched laughter which seemed mechanical and without meaning.

I came to the conclusion that for the most part this was genuinely an institution for people mentally afflicted, but I thought it might well hold one or two others like myself, quite sane but imprisoned here on the pretext of madness because somebody, whether family or enemy, had reason to keep them shut away from the world.

Once, during my third week, there was a commotion from the floor below while our rooms were being cleaned, and Nurse Webb went hurrying down the stairs to see if help was needed. Stella and the other girl were busy in two of the rooms, and at once I ran to the end of the passage to peer over the banister of the stairwell. I could see little of the corridors below, only that the stairwell dropped four floors to a large hall which I took to be the ground floor. Dr. Thornton was coming up from the second floor, one hand on the banister. I hurried back to my chair, and that was the end of the incident, except that I was now sure I could reach the ground floor direct by way of those stairs.

The door of my room was very solid and I could hear little from beyond when it was closed. Sometimes I would stand with my ear pressed against it and hear faint sounds of movement and doors bei unlocked in the passage. I guessed that these were times when n fellow inmates were allowed to join others in the common room D Thornton had spoken of. My heart sank when I recalled that he ha said I must prove of good behavior for several months before I mig join them.

Dr. Thornton paid me a visit twice weekly, always accompanied Nurse Webb. Wearing an artificial smile on his egg-shaped face, would gaze distantly past me as he asked how I was, would ignore ar answer I gave, feel my pulse, assure me that I was fortunate to be such good hands, and then depart.

On his third visit I asked if I might write a letter. He gave me shrewd, questioning glance, then beamed in his usual vague mann and said, "Why not? Why not? Whom were you thinking of writir to, Miss Smith?"

"To the gentleman who employed me," I said slowly, trying to a pear as lethargic as I had felt when I was taking the nightly drug. "H name is Mr. Ryder."

"Oh, but he knows you are here, Miss Smith. Don't you remembe It was he who called in the doctors when you were in a condition of ah—mental distress."

"I would like to write and thank him," I said.

"Very well, very well. Nurse Webb will provide whatever you requir We all wish you to be happy here. How well you are looking, Mi Smith. I'm sure that rest and quiet are having a profoundly benefici effect. Do resist any tendency to become excited, won't you? Goc morning, good morning."

Next day Nurse Webb brought me a thin pad of plain paper, pe and ink, and a single envelope. I was disappointed, for I had hoped steal an envelope for the letter I planned to write to Mrs. Hesketh preparation for my escape. As it was I stole two sheets from the pa and with these and a great deal of care I later fashioned a rath unsightly but adequate envelope, using jam to gum the edges togethe

I knew very well that the letter to Mr. Ryder would never be poste and so I wrote only a few lines, saying that I could not remember bei taken ill, apologizing for any trouble I had caused, and hoping th somebody might one day come to visit me. The second letter I wro was to Mrs. Hesketh. In as few words as possible I begged her to he me and told her that I had been abducted and was being held in a institution for the insane under a Dr. Thornton, standing I knew not where, but near a village on the edge of moorland. I addressed my homemade envelope, put the letter in it, and hid it under the paper lining of the drawer in which the Bible was kept.

That was a good day, for I felt I had achieved something, but for most of my waking hours I was struggling against fear and a dreadful sense of utter loneliness. There was nobody with whom I could share a single thought. I had a fear of Nurse Webb that went beyond reason, to the degree that I could feel my heart begin to pound whenever I heard the key in the lock and knew I was about to see her. I was also afraid of failure, for I dreaded to think what would become of me if I did not escape.

To keep such weakening thoughts at bay throughout the seemingly endless hours of the day, I began to occupy my mind by settling down to read the Bible through from the beginning, one book each day. I also made a point of taking off my nightdress twice each day to do a full hour of the physical exercises Mam'selle Montavon had required all her students at the college to practice regularly. Apart from passing the time, these exercises were important to me now, I felt, for I did not know what lay ahead, and I wanted to avoid having my body become slack and weak from enforced idleness.

The worst times came when the light was turned out at eight and I found myself lying awake for two or three hours before sleep came to me. Then I had to depend on happy memories to hold back my fear. There were not many, but the best memories were of times I had spent with Toby Kent, in Paris or in Chelsea, and best of all was my memory of the day he had taken me to the circus. I relived that day in every minute detail, again and again, remembering how we had laughed together, and it never failed to drive back the shadows and bring me a kind of peace.

By the end of the fourth week I knew that Nurse Webb had a regular day off each Thursday, and it was only then that I was able to form a definite plan. Every Thursday, from breakfast onward, she was replaced by Mrs. Gregg, a short stocky woman with a sour manner and a smell of gin about her. I did not like Mrs. Gregg, but neither did I fear her, and this made it possible for me to plan something I would never have dared to attempt on a day that Nurse Webb was on duty.

First I had to make sure that Mrs. Gregg's duty period extended into the night, and there was only one way to do this. On the fifth Thursday of my imprisonment, soon after midnight, I mixed up some strong soapy water and kept sipping it until I felt close to being sick. Then, with much apprehension, I tugged the bellpull I had been warned to use only in emergency.

I heard no sound from outside, neither did I expect to, for I had seen no bells outside the doors in the passage, and I surmised that the bellpulls were connected to a room where somebody would be on duty to note the call and alert the nurse in charge of that section.

Five minutes passed. I finished the last of the soapy water and struggled to hold it down. There came the sound of the key in the lock. I ran into the water closet, touched the back of my throat with a finger, and immediately began to be sick as I knelt with my head over the bowl.

When the retching eased I lifted my head. The gaslight in the room had been turned up and Mrs. Gregg stood in the open doorway of the water closet, scowling down at me, wearing a nightcap and a dressing gown over a flannel nightdress.

"What's amiss?" she snapped. Like Nurse Webb she had a northern accent, and this helped to confirm my impression that the moors I could see from my window were probably part of the Yorkshire moors.

I gasped for breath, wiped my face with the towel I had snatched up, and retched again. It must have been obvious to anyone that I was making no pretense. "I'm sorry," I faltered, panting. "I had such pains . . . in my stomach. I was afraid . . ."

She scratched her chin and stood pondering, no doubt trying to decide whether or not I was seriously ill. After a moment or two she said, "Have you finished?"

I got slowly to my feet, a hand to my sweating forehead. "Yes. I . . . I think so, Mrs. Gregg. I'm sorry. I woke up with the pains, and then . . ."

"Come under the light." She took me by the arm and pulled me under the gaslight, feeling my brow and peering at my face, which I knew must look pale and waxen. "Is the pain still there?" she demanded.

"No," I said shakily, "it seems better now I've been sick."

"Must have been something you ate," she grunted. "Get into bed and keep warm."

I obeyed gladly, for I was feeling shivery. She stood regarding me uncertainly for a few moments, then said, "You going to be all right now?"

"Yes." My face was hidden in the bedclothes. "Yes, I'm sure I shall be."

She shuffled out of the room, closed and locked the door. The gaslight dwindled and vanished except for the tiny glow of the pilot flame. I hugged the bedclothes about me and felt mingled triumph and fear. I had confirmed that on Thursdays the person on night duty was Mrs. Gregg, and I had done so without getting into trouble and being subjected to what Nurse Webb had called the calming down treatment. But I was afraid, too, because the next step in what I planned would commit me to an attempt at escape, and I felt that my very life and sanity would hang upon this.

I waited two weeks before taking the step from which there was no turning back, and I did so because I thought it unwise to use my emergency alarm to call Mrs. Gregg on consecutive Thursdays. During that fortnight I increased my exercise time to three separate hours each day to ensure that I was in good physical condition.

When the final moment came there were few preparations for me to make. It was one o'clock in the morning. I put the hidden letter to Mrs. Hesketh in my dressing-gown pocket and moved my chair so that it stood beside the water-closet door, which opened outward. I set the door ajar, then said a prayer, screwed up my courage, and tugged at the bellpull.

Five minutes passed. I was kneeling on the floor on the far side of the bed when the gas was turned up from outside and I heard the key in the lock. At once I lay flat beside the bed, hidden from anyone coming into the room. I heard the door open, the scuffle of slippered feet crossing the room below the foot of the bed. Mrs. Gregg came into view, wearing nightcap, nightdress, and dressing gown, as before. She was sideways-on to me, and moving past, so she did not see me lying close against the bed as she made for the water closet.

As she pulled the door wide her back was toward me. I came to my feet, ran forward, and gave her a push that sent her stumbling through the doorway with a grunt of surprise. Next instant I had slammed the door and was setting the top of my chairback under the handle to keep it tightly shut.

I heard Mrs. Gregg give an angry shout as I ran to the door she had left open. The key was in the lock. I went out, closed the door quietly, and turned the key with a shaking hand. Now I was committed, ar the rest of my escape was in the lap of the gods, for I did not kno enough about the house or surroundings to have formulated a sour plan. As I turned from the door I could still hear muffled shouts fro Mrs. Gregg, but the sound did not carry, for the water closet w against the outer wall, and by the time I reached the head of tl staircase I could hear nothing.

It seemed my heart was making more noise than my feet as I bega to run down the stairs. There were three short flights between eac landing, and on every floor a gaslight had been left on, burning lo Boards creaked, a window rattled, but I saw nobody, and no voi called out to me to halt. No lamp burned in the large square hall at tl foot of the stairs, but enough light came from above for me to see tl heavy front door with two stout bolts.

I eased the lower bolt back without difficulty, but then found would have to stand on a chair to draw the upper one. For long secon I was almost senseless with panic at the delay, but with a huge effort made myself move steadily about the task until at last it was done. climbed down from the chair, carried it carefully back to its pla against the wall, then went to the door again and held my breath as grasped the handle. The door opened, and a cool night wind touch my sweating face.

Thirty seconds later I stood in a moonlit courtyard with my back the wall of the house, peering toward heavy wooden gates which I kne must lead out to the road. I could make out the stables and coach hou on my right. This was a moment I had thought about many times. was shod only in bedsocks, and the road to the village would no dou be rough. There were horses in the stable, and if I could saddle one ar move away at a quiet walk I would surely save myself the pain bruised and bloody feet. But I was unfamiliar with the stables and n greatly experienced with horses. I would have to find saddle and brid for I had no confidence in my ability to ride without, and I simp could not bring myself to linger so long with the chance of bei discovered.

My eyes had grown accustomed to the darkness now, and I ra across to the gates. There was no lock, only a wooden bar resting in socket, and a bolt at the foot. I eased one gate open just wide enoug for me to squeeze through, and pushed it to behind me. In the distan I could make out one or two tiny lights. These would mark the sleepi village. The road leading to it lay before me, a narrow and unmade road, but one which I prayed would carry me to freedom.

Five minutes later I looked back and saw the silhouette of the institution, my prison, rising solitary from the moor. The night was mild and I was warm from exertion, but even so I shivered at the sight and turned my head quickly away as I hurried on. In another five minutes I was limping from the grazes and bruising my feet had suffered, but I did not care, for hope was rising within me at every step.

When I reached the village I would first seek a postbox and post my letter to Mrs. Hesketh. Once that was done, then whatever happened I would no longer feel utterly alone, and I could hope for help. When the letter was posted, I planned to seek the vicarage and tell my story there, hoping to convince a man of some authority in the village that I was sane.

One of the lights I could see appeared to be moving, growing larger. I caught my breath in alarm as it suddenly dawned on me that the light was moving along the road toward me. A slight breeze from behind me must have carried away all sound of an approaching carriage, but now I heard it, the steady clop of hooves and the rattle of wheels from no more than a hundred paces away.

I froze, then turned and limped off the road as quickly as I could, to find myself amid thick tussocks of grass in a marshy patch of ground, my feet sinking in at each step. The carriage drew nearer, then to my horror it came to a halt. I crouched where I stood, not daring to move.

A voice, the coachman's voice perhaps: "It were something moving, sir. Too big for an animal. Saw a flash of white, I did."

That must have been the skirt of my nightdress showing below the dressing gown. Another man spoke, and terror gripped me, for it was the voice of Dr. Thornton, sounding both angry and disturbed. "Are you sure, Jackson? If it was too big for a wild creature it can only be human. Where did you say?"

"Just about 'ere, sir. Moving off the road it was." The coachman was standing up in his seat now, lifting a lantern high to throw a wider circle of light, and I saw the figure of Dr. Thornton moving closer to the edge of the road.

"I can't see anything," he said. "No, wait . . ." He was looking in my direction. "Something there. Let's see." He moved toward me, and I knew I was lost. Rising from my crouched position, I turned and tried to run. There came a shout from behind me: "Yes, by God! It's a woman! Lend a hand Jackson! Quick, damn you!"

First my feet sank in the marshy patch, and then as I struggled on my ankles were caught by heather or coarse grass and I sprawled headlong. Sobbing for breath I dragged myself up and blundered on. Booted feet crunched on heather behind me, drawing closer despite all my efforts. I crumpled the letter to Mrs. Hesketh and dropped it. Another ten agonizing paces and I heard the breath of the man at my heels. A hand caught my shoulder, jerking me off balance so that I fell sideways.

The sky was blotted out as the man loomed over me, crouching to pin me down with a hand on my chest. "Got 'er, sir!" cried the coachman. There came the sound of feet approaching at a steadier pace, and I looked up fearfully as the coachman moved aside. Dr. Thornton stood peering down at me. I could not see his face for he was silhouetted against the moon, but he could see mine, and I heard his sharp intake of breath as he recognizd me.

"By Christ," he said incredulously, *"it's the McLeod girl!"*

I was never to know how Dr. Thornton chanced to be coming from the village in his coach at so late an hour. Perhaps he had been carousing at a friend's house, for when he dropped slowly to one knee and leaned over me I smelled whiskey on his breath. I only knew that I had failed, and the knowledge of what this portended was a blow as brutal as if I had been struck with a club. Despair was like a giant hand crushing me into the ground as I thought numbly of the room that was my prison, of the endless empty hours and countless empty days that awaited me. And my failure was all the more cruel because I had so nearly succeeded.

Taking my arm in a painful grip Dr. Thornton stood up, drawing me to my feet, his face close to mine, glaring in fury. His mouth was loose, and again I smelled whiskey. Perhaps he had been a little drunk, but he was rapidly becoming sober, for behind the fury lay shock and fear, no doubt springing from the realization that I had come so close to escaping.

With a thrust of his arm he sent me staggering against the coachman. "Get her into the carriage," he said thickly. "I'll deal with this as soon as we reach home."

Fourteen

We entered the institution by a side door which Dr. Thornton unlocked with a key, and I was taken straight to the main hall. Within five minutes there was much hustle and bustle as servants were brought from their beds in hastily donned clothes, one sent to rouse Nurse Webb, another to my room, and a third to the laundry, though for what purpose I did not hear.

I had spoken only once since my capture. When asked how I had got out of my room, I answered that I did not remember, that Mrs. Gregg had opened the door and I remembered nothing beyond that. I did not expect to be believed, but felt it better to pretend a kind of innocence than to admit that I had carried out a carefully planned escape.

I sat in a chair in the hall, guarded by a male servant I had never seen, and waited for whatever was to be done with me. When Mrs. Gregg was released from the water closet and came down to the hall, Dr. Thornton raged at her for allowing me to escape, and she in turn raged at me, calling me a crafty little cow. Nurse Webb appeared. Her cropped hair was a little untidy but she was fully dressed. She listened impatiently while Mrs. Gregg repeated her tale, then sent her to bed in obvious displeasure.

Dr. Thornton paced up and down the hall, hands behind his back.

He was still shaken and angry, but controlled now and completely sober. "I don't want this happening again, Harriet," he said forcefully to Nurse Webb when Mrs. Gregg had gone. He stopped to look at me with narrowed eyes. "Hard to tell if this girl just seized an opportunity offered by that stupid woman or if she planned the whole business."

Nurse Webb folded her powerful arms and eyed me with an air of anticipation. "Whichever it was, the patient is suffering from being overexcited, doctor," she said. "I recommend immediate corrective treatment."

Dr. Thornton nodded. "I've given orders to prepare for it," he said. "All right, carry on, please. I rely on you to make sure she gives no further trouble, Harriet."

"Very well, doctor."

He turned away down one of the passages off the hall. The man who had been sent down to the laundry reappeared. Nurse Webb said to him, "You and Kearley bring her down. Don't stand any nonsense."

The man standing guard over me took my arm in a hard grip and said, "Come on." I did not resist. Whatever was in store for me, I knew that to resist would only make it worse. We passed through kitchens to the laundry, Nurse Webb leading, the two men walking one each side of me, holding my arms. In a corner of the laundry was a long stone trough filled with water. Nurse Webb stopped by it and said to me, "Take your dressing gown off, Miss Smith."

I was sure she wanted me to disobey, but I complied, now wearing only my nightdress.

"Lie down," she said.

I looked about me. There was only the stone floor. I sat down, then lay back, shivering at the touch of the dank stone through my nightdress, deeply afraid, but trying to hide my fear. Nurse Webb took two long rubber aprons from a hook and tossed one to the man she had called Kearley. "You take her shoulders," she said, and began to put on the other apron.

When she had tied it in place she bent to grip my ankles in her strong hands, and Kearley crouched to grasp my shoulders. Now I was sure I knew what was to happen, but I had barely time to draw and hold my breath before I was plunged into icy water, completely immersed. The shock seemed to strike at every nerve in my body. I tried to lift my head, to get my mouth and nose clear of the water so I could breathe, but I was too deep, and they held me down . . . held me down . . . held me down . . .

Panic seized me and I began to struggle wildly, but I could not break free. My lungs were bursting and I wanted to scream. When I was sure I must breathe in and drown, I was suddenly lifted clear of the water and held inches above it. With blurred, water-filled eyes I saw the shape of Nurse Webb as she held my ankles. My nightdress was rucked to my thighs now. She said, "You will not try to run away again, will you, Miss Smith?"

Before I could answer I was plunged under the water for a second time. Once more I went through the terror of near drowning, and once more I was lifted out when I was at the end of my tether. This time I could see nothing, I could only hear the voice of Nurse Webb saying, "You will not try to run away again, will you, Miss Smith?"

I was trying to speak when the water closed over me and the ordeal began anew. I lost count of the times I was plunged into that trough of water. Each time I was lifted out, Nurse Webb put exactly the same question. At one stage I was trying to gasp, "No! I promise!" For I would have said anything to stop the torment, but she was not concerned with any answer. The ordeal went on and on, and I was never to remember the end of it, for there must have come a point at which I lost my senses.

When I came to myself again I was in darkness, lying on the linoleum covered floor of a tiny room, a cupboard perhaps, shuddering with cold, still in my soaking nightdress. Slowly I sat up and groped about me. It was two or three minutes before I was able to guess that the cramped place where I lay was a water closet. When at last I stood up, on unsteady legs and pain-racked feet, groping in the darkness, I found a broken handle on the end of the chain hanging from the cistern, and knew that I was in the water closet of my own room, where I had earlier imprisoned Mrs. Gregg.

I did not know how much time had passed. My teeth were chattering and I felt cold to the bone, but the chill in my mind was deeper and worse. I had failed, and now I had experienced the treatment meted out to inmates Dr. Thornton decided were in need of calming down. Death could not have brought worse torment, for the treatment had rendered me unconscious, and I would have felt no more if I had died under Nurse Webb's ministrations.

I tried the door, but it would not move. Slowly I peeled off my nightdress, wrung it out in the lavatory bowl as thoroughly as I could, then hung it from the cistern and forced myself to begin doing physical exercises as vigorously as I could in the cramped space, jumping up and down with my arms at my sides, running on the spot with arms held high over my head, pushing myself off one wall with flat hands, turning to fall against the other, and pushing myself off again. These were all exercises in which Mam'selle Montavon instructed her students to help them keep in good health, supple, and attractive in figure.

Later I was to think the exercises that night may have saved my life, but after an hour, although the chill had been replaced by a glow of warmth, my torn feet hurt badly and I was almost exhausted. My nightdress was still very damp and offered no warmth, so I decided I would rest for ten minutes but then continue with less energetic exercises, of just sufficient vigor to prevent my becoming chilled. Sitting down on the floor in a corner of the tiny closet, I leaned my head back against the door, closed my eyes . . . and fell asleep.

When at last the cold woke me I knew I must have slept for at least two hours. I was stiff in every muscle, and the penetrating chill had taken me in its grip again. My head felt thick, my brain sluggish, and to drive my body into renewing the exercises was too huge an effort. The best I could manage was to stand up and keep walking in the tiniest of circles, on and on and on, feeling the strength running out of me, my chest tightening, and my head growing hot.

There came a moment at last, after I had lost all sense of time and almost all sense of place, when I heard the door handle rattle as the chair outside was moved from it. The door opened and Nurse Webb stood there, the early morning light from the window behind her. "Come out, Miss Smith," she said. Every hair was in place, and she looked exactly as she had always looked in her gray dress with the leg-of-mutton sleeves. I trembled as I walked past her.

A clean dry nightdress lay on the bed. I picked it up and put it on without being told. My hair had dried now but was lank and tangled. "Get into bed," said Nurse Webb, and I obeyed. "Dr. Thornton has recommended that you fast today," she continued. "We trust you will not again try to run away from those responsible for your welfare, Miss Smith."

I turned on my side without answering, and after a moment heard her go out and lock the door behind her. I knew that I was going to be ill, perhaps very ill. In that state I would have little strength and determination, so as I lay in bed now I thought of my mother, Kathleen McLeod, and I told myself that for her sake I must never give in. I had perforce endured four years at the College for Young Ladies before being able to free myself from that life, and if I had to wait as long again to escape from the asylum where I was now a prisoner, I would wait without ever losing a scruple of the determination I would need.

I would be endlessly patient. I would be quiet and obedient, and convince everyone that my spirit was broken. In time I would be allowed to use the common room. I would learn more about my prison. I would think and plan, and in the end I would again break free, better prepared next time. Somehow I would succeed. Somehow . . .

With these thoughts I lay fighting to rebuild my spirits before the coming illness took my strength, never dreaming that I was bracing myself for a struggle which would soon be taken out of my hands.

By nightfall the fever was upon me, and in the following days I seemed to be in a delirium when awake and in a nightmare when I slept. A demon sat on my chest, squeezing, crushing, preventing me from dragging into my lungs the air I craved.

Occasionally there were brief periods of lucidity when my mind felt unnaturally clear and perceptive. Twice I was aware of being fed warm soup from a bowl by a woman in a gray dress who was not Nurse Webb. Once I came to myself while Dr. Thornton was present and talking to Nurse Webb as he took my temperature. Several times when alone I experienced these curiously lucid moments, waking from a feverish sleep with a sense of deep comprehension. In one such awakening, during the night, I understood with absolute clarity that Dr. Thornton would not be at all dismayed if I were to die, but was taking great care to ensure that he could not possibly be accused of neglect.

Then at last came a day when the fever was gone, and with it the nightmares and the times of strange perception. My only feeling was one of utter weakness, for I had barely the strength to move a finger, yet I could feel a thread of stubborn satisfaction in my mind, for I knew that the crisis was past, and I had survived. Now, slowly and patiently, I would work to build up my strength both in body and spirit until I was fully restored, and could embark upon the long ordeal I would have to endure if I ever hoped to be free.

Three days later I was able to summon enough strength to get myself from the bed to the water closet unaided. As I returned, pausing to steady myself against the wall, I caught sight of my face in the small looking glass attached to the wall above the table, and it was the face of a stranger. Beneath a tangle of hair, my eyes were dark hollows sunk deep in my head. My skin was waxen with red blotches. My cheeks had fallen in, my lips were puffy and sore.

I climbed into bed and lay back, panting a little from the effort, telling myself that my present appearance did not matter. I was able to eat now, and although the food was neither plentiful nor well cooked, it was sufficient and nourishing enough to restore me to health in the course of time, which was all I wanted. If there was one thing I did not lack it was time.

Breakfast had been brought to me an hour ago. Nothing more would happen now till the noon meal came. Dreadful though I might look, I felt better and stronger than I had yesterday, and sleep was nourishment for my weakened body. I said to myself, "Patience, Hannah, patience," as I had said many times before, then closed my eyes and slept.

It was perhaps an hour later that I woke to such noise and commotion as I had never before heard since the night my imprisonment began. There were shouts from the corridor, raised voices, scuffling, then a sudden rattling of the key in the lock. By this time I had managed to lift myself on an elbow and was staring toward the door, startled and beginning to feel afraid.

The door was flung open, a man stormed in and stopped dead, staring down at me with widening eyes. Then my fear was gone, and for the first time in years I gave way to tears, for the man was Andrew Doyle. Long seconds passed while he stood gazing as if he scarcely knew me, his face slowly becoming a mask of fury.

"Please . . . . please, Mr. Doyle," I said in a croaking whisper, "don't let them keep me . . . . it's a prison . . ."

A heavy riding crop hung by a loop from his wrist, and he wore neither topcoat nor hat. Outside in the corridor there was still much noise going on. I could hear Nurse Webb's voice raised in anger and indignation, but Andrew Doyle ignored all that was happening outside. He came to the bed, and his rage was such that his eyes seemed to glow with it, but that rage was not for me. Kneeling, he tucked the blanket and sheet about me very tenderly, then slid his arms beneath me and stood up, lifting me easily and holding me cradled like a baby. "You're safe, Hannah," he said in a shaking voice. "You're quite, quite safe now."

There came a scream of wrath, and when I turned my head a little I saw Nurse Webb coming through the door in the grip of one of the biggest men I had ever set eyes on. His face was like rough-hewn mahogany, the flesh hard and battered. His huge hands were even darker brown, and glistened slightly as if the bones were covered with shell rather than flesh. Nurse Webb was a powerful woman, as I had reason to know, but this man held her by the back of the neck with one hand, bent forward a little, and clearly quite powerless in his grasp. The man's blue eyes were twinkling as he said with a placid air, "Th'ole bitch tried to bite me thumb, zur." His eyes moved to me, and lost their twinkle. "Dear Lor', is that the young leddy? Don't look to weigh more'n a feather, do she?"

Nurse Webb was still screaming threats. Andrew Doyle said, "Calm her down, Jake."

"Pleasure, zur." Again the blue eyes twinkled. Without seeming effort the big man ran Nurse Webb to the washstand, poured the whole jug of water into the bowl, and plunged her face down into it, holding her there. "I don't reckon Owd Jim's 'aving much trouble with them folk outside," he said reflectively, scratching his leathery cheek with his free hand. "Talks very persuasive does Owd Jim."

Nurse Webb's arms were frantically clawing the air, and great bubbles were bursting all round her submerged head. I should have been glad, but I remembered my own terror and said, "Please, Mr. Doyle . . . stop him. They did that to me when I escaped."

"We know," he said grimly. "We know, my sweetheart. All right, Jake, that will do. We'll go now."

Jake plucked Nurse Webb's head from the bowl, and with a swing of his arm tossed her bodily onto the bed, where she lay gasping and sobbing. Andrew Doyle carried me carefully through the doorway. There were half a dozen people in the passage, three men and two women in the gray uniform worn by the staff, and another man as huge as Jake. My head was whirling with bewilderment and relief, but I realized that this must be Owd Jim. In fact he looked no older than Jake, but he wore a morose expression in contrast to Jake's amiable look.

Owd Jim was saying not a word, and it was evident that if he "talked very persuasive" as Jake claimed, then it was with his fists that he talked, for of Dr. Thornton's three men present, only one was on his feet, and he stood pressed against the wall, eyes rolling in fear. A second man lay on his back unconscious, and a third sat against the far wall, moaning and holding his jaw. The two women were huddled together, shocked and fearful. It dawned on me now that Jake and Owd Jim must be prizefighters—or perhaps former prizefighters, for neither was young—great muscular gladiators of the prize ring, faces toughened by years of battering, their fists pickled in brine to make them hard as brick.

Andrew Doyle said, "Lead on, Jim."

Owd Jim nodded gloomily and moved toward the stairs. Andrew followed, and Jake came behind. I saw now that each prizefighter carried a beknobbed cudgel at least a foot long hanging from his belt, but I could not imagine that these would be needed. As we started down the stairs I struggled for control to prevent myself crying again, and said in a feeble voice, "I did try to escape, Mr. Doyle, I tried so hard, and I was going to try again once I was well, but . . . oh, thank God you came."

"We know you tried," he said, and I could feel the anger in him as he held me close. "We know about the water treatment, and how you almost died."

I wondered whom he meant by "we." I wondered how they could know what had happened, and how they had found me, but these were only vague, half-formed questions in my mind, and they could be answered later. All that truly mattered for the moment was the miracle of the past few minutes, the miracle by which I had suddenly found myself safe in the arms of a man who had befriended me. Safe, and a prisoner no longer.

We passed other men and women of Dr. Thornton's staff on the lower landings, but nobody made any attempt to stop us until we were nearing the big hall on the ground floor, and then I saw Dr. Thornton himself appear, running from a passage which led to the back of the house and obviously in great alarm, as if he had only just been told what was happening in his institution. Two men followed him, halting at the foot of the stairs as he began to mount. Four steps up, he came face to face with Owd Jim, but looked past him to Andrew Doyle. "How dare you, sir!" he cried. His face was white and sweating, perhaps with a blend of anger and fear. "Release that patient at once, or I shall send for the police!"

Andrew Doyle said, "Leave him and move those other two away, Jim."

Owd Jim walked past Dr. Thornton on the stairs, spread his arms to catch each man round the neck as he walked between them, and simply continued walking, half carrying half dragging them with him to the side of the hall. Andrew Doyle said, "Are you Dr. Thornton, principal of this institution?"

"I am, sir! And I'll have you know—"

He was unable to say more, for Andrew Doyle lifted one foot and thrust hard at his chest, hurling him back down four stairs to go sprawling on the floor of the hall with a cry of shock and pain. We followed, and as Andrew Doyle cleared the stairs he turned to Jake, behind him. "Hold her, Jake," he said, "I've something to attend to." The big man took me very gently in his great arms, and Andrew Doyle turned to Owd Jim. "If anyone tries to interfere," he said, freeing the crop that hung from his wrist, "break their heads."

"Right," said Owd Jim lugubriously, and took the cudgel from his belt.

Dr. Thornton had struggled to his knees when Andrew Doyle suddenly seized him by the lapels of his jacket, flung him against the wall with stunning force, and then, as he fell, bent and dragged the back of the jacket up over the man's head. "Who paid you?" he said in a voice with an edge like a sword blade, and with those words the crop whistled down across Dr. Thornton's back. There came a muffled shriek of pain from beneath the jacket, and he tried frantically to crawl away, but Andrew Doyle pinned him against the wall with one foot and brought the crop down again . . . and again, and again, each time repeating the same question in the same iron-hard voice. "Who paid you? Who paid you?"

I saw the shirt split across Dr. Thornton's back as his screams grew louder, and I hid my face against Jake's massive chest. "Now jest you don' fret, miss," he rumbled softly in my ear. "Bit of a whippin' 'll do 'im a power o' good."

"Tennant!" The word came in a sobbing shriek, and I heard the crop bite once more. *"Sir John Tennant! Tennant! Tennant!"*

I peered from one eye and saw Andrew Doyle step back from the cowering man on the floor and fling the crop aside, muttering to himself a word or two in Spanish I did not understand, then speaking in English with his American accent. "There's nothing more I want from you, Thornton. Just that name. By all means tell the police about this i you dare, you goddamn scoundrel. My name is Andrew Doyle, and I'l be talking to the police myself. All right, Jake." He took me in his arm again, smiling down at me reassuringly, and only seconds later I passe through that forbidding front door for the last time, with Owd Jin leading and Jake following.

A carriage waited in the courtyard, the coachman in his seat. The gates stood open. Owd Jim swung up beside the coachman. Jake opened the door and I gave a little cry of pleasure, for there was Mrs Hesketh, anxiety struggling with relief in her eyes as she reached out to help Andrew Doyle lift me into the coach. She settled herself beside me, holding me with her arms about me as the two men climbed in and closed the door. The carriage began to move, and I almost wept with joy, but managed to hold back tears as I whispered, "Oh, thank you thank you, thank you . . ."

"Hannah, my poor Hannah, what have they done to you?" Her voice was choked, and she stroked my cheek gently as she spoke. "Dea heaven, that stupid girl from the village told us about the calming down treatment and how she thought you were going to die of pneu monia, but I didn't dream you'd look so . . . so . . ."

Her voice failed her. I felt weak with happiness as I said, "I'm much better, Mrs. Hesketh, and now I'm free I'll soon be my old self again, promise. I'm really a very strong person."

"You are indeed, child," she said in a low voice. "God knows you have needed to be."

I pressed my cheek to hers, and said shakily, "I can hardly believe I'm not dreaming. Who did you mean just now, when you spoke of a girl telling you I had been ill?"

"One of the village girls they employ for daily cleaning," said Mrs Hesketh. "Stella. The one who cleaned your room."

"She *told* you? I thought they would all be too frightened of Nurse Webb and Dr. Thornton."

From the facing seat, Andrew Doyle said, "Oh, sure they're frightened of those two." He laughed, and I saw that the tension had at last gone out of him. "But by the time Mrs. Hesketh had finished with Stella, the wretched girl was terrified that the wrath of God and all the might of the law would come crashing down on her if she didn't tell the truth."

I had seen Mrs. Hesketh deal with people, and I could well imagine the effect she would have on Stella. The thought made me giggle, and because I was so weak I almost wept again.

"Don't talk now, dear," said Mrs. Hesketh. "Just rest. There's a train leaving for London in an hour, and we have reserved a first-class compartment for the journey. You can ask questions then, if you feel up to it, and we'll tell you how we found you." She looked across the carriage at Jake. "I hope you boys didn't do more damage than necessary?"

Jake's blue eyes smiled at her reproachfully. "Damage, Mrs. 'esketh? Ah now, you know us better than that. Like lambs we was, Owd Jim an' me. If we'd been any gentler we'd 've been preachin' a sermon. You ask the gennelman."

"They were perfect, Mrs. Hesketh," said Andrew Doyle, leaning back and stretching his legs with a little sigh of contentment, his eyes resting steadily on me. "They did exactly what I required of them, and I'm most grateful to you for recommending such a reliable escort."

I groped for Mrs. Hesketh's hand, and pressed it with what little strength I could muster. "I'm grateful, too," I whispered fervently.

The next few hours seemed like a dream after my long weeks of imprisonment, and I had to keep reassuring myself that I was truly awake. I lay on one side of the train compartment, a pillow under my head, while Andrew Doyle and Mrs. Hesketh sat on the other side and talked to me. Jake and Owd Jim were in another compartment.

"At first we all thought you had run away," said Andrew Doyle, "because a suitcase full of your clothes was found to be missing. One of the maids gave notice a week later, so we think she must have been bribed to pack a case with your clothes and get rid of it, then perhaps became frightened that she might be found out."

I said, "So because of that, even Mr. Ryder believed I had run away?"

"Yes, and he was frantic. He at once sent a message to the Hesketh Agency instructing them to use all possible resources to find you, and in return he received a message from Mrs. Hesketh telling him her agency had no intention of working for him again. I saw him a few days later when I paid a call, and that was when I heard the news. He was beside himself with anger toward you. I don't think it crossed his mind that you might have been abducted."

Mrs. Hesketh said, "It may well be that he could not bear to consider the possibility of Sir John Tennant having outwitted him." She leaned forward and touched my hand. "Forgive me, Hannah, but it became necessary for me to tell Mr. Doyle all that I had told you about your birth and your true parents."

I shook my head. "It doesn't matter, Mrs. Hesketh. Nothing matters beside my being free from that dreadful place. Does anybody else know?"

"Well dear, Mr. Doyle and I proposed to tell Toby Kent, and we sent him a telegram in Paris when we first came to believe that you had been abducted, but that was weeks ago and we have had no reply, so we think he must be away on some travels."

"I'll tell Toby the truth about myself when I next see him," I said. "The one person I don't want to know is my real mother, Mrs. Ritchie."

Andrew Doyle moved his shoulders in a shrug. "Sebastian Ryder knows, and whether or not he tells her is in the lap of the gods."

"Yes . . . I realize that." I spoke slowly, pausing often to get my breath. "But I won't be an instrument of his revenge, Mr. Doyle. Short of using force, nobody can make me show my butterfly mark, and without that he can prove nothing." I waited for a moment as the train rattled through a small station without stopping, then: "How did you first come to suspect that I had been abducted?"

Mrs. Hesketh made a wry grimace. "I was the one who should have suspected, but to my shame I failed to do so. It was Jane Ryder who felt sure something was amiss."

"Miss Jane?" I could scarcely believe it.

Andrew Doyle nodded in confirmation. "She said as much to me when I called and first heard that you'd gone. She told me it simply wasn't in Hannah McLeod's nature to run away under such circumstances. She had said as much to her father, but he flew into a rage and told her not to be stupid."

"Jane . . . ?" I said wonderingly. So it was blunt, businesslike Jane who had shown enough perception to doubt what all the evidence attested.

"While I was there," said Andrew Doyle, "she had a sudden notion, and took me up to your bedroom. There she went through the wardrobe and drawers to see what had been left, and at the back of one drawer she found . . ." He broke off and stood up to take a small suitcase from the rack. Another suitcase lay beside it, and I realized that in order to be at the institution this morning, Mr. Doyle and his party must have stayed in a nearby town overnight.

He opened the case and took from it the old tin box in which I had always kept my valuables—my birth certificate, which I now knew was false, my foster mother's birth certificate and wedding ring, the letter she had written me before she died, her prayer book, the small empty purse, and the ring of Mexican silver engraved with the initials R.D.

"Perhaps you would like to make sure everything is here," Andrew Doyle said, taking off the lid and holding the box so that I could see. "This confirmed Jane's suspicion, for we both felt sure you would never have left these things behind if you had run away. Forgive me for reading the papers it contains, Hannah, but I thought something might offer a clue." He hesitated, then continued, "I thought the letter from Kathleen McLeod, writing as your mother, was the most touching and wonderful document I have ever seen." He smiled. "Except for the final words, urging you to trust no man. We can understand her bitterness, but there are some who can be trusted, Hannah."

"I know that, Mr. Doyle." I managed to return his smile. "I've become quite a good judge." I looked through the box and nodded, deeply thankful that these few precious things had not been lost to me. "Yes, everything is there, thank you." I looked at Mrs. Hesketh. "May I ask you a favor, please?"

"Of course, child."

"If you have a brush and comb in your case, would you help me sit up and then brush my hair and make it tidy? I haven't been able to do it since . . . since the water treatment, and it feels so horrid."

She jumped up, clicking her tongue in annoyance. "Good heavens, where are my wits today? And yours too, Mr. Doyle! Have you not the sense to imagine how the poor girl must feel with her hair like an old bird's nest? And with you sitting staring at her every moment? For shame on you, Mr. Doyle."

He grinned as he lifted down her case. "I find Hannah McLeod beautiful under any conditions," he said. Then, to me: "Would you believe that Mrs. Hesketh has told me off for one thing or another almost every day since we began trying to find you?"

"Yes, I can believe it, Mr. Doyle." I was close to tears once more with the joy of being able to talk and joke again. "Mrs. Hesketh very properly believes that gentlemen should be kept in their place."

He laughed, then came and lifted me, seating himself on the edge of the seat so that he faced me, and holding my shoulders gently to support me in a sitting position while Mrs. Hesketh moved behind me and began the task of brushing out my matted hair. So it was that between them they told me the rest of their story.

The Willard family had returned to Europe, where Benjamin Willard had further business, and they would shortly be going home to the United States. Andrew Doyle had first tried to find Toby Kent to enlist his help in seeking me, but failing in this he had recalled that it was through the Hesketh Agency that Toby had first found me in England, and so he had called at the office in Chancery Lane and made the acquaintance of Mrs. Hesketh. When she learned of his fears, and examined the little box of my possessions he brought with him, she had immediately seen the hand of Sir John Tennant behind my disappearance. It was then that she decided she would have to tell Andrew Doyle the truth about me, so he would realize why Sir John, my grandfather, desperately needed to have me removed, and following this they had sent a telegram to Toby Kent's address in Paris, but received no response.

They had some fear that I might no longer be alive, yet could not quite believe that Sir John would bluntly order my death. He would, they felt, be more subtle than that, and Mrs. Hesketh had suggested that I might be held in a nursing home somewhere far from London, a place where Sir John's money and influence ensured that I would remain a prisoner.

"We could find no corporate or financial connection between Tennant and any such establishment," said Mrs. Hesketh, working gently on the tangles of my hair, "and so we had to seek other ways of finding a connection. After considering the matter I instructed Boniface to take charge at the office and deal with all other business while I rented a small cottage for two months in the village of Lyndonbrook, which is Sir John Tennant's village."

I looked wide-eyed at Andrew Doyle as he sat holding me. "Boniface had been there before in the course of his inquiries," he explained, "but Mrs. Hesketh had not, and she used a false name both in renting the cottage and bribing the squire's post boy."

"Post boy?" I echoed dazedly.

Mrs. Hesketh said, "I bribed the boy who daily brought all letters from the manor to post them in the box by the village post office. He is a simple lad, and since I convinced him that I have powers of witchcraft and could lay a most fearful curse upon him, I had no fear that he would speak of me to his employer."

"But . . . what did you bribe him to do?" I asked.

"Just to call at my cottage each morning and enjoy a cup of tea on his way to the post office. He would leave his letters in the kitchen and take his tea in the little living room, never lingering for more than five minutes. That was more than long enough for me to go through Sir John Tennant's letters."

Sometimes, she said, there had been only one or two, sometimes as many as six. Most bore business or domestic addresses which were clearly beyond suspicion. A kettle was on the boil ready to steam open any letter about which she felt some doubt.

"Apparently," said Andrew Doyle solemnly, "it takes only a few seconds and leaves no trace. I've greatly expanded my education under Mrs. Hesketh's tuition."

She had reasoned that if I were alive, I must be held in a private institution of some kind, whether here or abroad, and that this must involve the payment of regular bills, but it was not until her sixth week in the cottage that the post boy brought the letter she wanted, a letter addressed to Dr. Reginald Thornton at the Moorside Institution for Mental Defectives near the Yorkshire village of Dornington. Inside was a check for fifteen pounds ten shillings, made out to Dr. Reginald Thornton, and nothing else.

"That was three days ago," said Andrew Doyle. "The place is a registered institution and we could find no record of complaints about it, but we did discover that a bed there had been endowed by Sir John Tennant many years ago." His mouth tightened with anger. "Perhaps he has had occasion to remove people before, or felt it wise to be prepared if the need arose. Who knows with such a man?"

Behind me, Mrs. Hesketh sighed. "Your Mr. Doyle would have rushed up to Dornington alone," she said, "but I felt it wise to call in two large acquaintances of mine for the occasion, and we all traveled up yesterday. It took a few hours to discover which of the village girls did daily work at the institution, but Mr. Doyle had a wee pencil sketch of you that Toby Kent had scribbled at some time, and with that we managed to find out that your name was Miss Smith and that the girl who cleaned your room was Stella, the cobbler's daughter."

"She didn't go to work this morning," said Andrew Doyle. "Mrs.

Hesketh told her not to, for we didn't want Thornton to have warnin that we were about to descend on him. I think you know the rest."

I nodded, feeling suddenly very sleepy now that the first wonder an excitement at being free had passed. Mrs. Hesketh laid aside the brus and began to plait my hair. "That's the best I can do for now, dear, she said. "You can have it washed in a day or two, when you feel a littl stronger."

"Thank you, Mrs. Hesketh, you're very kind." A thought came t me, and I said, "Do you think . . . is it possible to find me a roo somewhere, very cheap, where I can rest? I don't want to go back t Mr. Ryder, and . . . if I refuse to let him use me he won't want m anyway. Oh, I'm very grateful to Miss Jane, and I'll write to her, but can't go back. I've saved some money, enough to pay rent for a week c two—"

Andrew Doyle gave me a very gentle shake. "Will you stop talkin nonsense, Hannah?" he said. "You're going to a convalescent hom near Green Park, where Mrs. Hesketh can visit you easily, and I sha be visiting you too, until I leave for Mexico."

"But who is to pay for everything, Mr. Doyle?" I said, sudden feeling distressed, my thoughts muddled now in the aftermath of a that had happened. "Who paid for the cottage Mrs. Hesketh rente and for the two prizefighters, and everything else?"

He smiled. "An admirer, Hannah."

"Admirer? But I haven't got—oh no, you mustn't say things lik that." My voice began to tremble.

"Very well, I won't for the moment," he said soothingly, "as long a you promise to stop worrying about who pays for this and that."

I could find no strength to argue. Mrs. Hesketh had finished my ha and was helping me to lie down again. "All right, Mr. Doyle," I sai and tried to smile. "I'll stop worrying. I'm so grateful to you both."

The remainder of that day was like a half remembered dream for m Throughout most of the train journey I slept, and for the rest I wa only partly awake. There came a time when I was vaguely aware c being in a wheelchair, then in a carriage, with Andrew Doyle holdin me in his arms as I lay across his lap.

A house. A cool room. A bearded face with a stethoscope hung abou the neck. Voices. Mrs. Hesketh answering questions. Another fac bright and reassuring, surmounted by a nurse's headdress, then nothin more as I sank into a long, untroubled sleep.

Fifteen

I learned later that I was still asleep when Mrs. Hesketh visited me the next day, but by the second day, when she came in the afternoon, I was awake and like a new person. I had been given a bath, my hair had been washed and then brushed till it was silky smooth, and I had been able to stand by the window of my bright and well-appointed room, looking out over Green Park for almost ten minutes that morning without feeling tired.

The food was delicious and temptingly served. My appetite was returning, the hollows under my eyes were beginning to fill out, and Dr. Sullivan was both surprised and delighted by my progress. I was sitting up in bed reading a book when the nurse showed Mrs. Hesketh in. She looked very elegant in a dark red costume and a pretty straw hat. When the nurse had gone she bent to embrace me, and I hugged her tightly, whispering my thanks anew.

"Oh, nonsense child," she said, kissing my cheek, then drawing up a chair to the bedside. "I'm simply delighted that I have been able to purge my feeling of guilt toward you, at least to some extent. Now, if you find yourself becoming tired, you must say so at once. Dr. Sullivan tells me you're making splendid progress, but you mustn't overdo things."

I had spent so long alone in the past weeks that it was a joy to have friend to talk with. I told her how I had been abducted that afternoc when I left her house, and she in turn recounted more details of th way in which she and Andrew Doyle had contrived to discover m whereabouts. She wanted to know about my attempt to escape, an blinked away tears when I spoke of the letter I had intended to post her, and how by black mischance I had been caught when so close success.

"Have you given any thought to what is to be done about Sir Joh Tennant, my dear?" she said. "There is absolutely clear proof that h contrived to have you shut away in that dreadful place, and the abdu tion was certainly a criminal act."

"Yes," I said slowly. "My grandfather is an evil man. I hate an despise him for what he has done and what he would have done to m But I can't bear the thought of legal proceedings, of giving evidence court, and of reliving all that horror again in public, Mrs. Hesketh. All want is to be free of the whole business, and to be sure he won't c anything to harm me again."

"Have no fear of that, child," Mrs. Hesketh said with an angry gli in her fine eyes. "Andrew Doyle went down to Lyndonbrook this mor ing to see the fellow and to tell him that it rests in *your* hands wheth or not he's dragged through the courts to end up in prison. Be sure he never dare raise a finger against you in future." She looked at the litt fob watch on her lapel. "You will see Andrew Doyle later, for he'll b visiting you on his return to discover what action, if any, you wish take." She patted my hand. "I hate to see a scoundrel go unpunishe but for your own sake, I think you have decided wisely. Now let us ta of something else."

When I inquired after Mr. Boniface she rolled her eyes upward. "I excellent health, as always, but still as irritating as ever. Year after year ask myself what on earth I see in the wretched man, and yet"—sh shook her head and sighed—"he's an affliction I should sorely mis Boniface is excellent at his job, mind you. We now have another assi tant besides Charlie Grindle—he was the one you saw in Paris pretend ing to be an embassy man when Boniface played that disgraceful tric on you. I must say Charlie seems much improved since the day whe dear Toby Kent came and banged his head against the wall. I wonder . . . ?"

She gazed into space for a moment or two, then collected herself an went on, "Well, as I say, we now have two assistants, and both they and Boniface are all busy working on rewarding cases. Yes, I must admit that Boniface really does very well, and the agency is thriving, but outside his work he has no flair, no flair at all. I do so like a man with flair . . . like young Toby Kent, one might say."

She looked at me with a hint of apology. "You have no intimate connection with him, dear?"

I smiled. "No. He's been a very kind friend to me, but no more. He's quite free, Mrs. Hesketh."

"Ah. Then I shall hope that he may call upon me again one day soon." She frowned. "It's strange that our telegram failed to bring him posthaste to help us find you."

"Oh, I'm sure he would have come if he received it, but he may have moved, or decided to tour Europe, or perhaps gone to America. You never know with Toby."

Mrs. Hesketh sighed again and stood up. "I like that," she said. "You *always* know with Boniface, I'm afraid. Such a dull man." She laughed, as if at herself. "Well, I must be going, Hannah. Don't try to do too much too soon, dear."

It was late afternoon when Andrew Doyle was shown into my room. I was warned of his arrival when the nurse came five minutes before, to see that I was respectably clothed in a long dressing gown and sitting up in a chair by the window instead of in bed. I was secretly amused, remembering a night in Paris when Andrew Doyle had lain unconscious in my bed and I had crept in beside him to save myself from freezing.

He was smiling when he entered, but I sensed something of gravity in him as he took my hand and bowed over it. The nurse said apologetically, "The gentleman has some private things to talk about, Miss McLeod, so Dr. Sullivan says I'm to leave him with you."

I gave her a reassuring smile and said, "Yes, I'll be quite all right thank you, nurse."

When she had gone, Andrew Doyle sat down facing me. "I went to see Sir John Tennant this morning, Hannah," he said quietly, "but I was unable to do so. I have to tell you that he is dead."

"Dead?" I stared in shock.

"He went out with a shotgun before breakfast this morning," said Andrew Doyle. "An hour later he was found on the edge of woods adjoining the manor, with a gunshot wound in his head which the doctor says would have been instantly fatal. He appears to have dropped the gun by chance in such a way that a twig caught the trigger and discharged it. His death will be considered an accident."

I shivered. "And . . . it wasn't?"

He shook his head. "The coincidence is too huge. I made some inquiries, and learned from a servant that Tennant received a telegram yesterday morning. He spent the rest of the day shut in his study, and took no meals. The telegram can't be found, but some paper ashes lay in a large ashtray in the study. Sir John Tennant hasn't been out shooting for five years now, and the servants were astonished that he went out this morning."

I said, "You think the telegram came from Dr. Thornton, warning Sir John? Saying that you had taken me away from the institution, and that we knew who paid for me to be held there?"

"I'm sure of it, Hannah. Imagine the effect on that wicked man. Hannah McLeod is free. She knows who abducted her, because Thornton confessed it. Whether or not she knows *why* she was abducted doesn't matter. The point is, he's forced to realize that you're not alone, that you have friends with enough power and determination to have tracked you down against all the odds, and then to storm your prison and bring you to freedom and safety. As Sir John Tennant sits alone in his study with that knowledge, he could never dream that you might take no action against him. He faced scandal, a trial, certain imprisonment, and perhaps a revelation of the truth, that you are his daughter's child. A man of his position and pride couldn't face it, Hannah."

We sat in silence for quite a little while as I tried to absorb what had happened. At last I said, "So Mr. Ryder has gained the fitting revenge he wanted, and much more quickly than he expected. I suppose I ought to feel pity for my grandfather, but I don't feel anything. Is that very bad, Mr. Doyle?"

"Bad?" He looked at me, tight-lipped. "The man was a monster who intended you to suffer in a living hell till you died. You could well be forgiven for feeling glad."

"No. At least I don't feel that. I just keep feeling so thankful to be here."

He stood up, pacing away slowly and then returning to stand looking down at me. "I've just sent a note to Sebastian Ryder telling him all that's happened, including the fact of Tennant's death," he said. "I also told him that you had no wish to continue in his employ. That's still your feeling, Hannah?"

"Oh yes, Mr. Doyle. I wrote to him myself this morning as a matter of courtesy, and I also wrote to Miss Jane to thank her."

He nodded. "I'll make a point of seeing Ryder myself in the next day or two, so I can make plain that you don't want the truth about your parentage made public. I'll advise him that if he ignores your wishes, then *I* shall make public that he was using you as an instrument of blackmail. I think you can be quite sure he'll see reason, Hannah."

I felt great relief, and said, "That's very comforting, Mr. Doyle. I shall be so glad to put all this behind me and never think of it again."

"You've had to do that far too often in your young life," he said somberly. "But please God this will be the last time. Do you have any plans for the future?"

"Yes, I've been thinking about that. I can't hope to repay you for all you've spent and are still spending on me, Mr. Doyle, and I think you would be upset if I tried, so I'm just accepting all you've done as a gift, with my gratitude."

"You once risked more for me than I've ever risked for you, my sweetheart," he said softly.

I remembered now that he had used the same endearment when carrying me out of Dr. Thornton's institution. Then it had been almost as if he were speaking to a child, but now I felt myself flush a little. It seemed a too intimate endearment, but I told myself that perhaps it was much less so in America or Mexico.

"About future plans," I went on rather hastily, "I think, to begin with, I shall have to go into service. If I'm lucky I might get a position as a lady's maid. When I was at the college we used to do each other's hair, so I'm quite good at that, and I'm hoping perhaps Mrs. Hesketh might help with advice. Once I'm settled and earning my keep I could start to look for something better, a position teaching French in a school, perhaps. I shall have to tell lies about my years in Paris, for nobody will employ a girl who has been what I have been. I suppose I should have suspected something amiss when Mr. Ryder seemed not to mind employing me even though he knew the truth, but I was rather confused at the time—"

"Wait, Hannah," Mr. Doyle broke in, lifting a hand to halt my flow of words. I stopped, and he stood looking down at me curiously, half smiling. After a moment or two he said, "We've come to each other's help in moments of great need, and there are strong bonds between u Can you bring yourself to call me Andrew?"

I made myself meet his gaze as I said, "It isn't a question of bonc Mr. Doyle. It's a question of position. You are a wealthy gentleman excellent family and background. I am . . . well, nothing really. A my background is beyond the pale."

"I don't concern myself with family or background," he said p tiently. "You know that, Hannah. You've heard me speak of the cou try of my birth, Mexico, and you know my heart is more with t peasants than with the great families like my own. Please call me A drew."

I decided it would be churlish to argue further, and said, "Very we Mr.—Oh dear. I will try . . . Andrew."

His dark eyes smiled. "That's the first step. Now for the secon Would you like to go to another country and build a new life the Hannah? A life on the other side of the world, where you would nev need to fear that one day the secret of your past might be uncovered

"Do you mean Mexico, Mr. Doyle?"

"Andrew."

"I'm sorry. Andrew."

"Yes. I mean Mexico."

"I think," I said slowly, "that I would like to begin afresh, but sure I would have little chance of finding work in service there? After all, don't speak Spanish. I could quickly pick it up, but—"

"I'm not suggesting that you go into service there," said Andre Doyle. "I'm suggesting that you should be my wife."

"Your *wife?*"

For a moment I thought he was making a cruel joke, but then sa that he was entirely serious. "But you *can't!*" I said incredulously. "O please think, Mr. Doyle—I mean Andrew. Please think!"

"I have thought at great length," he said calmly. "I look at Hanna McLeod and my heart swells with love and admiration. I see a you woman I would trust with my very life."

Temptation came upon me, swift and sudden. To begin afresh, security and comfort, with a man I liked, a man I knew to be kind a loyal . . .

"No," I said desperately. "Oh dear heaven, I'm so touched I cou weep, but it would be madness, Andrew. Think of your family. Ho can you inflict me upon them? I am *la professeuse,* from a Paris bordello. How can you inflict me upon yourself?"

"I want you for myself because I love and respect you for your courage in rising above the horrors that were inflicted on you," he said in the same calm voice. "There is no question of inflicting you upon my family. I shall present you as an English girl of good family, which is true, but now orphaned. Your past is none of their business."

"But Mr. and Mrs. Willard know. Clara knows."

"They will keep their own counsel. Nothing could persuade them to harm me, or you either for that matter."

"I . . . I suppose so. But you say that being so far away means my secret could never be uncovered. It isn't so, Andrew." I swallowed a lump in my throat and spoke with deliberate brutality. "Foreign men come to Paris, as you and the Willard family did. I have lain with men from countries half a world away, both east and west, men who might recognize me."

He nodded soberly. "Nothing in life is completely certain. We must accept that, just as we accept that we may be struck by lightning or trampled by a runaway horse . . ." He went on speaking, but I was suddenly overcome by a great weariness of mind that brought inertia to my thoughts and was like a waking sleep. I know that I resisted, argued clumsily, tried again and again to make him realize the folly of what he was asking, but he countered all my arguments with smiling affection, and gradually I came to feel that perhaps . . . perhaps it was possible.

I had made a vow, on the day I walked from the College for Young Ladies as a free woman, that I would never again take a man to my bed, but I had not dreamed then that any man would wish to marry me. It meant nothing that I was not in love with Andrew Doyle, for after the life I had lived I had long been certain that I could never know what it meant to fall in love, if indeed there was any real meaning in those words. Moreover, I did not believe in the notion that a woman could feel true love for only one man in the whole world, or that a man could feel love for only one woman. Surely most men and women could find reasonable contentment with many a different partner, as long as they were in harmony one with another. I liked Andrew Doyle, I respected him, trusted him, admired him. That would suffice for me to give him happiness and a lifetime of loyalty.

There came a moment when he stood holding my hands and I could struggle no longer. As if from a great distance I heard myself say, "Yes . . . yes, Andrew, if that is truly what you wish . . ."

The next few days had a dreamlike quality about them, and only gradually was I able to accept the reality of what had happened. Some shadowy doubts remained, but I would not allow myself to dwell on them for I had given my promise now.

Mrs. Hesketh had no doubts whatsoever. "Good heavens, child, you were quite right to accept. You've not deceived the dear man, and if he has the good sense to want a fine young girl like you, then you'd be foolish to deny him. It's a great pity that some of his honorable intentions can't rub off on Boniface."

My fiancé, Andrew Doyle, came every day to visit me, bringing me a beautiful diamond eternity ring the day after his proposal. When he came to see me two days later, I was dressed and sitting out in the garden for the first time. He kissed my lips gently in greeting, drew up a chair so that he faced me, and told me that in Dr. Sullivan's opinion I would be fully restored to health in another three weeks.

"Hannah, my sweetheart, I want to arrange for you to make the voyage to Veracruz as soon as you leave here," he said, holding my hand. "But I shall have to go on ahead myself in only a week from now. There's some important business I have to attend to, and of course I want to tell my family how wonderful you are, and have them prepared for your arrival. I've sent a long telegram and written a long letter, but it's better that I go in person to pave the way for you."

"Yes, of course, Andrew. I'm going to be very nervous. The more you prepare your family the better."

"I want to take them a photograph, so I must arrange for a photographer to come and take your picture before I leave. The only thing I have at the moment is Toby Kent's sketch." He felt in his pocket and took out a wallet. Tucked inside was a miniature pencil sketch of my head and shoulders. I thought it flattered me a little, but the likeness was excellent.

"Did you ask Toby to do it for you?" I said.

"Good Lord, no. He's got a drawer full of them. I saw them in his studio one day, and asked if I could have this one." Andrew grinned. "Incidentally, the wanderer must have returned to Paris at last and found the wire Mrs. Hesketh sent him weeks ago. She received this telegram at noon today."

From another pocket he took a pale orange envelope and handed it to me. The telegram read:

> RETURNED VIENNA ONLY THIS MORNING STOP WILL ARRIVE HESKETH AGENCY TONIGHT STOP IF ANDREW DOYLE STILL IN ENGLAND PLEASE ADVISE HIM MY ARRIVAL STOP IF HANNAH NOT YET FOUND I INTEND MOST DIRECT ACTION AGAINST TENNANT STOP REGARDS TOBY KENT.

I laughed as I handed back the telegram, and said, "That's Toby."

"What do you imagine he means by 'most direct action'?"

"I shudder to think. He's half Irish, and as a seaman, he must have had his share of brawls."

"Mrs. Hesketh told me he has a way of banging heads against walls."

"Yes. I'm very glad she and you managed to find me by more subtle means before Toby came on the scene."

We talked about the journey to Mexico, and Andrew said I must have a lady companion with me. I did not think this necessary, but he was very firm and said he would hire a suitable person to accompany me. I told him I wanted to learn Spanish, and asked him to bring me a textbook next day and to spend at least half an hour of each visit talking to me in Spanish, so that I could repeat his words and begin to acquire a good accent.

This pleased him, and with much enthusiasm he began to point out various objects, naming them in Spanish with their genders, and listening carefully as I repeated the words after him. Later, when he kissed me and left, I felt so moved that I was close to tears. I had been kissed many, many times, but Andrew Doyle was the first man ever to have kissed my lips with love.

Next morning before luncheon I was again sitting in the garden reading a book when I heard feet on the brick path beside the lawn. I thought it was one of the staff, or another convalescent patient, until the feet halted and a familiar voice said, "So who's going to give you away then, young McLeod?"

"Toby!"

He stood smiling down at me, dropping his cane and a smart gray top hat on the table beside me, very elegantly dressed in a fine gray suit, a small rose in his buttonhole, his red hair as unruly as ever. I laid my book aside and reached out my hands. He laughed and took them gently, his gaze very keen as he studied me. "You look a great deal better than I feared," he said. "When Flora told me what had bee done to you, I was frightened out of my wits until she reassured me.

"Flora?"

His green eyes twinkled. "The peerless Mrs. Hesketh. I arrived a Chancery Lane last evening in great haste, believe me. I'd been trave ing, you see, spending some time in Budapest then Vienna, and when got back to Paris there was this weeks-old telegram waiting for me t say you'd vanished and had probably been abducted by Tennant. wondered what the devil could be going on, for I didn't know then tha . . ."—he paused, looked about him as if to make sure we could not b overheard, and went on—"didn't know that certain discoveries ha been made about your birth and parentage, me beauty, and there's hair-raising story if ever I heard one. But anyway, a fine old panic I wa in when I arrived, I can tell you."

"I'm so sorry you had a lot of needless worry, Toby." I released hi hands and touched the chair beside me. "Sit down and tell me wha happened when you reached Chancery Lane."

"Not much to tell," he said, taking the chair. "Flora Hesketh wa waiting to tell me the whole story, including the fact that you wer safe, that she and Andrew Doyle had rescued you, and that Tennan had made a good job of shooting himself. So I was able to relax an allow her to soothe my troubled soul."

I laughed and patted his arm. "I'm sure she enjoyed that, for she wa hoping to see you again soon. But . . . I do wish Mr. Boniface woul marry her. That's what she really wants."

He smiled ruefully. "I'm no matchmaker, Hannah. Oh, before forget, I bring you good wishes from Jane Ryder and her brother Ger ald."

I stared. "When did you see them?"

"Not an hour ago, when I went to Portland Place to have a wor with Sebastian Ryder." Toby scratched his chin thoughtfully, and glint touched his eyes. "I had in mind to point out that he'd damn nea killed you with his vicious plots."

"Oh, Toby. You didn't—?"

"I never lifted a finger. The man's no more than a ghost now. A walking husk."

"A ghost? Whatever do you mean?"

Toby shrugged. "I mean he's a man who's lost the most importan thing in his life, the thing he worked twenty odd years to achieve. In way he's been cheated of his revenge, Hannah, for he planned to play cat and mouse with Tennant for many a long day. Now his victim's dead, and it's taken the heart out of him, at least for the time being. No more than he deserves, say I. However, young Jane and Gerald caught me as I was leaving and asked to be remembered kindly to you. Jane was glad to have a letter you'd written her."

"Yes. She was the one who didn't believe I'd run away, and I wrote to thank her."

"So Andrew told me."

"You've seen him?"

"When I left Chancery Lane this morning I called first on Andrew to congratulate him."

I looked down at the ring on my finger, feeling a little shy. "You know we're to be married, then?"

"Can you imagine Flora Hesketh not having told me? Of course I know, and you have my true and sincere felicitations, Hannah."

I looked up, the shyness gone. "Bless you, Toby. You don't think it was wrong of me to accept? I mean, in view of what I was?"

"It could only be wrong if Andrew didn't know," he said gently. "Even so, he tells me you argued interminably, which was right, and what I'd expect of you, but it was neither wrong nor unwise to accept in the end. He's a good man, Hannah, and he'll care for you well. A dreamer and an idealist, yes, but that's no bad thing."

A thought had been tickling the back of my mind, and I voiced it now. "Toby, what was it you first said to me when you arrived here, something about giving me away?"

He looked at me with a lifted eyebrow. "I just asked who's to give you away at your wedding. Since I'm the oldest friend you have, I'm offering myself for the job, Hannah McLeod."

I sat startled, a hand spread on my breast, looking at Toby in astonishment and delight. "Oh! I simply hadn't thought about that. Would you really do it for me? Would you come to Mexico and give me away at my wedding?"

"If you ask anyone else, I'll bang his head against the wall till he withdraws," said Toby amiably. "Andrew tells me he's booking a passage for you and a lady companion in about three weeks, so I thought I might make the voyage at the same time. I understand you're to live with Andrew's family in Monterrey for six months or so before the wedding, so during that time I can travel here and there about Mexico and get some fresh inspiration for painting."

"That would be wonderful, Toby. Was it for inspiration you were in Budapest and Vienna?"

"Partly. I'd done a lot of painting in a fairly short time, and I wanted to go somewhere fresh, to think and experiment."

"Was it successful?"

"Not too bad, me beauty, not too bad. At least I'm selling well, so they tell me, and becoming outrageously rich."

"That's lovely. You won't ever forget that I was your butterfly girl though, will you?"

"We-e-ell," he said doubtfully, "maybe not. I'll probably manage to remember."

I laughed, then looked at him carefully and frowned. He was sitting at ease, the hint of a smile on his lips, gazing with lazy interest and his painter's eye at some tall purple dahlias in a nearby flowerbed. I could see only the side of his face, yet I felt sure that I sensed, as if from afar a shadow upon his spirit.

I said, "Toby, look at me."

His smile grew a little broader, but he continued to look at the dahlias and said, "Now don't distract me when I'm trying to fix a color in my mind."

"And don't you try to fob me off, Toby Kent." I leaned forward and reached out to cup his chin in my hand, turning his head toward me so that I could study his face closely. He submitted with a look of amusement, and after several seconds he said, "You're a fearsome sight when you glare at a fellow like that, young McLeod."

"Never mind what sort of sight I am. You're sad, Toby. What's happened?"

"Sad? Nonsense. Why should I be sad, you daft girl?"

"That's what I'm asking you, and don't try to deny it." I took my hand from his chin. "Heaven knows I may be daft, but if there's one thing I know about it's men. I'm not proud of that, nor ashamed of it either, but it's a fact, and I can see sadness in you, Toby—" I stopped short with the sudden realization that I was presuming greatly. "Oh, I'm sorry. Is it something you don't want to tell?"

He sighed and looked at me with smiling resignation. "Now when did I have secrets from you, Hannah? All right, I'll confess. There was a girl I met in Vienna, of an aristocratic family, and I was commissioned paint her. Well . . . for the first and last time, Toby Kent lost his icked heart to a girl the moment he set eyes on her, but she didn't se hers to him, and there's an end of it."

I said, "Oh, I'm sorry, Toby, so sorry. I hope you won't be sad for ng." I had listened to countless men talk endlessly to me about every maginable problem, and I had grown to have little belief that love at rst sight was an enduring thing, but I knew the folly of trying to omfort Toby with words of reason. The best way for him to exorcise er memory would be by talking about her rather than keeping her ocked away in his heart, and I said, "If you want to tell me all about er, I'll gladly listen at any time. You might find it a help."

He gave a little laugh and said, "We'll see, but let's change the ubject now." He stood up and turned slowly round. "All this time and ou've made no comment on the amazing elegance of the figure I'm utting these days. I'm hurt, me beauty. Cut to the quick, so I am."

I picked up his mood and said, "A thousand apologies, *mon vieux*, ut the only reason I've said nothing is that I've been completely lost or adequate words, whether in English or French. You look so . . . so . . ."

"Posh?"

"Ah, posh! *Le mot juste.*"

We both dissolved in laughter and he sat down again. "Am I tiring you, Hannah? Would you like me to be going now?" he asked.

"No, no, you're restoring me. I was so alone in that awful institution, I love having somebody to talk to now."

His eyes grew somber. "I've heard something about it from Flora Hesketh and Andrew Doyle," he said, "but I'd be glad to hear the whole tale from yourself, Hannah."

"Very well, but promise you won't seethe and fume and grind your teeth. It's all over now."

Toby Kent laid a hand on his heart. "I promise," he said.

During the week that followed I grew steadily stronger. Andrew visited me every afternoon. There was much to talk about and I was eager to practice the Spanish I had been studying in the textbook he had brought for me. Toby Kent and Mrs. Hesketh took turns to visit me each morning for an hour, so I did not lack for company each day.

From Paris I received a kindly letter from Mrs. Willard and also one from Clara. I read them somewhat nervously. Both welcomed the news of my engagement to Andrew and I was unable to detect any hint dismay, but I could not believe they were truly happy for Andrew marry a girl with my past. It seemed more probable that they wer inwardly horrified but had felt obliged to accept his decision as unchangeable. This being so, and since they had seemed to like me an realized I did not spend those years at the college in Paris by choic they were perhaps accepting the inevitable without resentment. Fro their letters I learned that they would be going home with Andrev joining the ship at Le Havre and spending a few weeks in Mexic before going on to their own home in Virginia.

On Mrs. Hesketh's first visit following Toby Kent's return, I was ver happy to see her, but noticed that like Toby himself there was a sadnes in her which she tried to conceal. When I spoke of this she sighed an said ruefully, "It's just men, dear, men. I sometimes think they wer born to make women sad."

"Oh dear. Is it Toby?"

"Heavens no, Hannah. Toby Kent is a joy, but I'm older than he i by eight years, and we're no more than ships that pass in the night, h and I. No, it's that good-for-nothing Boniface, as it always was. He's a home again, working in London for a while, and last night I so swallowed my pride as to ask the wretched man if he *ever* intended to marr me, and do you know what he replied? 'That is a question, Mrs. Hesketh,' he said, 'which no gentlewoman should ever ask of a gentleman. I was so humiliated I could have wept, though of course I did not When I think of all I do for Boniface . . . you know, his busines would be in ruins instead of thriving, if it were not for me. Oh, I know I'm sharp with him, but only because he behaves with such indifference, and I look after him very well, indeed I do, Hannah. I'm always there when he returns from working on a case; I cosset him with his favorite foods, and I'm most generously affectionate with him in our private concerns. But there, I didn't mean to run on so, child. Whatever can you think of me?"

I said, "I think the world of you, Mrs. Hesketh, and I think Mr. Boniface is utterly spoilt. He needs to discover what it is like *not* to have you there to make his business run smoothly, and to care for him and cosset him. He takes you completely for granted—" A sudden thought struck me, and I almost gasped with the surprise of it. "Mrs. Hesketh, I have a wonderful idea. Will you come to Mexico with me at the end of the month?"

She put a hand to her head in bewilderment. "Mexico? But . . . oh, I don't understand."

"I need a lady companion, and Andrew is going to hire one for me, but I would love to have *you* for my companion. Then you could stay a little while, or return almost at once if you wished, but at least you would be away for a month or six weeks, and Mr. Boniface would have to fend for himself."

She blinked, startled. "Fend for himself? The shock would kill him, Hannah."

I laughed. "Oh, no it wouldn't. It will teach him a lesson he should have learned long ago. I can't promise that he will immediately ask you to marry him, but if he thinks you might leave him alone again, I really believe you will find him more appreciative and more anxious to please, and I'm sure you'll bring him to the point before long. If that's what you want."

Mrs. Hesketh looked at me rather dreamily and with much affection. "I'm a fool, of course," she said softly, "but that is what I want, Hannah. You're very wise for your years, child."

I made a wry grimace. "I'm very old for my years, but it can't be helped now."

Sixteen

I was delighted that Mrs. Hesketh agreed to accompany me, and on a bright October day we boarded a ship called *Maid of Troy* and set sail for Mexico by way of Bermuda, Nassau, and Havana. Our destination was Veracruz, where we would be met by Andrew and taken by train to Mexico City. After a night's rest we would continue our journey by the railway running north for five hundred miles to Monterrey, with one overnight stop at San Luis Potosí.

Mrs. Hesketh was to remain in Mexico City for a little over two weeks, staying with a branch of Andrew's family on his mother's side. She would then be escorted to Veracruz and return to England on her own, all her journeying being first class and at Andrew's expense. He was delighted to know that I would be accompanied by the formidable lady who had proved such a powerful ally to him in helping to find me.

During the three weeks before our departure, Toby Kent had brought me maps and books about Mexico so that I could begin to learn something of the country which was to become my new home. During his visits I would tell him what I had learned, and he would test my small but increasing Spanish vocabulary from the textbook. I discovered that he had a smattering of the language himself, having

:rved for some time on a Spanish cargo ship, and now he was glad to •in me in learning more, since he intended traveling in Mexico.

Mrs. Hesketh had also continued to visit me, but she had no inten- •on of learning a word of Spanish or any foreign language. "To learn a)reign tongue is entirely unnatural, child," she declared. "It was God ı His wisdom who started all these different languages as a punish- ıent for building the Tower of Babel, and it is not for me to try to vade His judgment."

There was a twinkle in her eye as she said this, and she was alto- ether happier now, for Mr. Boniface's response to her impending eparture had been one of alarm. "The poor creature couldn't believe at first," Mrs. Hesketh announced with delight. "Then he was furi- us and now he's distraught, verging on pathetic. Dear Toby took him ut and got him drunk the other night, and in his cups Boniface oured out what passes for his heart. Toby assures me that by the time return from Mexico the wretched man will be on his knees begging ıe to marry him. Toby says I'm to make him wait awhile, then allow ıyself to be reluctantly persuaded."

"And don't do anything for him while he's waiting," I said. "Any- ıing at all, Mrs. Hesketh, neither bed nor board."

"I had that in mind," she said with a soft laugh, and reached out to ıke my hand. "You're better than a daughter, Hannah, dear. A daugh- :r would be shocked out of her wits."

My cabin on the *Maid of Troy* adjoined Mrs. Hesketh's, and Toby's abin was on the same deck. The weather was mixed at first, and for vo days Mrs. Hesketh and I felt queasy, but then we found our sea :gs and began to enjoy the voyage. The weather improved, and in the esh sea air I soon began to feel bursting with good health, the mem- ry of my recent ordeal fading to an almost forgotten bad dream.

I continued to study my books on Mexico and to practice the lan- ıage with Toby. Mrs. Hesketh read novels from the ship's library and ecounted instalments to us each evening at dinner. Toby sketched, nd occasionally painted a picture, working very quickly as he always id. Mrs. Hesketh did not like his paintings, but I found myself grow- ıg to like them more and more. To tease her, he painted a perfect keness of her, so exact that it was like a photograph in color, and she as delighted with it.

The three of us made good company together. We talked, read, rgued, played deck games, struck up acquaintance with other passengers, listened to the ship's orchestral trio in the lounge of an evenin and played draughts, chess, and some card games that Toby taught u

There were times when I had terrible qualms about what I had dor in agreeing to marry Andrew. No matter that he knew the truth abo me, no matter that as a child I had been brutally forced into a shamef way of life and had escaped as soon as I could. The fact remained th nothing could undo my past, and this was a dreadful dowry to bring my husband. I said nothing of these anxieties to Mrs. Hesketh or Tob The burden was mine to carry, and it would have been cowardly to a for comfort and reassurance.

On a fine warm day our ship tied up at the quayside of Mexico oldest port, Veracruz. During the past few days I had made an effort cast all anxiety aside, and I was full of excitement as I stood by the ra watching the hustle and bustle below and hoping in vain for a glimp of Andrew. We disembarked, our trunks were unloaded, and we we passed through customs without delay. In the hall beyond there w still no sign of Andrew, but almost at once a tall man with silver-gr hair and fine aristocratic features approached us. He wore a light gr morning suit and carried a top hat and a cane with an ivory kno Moving at a respectful distance behind him were two men in son kind of livery, whom I judged to be servants.

The tall man bowed to us and addressed Toby in good Englis though with a strong accent. "May I ask, sir, if I have the pleasure address Mr. Toby Kent?"

"Myself, sir," Toby said, taking off his hat and bowing in respons

"I am Enrique del Rio, a cousin of the mother of Señor Andre Doyle."

"A pleasure to meet you, sir," said Toby. "Ladies, I present Señ Enrique del Rio. Señor, I present to you Mrs. Flora Hesketh and Mi Hannah McLeod."

We shook hands, and I forgot all the Spanish I had learned, but th was of little moment, for Enrique del Rio continued to speak rath urgently in English. "I am meeting you on behalf of Andrew becaus he is not able to attend upon you." He glanced to either side, an lowered his voice. "There is some rather distressing news I have to te but I must not speak of it in a public place. It must wait until we are o the train."

My heart lurched, and I said in a whisper, "Is Andrew ill? Has h been hurt?"

The man shook his head. "No, señorita. We believe him to be in good health at present, but please permit me to say no more until we are private."

I felt Toby take my arm and heard him say, "Very well, señor, we are in your hands."

Enrique del Rio spoke a few words to the servants and offered his arm to Mrs. Hesketh, who took it with much dignity. A carriage was waiting to take us to the railway station, and another followed with our luggage. Nothing was said on the brief journey, except that we replied to a polite inquiry as to whether we had enjoyed a comfortable voyage.

A first-class compartment had been reserved on the train, and for a moment I recalled in a dreamlike manner that only a month or two ago I had lain in another train compartment thousands of miles away, frail and sick, while Mrs. Hesketh and Andrew Doyle told how they had contrived to find and save me. Now I was well and strong again, but racked by anxiety for the man who had befriended me, who had gone to such lengths for me, and had honored me by asking me to marry him.

When we were settled in the compartment, Enrique del Rio said quietly, "It was arranged that you were to stay tonight at my home in Mexico City, then proceed by train to Monterrey, except for Mrs. Hesketh," he bowed his head to her, "who was to be our guest until her return to England. But now we feel it is better that you all remain at my house until . . . until the situation is resolved."

I said, "Please, what situation, señor?"

He looked at me with sympathy. "Andrew is less than discreet," he murmured, "and I think you must know that he is a political person, a man of good intention of course, but one who wishes to make all things perfect for all men without delay."

Toby said, "We know Andrew has great sympathy for the less fortunate people of your country, sir. He has made no secret of that."

Enrique del Rio nodded somberly. "I regret to say that he is regarded by the family as a young fool with a very hot head. We are a family of much influence, and there are several of us who hold high position in government, so Andrew has given us much cause for worry since he is on the side of people who are against us." Enrique del Rio gave a resigned shrug. "But . . . he is of our family. Even though his father was *americano,* he is still of our family, and so for the sake of his mother we have turned our eyes away from some of the foolish things he has done. But now he has put himself in a very dangerous situation."

I leaned forward, my hands clenched together, and said, "Please tell me where Andrew is now, sir, and what danger he is in."

"Andrew is somewhere beyond Oaxaca, in the hills of the Sierra Madre del Sur," he said slowly, "and he is the prisoner of a rebel band who threaten to take his life."

I stared, speechless, and began to shiver. Mrs. Hesketh put an arm round me. Toby Kent said, "But I cannot see the sense of it, sir. Surely Andrew is a friend of the rebels?"

Enrique del Rio smiled without humor. "Oh, certainly, Mr. Kent. He tries to help them, to bring provisions and guns to them, and if we had not protected him, he would be rotting in prison now. But in truth he has been prevented from giving them much material help, and so they have seized the opportunity to use him in another way. As soon as he arrived from England, he went to Oaxaca and on into the Sierra Madre del Sur to talk with the man who leads these rebels, a man who was once a gentleman, and much like Andrew in many ways."

I said in a voice that sounded unlike my own, "Is his name Ramon Delgado?"

"Ah, so Andrew has spoken of him to you. Yes, Ramon Delgado is the man who is hoping to fan the spark of revolution into a great fire. I assure you he will not succeed. For twenty-five years we have had peace in Mexico under Porfirio Díaz, following a long series of wars and internal struggles. The people are thankful for peace, even the poor people. There was a time when our country swarmed with robbers and bandits, and it was the poor people who suffered most. But now banditry has almost disappeared, destroyed by government forces. We have cleared enormous foreign debts, and Mexico has now the opportunity to make steady progress to prosperity."

Enrique del Rio had become impassioned as he spoke, and now he seemed to realize this, for he broke off sharply with a gesture of apology. "Forgive me. I become angry to think that Andrew may lose his life because he will not be patient. He is a foolish boy, but his heart is good and we have great affection for him. Ramon Delgado has not the least chance of success. His band of rebels is small. It survives only because to mount a military operation in those hills is a waste of time and money. Delgado's following will gradually wither away as the men lose heart. Let me say that I admire his courage and respect his motives, but I know that he will achieve nothing."

I had found it difficult to contain myself while Enrique del Rio talked and talked without explaining how Andrew was threatened, and the moment he stopped speaking I said quickly, "You say that the rebels are using Andrew in a different way. How does it help them to threaten his life, señor?"

With a great clanking and hissing the train began to move. Enrique del Rio waited for the noise to die away somewhat, then he said, "A few weeks ago the *Guardia rural* caught a group of Delgado's men. Six of them. At present they are in Oaxaca awaiting trial. It is quite certain they will be found guilty of rebellion and sentenced to be shot. When Andrew arrived in Mexico, he went to Ramon Delgado as a friend, but they have taken him as a hostage, and they have sent a message to the state governor, secretly, saying that if the six rebels die, then Andrew Doyle will be hanged."

For long seconds nobody spoke, then Toby said, "This is the way Delgado treats a friend?"

The older man shrugged. "He is desperate to maintain the morale of his band. If he can save six prisoners from execution, it will give his men more confidence for a while. And remember, to them Andrew is a young man of rich family who in their eyes only plays at being a rebel, so he is a very suitable sacrifice."

Toby said thoughtfully, "Are you sure Andrew isn't cooperating with them in a plot?"

"Quite sure, señor. It has been necessary to establish a go-between, a trusted man, so that the governor can negotiate with Delgado. This go-between has seen Andrew and spoken with him. He has no doubt that the threat is genuine, and says Andrew is shaken and embittered at this cruel betrayal by men he has sought to help."

I said to Toby, "If he appears so, then it must be true. Andrew is no actor." I looked at Enrique del Rio. "You spoke of negotiations, señor. Does that mean the governor may agree to release the prisoners?"

He lifted a protesting hand. "Not for one moment, señorita. I beg you not to hope for that. As I have told you, this whole matter has been kept secret, but of course our family was informed at once. Andrew's mother has gone down to Oaxaca, with one of her brothers and his wife to accompany her, staying at the house of a friend. The *americano* members of the family are also staying there, her sister-in-law, Señora

Melanie Willard, with her husband and daughter. Between us all we have strong influence with the government, but we know that Porfirio Díaz will never bring pressure upon the state governor to yield to rebels, and we of the family acknowledge that it would be wrong to do so."

Mrs. Hesketh spoke for the first time, and sternly. "Then what are the negotiations about, sir?" she demanded.

"It is a question of playing for time, señora," he replied. "The governor pretends to offer hope that an arrangement may be agreed, but this is no more than a device to gain time."

"So that you may send soldiers in?" asked Mrs. Hesketh.

"No, señora. If soldiers enter those hills, the rebels will see them from miles away. Andrew will die, and Delgado's men will disperse into hiding until the soldiers have gone. The governor seeks to gain time in the hope that something in the situation may alter. Delgado may change his mind perhaps, or Andrew may succeed in escaping, or the rebels may realize they cannot win, and so lose heart." He paused as if seeking other possibilities, then added unconvincingly and with a helpless shrug, "Anything."

I said slowly, "There is one further possibility, señor, but we can talk of that in Oaxaca."

He looked taken aback. "But we are going to Mexico City, señorita. There is no point in your traveling to Oaxaca. It can only be distressing for you."

"There is every point in my traveling to Oaxaca," I said politely, "and you must remember I am Andrew's fiancée, señor. I have a right to be there."

He looked at me warily, and after a moment said, "Of course, señorita. It is for you to decide."

The journey to Mexico City took a little over six hours, but I think to us all it seemed endless. There was no more to be said about Andrew's danger, yet we could not speak of ordinary matters which might be of interest to us as newcomers to Mexico without seeming not to care that there appeared to be little hope of saving Andrew from death at the hands of the rebels.

For most of the journey we were silent. Occasionally Enrique del Rio would hesitantly point out something of interest and we would murmur a polite response. It was a relief to go to the dining car, but we only toyed with our food. I had longed to see the great stepped pyramids of the Aztecs I had read about, but when we passed a group of them as we neared Mexico City, I barely took notice of them, and when at last the train clanked to a final halt we were all weary from the ordeal.

We spent that night in Enrique del Rio's beautiful house. His family was large, and everyone was very polite to us, but I soon sensed that Andrew's decision to marry a strange English girl was unpopular. Before we went to bed that evening it had been arranged that we would board the first available train for Oaxaca in company with Enrique del Rio. I did not want Mrs. Hesketh to endure the three hundred mile journey, and asked her to remain in comfort in Mexico City, but she would not hear of it. "I shall be a great deal more comfortable with you than on my own with these foreign persons who clearly wish we were not here," she declared firmly.

The three of us had been left alone for a few minutes in a room adjoining the dining room, where we had sat awkwardly through a glum and almost silent meal with the family. Toby said quietly, "What have you got in mind, Hannah? What's this other possibility you mentioned?"

I kept my voice almost to a whisper as I replied, "I know Ramon Delgado. He was in Paris two years go, for about a month in the summer, and he came several times to the college."

Toby said, "To you?"

"Yes. Mam'selle Montavon recommended me the first time, and after that he would only come to me. Before he left he said he would always help me if ever it was in his power to do so."

"Well . . . it's in his power now," said Toby slowly, "but he may not want to be reminded. Why did he say such a thing, Hannah?"

"Because he believed I had saved his life. He's a very emotional man, far more so even than Andrew. The first night he came to me he was in black despair, on the verge of suicide, and completely impotent. But I was able to coax him into talking to me. He talked and talked, and I listened and tried to comfort him. After awhile he asked how I came to be a student at the college, and though I named no names I told him the truth, which was something I rarely did when that question was put. I think it made him count his blessings and feel ashamed of falling into despair. After one or two more visits he was no longer impotent, and he said I had saved his life and restored his manhood. At the end of his stay in Paris he gave me a ring as a token, which I've kept, and an address to write to, which I didn't keep, and he said that if ever needed his help I had only to ask."

There was a silence when I finished speaking, and in it both Tob and Mrs. Hesketh gazed at me in the same odd fashion, with a kind o affectionate wonder.

"You're a remarkable young lady, Hannah McLeod," Toby said a last. "And that was a very large debt you laid upon our friend Ramo Delgado." He leaned back in his chair as there came the sound o footsteps approaching across the tiled floor of the adjoining room. "I might even be large enough," he added softly.

Two days later and less than an hour after our arrival at the house i Oaxaca, I sat at a long oval table with seven other people. Toby was o my left and Mrs. Hesketh on my right, very elegant and self-possesse in a long cream-colored dress. Enrique del Rio sat at the head of th bare table. Facing us across it were two women and a man. Andrew' mother, Señora Maria Gabriela Doyle, was in the center flanked by he brother and his wife. All were soberly dressed in clothes of the fines quality. Señora Doyle was perhaps fifty, a handsome lady whose eye and broad brow reminded me very much of Andrew. She sat wit delicate long-fingered hands folded on the table, her face almost impas sive except that deep in her dark eyes I could glimpse mingled pain an anger. Her brother, ten years older at least, was a big man with a gru voice and restless manner. His wife, a tall thin lady, had a way of tiltin her head back and literally looking down her nose with a haughty ai that quite belied her nature, for she was gently spoken and conciliator in tone.

All three were polite, as Enrique del Rio had been throughout, bu once again I could not help being well aware that Andrew's choice of future wife was considered as unwise as his escapade with the rebel which threatened to cost his life. Though no word of disapproval ha been spoken, it was clear that they thought a young English girl o vague background was a highly unsuitable match. For the moment was indifferent to their opinion, except that at the back of my min hovered the thought that if I could save Andrew they might warm toward me, and I wanted this for his sake.

At the end of the table, facing Enrique del Rio, sat Señora Doyle' brother-in-law by marriage, Mr. Benjamin Willard, and I was thankfu for his presence since he was acting as a bridge between myself an ndrew's family. The discussion had been going on now for some ıirty minutes. It was tediously labored because neither Señora Doyle's rother, Señor Amado, nor his wife understood English, and on our de we had no Spanish, so translation both ways was necessary.

Señor Amado had been speaking, and now Enrique del Rio trans-ted. "He says again that it is impossible for you to go into the hills ıd speak with Ramon Delgado."

I shook my head. "As long as the man who is your go-between will ct as guide, there is nothing impossible about it, señor. You have said will take two or three days by mule. I am not a skilled rider, but I can t on a mule for three days if need be."

"Such a journey will be very exhausting, very dangerous. It is wild ountry. A rebel seeing two persons approach might shoot and kill ou."

Toby said, "Three persons, sir. Andrew placed his fiancée under my are. He would probably wish me to dissuade her from the attempt she to make, but that I cannot and will not do. It is her right to do all ıat lies in her power for the man she loves. However, I shall certainly ccompany her. Let there be no doubt of that. Andrew Doyle is my iend."

Enrique del Rio translated. Señor Amado declared the whole idea bsurd. His wife felt that the intention was good but that we would nly be presenting Delgado with more hostages. Benjamin Willard isagreed. Looking at Andrew's mother, who had not spoken for several ıinutes, he said gently, "Maria, I feel your brother and his wife speak s they do because they find it hard to believe that Hannah can per-ıade Delgado to spare Andrew's life. But as we have heard, the man is her debt for a very important service her family was able to render im when he was in Europe. Let us remember that although Ramon elgado is a rebel he is not without honor. He once promised to repay ıe debt if ever Hannah called upon him to do so. It is at least possible ıat he may keep his word."

Señora Maria Gabriela Doyle listened carefully but without taking er eyes from my face the whole time. When Benjamin Willard opped speaking, she said in good English, "Please tell me, Miss IcLeod, what is the nature of the service your family performed for elgado, and when did it take place?"

I was prepared for this, and answered without hesitation. "It was in

Paris, a little more than two years ago, señora, but I am not permitte to say more because the matter was highly confidential."

She considered me for a long moment, then said, "I understoc from Andrew that you have neither father nor mother living. Presur ably they have died since performing this service?"

"Yes, not very long after," I lied, meeting the gaze of her dark eye

"Is it possible that your family gave him aid as a rebel by providi weapons for him?"

Before I could reply, Benjamin Willard broke in sharply. "Please c not ask Hannah to break a confidence, Maria," he said. "And plea remember that even if what you suggest is true, it would be no mo than Andrew himself has attempted to do in aid of Ramon Delgadc cause." He looked down the table at Enrique del Rio, and anger tinge his voice. "Surely to God you will not allow some notion of family pric to stand in the way of saving Andrew's life?"

"No, of course not." Enrique del Rio broke into a gabble of Spanis for the benefit of the two who spoke no English, but before he ha finished Andrew's mother cut him short with a word or two.

Looking across the table at me with the same controlled expressic she said, "You must know that if Ramon Delgado refuses to acknow edge the debt, he may kill you and your English friend, or he may k your friend and keep you for other purposes. As a young English gi who must have lived a sheltered life, you seem strangely unafraid."

I shook my head. "You misjudge me, señora," I said truthfully. "I a very much afraid."

"But you believe you will succeed?"

"I hope to. I cannot say more."

"And you love my son?"

Love? I did not know the answer to her question, but I knew th answer I must give. "Yes, señora," I said. "I love him deeply."

She glanced to her left and right, spoke briefly in Spanish, the looked at me again, and once more I glimpsed in her eyes the wearine and fear she hid so well. "So be it," she said slowly. "Our prayers wi go with you. May God go with you also."

Clara Willard and her mother had been resting when we arrived a the house in Oaxaca, and I did not see them until after the discussic had been held. Mrs. Willard was drawn and distressed, but I wa shocked by Clara's appearance. Her eyes were sunken, with great blac smudges beneath them as if she had barely slept for days, her pretty face had become gaunt, even her body seemed to have shrunk, and all the fire and confidence I so well remembered had vanished.

We met after siesta, when we were all gathered in the large patio to be served with cool drinks, but in front of the family and our hosts we were restrained in our greeting. Later, when I was trying to decide what I should take on the journey I was to begin next day, Clara came to my room alone. She did not weep, but I could feel her trembling with the effort to hold back tears as she clung to me seeking reassurance.

"Can you truly save poor Andrew?" she said in a shaking voice. "Papa says he feels there is every hope that Delgado will honor his pledge, but . . . oh, Hannah, do *you* think he will? You're the only one who really knows him."

Since the Willard family knew the truth about my years at the College for Young Ladies, I had privately told Benjamin Willard on my arrival in Oaxaca the true grounds for hoping that I might be able to influence Ramon Delgado. I had also given him permission to tell his wife and Clara, for they would know that the story I proposed to tell Andrew's family, that Delgado was in debt to me for a service rendered by my parents, could not possibly be true.

I made Clara sit on the bed beside me and held her hands. "I have very real hopes of success, Miss Clara," I said, putting as much conviction into my voice as I could muster. "Ramon Delgado is a man of strong emotion and impulse, but I'm quite sure he is not an evil man, nor a cruel man. It seems from what I've been told that he is desperate at the moment, but I believe there is a good chance that his sense of honor as a Mexican will outweigh every other consideration."

She looked at me from haunted eyes. "I can't remember a time when Andrew wasn't there," she whispered. "It would be like losing a brother if . . . if he didn't come back." She looked down at her hands. "I'm ashamed, Hannah. The man you love is under threat of death, and it should be for me to comfort you, not you to comfort me. But you seem so strong . . ."

"I'm not really," I said. "But in some ways I'm much more used to being frightened, so I manage not to show it. Besides, there's something I can do that may help Andrew, which gives me a purpose. That's much easier than just waiting and hoping."

She lifted her head and looked at me. It was hard to recognize the fierce and menacing young woman I had first met on the stairs of number eight Rue Labarre. "You mustn't keep calling me Miss Clara now," she said, and tried hard to smile. "After all, we're to be cousins soon."

I pressed her hands, then released them and stood up. "Will you help me decide what to wear and take, Clara? You know this country, but it's all strange to me. I've only ever ridden sidesaddle, and I'm not very experienced even at that. Do you think they will have a sidesaddle I can use?"

She frowned, standing up to survey the clothes I had laid out, and was at once much more like the Clara I knew, for she had a purpose now. "You don't want a sidesaddle for a journey into the Sierra Madre del Sur," she said positively. "Papa says you'll be using mules because Anselmo declares they are best for the trip. More surefooted. Anselmo is the go-between, the man who will guide you to Delgado. No, what you want is breeches. Let me look at you . . ."

She stood back and moved round me, eyeing me thoughtfully. "Yes, Pancho the groom here has a son about your size. I'll get two pairs of trousers for you. You'll need some suitable underwear, too, and I think you should take plenty of cotton wool for padding. After two days on a mule you'll be dreadfully sore, not being used to the saddle . . ."

Seventeen

had by chance done Clara a service by enlisting her aid, for she threw erself into the task of making preparations for my journey. We left ext morning, soon after dawn, Toby, Anselmo, and I, riding three ules and with a fourth carrying food, bedding, and spare clothes. ndrew's family gathered to wish us good fortune as we left the stables. was a restrained and sober farewell. His mother held my hand for everal seconds, then said in a voice made harsh by strain, "I am grate-ul, señorita. I am grateful."

Mrs. Hesketh, Clara, and her father rode through the little town ith us in an open carriage, past the magnificent baroque church of anto Domingo and on to the *zócalo,* the main square where a cathe-ral with a great wooden clock stood, then through streets of houses ith balconies, elegant archways, and decorative grillwork, to a point here the road running to the southwest became a broad dusty trail ading to Monte Alban. Here, I remembered from my reading, stood e ruins of a city which had flourished more than two thousand years go.

On the outskirts of Oaxaca we said good-bye to Mrs. Hesketh and to lara and Benjamin Willard, then rode on toward the hazy hills of the ierra Madre del Sur. Anselmo was a dark taciturn man of about forty, with a long moustache and a nose like an eagle's beak. He had bee instructed to take me to Ramon Delgado, but had not been told wh and clearly disapproved of the expedition. He rode ahead at a ploddi pace, the baggage mule on a leading rein, and spoke only when he h to.

I wore a boy's shirt and trousers, a wide-brimmed straw hat, and t riding boots and gloves I had brought with me from England. My ha was in a single plait. On Enrique del Rio's advice, Toby had eschewe his own riding breeches in favor of borrowed trousers in heavy cali such as I wore myself, which were looser and more comfortable Mexican heat than the tight-fitting English breeches.

Soon we turned off the road and began to climb out of the ferti Oaxaca valley into the hills. Rich dark soil became yellow and barre and after a few more miles we were following no trail that I cou detect, though Anselmo led without pause or hesitation. We rode f four hours before pausing to drink from the water bottles carried by t spare mule, then another two hours before halting in the shade offer by a forest of holm oak.

I knew that the town of Oaxaca itself stood some five thousand fe above sea level. We had climbed much higher now, and with the i creased humidity and thinner air I could feel my lungs beginning labor. Toby, too, was panting slightly. We had spoken but rarely on t journey so far, for there was little to say, but his presence beside me w an abiding comfort. I had only to turn my head to receive a smile, dr or cheerful, and a word of encouragement.

We did not linger to cook, but ate tacos already prepared for us-meat, cheese, eggs, or vegetables folded into the thin flat pancak called tortillas and fried. After the halt, we rode on till sunset with on two brief pauses to drink.

Anselmo made a fire to heat water for coffee and warm throug some more tacos. My thighs were sore from the long ride, and I su pected that Toby was suffering the same discomfort, for he move stiffly, but neither of us spoke about it. That night we slept under t stars, each wrapped in a blanket with a saddle for a pillow, the mul hobbled nearby. The ground was not a comfortable bed, but I sle soundly till dawn despite that.

After breakfast next morning I went behind an outcrop of rock ar padded my thighs and buttocks with the cotton wool Clara had advise me to take. No doubt this gave me some protection, but by the end the second day's journey I was in agony. When we had eaten our supper, Toby took my arm and we walked a little way from the camp we had made. "You don't have to tell me," he said, "you're in a poor way from saddle sores. How bad is it, Hannah?"

"My thighs are raw, Toby. When I looked before supper they were bleeding a little. I'm sorry if I've been bad-tempered."

"You haven't, me beauty. Can you continue tomorrow?"

"Yes, I must. Anselmo said we only have another four or five hours to go."

"I'm damnably sore myself. Mules and seamen don't mix. I'll tell Anselmo that you and I will be walking tomorrow. It won't slow us down by more than an hour or two."

"Bless you, Toby. I didn't want to suggest it."

"Even walking won't be too pleasant. I've a big jar of grease Pancho gave me, animal grease of some kind. It looks vile, but you're to give the bad parts a good coating of it tonight, Hannah, and maybe it will stop the skin cracking."

I did as Toby had bidden me, and was still sore in the morning, but no longer felt that my thighs were on fire, and walking was not too painful. Anselmo disapproved of our walking, but since we each spoke only a few words of the other's language there could be no long argument on the matter, and he had to content himself with registering his opinion by much shaking of his head and rolling up of his eyes in disgust.

Toward midafternoon, as we moved along a shallow valley through which a small stream wound tortuously, there came the sharp report of a firearm from the crest of a low hill ahead and to our right. At once Anselmo drew his mule to a halt and turned to speak to us. "We near now," he said, and pointed to the hill. "Man there see three. He shoot gun to say stop. You wait now."

As he turned away I managed to find a few words of Spanish and said, "*Un momento por favor, Anselmo.*" Carefully I took the safety pin from the pocket of my shirt and drew out a tiny linen bag I had hastily made in Oaxaca for the ring of Mexican silver Ramon Delgado had given me. "For Señor Delgado," I said, handing it to Anselmo and abandoning Spanish. "You give to Señor Delgado, please."

He looked at the little bag in his palm, shrugged, then pushed it into his shirt pocket. "I will give," he said. Leaving the baggage mule he touched heels to his mount and moved on at a walk.

"A sentry on the hill," said Toby, beginning to unstrap my blanket roll from behind the saddle. "It's going to take a long time for Anselmo to reach the sentry, then go on to Delgado's camp, talk to him, and come back for us, so let's rest."

He unrolled my bedding and his own on the ground beside the stream, and we lay down thankfully, both choosing to lie facedown for comfort, our hats tilted back to protect our heads from the sun. I pillowed one cheek on my arm, looking at Toby, and said, "I've tried to keep my face shaded, but it feels very red and sunburned. Do I look too awful, Toby?"

His own face had been weathered by years at sea, but it was still burned and peeling a little. "To be honest I've seen you looking better, young McLeod," he admitted. "I'm afraid there's no denying you're red-faced and sweaty and none too clean, but I'm surprised at the question. It's the first time I ever knew you concerned about whether a man would like your looks, and this is a devilish queer moment to start, for it's a time and place where looks could hardly matter less."

"They might matter," I said. "It might be important for me to look . . . well, not too unattractive for Ramon Delgado."

"Yes," Toby said after a little silence, his green eyes somber. "I take your point."

I got to my feet and went to the mule for the small toilet case in the pannier containing my skimpy luggage. "I'm going to have a bath in the stream," I said. "Shout if you see Anselmo coming back."

I moved downstream a little, stripped off my clothes, and spent a good ten minutes beating the dust out of them and trying to sponge them into some semblance of cleanliness. The stream was little more than a foot deep in places, and for another ten minutes I sat in it, cooling my sore thighs while brushing diligently away at my hair to rid it of dust.

Finally I washed my body, dried myself partly on a small towel and partly in the hot sun, then put on my clothes again and went back to Toby. "At least I'm clean now," I said, "but my hair still feels grubby, even though I've brushed it till my arm aches."

Toby sat up and held out a hand. "Give me the brush and sit down," he said.

For almost half an hour he steadily brushed my hair till it felt smooth and clean. "That's fine and shining now," he announced. "Do it in two plaits, Hannah; that's how it suits you best."

Another hour and a half passed before Anselmo returned, and during that time of waiting with nothing to do, I found myself growing steadily more afraid. From the moment of reaching Veracruz until leaving Oaxaca I had been swept along on a tide of events with little time to reflect or consider, and over the past three days the hardships of the journey itself had been sufficient to prevent me thinking ahead. But now, suddenly, it seemed madness that I should be here in a wild and remote part of Mexico, about to place myself in the hands of armed men in rebellion against the government.

With all my experience of men, how could I have been so stupid as to think that Ramon Delgado had meant what he said? Or even if he meant it then, was it likely that his intention would still hold good more than two years later? Every girl at the college in Rue des Moulins knew very well that pillow talk, as we called it, rarely held any degree of truth. Now I had not only placed myself in danger, but had brought Toby Kent into danger too.

And yet, and yet . . . however much I cast about in my mind for alternatives, I could think of no other way I might have acted. I drew breath to say to Toby that I was sorry I had allowed him to risk his life, but then saw that he had fallen asleep. I could not sleep myself now, so I moved to sit with my shadow giving shade to his head, and used my damp towel as a whisk to keep the occasional fly away from his face.

At last I saw the distant figure of Anselmo coming down from the hill with two men on horses. I woke Toby and we rolled up our bedding and strapped it in place. When the men reached us, Anselmo announced, "Delgado say he will see you," and I was swept by a blend of fear and relief.

To keep as cool as possible I thought it best to ride now, and Toby also mounted his mule. The two men with Anselmo were in their thirties, poorly dressed and unshaven. Each carried a rifle and a bandolier of cartridges, and as we prepared to move they watched us with curiosity from beneath the brims of their sombreros. For an hour we climbed steeply. Anselmo talked quite a lot with his companions, but Toby and I were ignored. We wound in single file through a narrow defile between low rocky cliffs, and emerged to see only a quarter of a mile away the remains of what must once have been a village. It stood beside a basin where the stream made a miniature lake, and as we drew nearer I saw that many of the adobe houses were still intact, though most lacked doors or windows and some had crumbled under the onslaughts of wind and weather.

The sun was dropping toward the horizon as we halted at the end of what had once been a street, and slid down from our mules. Apart from the houses, ramshackle shelters roofed with crude clay tiles were scattered over a wide area, and I could see a dozen small cooking fires. Men began slowly to gather, murmuring together, staring at us with open curiosity. Every man carried a rifle, and some also carried pistols at their belts. I judged that Ramon Delgado had perhaps a hundred and fifty men here, and I realized how truly Enrique del Rio had spoken when he said that this small spark of rebellion had no hope of success.

After two or three minutes in which questions were called out by the men and answered by Anselmo, an older man who seemed to be of some authority pushed his way through the crowd. "You come," he said, looking from me to Toby and back again. "Come now."

I took Toby's arm and we followed the man along a dusty track between houses until he stopped at one that still boasted windows and doors. Inside, he led the way along a short passage, threw open a door, and stepped back. I released Toby's arm and entered. He followed, and I heard the door close behind us.

Ramon Delgado sat at a scrubbed wooden table. On it were scattered pieces of writing paper, some yellowing newspapers, a small pile of tattered magazines, and a well-thumbed folder which held what appeared to be some letters written on good quality paper. He had aged more than the two years which had passed since I last saw him, and he wore a small, rather untidy beard now, but I would have recognized him even if we had met unexpectedly, for the deep-set impassioned eyes were the same.

He rose as I entered, glanced thoughtfully at Toby, then gestured toward two roughly made wooden chairs facing the table. "Señorita, señor," he said politely, "please be seated."

He waited for us to sit, then followed suit. As he did so, I saw that my silver ring lay on a piece of white paper in front of him. He looked at me with raised eyebrows. "How may I help you, señorita?"

I said, "Allow me to present Mr. Toby Kent, who has escorted me here, señor."

Ramon Delgado inclined his head in Toby's direction, but said nothing. After a moment or two I continued, "Do you remember me, señor?"

He spread his hands in a way I remembered. "That is a delicate question, señorita. Let me first ask you, is Mr. Kent your husband?"

"No. He is a friend."

"Not . . . forgive me, not a lover?"

"No, señor. And allow me to say that there is no need for you to be discreet. Mr. Kent knows that I was a student at the College for Young Ladies of Mam'selle Montavon."

"Ah." Ramon Delgado leaned back in his chair and smiled. "Then I am able to say that I remember *la professeuse* very well indeed, and I shall never forget her." He looked down at the ring. "I well remember why I gave this ring to her, but imagine my complete amazement when it was brought to me today, and I learned that the girl of the golden butterfly was herself waiting no more than a mile or two from my camp." He shook his head with a look of incredulity. "I can hardly believe it even now."

Toby said quietly, "You once promised Hannah McLeod help if it lay within your power, señor. That is why she is here today."

Ramon Delgado nodded ruefully. "So I imagined. But as you must see, my power is very small at this moment. I am a hunted outlaw, with neither wealth nor influence, and it is hard to imagine any service that I am able to render the señorita."

I said, "There is one, Señor Delgado. You hold as prisoner a man named Andrew Doyle. I am engaged to be married to him, and I have come to ask you to set him free."

From Ramon Delgado came a sharp sound of indrawn breath, and my heart sank as I saw his face turn to stone. "Andrew Doyle?" he said slowly. "Engaged to *you?* Does he know what your profession is?"

"He knows what it was, señor," I answered, fighting to keep my voice steady. "I left the college two years ago, as soon as I was able to fend for myself."

"But . . . he knows?"

"Of course. Did you judge me to be dishonest, señor?"

"No, no . . ." He waved a hand in brusque apology, then shook his head with an air of astonishment. "But when I think of his family . . . ah well, it seems poor Andrew is a fool in more ways than one."

Toby stirred, and I said sharply, without turning my head, "Sit still, Toby. I'm not insulted."

After a moment or two his voice beside me said coolly, "I'll behave, Hannah, never fear."

Ramon Delgado stood up and paced across the little room. "Do you know what you ask when you request me to free Andrew Doyle?" he demanded grimly. "I will tell you, señorita. You ask me to destroy the one chance that is left to hold my men together. If I do not save their comrades, they will lose faith in me, and Andrew Doyle is all that I have with which to bargain." His voice rose, shaking with emotion. "You once gave me confidence and strength to pursue a cause that is the very core of my life, and now you ask me to destroy the last hope for that cause by my own hand."

Toby said, "No matter what happens to Andrew Doyle, your comrades in prison will not be saved from the firing squad, señor."

"That is what Doyle's family would have me believe."

"That is what you know in your heart to be true, Señor Delgado."

I said, "Please. It does not matter which of you is right. A Mexican gentleman once made me a promise, and gave me a token by which I could call upon him to keep that promise if ever I had the need. Now that time has come, Señor Delgado, and I ask if you will honor the promise you made."

He did not answer at once, but moved to light a lamp, for dusk was creeping into the room. As he set the lamp down, I saw that his face was drawn, his lips tight, his eyes bitter. "You have come among desperate men, señorita," he said at last. "If you were to die, my promise would no longer remain."

I controlled the sudden fear that seized me, and said in a voice which did not quaver too noticeably, "Of course you have the option of killing us, señor, and of living with murder on your conscience for the rest of your life."

Toby stretched his legs out and said ruminatively, "I sat up half the night before we left Oaxaca, and wrote out a careful account of exactly what we proposed to attempt. If we do not return, it will be published in every newspaper in Mexico, and many in Europe and the United States. You will be dishonored on a very large scale indeed, señor."

Ramon Delgado drew a long breath as if seeking to control himself, then he sat down again and looked at me with hostile eyes. "You will leave here unharmed," he said. "As regards the matter of Andrew Doyle, I will consider this and give you my answer in the morning."

"May I see Andrew?" I asked.

"No, you may not, señorita. You may have my word that he is well." Ramon Delgado picked up the ring and studied it. He called out somehing in Spanish, and two men with rifles entered. "You will leave us ow, Mr Kent," he said, still looking at the ring. "Go with my men, if ou please."

I felt a shock of new alarm, and my voice sounded almost shrill as I aid, "Please assure me that you intend no harm to Mr. Kent."

Ramon Delgado shrugged. "I give no assurances, señorita," he said. The men here are of independent spirit, and their response to disci-line is regrettably uncertain."

Toby stood up and touched my shoulder "Don't worry, I'll be fine," e said, then turned and went out between the two men, wishing them cheerful good evening with some of the few words of Spanish we had cquired.

When the door closed, Ramon Delgado laid down the ring and ooked at me. Even in the poor light of the lamp I could see that his yes held the gray weariness of a desperately tired man. "Will you share ny bed tonight?" he asked.

My heart sank. I said, "If it is the price of Andrew Doyle's safety or f Toby Kent's safety, I will. Otherwise, no."

He looked surprised. "What difference can it make to you after your ears in Paris? What is one more night with one more man?"

I tried to speak very calmly as I said, "You know my story, señor. I vas an abducted child under compulsion, not quite seventeen when ou last saw me, but almost ready to break free and fend for myself. I ut that life behind me, as I had always planned, and no man has nown me since. When you ask me to share your bed, you are not sking *la professeuse* of Rue des Moulins. She has ceased to exist. You re asking Hannah McLeod, another person."

"But you would still yield yourself to save Andrew Doyle?"

"Yes."

"Or Mr. Kent?"

"Yes."

He shook his head with a baffled air. "A Mexican woman would ather die than be so dishonored."

"We are speaking of my fiancé dying, of my friend dying. Besides, I ave much experience of being compelled to let a man use my body, ut I am not dishonored by it. The dishonor lies with those who com-el me."

He sat with chin on chest for a long minute, eyes half closed, then

roused himself with a sigh. "You will spend the night alone," he sai
"It will make no difference to my decision."

A man escorted me to the end of the tiny village, to a tumbledow
house occupied by two wrinkled old women, and spoke to them
Spanish far too rapid for me to follow. They showed great curiosit
chattering together, examining my clothes, and seeming greatly to a
mire my boots. When the man left, the women took me to a sm
room where a straw paillasse lay in the corner, and indicated by ge
tures that this was where I could sleep. I was thankful when the ma
returned a few minutes later with my bedroll, for the paillasse w
filthy.

He settled himself outside the only door of the house, presumably c
guard, and later I was brought water in a bottle and some chee
wrapped in tortillas. I ate and drank a little, then unrolled my bed ar
lay down. There was no lamp, only a wick of twisted fiber floating in
dish of oil.

For a while there were only the small and mainly distant sounds
be expected from the sprawling encampment centered on the aba
doned village, occasionally interspersed by bouts of chatter between th
two old women who sat in the room that opened onto the street. I w
never to learn what they were doing with the rebels, but thought th
might be original inhabitants of the village who had remained whe
others abandoned it.

Later came a sound that made me uneasy. At first I found it hard
identify, for it rose and fell like a distant wind gusting through a tunne
Then I realized that it was the sound of a crowd, all responding
something they were watching, the noise a distant murmur for th
most part, but rising every now and again to a roar of excitement.
remembered Toby taking me to the circus in England, and the aud
ence making just such a noise at the climax of some remarkable feat
acrobatics.

I got up and went into the other room, using my scanty Spanis
vocabulary in an attempt to find out what was happening, but thoug
the old women and the man on guard chattered and laughed, makin
all kinds of signs and gestures, I could not fathom their meaning, an
after awhile I went back to my bed. The worrying sound stopped soo
after, but I lay thinking of Toby and feeling sick with anxiety as
remembered Ramon Delgado's words, "*I give no assurances.*"

I had little hope of sleeping, and lay listening as silence came gradually to the encampment, leaving only the natural sounds of the night. It was in the early hours that sleep caught me unawares, when I was saying my prayers for the third or fourth time asking for Andrew and Toby to be spared.

I think my sleep was deep, but it cannot have been long, for the night was barely tinged with the gray of coming dawn when I roused to a hand shaking me by the shoulder. Anselmo, our guide, crouched over me.

"Come," he said in a low voice. "Bring bed and come. No talk."

The mists of sleep vanished within seconds as I rolled up my bedding, got to my feet, and followed Anselmo out of the house, passing the two old women snoring on their beds of straw in the front room. The guard had gone. Our four mules stood a few paces away, and my heart lifted with thankful joy as I saw Toby Kent holding them. Anselmo said again, "No talk."

Toby took my bedroll and began to strap it on the mule. In the half-light I saw that one side of his face was swollen and discolored. I put my hand to his other cheek gently, looking a question at him, but he gave a reassuring shake of his head, and a brief grin touched his bruised mouth.

Following Anselmo's signs, we walked the mules a hundred paces or so beyond the village before mounting. There was no sign of Ramon Delgado, no sign of Andrew Doyle, and I felt despair come upon me, for it seemed certain I had failed. When I touched Toby's arm and again looked a question at him he lifted his shoulders and spread a hand to indicate that he knew no more than I. We moved into single file to go through the narrow pass between low cliffs, and I felt tears running down my cheeks, for now it was plain that Ramon Delgado had rejected my plea, and all our efforts to save the man I was pledged to marry had been in vain. I began to be racked by a sense of guilt. Had my refusal to share Ramon Delgado's bed influenced his decision? He had said that it would make no difference, but now I wondered.

Five minutes later we came out of the narrow pass, and there, where the cliffs fell back, a mounted man waited in the growing light, and it was Andrew Doyle. I gave a sob of joy, and would have slipped from my mule and run to him if Anselmo had not gripped my arm. "Ride," he said. "Talk after. Ride now."

Andrew wore the kind of working clothes I had seen riders wearing on the cattle ranches we had observed from the train, but his horse was a fine creature. He came beside me and reached out to grip my hand as we rode side by side, though he was much higher in the saddle. For a while his face was no more than a blur, but then my tears dried and I was able to see him clearly. To my relief he seemed quite unhurt. His chin bore a stubble of beard, his clothes were dusty and travel-stained, his hair unkempt, but to me the greatest change was in his eyes. They were the eyes of a man betrayed, and shocked to his inmost soul by that betrayal. A romantic and an idealist, he had been far more cruelly hit than most other men would have been, and my heart went out to him.

We did not stop until we had descended through the broad valley where the stream ran, and passed on into the lower range of hills beyond. We could have talked long before then, but as if by tacit consent no word was spoken until Anselmo drew his mule to a halt and said, "We stop for drink. Five minutes."

Andrew was down, lifting me from the saddle and holding me in his arms. "Hannah!" His voice was a rough whisper. "Hannah, it was madness for you to do what you've done." Still holding me, he half turned his head to speak to Toby. "And are you crazy, too? Why in God's name did you let her?"

I heard Toby say amiably, "My dear fellow, I couldn't think of a way to stop her."

Andrew let me go and took my hands, gazing down at me with troubled eyes. "Delgado came to me before dawn," he said. "He told me of the debt he owed you. Told me exactly how it came about. He didn't . . . misuse you last night?"

"No, Andrew, no. But he wouldn't promise to set you free. Until I saw you as we came out of the pass, I thought we had failed."

"He released me and led me to my horse," said Andrew. "He told me to walk with it through the pass and wait for you there." He nodded toward Anselmo. "We had to be away before the camp roused. Some of the men could make trouble."

Toby handed me a water bottle and said, "Will they follow?"

"No." Andrew shook his head. "Now we're through the valley and out of sight, they won't give chase."

"Will Ramon Delgado be in danger from them?" I asked.

"No serious danger. But it means the collapse of his rebellion." Andrew shrugged, and his eyes were bitter. "It's well deserved. I befriended that man, I worked for his cause, I risked being an outcast om my family and yet he took me as a hostage and would have anged me to gain his ends."

"It's over now, Andrew," I said gently "We're going home." It was ill hard to believe my good fortune. I offered up a silent prayer of ratitude, then drank from the bottle and handed it to Andrew. Toby urned to tighten his mule's girth, and now I saw in the full light of norning the heavy bruising and swelling all down one side of his face. I inced in sympathy and moved toward him. "Toby, what on earth appened to you? Was it something to do with all the shouting I heard st night?"

"Well now, there was a certain amount of shouting as I remember," e said, and gave me a crooked grin. "The thing was, these rebel ellows of Delgado's seemed to take against me for some reason, can ou imagine that? I swear I was as peaceable as an archangel, but a few f them were set on making the gringo eat humble pie. There was one ho had lived in America, and he did the translation for us."

"They're men who like to fight," said Andrew soberly. "I'm surrised one of them didn't invite you to a first-blood duel with knives."

"Now isn't that exactly what happened?" said Toby. "But I rather ancied they were experts with a knife, so I said as a guest in their ountry I'd prefer to challenge any three in turn to an Irish standown."

I looked blankly at Andrew, who shrugged and said, "I've no idea hat he's talking about."

"You're an ignorant pair," said Toby, "so I'll explain. As you might xpect, an Irish standdown is a piece of sheer lunacy. You take turns to it each other with your fist, and when a man can't get up, he's lost."

A hand to my mouth, I stared at his bruised face. "And that's what appened to you?"

"You should see the other fellows," said Toby, and grinned again. They were wary at first, but when I said they could each have first trike, they couldn't believe their luck, thought I must be an idiot, and airly jumped at taking up the challenge. That suited me, for I reckned that if they were experts with a knife, it was unlikely they'd be nuch good with a fist."

Andrew laughed suddenly, and I felt glad that he was able to forget is bitterness, even for a few moments. "You were right," he said. There's no prizefighting here. Mexicans being serious people, they use nives or guns."

"That's what I had in mind," said Toby. "The first man went for n face, which is natural and painful but not effective. Then I hit hi before he could blink, and down he went for five solid minutes. An o shipmate of mine, Paddy O'Malley, taught me how to get a knuck into the solar plexus. If you do it just so, then even when they start come round they think somebody's made off with their legs."

I had torn a piece from my towel and soaked it in water so I could least sponge his battered face where the flesh was broken. "You stoc still and let three men punch you in the face?" I said incredulously.

"It was better than knives," he protested, "and anyway, why weren you there with your hatpin to protect me, young McLeod?" He had speak out of one corner of his mouth now, for I was gently swabbir the other corner. "The fact is," he continued, "I only got two fists the face, since the third fellow tried to copy my system, but little goc it did him, for he hadn't the benefit of Paddy O'Malley's instructio Then I dropped him, and the crowd decided the gringo had give them some good entertainment, and they became quite friendly."

"You did well," Andrew said quietly. "It isn't easy to win over suc people. They have little cause to like the gringo. I am half gring myself, and I know."

A few minutes later we set off again. Now that Andrew was safe ar we were on our way home, I felt as if I were not quite in my body. was an odd sensation, and not unpleasant. With the crisis past, I ha no responsibilities until we reached Oaxaca, and I could not best myself to wonder how Andrew's family would receive me then, or think about what problems I might have to face.

We did not hurry on that journey, neither did we talk very much, f I think we were all affected by the same dreamlike sensation, but w were at ease and comfortable with one another, and there was a goc understanding between us. If Andrew was subdued, it was not to b wondered at. He had been deeply hurt, he had lain under the threat death, and he still had his disapproving family to face.

The vile looking grease Pancho had given Toby was proving surpri ingly effective, for although I was stiff when we dismounted at eac halt, my thighs were no longer agonizingly raw. We spent three nigh on the trail, and on the morning of the fourth day, when we were on a few hours from Oaxaca, Anselmo rode on ahead at dawn to give th news that we were returning safely.

At midmorning we came over the last ridge and saw in the distanc the little town nestling in the valley For a while we sat in silence, all busy with our own thoughts. Then Andrew said slowly, in a rather puzzled way, "How was Clara when you left?"

"Very distressed and frightened for you," I said. "But she'll be rejoicing now."

He nodded, touching heels to his horse, and we began the long descent. When we had covered almost half the distance, we saw two carriages and two figures on horseback appear on the outskirts of the town and move out along the Monte Alban road for a little way before halting. Two men descended from the carriages, each putting on a wide-brimmed hat against the growing heat of the sun. The riders dismounted and the four men stood in a loose group, all faces turned to look up into the hills we were descending.

"A reception has been arranged," said Toby. "That's Anselmo and Benjamin Willard with the horses, and the gentlemen in the dark suits and gray hats are Enrique del Rio and Señor Amado, I fancy."

Andrew shaded his eyes and stood up in the stirrups. "Can you see Clara?" he asked.

"She'll be in one of the carriages with your mother and Mrs. Willard," I said. "It's too hot for them to stand out in the sun while they wait for us."

"The question is," said Toby pensively, "are they preparing to kill the fatted calf for the prodigal son, or are they preparing to half kill the prodigal son himself?"

Andrew reached out to hold my hand for a moment and gave me a wry smile. "We'll soon discover," he said.

Despite all hardships I had been strangely happy for the past three days, but as we drew steadily closer to our journey's end, I began to feel a growing reluctance to face the stiff formalities and cool politeness I had known with Andrew's family. We were still two or three hundred yards away when the trail we were following merged with the road. I was riding with Andrew on my right. On my left, Toby held the leading rein of the baggage mule.

Now there was movement in the waiting group ahead. The carriage doors were opened, and ladies were being helped to descend, Maria Gabriela Doyle and her Mexican sister-in-law from one carriage, Mrs. Willard, Mrs. Hesketh, and Clara from the other. The two Mexican ladies were in dark dresses, the others in light summer dresses, and all were carrying parasols.

We plodded steadily on at the pace of the mules. No wind moved within the valley to stir the ladies' skirts, and in the shimmering heat those nine motionless figures seemed to form a tableau. Imagining how dreadful I must surely look after a week of hard travel in the wilderness, my face burned and peeling, my hair and my borrowed clothes thick with dust, I had to suppress a nervous giggle at the prospect of meeting once again the elegant ladies and gentlemen of Andrew's family.

We were no more than thirty paces away when the tableau broke in an extraordinary fashion. Quite suddenly Clara dropped her parasol and began to run toward us, holding her skirt up a little to help her move more freely. Less than a second later Andrew almost threw himself from the saddle and ran to meet her. The pretty straw hat she wore fell unheeded to the ground. I could see tears pouring down her cheeks, and heard her sob as she reached out toward him. Next moment it was as if they had been transported to another world, for they were locked in each other's arms and utterly oblivious to all but themselves.

Stunned and uncomprehending, I drew my mule to a halt. Beyond Andrew and Clara, their relatives and Mrs. Hesketh gazed with the same bewilderment as must have shown on my face and on Toby's beside me. My fiancé and his cousin had half turned as they embraced, and I could see that both had their eyes closed. Andrew was touching his lips to her cheek, her brow, her eyes, again and again, smoothing his hand back over her hair, murmuring wordless sounds, and all the time Clara's arms clutched him as if she would never leave go.

It dawned upon me then that I was gazing upon a man and a woman who were deeply, fiercely, wholeheartedly in love, but who had never been aware of it, perhaps because as cousins they had taken one another for granted. Now, after the shock, the fears, and the long anxieties which had loomed like thunderclouds over them for many days, realization had burst upon them like an electric storm, catching them totally unawares . . . and the man was Andrew Doyle, who had asked me to marry him.

I felt pain, weariness, sorrow, yet somewhere deep in the core of my being was the glimmer of another feeling, strangely like relief. Benjamin Willard strode forward and called out hoarsely, "Clara! For God's sake, child, what are you about? Andrew! Come to your senses!"

Slowly, dazedly, they broke from each other but remained close together, holding hands. Two shocked pairs of eyes sought and found me, two faces showed the torment of remorse. "Oh . . . forgive me,

Hannah!" Clara exclaimed in a shaking whisper, and snatched her hand from Andrew's grasp. "I was only . . . I didn't mean to . . ."

Her voice trailed into silence. Andrew said, "Hannah, it isn't what you think. I mean, we were just carried away, because . . ." He stopped speaking, lifted his hands, then let them fall to his sides in a helpless gesture.

My mind seemed completely blank, but I heard myself say in quite a steady voice, "You were carried away because you and Clara are very much in love, Andrew, and you have only just discovered it. Please don't lie to yourself about that. I . . . I'm really thankful that you have found out now. In time."

He said with desperate intensity, "But Hannah—!" Then words failed him again as he realized that in honesty there was nothing he could say. Clara was facing me bravely, tears on her cheeks, hands clenched tightly together now as she said, "I'm so ashamed. I'll go away, Hannah, I promise—"

Again I heard myself say, as if it were the voice of another person, "No. Please let me speak. You owe me that, all of you." Andrew's mother, aunt, and two uncles stood like statues, their faces unreadable. Mrs. Willard moved forward to stand beside her husband, a blend of pain and pity in her eyes. Mrs. Hesketh closed her parasol briskly, walked forward, then turned to stand beside my mule as if guarding my flank.

I said slowly, "I will not become Andrew's wife. It would be quite wrong to do so. I thank God he is safe, and I bear no ill will toward him or toward Clara. I shall always remember their kindness and friendship. I have no wish to talk about what has happened, it will only cause embarrassment and unhappiness. I wish to go away as soon as possible, back to England or France."

Andrew's hand crept out toward Clara, and she took it. I felt very shaken and wanted to be done with talking, so I went on more quickly, "I should be grateful if you would all return to the house in Oaxaca now. I shall follow with Señor Kent. If there is a convenient train, I shall leave for Veracruz in the morning and take the first available ship to Europe. Until then I beg you to let me remain quietly alone."

There was a long silence. At last Enrique del Rio moved to a carriage and opened the door. "Andrew, Clara," he said. "Come, please."

Andrew drew breath to speak. I shook my head, looked down at my hands on the pommel, and closed my eyes. Mrs. Hesketh's voice said quietly, "I shall be waiting for you, Hannah, and I shall ensure that yo are not disturbed." There were sounds of movement, of doors openin and closing, the chink of metal as horses were mounted. A man spok in Spanish, and I sensed that somebody was taking charge of Andrew horse, Anselmo perhaps. Harness creaked, wheels turned gratingly o the gritty, hard-beaten ground, and there came the sound of hoove moving at an easy pace.

Gradually the blend of noises faded into the distance. After awhile opened my eyes but without looking toward Oaxaca, then slid from th saddle, walked my mule to the side of the road, and sat down where low outcrop of rock broke the hard-baked ground. Toby, still astride h mule, long legs dangling with feet close to the ground, studied me wit interest.

"If you can bear a small compliment, young McLeod," he sai thoughtfully, "I consider you comported yourself with great dignity jus now."

I waved some flies away from my sweaty face and said, "I was think ing it must have sounded very pompous."

He pushed back his hat and considered. "Slightly pompous pe haps," he acknowledged, gently fingering his still swollen cheek, "bu you needed a touch of that to compensate for looking like a sma walking scarecrow."

I heard myself laugh, and decided that although I felt very peculia in the aftermath of all that had happened, I was not suffering from broken heart. Thinking back, it occurred to me that I had accepte Andrew's proposal when I was feeling too weak to withstand his persi tence. Now, by a curious trick of fate, I would not become a fin Mexican lady after all . . . but perhaps that was no bad thing.

Toby stepped down from his mule, sat beside me, and offered me water bottle. I drank and passed it back to him. He drank in tur replaced the cork, and hung the bottle on his saddle again.

"Are you greatly set on touring Mexico and painting picture Toby?" I asked.

He shrugged. "Not especially. If you're going home, I think I'll g back with you."

I nodded. "Oh, I'd like that. Can you lend me the fare money? I' pay you back in time, when I've found work."

He said, "Do you want to hurt Andrew badly?"

I sat up straight and looked at him. "Of course not. You know me better than that."

"Then at very least you'll have to allow him to provide for your fare and Mrs. Hesketh's, and enough money for you to live reasonably for . . . let's say six months or so." Before I could speak he went on, "No, don't argue, Hannah. It won't be charity on his part, it'll be charity on yours. He already feels he's betrayed you, so if you reject such small help as that he'll hate himself, and it'll be the same for Clara."

I saw that Toby was right, and said reluctantly, "Yes, I suppose so. I don't want to have to discuss it with Andrew, though. It's best if we don't talk again, for there's really nothing to say."

"I'm sure that's understood." Toby pulled off a boot, shook some grit out, and put it on again. "I'm the one Andrew will approach," he went on. "He'll be wanting to settle an income on you, and I doubt that his family will object, for they're not unhappy to see you go, but I fancy you'll not be in favor of any such arrangement?"

"No. I'll accept only enough to see me home, and whatever you think sufficient for my keep for a few months. And I'll let you have my engagement ring to give back to Andrew before we go." I discovered that I was not feeling at all upset now, just rather sleepy and remote from myself.

Toby said, "Will you go back to London or Paris?"

"I haven't thought yet. Oh, wait, I have now. Paris would be best, at least to begin with. I don't want to run into any of the Ryder family or Mrs. Ritchie." It was strange to speak so formally of the woman who had borne me, but I would never think of anyone but Kathleen McLeod as my mother.

The sun was at its hottest. Toby lifted down a big goatskin water bottle and said, "We've no need to hoard this any longer." He lifted it and poured water over his head, chest, and back. "Ahh, that's better. Want some, me beauty?"

I smiled. "Why not? I'm sure it can't make me look any less like somebody's beauty."

He soaked my head and shirt, and I was glad of the cooling relief, though I knew I would be dry again in fifteen minutes. "If you like, you could have your old room in Rue Labarre for a while until you've sorted yourself out," he said. "I'll be glad to sublet it to you at an exorbitant rent."

I sat thinking for a while, then I said, "Even at an exorbitant rent, can't think of anything I would like more. Bless you, Toby."

"That's settled, then." He took my hand and we stood up togethe When I looked toward the town there was no sign of carriages or rider "We might as well go along now," said Toby. "I'm sure Maria Gabriel Doyle will have made arrangements for us to be discreetly received an accommodated when we arrive." He clapped my hat on my head an lifted me onto my mule. "Holy saints, I wonder what Flora Hesket will have to say about all this?"

"I can't imagine," I said, and watched him bestride his own mul "But it will certainly confirm her opinion of foreigners."

He looked at me in surprise, then threw back his head and laughe "By God it will," he said, and took the rein of the baggage mule. "Let go and listen to her hold forth, young McLeod."

The mules plodded off at a steady gait, and side by side we made ou way slowly along the dusty road leading into the town.

Eighteen

On a November morning of bright sunshine over Paris, a week after our return from Mexico, I sat by the window in Toby Kent's studio making a small repair in one of my petticoats.

Although my face was still rather brown, I could look in a mirror without wincing now, for my hair was clean and shining and my face no longer peeling beneath a layer of sweat and dust. I had returned to find my old room across the passage much improved since Toby had taken over the tenancy. It was comfortably furnished now, and there was always an ample supply of coal to keep it warm, brought up by Mme Briand's husband at Toby's expense.

Toby was at his easel, in shirt-sleeves, muttering, snorting, glowering as he went through his usual preliminaries before suddenly finding the way he wanted to attack the canvas. These preliminaries had continued for longer than usual but I was pretending not to notice, and trying to decide whether to go back to La Coquille if Père Chabrier would have me, or try to find better work as a nannie or perhaps even a governess, either in England or France, but deep in the country, far from London or Paris, so there would be little chance of ever meeting anybody from my past. The second idea was more sensible, but I knew that in the end I would decide to remain in Paris, for I could not face the thought of losing Toby as my neighbor I had no better friend, and we had con to know each other so well that nobody could possibly replace him.

There came a clatter as he threw down his brush and palette. looked up to see that he had stepped out from behind the canvas ar was glaring at me, hands on hips. "Now look here, me beauty," he sa sternly, "do you know what I did last summer? I bought a cottage dow in Cornwall and another in the south of France, in a tiny fishing villag you've never heard of, called Juan-les-Pins. All paid for with what I go for leasing *Butterfly Girl* to Andrew Doyle for a year, and with plent left over besides. That's what I did last summer."

"Well . . . it's nice for you to be a man of property, Toby dear," said, "but why Cornwall and Juan-les-Pins?"

"Because they're fine places for a fellow who likes to paint. I migh live awhile in one and awhile in the other. Summer in Cornwall, winte on the Mediterranean maybe."

I felt a pang of grief, but smiled and said, "That will be lovely fo you, Toby. I shall miss you very much, though."

"Ah, now that's what I'm coming to," he said, scowling. "Would yo consider marrying me and coming along with me, Hannah?"

I stopped my needlework to stare. "Marry you? Oh, Toby, that's th first time you've ever said anything to hurt me."

"*Hurt* you? For heaven's sake, how?"

"Well, not really, but you're sorry for me, and you're a good friend and perhaps you're worried about what will become of me, so quite suddenly you get the notion that you can put everything right by marrying me. You should know I don't want pity, Toby."

He shook his head slowly, the scowl fading from his face. "Oh, but you're wrong," he said very softly. "I don't pity you, Hannah. I'm not speaking on impulse and I didn't suddenly get the notion of marrying you. That might have been so for Andrew, but not for me. Dear God, d'you not know I've loved you almost from the beginning? Not quite the beginning, for it wasn't love at first sight, but it was love sure enough after you'd been just a few weeks here, and I'm a man who's traveled far and wide enough to know it was no passing fancy."

I sat with a dozen half formed thoughts making a kaleidoscope in my head, and with a curious warmth expanding steadily within me despite a shadowy apprehension which tried to prevent it. I said, "But, Toby . . . you told me when I was in the convalescent home that you had loved and lost a lady in Vienna, didn't you?"

He nodded resignedly. "Yes, but I was lying most outrageously, Hannah, for it was you that I'd loved and lost. You saw I was sad and you wanted to know why, but I could hardly tell you the truth of it when you'd just become engaged to Andrew, could I?"

"Oh, dear. No . . . I suppose not. It was too late then. But, Toby, long before that there was a time when you told me not to be so trusting, and to be more wary of everybody. Even of you. Why did you say that?"

"Because I wanted you," he said simply. "Not just as a girl, but as my wife. I wanted you more than anything in the world, and I didn't trust myself to keep from showing it one fine day."

"But why shouldn't you have shown it?"

"I was sure I'd lose you if I did. Lose you as a friend and companion."

I stared, baffled. "For heaven's sake, why should you lose me? I don't understand."

"Why?" He ran both hands through his hair in an angry gesture. "Because of what had been done to you, that's why. Because you had spent four years at Mam'selle Montavon's college being sold to men. Don't you see, you daft girl? After that I was sure you'd be repelled by the idea of any man so much as touching your hand, let alone sharing your bed. I was *stunned* when I heard that you'd accepted Andrew! I felt as if my brains had suddenly turned to porridge, and it was only then I realized what a mutton-headed fool I'd been . . . that it was too late, and I'd missed my chance."

I remembered how he had always been so careful never to touch me, until I took the initiative by holding his arm as we walked, and I said, "You weren't a fool, Toby. You were a very kind gentleman . . . and friend."

He made a wry grimace. "But stupid with it. Now I've been given another chance, and I meant to wait awhile before speaking, but I couldn't, so I'm hoping to God I haven't spoken too soon." He stood by the easel, his green eyes watching me anxiously, asking an unspoken question. I suddenly remembered learning from Andrew Doyle that Toby had a whole drawer full of pencil sketches of me, and I asked myself why this and many another small indication had not at least made me wonder if Toby's feeling for me might run deeper than simple friendship. Slowly some of the scattered, nebulous thoughts in my head began to come together and take more solid shape. I laid aside my mending, put out my hands, and said, "Come close to me, Toby There are things I must ask you and tell you."

He came and knelt beside my feet, facing me, holding my hands, his head only a little lower than my own, for he was a big man. I said, "I won't pretend I've suddenly fallen in love with you. I think that after what has happened to me, I'm not vulnerable to being smitten by a thunderbolt, as Andrew and Clara were, but . . . in these last few moments I've recognized feelings within me that I wasn't conscious of before."

"Can you tell me something of them?" he said gently.

"Well . . . when I think back, I realize there has never been a single moment in your company when I wasn't glad and happy to be with you. I realize that I've never had to watch my words in your company, but could always speak freely from my heart, for you would never misunderstand or take offense. I realize that I've always loved the way you talk to me, sometimes scowling and calling me a daft girl, but speaking so because you could feel free to, knowing that in my turn I would take no offense either."

He lifted one of my hands and touched it to his lips. I said, "I realize now that even after the first time you took me out to supper I trusted you completely, with never a shadow of doubt. Oh, I always appreciated how kind you were to me, and how thoughtful, but I've been blind in many ways. Why didn't I see that I've never felt a moment's unease with you? That we've always been so . . . so pleasant and comfortable with each other? That I've always enjoyed doing any small thing I could for you—cooking your breakfast, sewing on a button, sitting for you to paint me?"

A smile glimmered in his eyes. "Because you're a daft girl, maybe?"

I smiled back, and pressed his hands. "I expect so. But I see all these things now, and many more. I don't know what it is to fall in love, but I do realize that I've grown to love you, Toby, with all my heart, for you are the dearest and truest friend I've ever known or can ever hope to know."

"Then . . . will you marry me, my butterfly girl?" he said.

I drew him closer, set his arms about my waist, then put my own arms about his neck and held his head against my breast, wanting him to know that I was not repelled but happy to feel him close to me, and knowing a moment of rueful satisfaction that I could so easily do this, for at least I was far beyond feeling shy with a man.

I could feel my heart beating against his cheek, and would have iven anything not to say what I knew I must say, for I had glimpsed he chance of a happiness such as I had thought could never be mine, nd I shrank from losing that chance.

"Toby," I said, stroking his thick red hair, "if I were to marry you I vould be the truest and most loyal and loving of wives. But I can't wipe ut the bad years, my dearest friend. Four years, and many men. I felt othing for any of them, except a kind of pity for the young boys. I ook no pleasure in any one of them. In that way, you would be the first nan I have ever known, Toby dear. But I was sold to many others, and 'm afraid. Afraid that their ghosts would haunt you."

He sighed, held me a little more tightly, and moved his head against ne. "Their ghosts don't exist for me, Hannah." His voice was muffled, ut light and glad. "Try to understand, my beautiful. The girl I love is a irl who has been made what she is by all that has happened to her, the ad things as well as the good. If it wasn't for the college, I wouldn't now your courage and your power to rise above the worst that can appen. I've never seen you show bitterness, or heard you utter a word f self-pity or complaint, and that was the first thing to touch my eart."

I lifted his head and kissed his brow. "But have you thought how it night be if we were married?" I said. "Suppose one day in Cornwall, or n the cottage by the Mediterranean, some friend or acquaintance of ours recognized me? After all, the Ryders know about me, and the Ritchies. We'll probably never see them again, but . . . well, however t might happen, there's always the chance that somebody might know ne, and start gossip, and then you would be ostracized."

Toby smiled up at me. "Well, first it's a small chance," he said, "for 've no wish to mingle with the society nibs and nobs, but I realize it ould happen, and what I have in mind is this. If any man insults my vife I'll break his jaw, naturally. If any woman does, I'll paint such a ortrait of her that she'll wish she'd never been born, something recognizable but satanic, and I'll show it in a gallery in London or Paris. If it omes down to whispered gossip and being ostracized by certain people, then they're just the kind of people I've no wish to mix with, and e damned to them. Will you give me a kiss, young McLeod?"

I laughed, holding his head in my hands, and said, "Wait, Toby dear, ust a little minute. There's something else—"

"I know there's something else. There's the fact that I'm an artist, and you might say a successful one, and what do people expect an art to be? Bohemian, of course. I truly doubt that what happened to y will ever slip out, but if it does, well there we are, two bohemians, a as I'm a fellow who's mixed with all kinds I'll tell you this. Most m will envy me, and most women will *know* their men envy me."

I looked into his eyes and saw no shadow of doubt there. "Toby,' said slowly, "when I spoke of there being something else I meant . children. If we marry, and are blessed with children, there might o day come a time when they stumble upon the secret of my past."

He lifted a hand to rest it against my cheek. "The more years th pass, the less likely it is to happen," he said quietly, "but if it did, wh then, Hannah? Your spirit has been tempered in fires that few wom ever know. You live without illusions, as few women do, and you see t world through eyes far older than your years. All these things are a pa of why I love you, and why we have no barriers between us in o minds. If one day when they are old enough to understand, our ch dren discovered your secret, would it destroy you when you have ris above so much? And when you would have me beside you?"

"I want to tell you what I've decided," I said, struggling a little frame my thoughts in words. "I've decided that I will never tell story unless I have to, but I will set it down, just as it happened. If o day in the future there comes a time when the past overtakes me, time when tales are told of what I have been, then our children m read that story for themselves. If they turn against me because of wh was done to me, if they despise me for it, then I shall pity them anc shall be sad, but it will not destroy me."

Toby started to speak, but I said, "Wait . . . there's just a litt more." He smiled, turned his head to kiss the inside of my wrist, th looked at me patiently. I went on, "I will not beg for understandi from them or from anybody, and I will not apologize for anythi except whatever of wrong I have myself committed. I am first my ov woman, and after that, I will belong to no man but you, Toby. I lo you dearly, I believe I have much to give, and I will give it joyfully a faithfully, but only if you truly want me as your wife knowing t dangers and heartache I may bring you."

After several seconds of silence he lifted an eyebrow and said, "Ha you finished? Is that all?"

"Well . . . yes," I said, a little disconcerted.

"It was a bit pompous, young McLeod."

I gave his head a little shake. "Well, it had to be. It's all very serious, Toby. You mustn't rush into marriage without thinking of all the consequences."

"Rush? I've thought of little else since the moment we sat together on that rock outside Oaxaca and it dawned on me that you were free once more. Now look, you've said you would marry me as long as I appreciated the fearful dangers, and I do, and I don't care a damn, so it's all settled, and how much longer must I wait for a kiss?"

"Oh, Toby. Not another moment, my dear one."

His lips on mine brought me a happiness I had never known, and I was trembling when at last we ended our embrace.

He gave a great sigh and stood up, drawing me to my feet, holding me in his arms again and looking down into my eyes. Suddenly his expression became anxious. "You shouldn't be here in the studio with me, Hannah," he said uneasily. "I mean, people will think . . . you know."

Laughter broke from me and I leaned my head against his chest. "Toby, whatever they think they've been thinking it for a long time now, you daft man."

"I suppose so." He let me go and paced away, scratching his cheek. "Look, we have to get married as soon as possible, me beauty. Perhaps I can get a special license. Then where shall we go? Cornwall or Juan-les-Pins?"

"With winter coming, it had better be the Mediterranean, hadn't it?"

"Yes, of course. Right." He slapped a fist into his palm. "I'll go to *le mairie* this afternoon and make inquiries about getting married. Dear God, I'm a happy man." He swung away and snatched up brush and palette. "Sit for me, Hannah darling. No, wait, give me another kiss first."

I did so gladly, and some time later I sat sewing again, in the same pose but a different person now, for my world had been changed and was lit with golden sunlight for me by a man with green eyes and red hair, who had been my friend and was soon to be my husband and my lover.

For perhaps a minute or two he muttered, snorted angrily, scraped at the canvas, and glared. Then suddenly he gave a great exultant laugh and began to paint.